A Bull Rider's GRACE

A BULLS & BUTTERFLIES NOVEL

H.M. HOY

A Note From the Author

Content Warning

THIS NOVEL CONTAINS DOMESTIC violence scenes between the Female Main Character and her ex-boyfriend. As a domestic violence survivor myself, I acknowledge that these scenes may be difficult to read.

The following chapters each have at least one scene that may be triggering for some. Read at your own risk.
*Chapter 2
*Chapter 4
*Chapter 9
*Chapter 15
*Chapter 30
*Chapter 32

Dealing with domestic violence?
Help is available!

National Domestic Violence Support Hotline:
800-799-7233 or text START to 88788

Prologue

Two Years Earlier

HE'D FELT PAIN BEFORE, but nothing like this.

Colt Boone stood at the gravesite, wishing he were anywhere else. The pitying looks and mindless platitudes people kept giving him were getting irksome.

His wife was dead. His life lay in ruins. He wanted this thing to be over and for everyone to leave him alone. Especially those who seemed to think this was the right time to tell him he'd meet someone else. They probably meant for it to be comforting, but it only pissed him off.

There wouldn't be anyone else for him. She'd been it. Nobody could ever replace her. It felt like he was seconds from shattering into thousands of tiny pieces. Only anger and sheer determination kept him from falling apart. He'd be damned if he'd risk going through this hell again.

Colt tugged at the collar of his black western shirt then popped the top button. Today, the shirt seemed to be strangling him despite being one of his most comfortable.

He'd had no choice but to wear his Sunday best. It bothered him, but by the time he rolled into town this morning, it'd been too late to hunt down a suit. As it was, he'd needed to drive nearly straight through to get here in time for Sarah's burial. When he'd arrived at the graveyard, several attendees—his in-laws loudest of all—whispered snide comments about his apparel. Not that he cared. Sarah would have understood why he wasn't wearing a suit, and only her opinion mattered.

The minister leading the funeral service motioned for him to step up to the podium, but Colt couldn't get his feet to respond. His limbs were heavy as if filled with lead. The eulogy he planned to give felt hollow. Lacking. He wasn't ready to say goodbye to her. Never would be. Maybe that explained his reluctance to speak.

He took a deep breath, squared his shoulders, and started forward. He'd barely taken two steps before he paused again to gather himself.

A familiar hand clapped down on his shoulder. "You good?"

Colt glanced sideways at his best friend, Cash West, and jerked his head in affirmation.

Cash studied him for a moment, a mixture of concern, compassion, and disbelief clear as day in his vivid green eyes. "You sure? You don't have to speak. I'm sure nobody would hold it against you if you didn't."

That's where Cash was wrong.

Sarah's parents had never liked that their daughter fell for a rodeo cowboy, and they never let Colt forget it. Not even today. Days ago, they'd gone so far as to immediately reject everything he'd told them of his wife's funeral wishes. They'd had the audacity to claim he was lying. As if he'd lie about something like that. Only the knowledge that Sarah wouldn't want them bickering—again—made him hold his tongue and hand over the reins.

He'd never been good enough for her in their eyes, but he'd loved their daughter even more than he'd ever loved rodeo, and that was saying something.

No, his wife's family would condemn him if he didn't say at least a few words. Of course, they probably would regardless.

It didn't matter. After today, he'd never cross paths with them again. Not willingly anyway. Still, he needed to say something. He owed it to Sarah.

She'd always supported him. Encouraged him to chase his dreams. And he'd done the same for her. In spite of how her parents felt about him, his and Sarah's marriage had been nearly picture perfect. The sort people dreamed of having.

And he'd killed her. Nobody would ever convince him otherwise.

His gaze locked on the casket that held his heart within it, and he swallowed hard.

Rather than answering Cash, Colt forced himself into motion and stepped up to the podium. The expectant gazes of everyone gathered landed on him.

How the hell was he supposed to give a eulogy when his tongue felt thick in his mouth?

He cleared his throat and struggled to get his voice to cooperate. "Thank you all for coming." The hoarseness tinting his deep voice bespoke the turbulent emotions he struggled to hide. "We're here today to say goodbye to my wife, Sarah." He smiled sadly then took a deep, hitching breath. "I remember her finding a kitten during our honeymoon and insisting we sneak it on the plane with us when it was time to come home. She made security chase us through the airport for—"

A lump lodged itself in his throat at the memory, and wouldn't clear no matter how many times he swallowed.

It'd taken close to an hour for security to get her to tearfully relinquish the kitten. He and Sarah nearly missed their flight; if he hadn't insisted on getting to the airport early, they probably would have. He'd taken her to the animal shelter to pick out a cat the moment they returned home.

"She was a hell of a woman. Generous. Kind. Beautiful. You could count on her to always be there for you, no matter what." He swallowed thickly. "She wasn't just my wife; she was my best friend. I loved her more than I can find words to say. I'll miss everything about her, especially her big heart." His chin quivered. "Without her, I'm a broken man," he croaked out.

His gaze swept over the people gathered around the gravesite. Besides both of their families, several of Sarah's friends had shown up. Quite a few of his own had come to pay their respects as well, their black jeans and cowboy hats looking just as out of place as his own amongst the sea of dresses and suits.

A shudder rippled through him in the wake of the memories cascading one after the other through his mind. They seemed intent on torturing him.

Sarah racing down the stairs to fling her arms around him the second he returned home from the rodeo circuit. Her beaming up at him, her hazel eyes so filled with life and love.

Colt rubbed at the ache in his chest. He'd never again feel the warmth of her embrace. Never taste her kiss or see that smile. She was gone.

Fuck. The finality of it all hit him hard.

He should never have let her go the last time he'd held her in his arms.

"She was my whole damn worl—" His voice cracked, rioting emotions threatening to engulf him. His gaze dropped to the podium as his vision blurred. "I'm sorry, I can't—" He snapped his mouth shut and hurried away.

Colt rubbed at his burning eyes while his mother-in-law, Claire, stepped up to the podium and took over. After the last conversation he'd had with her, it wouldn't have surprised him any if she'd left him to flounder. When Claire called him several days ago to tell him about Sarah's car accident, she'd accused him of indirectly causing her daughter's death. It was the first, and only, thing he and Claire had ever agreed on.

A hand landed on his shoulder. His gaze swung over to see Cash standing beside him with a grim expression. No further words passed between them. None were necessary. If one person here could understand at least some of what Colt was going through, it would be Cash—the man had suffered more than his fair share of loss as well.

Colt's eyes landed on the casket in front of him as Claire continued droning on.

How was he supposed to live without Sarah? How was it possible she was really gone? It didn't seem real.

He took a shaky breath and blew it out slowly.

Mere minutes later, the service concluded and some of the crowd dispersed. Only Colt, a handful of his friends, his parents, and Sarah's family remained.

Two graveyard workers silently approached, their faces solemn. Colt tensed as the workers began lowering his wife into her final resting place. His chest constricted painfully.

This was it.

He tore his eyes away from Sarah's gradually disappearing casket, unable to watch any more.

"I've got to go," he gasped to Cash then bolted for his truck.

⬥

Colt sat on a barstool in the only bar in town, staring blankly down at the tumbler of whiskey he held.

He'd have to call his parents later. No doubt they'd be worrying about him, considering the way he'd run from the graveyard. Especially his mother—she'd always been a worrywart when it came to him. They would understand why he'd needed to leave.

Cash sat to his left; two of Colt's other close friends—Dusty McCoy and Brody Emerson—to his right. The three fellow bull riders had followed right on Colt's heels when he'd hightailed it from the graveyard. It didn't surprise him any. Whenever one of them was going through shit, the others rallied around him. It'd been that way for all the years they'd known each other.

The quiet presence of his friends filled him with gratitude. There was nothing anyone could say to make this situation better, and they seemed to recognize that.

"Thanks," Colt muttered, feeling as though he should probably say something.

"Hey, man, don't mention it," Cash replied.

Dusty and Brody nodded in agreement.

Colt rolled his glass between his palms for a moment, then took a small sip. Though he wanted little more than to get blackout drunk right now, he couldn't. There were too many things he needed to take care of at the ranch he'd shared with Sarah. Things he should probably be sober for.

He'd need to pack up her things and figure out what the hell to do with them. Maybe it'd be best to drop her clothes off at a woman's shelter. She'd approve of that. Then he'd need to rehome her horse, along with her cat. It'd be too difficult having them around, too much of a reminder she was gone.

Shit, what about the ranch? Should he keep it? Sell it? He had no real desire to be there without her. The place held too many memories.

A wave of guilt washed over him as he considered their home.

He should have been with her that night; Claire was right to blame him. Sarah's death *was* his fault. If he hadn't been off chasing his third National Bull Riding Championship title, he wouldn't be feeling like the Grand Canyon had opened where his heart should be right now. She'd still be alive.

Had he been home, where he'd belonged, she wouldn't have ended up on that lonely stretch of highway—dealing with a flat tire. The bastard who'd hit her would never have crossed paths with her that night. With no witnesses, there wasn't even a way to hunt down the hit-and-run driver to get any sort of justice.

Colt may not have killed her with his own hands, but she was dead because of him.

Sarah's best friend, Katie, told him they'd met up at the sports bar the next town over to watch him ride on the big screen there. If he hadn't been riding, there wouldn't have been a reason for Sarah to go.

It was his fault. All his fault.

She'd asked him to stay home for the first time in ages, but he'd gone anyway. She'd said she had a bad feeling about him riding that weekend. But, after a string of bad rides days before, he'd needed the points to recover his spot in the standings too much to stay home. He'd been so focused on earning that next championship title. *Too* focused.

And now, she was dead. All because of him and his damned career.

Jesus, he needed to stop thinking about it before he completely lost his mind.

"Have you thought about when you'll be coming back to the circuit?" Brody asked, breaking the heavy silence that had fallen between the four friends.

Colt shook his head. "I'm not coming back. I'm done."

All three of his friends looked at him as though he'd gone nuts, but he ignored them—or, tried to.

"What? Are you crazy?" Cash asked.

Colt shrugged. "Never been sane. You know that better than anyone."

Cash widened his eyes, disbelief written all over his face. "You're one of the top fifteen riders in the nation already this season! I thought you wanted another title. You're seriously giving it all up?

"There's no point to anything anymore. One of you guys take the title this year and every year after that. I'm just done." Colt grabbed his glass and tossed back its contents in a single swallow.

Cash shook his head. "Why? What the hell are you going to do if you're not riding bulls?"

Colt didn't know how to explain the chaos in his mind. All he knew was he needed a break from everything, especially the guilt and regret eating at him.

Too bad neither seemed to be going anywhere.

"Don't know what I'll do. Don't much care either. Maybe I'll get a real job."

Brody's head jerked up, his brows snapping together over moss-green eyes. "Riding bulls *is* a real job!" he sputtered. "How can you imply it isn't?" He sat up a bit straighter and squinted at Colt.

"His wife just died, man." Dusty shot Colt a look filled to the brim with compassion and understanding before he narrowed his dark brown eyes at Brody. "Leave him alone."

Brody glanced at Dusty then exhaled a long breath and gave his head a small shake. "I know that, but retiring? Permanently? That seems a bit rash. Riding might be a good distraction."

"Or might cause me to join her in the grave real quick." Colt leveled his gaze on Brody. "How the fuck am I supposed to ride when I can barely breathe? You know how dangerous not being completely focused is. Shit, it's dangerous enough as it is."

Brody grimaced and rubbed a hand over his ribs, probably thinking of his last buck-off. A wreck. It hadn't been pretty, and he'd ended up with three busted ribs for his trouble. All because his thoughts had been on something going on back home instead of the bull beneath him.

"We're worried about you," Cash said quietly. "If you need a break, take it, but don't quit."

Colt ignored him and stared into his empty glass. He knew his decision wasn't one that any of the other men could understand. Not even Cash. Bull riding was more than a career. It was life. Walking away from it was unthinkable to them. It had been that way for him too until now.

He got to his feet and tossed a few bills on the bar before turning to look at his friends. How could he explain that even thinking about riding again heaped so much guilt on his shoulders that it made it difficult to stand? Riding was why she was gone.

"Look, I appreciate what you're trying to do, but I'm done. I need a break. A long one. Maybe someday I'll come back, but for now I'm out."

He heaved out a weary breath.

This was harder than he'd expected—walking away. Not as much from the sport itself, but from his friends. Who knew when he'd see any of them again. The uncertainty of it made the ache in his chest expand. He missed them already. Sure, they could keep in touch, but it wouldn't be the same as hanging out with them nearly every day.

He couldn't stay on the circuit, though. It hurt too much.

"Thank you guys for coming out," Colt said. "It means a lot for you all to have been there today. Tell the other guys I said thanks too when you see them next."

He didn't wait for a reply; he turned on his heel and left the bar.

Chapter 1

Present Day

Colt stared at his reflection in the cracked bathroom mirror, hating the sight of his own face. This wasn't living. In the two years that'd passed since he quit riding bulls for a living, he'd bounced from one ranch to the next more times than he could count. He rarely stayed at any one place longer than a week or two.

Sure, he made good money as the ranch foreman of Crooked Creek, but he detested nearly every moment of the work. It was too repetitive. Dull. He missed the adventure following the rodeo circuit brought with it. The adrenaline rush. The freedom. Never having to ask permission for anything. Never having to answer to anyone, except maybe his fans on occasion.

He never had been good with working under someone else. It chafed being told what to do and when to do it.

If it weren't for how much his boss, Jesse Smith, paid him, Colt would have put this ranch firmly in his rearview mirror by now too.

Paid well or not, he wouldn't be staying much longer. After a month of hard work and long hours for little thanks, along with being frequently hit on by Jesse's adult daughter, Tiffany, Colt was ready to get the hell out of here. He just needed to figure out where to head next.

This wasn't what he wanted to be doing with his life. Sarah wouldn't want this for him either. She'd want him to be chasing his dreams, not helping Jesse chase his.

It'd been a mistake to quit riding bulls. Still, he couldn't deny that he'd needed the time away to clear his head.

Too bad it hadn't helped.

Most days, he felt more dead than alive, like they'd buried some vital part of him alongside his wife. The last time he chatted with his parents, his mom insisted it was well past time to forgive himself and consider moving on from Sarah. While he'd admit it could be possible his mom was right, he doubted he'd ever be able to do it.

No point thinking about it. He couldn't do anything to change what happened.

He slapped on the faucet and rinsed off what shaving cream remained on his face. He had too much to do today to be standing around in his tiny cabin, beating himself up for shit long in the past.

Colt blinked as he stepped outside into the blinding sun moments later. He tugged his hat lower to better shade his face. Tiny beads of sweat popped out across his forehead as the sun began baking him. It was unseasonably warm for April. Today would be another hot one. Why couldn't Kansas have a normal weather pattern?

Two ranch hands, Lucky and Alex, leaned against the fence of the closest pasture. Both men were supposed to be repairing the fence, not using it to prop themselves up. The duo slacked off more than they worked. They were lucky he liked them, and that Jesse was content to let Colt handle dealing with the hired hands. Jesse's lectures were far from joyous to endure.

"Aren't you supposed to be fixing that instead of gabbing?" Colt asked as he headed for them.

Lucky's head snapped toward him.

Nobody knew Lucky's real name, and while it'd piqued Colt's curiosity some back when they'd been introduced, he hadn't cared enough to question him.

The lanky cowboy flashed a grin, displaying his yellowed, crooked teeth. "Getting around to it, Boss. Me and Alex were just deciding whether to go to the rodeo a few towns over tonight." He tilted his head while squinting his eyes. "Didn't you used to rodeo? Broncs or something?"

Memories flooded back to Colt. The feel of a pissed-off bovine between his thighs, all raw power and danger. The crowd cheering his name, and the rambling of the announcer.

A heaviness settled into his chest. He never should have quit.

He crossed his arms over his chest and nodded slowly. "I rode bulls."

"Yeah, thought so. Want to come? Maybe see if we can pick up any of the hotties that follow you guys around?" Lucky laughed, sounding a bit like a sick donkey braying. "Think I picked the wrong occupation. Sure aren't any chicks worth chasing here."

Colt wondered if any of his friends would be there. Fuck, he missed them. Especially Cash. The man was more like a brother to him than merely his best friend. A pseudo-brother Colt hadn't spoken to in nearly a year.

Colt was a shit friend. It'd be a miracle if any of them would even be willing to talk to him after how he'd ghosted them.

"Wish I could," Colt answered, surprised to discover how much he meant it. The prospect of seeing his friends, even just for the evening, tugged at him. "Can't tonight, though. Boss man needs me to head to a stock auction for him today. I'll probably be gone until late. Maybe next time."

"Shame," Lucky said. "Maybe if you went and found yourself a girl, Tiff would stop chasing you around like a hound dog after a rabbit."

A loud laugh burst from Colt. Most days, it seemed like he spent more time fending off Tiffany's advances than getting anything done. It grated on his nerves.

"Yeah, fat chance of that happening. Maybe if one of you guys hooked up with her instead, she'd leave me alone. Might distract her long enough for me to get some work done for once."

"Hell no!" both Lucky and Alex said in unison.

Tiffany was attractive with her long blonde hair, baby blue eyes, and smoking hot body, but her looks were the only appealing thing about her. She was so much worse than most of the buckle bunnies—rodeo groupies always up for a good time and a roll in the hay—Colt had known in the past. At least most of them had backed off immediately if he said no. Even at twenty-three, Tiffany didn't seem to know the meaning of the word.

It didn't help matters he knew she wouldn't be happy with a casual fling with him. She'd demand a relationship, and that was something he would never give her. Wouldn't give any woman. These days, all he offered anyone was a one-night stand. Getting attached to someone else—letting his heart get involved—was too damn risky. He wouldn't do it. Never again.

Sarah had been the first and last to hold his heart.

Alex screwed up his face while making a cross with his fingers as though warding off a vampire. "She's a snooty, spoiled pain in the ass. Don't got time for that."

"Can't blame a man for trying," Colt said with a chuckle. "Don't let Jesse hear you talking about his precious baby girl like that either. You know she can do no wrong in his eyes."

"Shit, man, how do you think she got like that?" Alex asked. "He coddles the hell out of her."

Colt shook his head. "Who knows, maybe she'll take up with that new guy. What was his name? Wyatt? William?" He waved his hand. "Whatever. She seemed pretty damn interested in him when Jesse introduced them yesterday."

"Poor bastard." Alex laughed. "Better him than any of us, though."

There'd been a noticeable decrease in how many times she'd come around to bug Colt since then too. That seemed promising.

"True," Colt said.

While he sure wasn't interested in Tiffany any more than Alex and Lucky were, her constantly wayward fingers reminded him of how long it'd been since he'd last had a woman beneath him. Nine months? Ten? Too damn long, but the guilt that followed each encounter made it difficult to drum up the interest anymore. It felt too much like he was cheating on Sarah, even after all this time.

Colt glanced at the time on his phone. "I should get going. Never going to get any cattle bought if I don't get over there." He nodded toward the fence. "That better be done by the time I get back. No skipping out to the rodeo with it still half-assed. I'm not in the mood to get chewed out by Jesse again tonight."

"Yes, sir." Lucky smirked while giving Colt a mock salute.

Colt shook his head and headed for his truck.

❦

Colt pulled his truck and the largest of Jesse's stock trailers into an open parking spot and stepped from the cab. The sounds of the auction floated to him: the low drone of the auctioneer somewhere in the distance, the lowing of cattle, the scattered whinnies of horses. A faint undercurrent of excitement hung in the air. It almost reminded him of the rodeo. Almost. It was close enough to send a fresh wave of nostalgia skittering through him.

He shoved the feeling away and headed for the registration booth.

A short time later, a pudgy cowboy urged a group of eight black Angus cows into the sales ring. They mooed loudly, protesting as the gate clanged shut behind them.

Colt leaned forward to study the milling animals with a critical eye while the auctioneer told the crowd about them. The cows had good weight and decent conformation. This bunch would do nicely with the bulls Jesse already owned.

The moment the bidding opened, Colt waved his paddle to place the opening bid. These would be the last ones he needed to buy today. Combined with the two he'd won earlier, the trailer would be nearly full.

Within minutes, he was the new owner of the tiny herd of cattle. Well, his boss was, technically. Now he needed to go pay for them, and he could get out of here.

Colt had just stood to leave when an auction worker rode a pretty jet-black horse—with a sock on its right hind leg and a big star on its forehead—into the ring. The horse couldn't possibly be more than fifteen hands high, with a beautiful smooth stride. The auctioneer stated that the animal was a seven-year-old Quarter Horse mare as her rider whirled a loop above his head and loosed it toward a roping dummy another worker hurriedly placed in the ring. The moment the rope settled around the plastic horns of the dummy steer, the horse immediately sat back on its haunches, pulling the rope tight.

A roping horse then, and a decent one at that if she responded the same when roping a real calf or steer. She'd be sure to help catapult someone to the top of the standings for whatever roping event they competed in.

A weird feeling came over Colt, and he sat back down.

This was stupid. He didn't need a horse, didn't even want one, and he sure as hell wasn't interested in doing any roping events. He had no ranch, no horse trailer, and no desire to stay at his current job long enough to buy either of them. Nonetheless, he couldn't bring himself to stand up and walk away.

His breath caught when the bidding began absurdly low. She was too lovely to sell for so little. Colt found himself raising his paddle to place a bid on the animal. It wasn't like he couldn't afford it. The sale of his and Sarah's ranch had left his wallet feeling a whole lot heavier, and he'd hardly touched that money. Most of the work he'd been doing provided lodging and food, so there'd been little to spend it on. Until now.

But what in the hell was he doing?

There was no good reason for him to engage in a bidding war for this little mare, but he raised his paddle again and again to outbid the others vying for her, determined to win. The singular explanation he had was the strange feeling he needed her. It might not make sense, but he'd learned long ago to not ignore his gut about things. After all, if he'd listened to his gut a couple of years ago, he'd probably still have his wife.

Shit, this was a bit hairier than expected. Should he drop out? That one balding guy seemed to really want her. It'd probably be wiser to let the man win. It wasn't like Colt had any use for a horse anyway, especially not one like her.

The lingering feeling gnawing at his insides became more insistent. Colt sucked in a breath and raised his paddle yet again.

The tension gripping him finally eased when the bidding concluded with him as the winner. With luck, he'd be able to figure out later what the hell he was going to do with the mare. Right now, he didn't have a clue.

He glanced at his phone as he pushed to his feet and headed for the exit. If he hurried, he might be able to join Alex and Lucky at the rodeo. If any of his friends were there, maybe he'd be able to hang out with them for a while. Catch up a little.

Shit, if he got there in time, perhaps he'd see if there was late entry and climb his ass back on a bull for the first time in ages. See if he still had what it took.

Colt rushed from the building, half running as he wound his way through the throng of people separating him from the payment booth at the front of the auction grounds.

He was so wrapped up in his thoughts he didn't notice the woman who'd stepped into his path until he collided with her and nearly knocked her to the ground. With a muttered curse, he caught her by the shoulders to keep her from falling.

The apology he'd been about to utter died on his lips when she turned her startled gaze up to him. His mouth went dry, and his breath caught in his chest as her eyes hit him like a bolt of lightning. They were the eyes of a siren. Ice blue, with a slight upturn at the outer edges, and fringed with long lashes. They stood out in sharp contrast with the mane of silky-looking black hair that hung in soft waves past her slender shoulders.

He didn't dare look lower than that.

His gaze slid over her face, taking in high cheekbones, a faintly upturned button nose, and attractively full lips. Lips that parted slightly as she seemed to study him in return. Her features had an elegant air, like some fairytale princess.

Realizing he was staring dumbly at her, he licked his lips with uncharacteristic nervousness. Heat shot through him, and he abruptly released her.

"Uh, sorry about that," he stammered and forced his feet back into motion before she could respond.

He felt her gaze following him as he walked away and clenched his jaw against the urge to look back at her. The temptation to turn around and talk to her was strong, but he refused to give in to it. The last time he'd found himself so instantaneously attracted to a woman, he'd married her. He wasn't doing that shit again. Not ever.

He rubbed a hand over his mouth, attempting to force his focus back to the job he was here to do. What he needed to do was get the animals he'd won paid for and loaded so he could get out of here. He didn't need to be obsessing over a chance encounter with a pretty face.

Shit, a woman as gorgeous as that one probably already had someone anyway.

Shaking his head at himself, he continued to the payment booth at a slower pace.

⬥○⬥

Colt stood in his boss's office, hat in hand, and waited for the older man to acknowledge him. The sooner he got this over with, the sooner he could retreat to his cabin and relax.

After getting caught in a traffic jam on the way back to the ranch, then having issues unloading the animals, it was far too late to meet up with Lucky and Alex now. It was probably for the best.

Somehow, Colt figured Jesse had never seen a day of hard work in his life. His hands were smooth as a baby's bottom—a sharp contrast to Colt's calloused ones. Jesse ran the ranch almost exclusively from this huge, luxurious office. In the month Colt had been at Crooked Creek, he couldn't recall seeing the overweight, balding man do anything more than talk on the phone for hours at a time, whine about getting mud on his boots, and yell at his employees.

When Jesse finally looked up at him, Colt hastily spoke. "Most of the cattle there were junk, but I found a few gems. I won ten Angus cows for your herd. According to the information the auction provided, all of them successfully calved last spring. They all have nice toplines and are well balanced. They should pair nicely with your bulls." He hesitated a beat. "I also bought a Quarter Horse mare for myself. It was kind of spur-of-the-moment. I don't have a place to put her yet, but I should be able to figure something out in a few days. Would you mind me keeping her here until then? She's in the round pen at the moment."

"Hell, I don't care, Boone." Jesse's voice was surprisingly high-pitched for such a big man. "We have open stalls; you know that. You can keep her here as long as you need."

Thank fuck. Colt had suspected it would be alright, but Jesse was difficult to predict at times. At least Colt wouldn't need to scramble to find somewhere else to keep her.

"While you're here..." Jesse continued. "There's a cookout at Daniel Sullivan's old place tomorrow. Used to be Pine River. Maybe you've heard of it before. I think Dan raised a few broncs back in the day." Jesse paused and waved a hand. "Anyway, the couple who bought it last year have done a hell of a good job restoring the old place. They invited Tiffany and me to attend, but I have other obligations." Jesse smiled. "I want you to go in my stead and take Tiffany with you. She's very excited to meet the new neighbors."

Colt stifled a groan. He'd been having such luck avoiding her lately too. He doubted Tiffany was excited about anything other than having another opportunity to pester him some more, but he would never tell her father that. "Why can't she drive there herself?"

Jesse widened his stance and puffed out his broad chest. "No sense in her wasting gas when you're going too. Besides, she says her car's check engine light is on, and you know she won't drive any of the ranch trucks. The invitation was for both her and me. I'm sending you as my representative, but she needs to go as well. She represents Crooked Creek too."

Unless he quit, Colt saw no way around it. Attending the cookout wasn't a problem—free food was never a hardship to accept. It was being required to take Tiffany along that grated. "Fine, but just this time."

To his surprise, Jesse laughed. "Yeah, okay. Whatever. Now, get out of here."

Colt settled his hat back on his head, gave Jesse a curt nod, and hastily complied—all too happy to leave the room.

⚬

Colt stretched out on his bed in the foreman's cabin and stared up at the ceiling as he thought back on the day. He groaned out loud and scrubbed his hands over his face as his mind immediately jumped to the woman he'd nearly run over at the auction. For whatever reason, he couldn't stop thinking about her for very long. Every time he cleared his mind, she popped right back to the forefront within minutes. It was damn frustrating. Why hadn't he at least gotten her name? Maybe stayed and chatted with her for a bit?

Dammit. He didn't need to know her name or anything else about her. It was unlikely he'd ever see her again. Even if she were single, by some unlikely miracle, he didn't need to get involved with anyone. It wasn't as though he'd be in the area much longer anyway. Sure, she was the first woman to cause even a flicker of interest in ages, but still. This preoccupation with her had to stop. He growled at himself and shoved all musings of her away again.

Colt turned his ruminations to the little mare he'd purchased. It was still a mystery to him exactly why he'd felt so compelled to buy the animal. Nothing about his situation was likely to change, yet here he was anyway—the owner of a horse. One he didn't know what to do with now that he had her.

Maybe one of his friends would have somewhere he could house her until he got his shit figured out—if they were inclined to talk to him.

There was one way to find out.

He glanced over at his phone where it sat on his makeshift nightstand and grabbed it. Cash would probably be the best person to start with. He quickly dialed his best friend's number.

Even if Cash didn't have a way to help him, maybe he knew someone who could. As he waited with bridled impatience for his friend to answer, he realized it was late enough that Cash would probably be at his motel by now.

"Colt?"

Relief rolled through him. It didn't sound as though Cash had been sleeping, and from the lack of annoyance in his best friend's voice, he likely wasn't with a woman at present either.

"Yeah, man. It's me. I'm not disturbing you, am I?"

"Nah, what's up? It's been a long time since I heard from you."

That was an understatement. "Yeah, I know. I've been shit about keeping in touch. I've been … busy. I'm sorry." Colt sighed.

Cash grunted. "Don't need an apology, man. You're my best friend. Shit, may as well be my brother. You needed time alone to get your thoughts and shit together. I get it."

"Thanks, dude."

"Don't mention it," Cash said. "So, what's got you calling?"

"Uh, well, I was wondering would you, or any of the other guys, have anywhere I could keep a horse for a while until I figure out what to do with her?"

"A horse?"

Colt chuckled. "Yeah. I had to go to an auction for work today and ended up buying myself a mare I don't need. She's trained to rope. I don't even have a trailer to haul her with, so I guess I'll need someone to come pick her up too." He rubbed a hand over the back of his neck. "I know it's a big ask after I've ghosted all of you guys most of this past year."

Cash laughed hard enough to make Colt frown. "A roper? What the hell did you go and buy a horse like that for? You don't rope."

"I'm aware," Colt said dryly. "Honestly, I don't know why I bought her. I just felt like I needed to." He shrugged, even though Cash couldn't see it. Colt didn't have the foggiest idea how to explain why he'd felt like he needed to buy the animal. He hadn't even figured out the reason himself yet. "So, do you know of somewhere I could keep her? It'd just be for a month or three." He hoped.

"Fuck, man." There was a long pause before Cash continued speaking. "Yeah, I know where you can keep her. I have a ranch in Wyoming; I bought it about six months ago. You can keep her there as long as you need."

"You bought a ranch? Why? You thinking about finally finding a girl and settling down?"

Cash made a sound of disgust. "Hell no! I'm never settling down; you know that. I bought it to earn some extra money. Beef prices are up, and I got the place for a steal. Two horses and three hundred head of Herefords came with it. I figured it made a wise investment. I've been thinking about renting out the house or something. I'm rarely there, but I have a decent foreman and a few hands to look over my beef herd. They'll take care of your mare. I can send someone to pick her up if you tell me where the hell you are."

"I'm in Kansas, at a place called Crooked Creek. I'll text the address to you when we hang up. Thanks, man. I appreciate it." That took care of figuring out where he was going to keep his new horse once he moved on. "I'm sorry I haven't been a better friend."

Colt felt like he'd missed so much of his friends' lives. He'd tried to keep in touch—he truly had—but the jobs he'd been working often kept him so busy he barely had time to think. Which had been exactly what he'd wanted. What he'd needed too. But fuck, he missed his friends.

Regret stabbed him in the heart. They'd all moved on while he watched their lives from a distance. And here he was, still standing in the same figurative place they'd left him. Fuck, he was pathetic.

"So, how has it been going?" he asked. "I've followed the standings. I saw that you're in the top twenty already. Not bad."

"Yeah, I guess I've been doing alright. Been winning some, getting bucked off the rest." Cash paused for a long moment. "It's not the same without you. Have you ever thought about coming back?"

Colt tensed. At least at the rodeo, he'd always felt like he belonged—unlike at the string of dead-end jobs he'd been working. He missed riding bulls more than he'd thought possible. He missed his friends even more.

Colt blew out a breath. "Yeah, I have from time to time. Been thinking about it a lot today, actually. And I've missed you too, man."

"So do it. Come back."

Colt hesitated. "I don't know. I've been away so long I doubt I even have what it takes anymore. Shit, I haven't been on a bull since that 93-score ride." That was a ride he tried not to remember very often. It was the last one Sarah ever watched. It felt like a lifetime ago and yesterday simultaneously.

"Oh, bullshit. You'll have us all regretting my talking you into coming back in no time. Come on, Colt. You know you want to. Come back."

Cash sounded so hopeful that Colt couldn't help but smile slightly.

He glanced at the window, though he couldn't see anything through the dirty glass.

Go back? Was he ready for that? He wasn't sure. One thing he was certain of was that he was tired of working for guys like Jesse. Shit, he was tired of living like this, period. But could he really just go back to the circuit? He'd walked away from the sport for a reason. The guilt still weighed on him, but it'd eased over the years.

Could he? He wanted to. He wanted to so damn bad. Shit, he dreamt of riding more nights than not. What would it hurt to give it a try? He'd walked away once; he could do it again if it turned out riding was no longer for him.

Fuck it. It was time to move on from this job anyway, and the pull to return to the rodeo was far too strong to resist. "Fine."

Cash whooped loudly enough to nearly deafen Colt.

"I have a cookout to go to tomorrow for work," Colt continued once Cash quieted. "Then, I can meet you guys wherever you are. I'm sure my boss will be fine with me keeping my horse here until your guys arrive."

"We're in South Dakota. I'll text you our schedule for the next four or five stops, and you can meet us at one of them when you're able."

Guess that answered whether his buddies had been at the rodeo Lucky and Alex went to. Big fat no there.

"Sounds good. I guess I'll see you soon, then. Thanks again for the help with my horse."

"Don't mention it. I'm happy to help. See you soon." Cash's voice was more cheerful than Colt could remember it sounding.

He hung up and rapidly tapped out the address to Crooked Creek in a text to Cash, then sat the phone back down on the nightstand.

Was he making the right decision by going back? Sarah would be happy that he was. She knew how much he'd loved riding bulls, how big a part of him it was. If she'd been watching from heaven— or wherever she was now—she was probably sorely disappointed with him for having walked away at all.

It was about time he made things right with her memory.

Chapter 2

"Babe, get me another beer!"

Grace Parker paused in the process of leaving the kitchen as her boyfriend, Flint Michaels, called to her from the living room. She'd been running non-stop since just after daybreak, preparing for the cookout they were hosting this afternoon.

It was all his idea. He'd said a cookout would be a good way for them to officially meet their new neighbors and show off the renovations they'd made to their ranch. That might be true, but when she'd agreed to it, she hadn't expected to be the only one doing all the work.

She should have known better. He'd roped her into similar things many times over the course of their relationship and rarely lifted a hand to help. Why had she dared to hope that this occasion would be any different?

Why did he get to sit on his ass all the time while she ran around frantically, making sure everything that needed doing got done? How was that fair? He took her for granted.

She had half a mind to tell him to get his own damn beer. He had two working legs. Her jaw ached as she clenched her molars together. She should never have agreed to move to Kansas with him. What had she been thinking? Her friends had told her not to do it, that there was something off about Flint, but she hadn't listened—thinking they were jealous. The truth made her want to laugh now. It was obvious they'd seen the glaring red flags she'd been blind to. Now, it was too late. She was stuck.

Grace shifted the serving platter she held in her hands. Damn, this thing was heavy. Who knew burgers and hotdogs could weigh so much? She still didn't understand why Flint demanded she prepare all of the food in advance. It didn't make a lick of sense to her, but she'd gotten it all done in record time regardless. The homemade coleslaw and potato salad already waited outside on the long white tables she'd set up earlier.

"I'll be there in a sec," she called back. "I need to run this food outside real quick." She started toward the back door.

"No, get it now!" Flint's slightly nasal voice cracked like a whip through the otherwise quiet house.

Her eyes widened, her gaze darting toward the other room as she froze mid-step.

"*Now*, Grace."

The threat of violence lacing his voice spurred her back into motion. While he'd never raised a hand to her before, she was no longer sure of anything where he was concerned.

Their relationship was in a downward spiral, and had been for some time now. The longer they were together, the more unpredictable and volatile Flint became. The three holes he'd recently punched in the living room wall were a testament to that fact.

Was the volcano he'd become the real him or just another mask? He sure hadn't been like this when she met him. She wished she knew what caused him to change so drastically. No matter how many times she thought back over their time together, she couldn't pinpoint a specific event that could have done it.

She swiveled on her foot and sat the platter on the kitchen counter. Nothing good would come from pushing him.

Grace grabbed a beer from the fridge, opened it, and hastily delivered it.

"Lazy bitch," Flint muttered under his breath as he snatched the bottle from her hand.

The slur failed to wound her. He'd called her that—and worse—more times over the past year than she could keep track of. While being spoken to so harshly stung at first, it barely even registered with her now. He did it far too frequently. The time she'd finally had enough and asked him why he kept speaking to her so cruelly, he'd told her he'd been joking around. When she confessed how much his words hurt her, he'd gotten mad and screamed in her face that she was being an oversensitive harpy, then stormed out of the house. He hadn't come home until well after midnight.

That'd been months ago. It was obvious now that he'd never been joking at all. Not that she'd ever believed he had been.

The sound of his voice grated on her nerves. There were days she wondered what she'd ever seen in him. He wasn't her usual type at all. She'd always gone for the cliché tall, dark, and handsome guys before. Flint didn't check any of those boxes. Just two inches taller than her own five foot five, he was stocky and a bit soft around the middle. Probably from all the beer he drank. His strawberry blond hair was almost always slicked back with a ridiculously expensive pomade. If it weren't for how charming he'd been when they first met, she doubted she'd have even looked at him twice.

She wished she'd listened to her gut and walked away when she'd had the chance.

Flint took a sip then glared up at her with disdain. "Don't know why I even had to ask for another. You should be checking to see if I need one."

Grace sucked in a deep breath and dropped her gaze to the plush carpet covering the living room floor. Resentment burned in her gut, but she fought hard to hide her ire from him in hopes of avoiding another fight. She simply didn't have the energy for another argument. Not today.

"I'm sorry," she said carefully. "I haven't had time. I've been busy getting everything ready for this cookout you insisted we should have. I've barely had a moment to sit down in days."

Flint scoffed. "You've got an excuse for everything." He returned his gaze to the television. "Why are you just now making the food anyway? People will be here any second; you should have had the food done already."

Grace bit down on her tongue to keep from snapping the retort that bubbled to the surface, then took another calming breath before answering, "I do have it done. The burgers and hot dogs were in the oven to keep warm, and the rest is already outside. I could really use your help."

He grunted in response and took another long swig of beer, then waved a hand dismissively. "I'm watching the game. Quit your whining and get out of the way. I can't see the TV with you standing there."

Grace shook her head and left the room without another word.

Never again. The next time that damn man had a grand idea for something like this, he could do it all on his own.

She was weary of the way he treated her.

What happened to the sweet man she'd first met? For the first year of their relationship, he'd been gentle, kind, even doting. She'd been immediately smitten. He'd clearly fooled her, considering his behavior changed after they'd bought this ranch and moved in together a little over a year ago.

It happened slowly at first. Just little things, initially. A backhanded compliment here. A not-so-funny joke about her there. Hidden barbs intended to wound her in the most insidious ways and make her seem like the oversensitive harpy he so often accused her of being. He grew mean so slowly that she hadn't realized how bad things had gotten until recently. Now, she wanted out.

He had her trapped and seemed to know it. Maybe that'd been his intent when he talked her into moving here—to Nowhere

Special Kansas, away from all of her friends back home in North Dakota. They'd probably given up on hearing from her by now. Since moving, he'd made her block their numbers and monitored her phone calls. Cut off from her friends, and with her parents—both birth and adoptive—passed on, she was alone.

All alone.

Grace retrieved the serving platter from the kitchen. She sat it on the table outside then stood back to survey the backyard once more. Flint would probably find something wrong with it; he always found fault with everything she did.

She sank into one of the lawn chairs she'd set up for their guests and closed her eyes. This damn cookout hadn't even begun yet, and she was already exhausted. At this rate, it'd be a long afternoon.

She hadn't even been sitting for five minutes when the first of their guests arrived. Grace shoved herself to her feet, pasted on a smile, and went to play host. Mere seconds later, people began pouring into the backyard as though the floodgates had been opened.

Flint came out of the house, a broad smile spreading his thin lips, and acted like a social butterfly as he worked the crowd. Grace had to stifle the urge to roll her eyes.

The gentle breeze carried his voice over to her. To listen to him talk, he'd toiled for hours and hours on this cookout. Anger churned in her stomach at his words. He was taking all the credit for her hard work again. She wondered what everyone would think if they knew he hadn't even grilled any of the food.

Grace bit her lip and reloaded the cooler—nestled in the grass at the end of one table—with cans of soda and bottles of water.

"You've done a great job with this old place. It looks great!"

Grace swiped her sweat-dampened hair out of her eyes as she straightened then glanced over at the woman who'd spoken. "Thanks, it's been a lot of work." Most of which she'd done on her own while Flint sat on his ass.

The blonde woman chuckled. "Oh, I bet! The old owner, Daniel Sullivan, really let this place go. Last time I was out here, it was a real mess. It looks wonderful now. I like the improvements you've made." Her dark blue eyes widened. "Oh! I should probably introduce myself, huh?" She thrust her hand at Grace. "I'm Sissy Marsh. My husband, Jeremy, and I live about five miles down the road."

Grace smiled and shook Sissy's hand. "Nice to meet you, Sissy. I'm Grace Parker."

"Oh, I know, honey. Everyone in town has been talking about you and your husband since you two bought this old place. Flint, is it?"

Grace's shoulders stiffened. "Boyfriend," she corrected softly.

Once upon a time, she'd dreamed of marrying that man. He'd used the promise of them getting married to talk her into so many things she now regretted, like putting her paycheck in his account instead of opening her own. Now, it was a relief that he'd never proposed. She didn't even want to think about the fit he'd throw if he ever did and she told him no. There was no way she'd ever agree to marry him. He'd lied about so much.

What had once seemed like a daydream was now a living nightmare.

A smile curled on Sissy's lips. "Oh. Shows me for assuming. Sorry about that."

Grace gave her head a slight shake and waved off the apology. "So, what is there fun to do in this town? Please tell me there is more than endless cookouts and gossiping, or I might go crazy. Between working on things here, and my job, I've been so busy that I haven't had time to explore."

Sissy laughed. "There's plenty of shopping downtown too. Oh, and there's the rodeo. We have a small one in the summer and a bigger one in the fall."

"I've heard about the rodeo. I'm a sports journalist for *Rodeo Unlimited*. I have always loved the sport. Back in high school, I used to do breakaway roping. Man, that seems like ages ago now!"

Grace couldn't even remember the last time she sat on a horse. It had probably been years. Well before she met Flint, for sure. He'd never let her ride, or do much of anything he suspected brought her joy.

"You'll have to come to the next one, then. You can sit with me. It'd be great to have female company. My husband used to do a bit of team roping back before we got married, so we always go. Sometimes, I think..."

Grace nodded absently as her gaze snagged on the tall cowboy who'd entered the backyard. A willowy blonde clung to his arm.

She recognized him as the man who'd nearly run her over at the stock auction she and Flint attended yesterday. Thankfully, Flint had come home without any of the cattle he swore he wanted to raise. The poor animals deserved a better owner than him.

Her eyes slid over the cowboy, taking in every detail. He was as good-looking as she remembered. His dark blue western shirt strained over broad shoulders as the muscles hidden beneath it bunched and flexed with every movement he made. He had to be at least six feet tall and, from what she could see, was built more athletically than most of the other men she'd seen in the area.

Was he a hired hand somewhere near here? A local rancher? Who was the woman he was with?

Her heart rate kicked up a notch as he swaggered through the crowd. He turned slightly, giving her a good view of his profile. A faint shadow of stubble covered a strong jawline. His nose seemed vaguely crooked, as though it'd been broken a time or two. With as rough-and-tumble as cowboys were, it probably had. Rather than detracting from his appearance, it gave him a somewhat rugged, all too appealing look. Dark brown hair—long enough to tempt a woman to slide her fingers through it—peeked out from beneath his black cowboy hat.

She remembered his eyes were a bright shade of blue, reminiscent of the ocean on a sunny day. They had held a prominent part in her dreams last night. A girl could absolutely drown in them. Sadness had lurked deep in their beautiful depths. That hint of pain had spoken to her own, and made her want to know what put it there and take it away somehow. Too bad she couldn't see his eyes from where she stood.

Her gaze drifted lower to his narrow waist. He wore a trophy buckle on his belt, but from this distance, she couldn't make out what it was for. As he walked further away, she struggled to keep herself from gawking at the way his worn Wranglers molded themselves to his ass. It wasn't the easiest endeavor—it was a really great ass.

When had she ever seen a more gorgeous man?

A flicker of guilt sparked. She had a boyfriend; she shouldn't be finding this man so damn attractive and difficult to look away from. There was no way she should have dreamt about the guy either, or woken up from that dream needy and aching like she had.

The pretty blonde hanging on his arm said something and tugged him toward a small group of people Grace hadn't met yet.

"That's Colt Boone."

Grace jumped. She'd been so focused on the cowboy that she'd completely forgotten Sissy was still standing beside her. Warmth flooded her face as she turned to look at the other woman; it was probably a bright shade of crimson by now. The knowing gleam in Sissy's eyes made Grace's face heat even further.

"He sure is easy on the eyes, isn't he? If I were a single woman, I'd try my best to rope that man." Sissy laughed. "It's hard not to stare at him."

Had Grace been staring at him? Geez, she hoped not. "Is he a local?" She allowed her gaze to drift back to the man in question.

"No. He blew into town last month. He's the foreman over at Crooked Creek. That's Tiffany Smith, his boss's daughter, with him. Horrible woman. I pity the man for having to deal with her."

Grace glanced at Sissy, half hoping she'd continue talking about Colt. She was unquestionably far more interested in learning more about him than she should be.

What she should do was change the subject to something safer before Flint overheard their conversation. He would kill her if he knew she was eyeballing some other man. It wouldn't matter that she had no intention of even saying hi to the guy. Flint's jealous streak had to be at least ten miles wide. If she had a dollar for every time he accused her of cheating, she'd have more than enough money to move somewhere far, far away from him by now.

Her gaze traveled over to her boyfriend of its own accord, and she barely concealed a wince. From the thunderous way Flint was glowering at her, she surmised he'd seen her watching Colt.

Great. Was it too much to hope that he'd forget about it before the cookout ended? Probably. She really didn't have the energy to deal with his jealousy tonight.

It wasn't as though looking was a crime anyway. There was no harm in it. Considering Flint often actively hit on other women right in front of her, he didn't have room to talk. Regardless, an anxious sensation spread through her. She looked away and dropped her gaze to the grass at her feet.

"Rumor has it Colt was a bull rider on the pro circuit until a couple of years ago. Our summer rodeo is coming up; if the rumor mill is right, maybe he'll ride in it."

A bull rider. Well, that explained the buckle.

"Supposedly, he retired when his wife died in some sort of accident." Sissy paused, a thoughtful expression crossing her face.

His wife died? Grace sucked in a breath at that news, and her heart clenched. No wonder there'd been such pain lurking in his eyes. She couldn't even imagine. How awful! It made her want to hug him. Not that she would. Flint would likely lose his mind if she even said hello to the man as it was.

"Hey, would you want to go to lunch tomorrow?" Sissy asked. "My treat! I can show you around town and fill you in on more gossip."

Grace lifted her eyes back to Sissy and forced a smile. She could still feel Flint's glare boring through her. Her stomach quivered. If he didn't forbid her from going, hanging out with Sissy for a while would be great. Who knew, maybe she'd even end up with a friend here.

"Sure, that sounds fun," she answered. "Where should I meet you?"

Sissy waved a hand dismissively. "Pfft, I'll come pick you up. No sense you wasting your gas." She smiled brightly. "Around ten sound okay to you?"

"Sure, that'll be great."

"Awesome! Well, I had better go save your boyfriend from my husband. Jeremy will talk his ear right off his head. I'll see you tomorrow!"

A smile twitched on Grace's lips as Sissy hurried away. It'd been so long since she'd last had someone other than Flint to hang out with.

Her eyes drifted back over to Colt before she could stop herself from looking. He glanced up right at that moment, and their gazes collided.

Her heart leaped in her chest then beat faster. Recognition sparked in the blue depths of his eyes, and one corner of his mouth tilted upward. Her breath caught. Oh, that smirk was dangerous. He was good-looking to begin with, but that smirk made him doubly so. Grace's lips curled into a small smile of their own accord as she nervously ran a hand over her hair. Her stomach quivered.

All too aware of Flint standing nearby, his heavy gaze still on her, she yanked her eyes away from Colt's and busied herself with making up a plate of food, trying her best to keep from looking at him again.

⎯⎯◆⎯⎯

"You cheating on me?"

Grace whirled around to face Flint, her eyes widening. The dish she'd been washing nearly slipped out of her hand.

Where had he even come from? She certainly hadn't heard him enter the kitchen, and the moment the cookout ended, he'd disappeared.

That'd been nearly three hours ago. It wasn't like she'd thought she'd have any help to clean up, but it would have been nice.

"What? Why would you ask that?"

"That wasn't a no." Flint's dark brown eyes narrowed on her as he squared his shoulders and lifted his chin.

His scrutiny made her feel a bit like a bug under a magnifying glass. Leashed fury radiated from him in nearly palpable waves while he clenched and unclenched his hands at his sides.

Her stomach knotted. "No, Flint. I'm not cheating on you. Why the hell would you think I am?" Grace turned back to the sink and scrubbed the dish she was holding a little harder than necessary. A mixture of anxiety and anger surged through her system.

"I saw you looking at that cowboy pretty hard earlier. He who you've been cheating on me with?"

Grace widened her eyes in disbelief. "I'm not cheating on you! I don't even know the guy. I'm not interested in him."

Okay, maybe that last bit wasn't entirely true. She was admittedly a little interested, but it wasn't like she'd ever do anything about it. She wasn't a cheater. Not even with as hellish as this relationship was.

"Am I not allowed to even look at other men now?" she asked incredulously.

"Hell no, you shouldn't be looking at other men!" he barked. "I'm your boyfriend, or did you forget? Other men shouldn't even exist to you!"

Was he for real? Flint's jealousy was seriously out of control.

Grace rinsed the dish and sat it in the strainer before turning to look at him. "Other guys shouldn't even exist to me? Are you being serious right now? What about that chick you were all over at the auction yesterday? You did a hell of a lot more than just look at her! If I recall, you asked for her number while I was standing right beside you! How was that okay?"

"How dare you talk to me like that after all I do for you! You ungrateful bitch," Flint snarled as he advanced on her with surprising speed, his hand lifting.

Grace didn't have time to realize what he intended to do before she found herself on the floor with her jaw aching and head swimming. Her hand went to her face as she stared up at him with wide eyes.

He'd hit her! He'd truly done it.

Anger churned in the pit of her stomach like dozens of rattlesnakes ready to strike. Only, those snakes lacked fangs. It's not like she could retaliate even if she weren't afraid to. He could easily overpower her.

Tears sprang to her eyes at the injustice. How had this become her life?

"Now look what you made me do!" Flint said, his voice full of accusation. "Why'd you have to piss me off like that?"

Flint stood next to her, hands on hips and shoulders back. His face was flushed, dark eyes bright and gleeful. He almost seemed proud of himself.

Flint arched one eyebrow and tilted his head as he loomed over her. "You gonna cry now, like a little baby?" He gave a snort of disgust. "I don't want to see that shit," he said with a sneer. "I'm outta here. Don't bother to wait up."

She said nothing as he stormed out of the kitchen. The front door slammed hard enough to rattle the windows mere seconds later, making her jerk.

Had that really just happened? Her aching face assured her it had. She wanted to cry, but she refused to. He wasn't worth any more of her tears.

She pushed herself back to her feet, using the countertop for support, then shuffled to the bathroom and studied her reflection. Her jaw was bright red and already bruising. Could she cover it with makeup? She rarely wore the stuff, but she was going to have to try. Her lunch date with Sissy tomorrow would be far from fun if she had to field questions about the bruise the entire time.

Grace sighed and turned away from the mirror. She returned to the kitchen, feeling strangely numb.

She needed to leave before this got any worse, but how could she? He had all her money. Even if she had the means, where could she go? Her parents were gone, and her friends were states away and had probably long since forgotten about her.

The beginnings of a headache throbbed in her temples. There was no way out. None she could see, at least. She needed time. Time to think, to plan.

Her gaze drifted around the room. While she couldn't do anything about escaping this situation yet, she could do something about this clutter. There was so much to clean up still. Grace rolled her shoulders and took a steadying breath, then grabbed the washrag from the sink and began scrubbing the countertop. She threw herself into the task wholly, intent on having the kitchen sparkling before Flint returned home. He would undoubtably have a complete conniption if he came back and found that she hadn't finished straightening up. She'd definitely ticked him off enough for one night.

A thought roiled to the surface, sending an icy chill down her spine, and she froze.

What if he hit her again?

Chapter 3

"GOOD LUCK, COWBOY." THE attractive brunette who'd spoken trailed a red-tipped finger across Colt's chest as he passed her on his way to the chutes.

He spared her a brief, distracted glance but muttered a thanks.

Since he returned to the pro-rodeo circuit a month ago, he'd been getting great draws. Well, great by his standards. Most said he had a death wish, but he didn't. Not really. He loved the rush the risk produced. The bulls he'd been getting were ones rarely ridden to the buzzer—many super rank, some simply powerful. He loved it.

His mind circled tonight's ride. He'd drawn a huge white bull named Hocus Pocus. The animal was well-known to be dangerous, both in the chute and in the arena. He'd landed more than one unlucky cowboy in the hospital in the five years he'd been on the pro-circuit. This bull was quite the challenge to ride the full eight seconds, but Colt was up for it.

Hocus Pocus rattled the chute with his horns as Colt crouched to talk to him—the same as he did with every bull before every ride. He couldn't remember when he'd picked up the pre-ride ritual, but he hadn't had a serious wreck since he started doing it, and his scores had stayed consistently high, so he superstitiously clung to it. It was silly, but it's not like it hurt anything.

Colt reached through the railing and ran a hand over the bull's muscular shoulder. He murmured quietly, wishing the bull luck and asking for a great ride. As he spoke, his eyes drifted closed.

He envisioned himself and Hocus Pocus out there in the arena. Saw himself make it to the buzzer and dismount safely. Saw a high score light up the scoreboard. Heard the crowd cheer for him.

He opened his eyes, gave Hocus Pocus one last pat, then pushed back to his feet.

"Talking to your ride again?"

Colt flashed a grin at the cowboy who'd spoken—Stetson Dalton, his spotter for the evening. At least he knew he wouldn't be slipping beneath Hocus Pocus's belly while trying to get settled on the animal's back. A fellow bull rider, Stetson knew his way around the chutes and would never let that happen. Since they met four years ago at a rodeo not unlike this one, Colt counted the cowboy among his extended circle of friends. Colt didn't know him as well as he knew Cash, Brody, and Dusty, but he knew Stetson well enough to trust him with his life.

"Of course. Maybe you should try it next time you ride. Maybe you won't get hung up again and end up having to spot me instead of riding."

Stetson winced. "Don't remind me. Maybe I'll try it sometime."

Colt bounced on the balls of his feet then shook himself out to loosen his muscles before climbing the railing. He felt Stetson grip the back of his safety vest as he cautiously lowered himself onto the bull's broad back. The moment he was seated, Stetson shifted his hand to his chest to protect Colt from getting slammed in the face by the back of the animal's hard head. All spotters were supposed to do it, but not all of them did. Colt appreciated it, especially considering Hocus Pocus was well known to act up in the chute on occasion.

A heady dose of adrenaline surged through Colt's veins when the enormous animal rattled the chute with his horns again. God, he'd missed this. The thrill, the rush, the danger. He should never have quit. It was great to be back. He felt at least partially alive again.

Colt flipped his chaps up out of the way while he got his legs into position, then shifted his hips around until he felt comfortably centered on the bull's back. He reached for the tail of his bull rope to tie his gloved hand in, a millisecond before Hocus Pocus attempted to rear up and jostled him.

Colt waited him out. The moment the animal settled, he swiftly wrapped the end of his rope around his fingers several times to tie in before the bull could act up again then wiggled his fingers to check his grip. Satisfied that it was as good as it was going to get, a lazy smile spread over his face and he dipped his chin toward his chest.

He raised his free hand high above his head then nodded to the gateman, who yanked the gate to the chute open. Hocus Pocus burst out of the chute with a bellow, leaping high and kicking out straight. Colt stuck with the bull as the animal bucked explosively, leaped, and spun—using his core muscles and thighs to keep himself as centered as possible.

His thoughts homed in on the bull between his legs, anticipating each of the powerful animal's movements. Exhilaration soared through Colt's veins, chasing away the dark cloud that'd been haunting him since losing Sarah. Here, in these eight seconds, he felt light, almost happy.

Too fucking bad it couldn't last forever.

When the buzzer sounded, signaling the end of the eight-second ride, he pulled the end of his bull rope to release his hand then used the next powerful buck to smoothly dismount with a backflip. He landed on his feet as gracefully as a gymnast and sprinted for the arena fence, with the bull right on his heels.

Colt scrambled up the fence railing and clung to the top, out of the bull's reach. The bullfighters rushed in to distract the animal's attention and drew it away from him. He dropped back to the dirt as his score lit up the scoreboard above the arena. 84.2. It wasn't as high as his scores had been before he'd walked away from the sport, but that wasn't surprising with as out of practice as he was. He'd take tonight's score happily. Shit, he could have scored in the 70s, like he'd half expected he would. Now that would have been a disappointment.

He grabbed his hat from where it'd fallen during his ride, slapped it against his leg to rid it of some of the dust coating it, and plopped it back on his head while he walked from the arena.

Dusty met him behind the chutes and handed him his bull rope.

"Thanks," Colt said.

"No problem." Dusty clapped a hand on Colt's shoulder. "I'm sure not looking to flirt with the grim reaper like you are, but I wish I had a bit of your luck with draws. At least your bulls pose a challenge. I keep drawing boring ones. They about rock me to sleep while I'm on their back."

"Guess I'm just lucky," Colt said with a crooked grin. "Who'd you draw tonight?"

Dusty made a face. "Nothing To It."

Colt groaned. The little brindle bull bucked like a seesaw and rarely scored very high. "Damn, I'm sorry. That's rough." He slapped his friend's back. "Who knows, maybe he'll surprise everyone and buck halfway decent tonight. A cowboy can dream, right? Good luck, man."

Dusty laughed. "Thanks. I think I'm probably going to need it. Maybe you can let me have some of your luck so I can get a good draw for once too."

"I'll see what I can do," Colt said with a laugh.

"Appreciate it." Dusty flashed a broad grin, displaying the dimples that won him so much attention from both buckle bunnies and female fans alike. "Well, I'd better get. I'm up soon and still need to finish prepping my rope."

Colt gave his friend a nod then headed for his truck to stash his gear. This particular rodeo didn't have a proper locker room for competitors. Everyone laid their equipment in piles in a set area of the grounds that was roped off to keep spectators from entering.

While he didn't normally mind, he was partial to his bull rope and didn't want anyone picking it up by mistake. Better to put it in his truck instead. Besides, it saved time packing up to head out in the morning.

He was on his way back to the arena to watch the last of his friends ride when he spotted a pair of familiar faces by the concession stand. His heart leaped in his chest, and he stopped in his tracks.

Cash didn't interest him any, but the woman he was talking to sure did.

It was her, the woman from the auction. The very woman who'd haunted his thoughts for weeks after seeing her again at the cookout she and her boyfriend had hosted. It'd almost seemed like fate for that cookout to be hers. Not that he believed in that sort of thing.

If it hadn't been for the fact her boyfriend kept giving him dirty looks at the cookout, Colt might have talked to her there. He hadn't wanted to make trouble for her. It was clear her boyfriend didn't like him, for whatever reason. He didn't know or care why. It wasn't like Tiffany would have left him alone long enough to say anything beyond hello to the woman anyway.

Tiffany wasn't here now, though. And neither was the woman's boyfriend, as far as Colt could see. Thank fuck.

She stood in front of Cash, scribbling furiously into a notebook every time his best friend said something. He'd ridden right before Colt, though he'd gotten bucked off six seconds in. From appearances, she looked to be interviewing him.

A reporter?

That figured.

He had never enjoyed talking to reporters much. His dislike for their probing questions only increased after Sarah's death. The way they always pried into his private business tended to set him on edge. Not even stepping away from the sport had stopped them from hounding him. They always found him, no matter where he went.

His gaze slipped down the woman's body. Reporter or not, the temptation to talk to her was strong. Her hair hung in ebony waves to the dip of her waist, nearly to the gentle curve of her hips. Fuck, the woman was even more gorgeous than he remembered.

She turned slightly, giving him a good view of her shapely backside, and he sucked in a deep breath. The way her denim jeans hugged her ass made his dick twitch.

Colt dragged his gaze back up to her slim shoulders and tried to will himself to walk away.

This was stupid. Why the hell was he standing around, hoping Cash would walk away soon so he could talk to her himself? She had a boyfriend. He'd never once made a move on another man's woman and never would. There was no reason to speak to her. So why wasn't he continuing on to the arena before he missed watching Dusty and Brody ride? Damned if he knew.

The moment Cash sauntered away, Colt slowly made his way over to the woman. He shouldn't be doing this. He knew it, but he couldn't stop moving toward her.

Those damn eyes of hers could probably draw in pretty much any man, but that wasn't what drew him. She was undeniably beautiful, sure, but loads of pretty girls were at the rodeos. No, it wasn't her looks. It was something else. Something nameless and powerful, incapable of being described. Whatever it was, it pulled him to her like a magnet—as doomed as a hapless person being lured by a kelpie.

"Hi," he said as he stopped in front of her. Every single thing he'd planned to say fled in an instant as his mouth went dry.

His knees shook when she glanced up at him and their eyes met.

Recognition sparked in her pale eyes, and a pretty blush colored her cheeks.

Interesting. What was that about?

He racked his brain for some way to start up a conversation. Now that he was here, he didn't have a clue what to say to her. Especially with that enchanting gaze on him again.

Her press badge caught his attention. Yep, a reporter. Grace Parker.

He shuffled awkwardly on his feet. "I'm Colt Boone."

"I know," Grace said with a slight smile. "My friend Sissy told me who you were when you came to the cookout my boyfriend, Flint, and I had." Her face turned a deeper shade of pink.

He found it strangely alluring.

"At least you didn't try to turn me into a pancake like you did at the auction," she teased.

Colt cleared his throat as warmth spread up the back of his neck and heated the tips of his ears. He'd hoped she'd forgotten what happened at the auction. "Yeah. Sorry again about that. I really should have been paying more attention to where I was going."

Grace laughed, and the sound did something funny to his insides. He was fairly sure he could listen to the sweet sound all day.

"Don't worry about it, Colt. I was just picking on you." Her lips twitched upward.

He glanced at her press badge again. "So, you're a reporter?"

"I'm a sports journalist for a small weekly newspaper called *Rodeo Unlimited*. I mostly interview stock contractors, but every once in a while I get assigned to interview a contestant. Usually a roughstock rider." She paused. "I should probably introduce myself too, huh? I'm Grace Parker."

"I know. I read your badge." Colt smirked and poked her press badge with a calloused fingertip.

Her face turned pink all over again.

"It's nice to officially meet you, Grace." He tilted his head slightly. "Do you always blush this easily?" God, she was adorable.

"Um, no, not normally."

It felt like hundreds of butterflies were beating their wings in his stomach. Chatting with an attractive woman never made him feel like this. At least, not since he was young and chasing around his first crush. Grace was different somehow.

She cleared her throat and tucked a strand of hair behind her ear. "So, uh, how did your ride go tonight? I was doing an interview and didn't get to watch." She nibbled at her lip.

The action drew his gaze to her mouth, and he found himself wondering what those lips tasted like.

He shut that train of thought down immediately. He wasn't going there. She was taken. Even if she weren't, he still wouldn't go there. Not with her. Not with anyone. Never again.

He shouldn't have approached her. This had been a mistake. There was no doubt in his mind that he was in trouble here. And yet, he couldn't bring himself to walk away.

He took a deep breath and focused his gaze higher on her face. "I saw. That was my best friend you were interviewing." He chuckled. "I had a pretty great ride. Scored 84.2. Hocus Pocus is a mean devil, but he's fun to ride."

Colt canted his head at her and made a face. "Was that question on the record, or is Cash the only bull rider lucky enough to be interviewed by you tonight?"

Grace laughed, her eyes lighting as she briefly touched his bicep.

Sparks spiraled up his arm from the point of contact and made his heartbeat quicken. He did his best to ignore it.

"Off the record," she said. "Unfortunately, you're not on my list for tonight." She gave him a smile that seemed a bit shaky. "I was curious. I heard the announcer talking about you while I was interviewing your friend."

"That's too bad. I have loads of tales I could tell you." He winked.

"Hmm, I bet you could." Grace's lips curled upward.

He nodded in the direction Cash had gone. "A bunch I could tell you about Cash too. He may as well be my brother. We grew up together."

"Maybe next time," she said with a laugh.

He shifted on his feet and cleared his throat, strangely unsettled. The sensation of her hand on his arm lingered—like the fleeting touch had somehow scorched his skin with the heat it had produced. He couldn't remember a time a woman's innocent touch left him feeling like this. Not since Sarah.

Yep, he was definitely in trouble here. If he was smart, he'd shut his mouth and walk away right now. Too bad he was enjoying the conversation far too much to do it.

"Where are you riding next?" Grace asked.

"Over by Grand Bend." Colt's lips twitched. "Why? You gonna come watch me?"

The idea of her watching him held more appeal than he'd admit. It had been ages since he'd had anyone special sitting in the stands rooting for him. His parents no longer attended the rodeos. Not even the ones local to them. His mom had seen him have one wreck and told him she couldn't watch anymore. Not that he blamed her. It had been a pretty nasty one; he'd come dangerously close to breaking his neck that time around. It still shocked him that he hadn't.

Another faint blush crept onto Grace's cheeks as she shook her head. "I'm headed home after I finish tonight's interviews. I normally do watch whenever I'm interviewing at a rodeo you're at, however."

He didn't know what to say to that, so he said nothing.

Why did she watch him? Was she as intrigued by him as he was by her? He pushed his curiosity away. It didn't matter.

Grace pulled a beat-up flip phone from her pocket and glanced down at the tiny screen displaying the time. "Speaking of tonight's interviews, I should probably get back to work. I still have three more people to interview." She looked back up at him and smiled brightly. "I've enjoyed talking to you."

"I've enjoyed it too." More than he would ever let on. A crooked grin played on his lips. "Thanks for the chat. Maybe next time, we'll be able to talk longer."

If there was a next time. He hoped there was. Even if it was foolish, he wanted to talk to her some more. Wanted to listen to that sweet voice of hers. Maybe make her laugh again.

"Have a good night, Grace." Without further delay, he forced himself to head for the arena, once again resisting the urge to look back at her.

Colt's gaze shifted over the occupants of the crowded bar as he followed Cash and Brody through the door.

He'd half hoped Grace would show up, but it didn't seem that she had unless she was hidden by the masses. With as packed as the place was tonight, that was a distinct, though unlikely, possibility.

Why did her not showing up to the afterparty have him feeling so damn disappointed? She'd said she was headed home after she finished her interviews. It made sense for her to have not attended. Besides, she had a boyfriend. Despite their conversation being brief, Colt could already tell she was the sort of woman who was worth more than a mere one-night stand, even if she were single. Which she wasn't, he reminded himself yet again. He had no business even thinking about her.

So why couldn't he get her off his mind? Hell if he knew.

"Who are you looking for?"

Colt glanced sideways at Cash. "Huh? Nobody. Just seeing who all showed up tonight."

The look Cash gave him in response said he didn't believe him. No surprise there. Colt had never been able to hide much of anything from him. They knew each other far too well for that.

Cash gave him a playful shove, his vibrant green eyes twinkling with good humor. "Well, I don't know about you, but I'm not standing around all night. I'm going to grab a seat before they all disappear. You comin', or you gonna stand around looking for nobody all night?"

"I'm coming." Colt shook his head as he followed Cash to the bar.

Where Brody had disappeared off to was anyone's guess. The quiet cowboy was probably off in the corner nursing a beer or something. He kept to himself more often than not. Broody fucker.

Like Colt was one to talk. He was pretty damn broody these days himself, or so he'd been told.

Cash plopped onto a barstool and signaled to the bartender. Colt seated himself beside him then allowed his gaze to roam over the people surrounding them once more. Besides the usual rodeo crowd, a large number of rodeo fans and reporters loitered everywhere. No doubt this tiny building was well over capacity. The owner of this place had better hope the fire marshal didn't show up. Colt wondered whose idea it'd been to have the afterparty at this venue.

A scantily clad brunette dropped onto his lap without warning, slung her arms around his neck, and planted a kiss on his cheek. "Hi there, Colt," she purred.

He recognized her as the same buckle bunny who'd wished him luck before his ride. Her name escaped him, but he knew she was a common face around the circuit. She was pretty, but he felt nothing. Not even a flicker of interest. Maybe if her hair was black and her eyes ice blue...

He inwardly groaned and shoved thoughts of Grace away once more.

Reaching up, he gently unwound the bunny's arms from his neck. "Not tonight, sweetheart."

A pout formed on the woman's lips, but she didn't argue. She simply slipped off his lap and transferred her attention to Cash instead.

His best friend pulled the woman onto his lap and caught her crimson-tinted lips in a brief kiss. Typical Cash there; he rarely turned down a willing woman. Not unless she'd been drinking anyway—his best friend did have *some* standards.

Colt had been the same once upon a time, well before Sarah. No, he'd probably been worse.

Colt took a small sip of the whiskey the bartender sat in front of him and stared blankly down at the bartop as he considered the events of the day. He was so deep in thought he startled slightly when Cash nudged his arm several minutes later. His gaze swung toward his friend, finding him standing a couple of feet away with his arm slung across the brunette's shoulders.

"I'm getting out of here. Meet you for breakfast?"

Colt gave Cash a quick nod then turned his attention back to his drink. He tossed back the contents of the tumbler in a single swallow. Another appeared in front of him before he could even lift a finger to signal the bartender. Impressive service, even as busy as it was tonight. He tossed that one back too, and a third appeared as if by magic. Yep, exceptional service.

The more he drank, the more his thoughts centered on Grace. Their conversation had been the highlight of his evening. Sure, his ride on Hocus Pocus had been fun, but talking to her had been so much better—seeing her smile, hearing her laugh. He could easily find himself addicted to being around that woman. If he was smart, he would stay far, far away from her instead of sitting here plotting a way to talk to her again.

But that was exactly what he was doing. Maybe he'd fallen on his head one too many times.

Colt's phone rang as he reached for his glass again. He snatched it off the bar and glanced at the screen. It wasn't a number he recognized. For a moment, he contemplated ignoring it. He was close to drunk; it was doubtful he'd even be able to speak without slurring. Regardless, he hit the button to answer and put the phone to his ear.

As the man on the other end of the line introduced himself and stated the purpose of his call, a slow smile spread over Colt's face. It seemed he might get his wish to talk with Grace some more after all.

Chapter 4

"GET UP!"

Flint's angry voice penetrated through the thick haze of sleep, rudely awakening Grace. Her eyes snapped open.

What now?

She thought back on the previous night. What had she forgotten to do to have caused him to wake her when the sun was hardly up yet? She came up with nothing.

"What's wrong?" She struggled to sit up as she gave him a questioning look.

"I'm hungry. Get up and make me some breakfast. And don't forget the extra butter on the toast this time. You always forget."

"Are you serious right now? Why can't you make your own breakfast?" she asked without thinking, too drowsy to remember it wasn't safe to speak to him like that anymore.

When Flint's face turned a bright mottled red, she realized her error, and a frisson of fear crawled down her spine.

In the past month and a half since the cookout, she'd gained more bruises than she could count—courtesy of his fists.

Sleep forgotten in an instant, she scrambled from the bed and mumbled a hasty apology while warily rushing past him, hoping—praying—that he didn't hit her.

When she made it to the kitchen without being struck, she leaned heavily on the countertop and inhaled a shaky breath through her nose. Her eyes slid shut as she exhaled softly through parted lips, a minute amount of tension easing from her battered body.

She couldn't risk relaxing too much. Flint was far too mercurial for that.

Grace shoved away from the counter and flung open the refrigerator door. What would he want to eat?

Not getting it exactly right would be a disaster of epic proportions. Flint was the king of overreacting. She was far too tired and sore to deal with the consequences of upsetting him again right now.

There was no making him happy. No matter what she did, this situation kept getting worse.

After perusing the meager contents of the fridge for a minute, she selected a few ingredients and got to work. It wouldn't do to keep him waiting long.

Flint entered the kitchen a moment later and seated himself at the table to watch her. To her dismay, she wasn't able to read his expression this morning. She'd have to be careful.

She sat a plate heaped high with scrambled eggs, link sausage, fried potatoes, and toast with extra butter in front of him. He didn't say a word, not even a thanks. Instead, he dug right in and ignored her completely.

Grace stifled a sigh and moved to return to the bedroom. Since she didn't need to be at work for a couple of hours, she had plenty of time to take a quick nap. She badly needed more sleep.

She'd gotten in late last night after doing interviews all weekend, ready to fall into bed and sleep for a week. Flint had taken one look at her and insisted she make popcorn and stay up to watch a movie with him instead of letting her go to bed. She hadn't dared to protest.

"Where do you think you're going?"

The question froze her in her tracks. As she looked back over her shoulder at Flint, her brows pulled together in puzzlement. "Back to bed for a bit."

"No."

Grace's heart raced as her body tensed. He was going to do it again, wasn't he? Maybe she'd been mistaken. "What?"

"I said, no."

This was far from new. He did this a lot these days. The not letting her sleep thing. It gave him great joy to torture her in any way he could think of.

Flint motioned to the chair across the table from him. "Sit." When she didn't immediately do as he demanded, he narrowed his eyes at her. The promise of violence colored his voice when he said with eerie calmness, "I said. Sit. Down."

She sat, and he turned his attention back to his food.

Inwardly, she seethed. It was too dangerous to let him see her anger, even just a hint of it. It would do nothing but earn her a beating and make him giddy. He seemed to love nothing more than to push her until she had some sort of emotional outburst. It didn't seem to matter much what it was.

While he ate, she nervously picked at the wood veneer that covered the table. Some dark part of her she never knew existed wished he'd choke. The unbidden thought made her feel wicked. It wasn't like her to wish someone harm. It wasn't who she was. It wasn't who she wanted to be.

She needed to get away from him before she lost herself completely.

One hundred dollars. That's all she'd managed to squirrel away in the shoebox hidden deep in the shadows of the closet. Just a few cents here, a dollar or two there—whatever change she had left after grocery shopping each week. Miraculously, Flint never questioned her or demanded to see the receipts when she said there wasn't change.

One hundred dollars wouldn't get her far. Not yet. She'd need to wait a bit longer to make her escape.

Flint said nothing more until he'd emptied his plate. He smirked and shoved it across the table to her. "Once you clean up the kitchen, you can go back to bed."

Her gaze traveled to the wall clock, and she had the sudden urge to cry. Her alarm would go off now in a paltry forty-five minutes. After she cleaned, there wouldn't be time for a nap.

"If I were to try, I'd probably be late for work," she said quietly.

Once again, he'd figured out a way to prevent her from getting adequate sleep.

"I don't like you being gone all weekend, and I don't like you interviewing all those cowboys either." He gave her a suspicious look. "Do they make you interview the one from the cookout too? I remember someone saying he's a bull rider." His expression hardened. "I'm not okay with it if they do. I don't want my girlfriend talking to the guy she was fucking around on me with. Nuh-uh. In fact, I forbid it. You won't like what happens if I find out you've talked to him." Flint sneered, making her skin crawl.

Heaven forbid Flint ever found out she had indeed spoken with Colt the weekend before last. It wouldn't matter that the conversation had been innocent enough and in a very public place. Flint would be beyond livid. The idea of him finding out terrified her.

At least he didn't know Colt's name. If she was ever instructed to interview him, Flint would never know Colt was the cowboy from the cookout—unless someone local told him. The prospect of that happening was almost too frightening to contemplate.

"I never cheated on you, Flint. I don't know why you keep insisting that I did."

Flint gave a derisive laugh and rolled his eyes. "Yeah, sure you didn't. Protesting too much to be innocent." He licked his thin lips and sat back in his chair. A smug smile crept onto his face as his cold brown eyes moved over her face. "I don't understand why you're even working. Come to think of it, I think you ought to quit. I'm not comfortable with you working anymore."

A chill slid down her spine, and her stomach knotted. It was a good thing she hadn't eaten, considering the way she suddenly felt like she might throw up.

Her job was her lifeline; she couldn't lose it. It was the one thing keeping her sane in this nightmare. Maybe she could appeal to his greed—her paycheck was bigger than his.

Grace swallowed hard and crossed her fingers beneath the table. "If you make me quit, you'll be short my paycheck. Are you sure you want to lose the money I bring in each week?"

He gave her a sharp look, silencing her. "Hmm, didn't think about the money." A calculating gleam entered his eyes. "You should tell your boss you need a raise. You're away all weekend. You need more money for the inconvenience."

It was hardly an inconvenience to her. More like a vacation away from hell, but she'd never tell him that.

Her gaze flicked back to the clock, and she slowly got to her feet. "I'll do that."

Despite her words, she had no intention of doing any such thing. Her wages were already more than fair. Not that she ever got to see even a dime, thanks to the jerk across from her. Never again would she be such a freaking fool.

Grace picked up Flint's plate. She waited until he gave her a nod—permitting her to leave the table—to walk to the sink. By the time she was finished cleaning, there wouldn't be time enough to do anything beyond toss on some clothes and dash out the door. Thankfully, she'd showered before bed last night.

Once the room was as sparkling as she could get it within such limited time, Grace hurried to the bedroom to get dressed. As she entered, the telltale sound of the shower running and Flint's horrible off-key singing drifted through the closed door of the ensuite. That answered where he'd disappeared off to while she'd been busy.

Maybe she could get out of the house before he finished. She sure hoped so. She was already running behind as it was, and the risk of him delaying her was far too high.

Grace grabbed her brush from its spot atop the dresser and ran it through her hair, then pulled her first coordinating outfit from the closet and threw it on.

The shower shut off, and panic gripped her. With wide eyes, she snatched her purse off the chair and bolted from the house. It wasn't until she was in her truck and backing down the drive that she could breathe easily again.

Something had to give. She couldn't keep living this way.

⚬

Grace stood in line at the time clock, wringing her hands. She hoped like hell she'd be able to punch in on time. Traffic had been fairly light, but after leaving the house nearly ten minutes later than she normally did, she'd had to speed to get here.

Patrick Johnston, her boss, was amazing, but even he had a limit to his patience for tardiness. Flint had probably made her use up all the tolerance her boss had for her, considering how often she'd shown up for work late because of him.

Despite Flint's objections about her working, she already knew he'd flip out if she lost her job. If she did, he'd undoubtably absolve himself of having any part in causing it. Flint never did any wrong. Ever. Not in his own eyes, at least. Anything bad that happened was always someone else's fault—usually hers, according to him.

She couldn't afford to lose this job. There was no way she'd be able to find another that paid as well as this one either. At least, not in this town. Gas prices were too high to commute. Not that Flint would ever allow her to.

The amount of control he had over her life infuriated her. She never thought she would end up in a situation like this. In the past, she'd told herself that the second a man so much as threatened to raise a hand to her, she'd leave. Immediately. The ease of that ideal lacked practicality while living the scenario, however. She hadn't understood why battered women didn't just walk away. Not until she became one too.

How had she even gotten to this place? She barely recognized herself anymore.

Once upon a time, she'd been so confident and assertive. Now, she jumped and trembled any time he so much as looked in her direction. It didn't help that, during a fight two weeks ago, he'd threatened to hunt her down and kill her if she ever tried to leave him. The expression on his face when he said it had shaken her to her core. She had no doubt he'd absolutely meant it.

Grace had just plopped into the seat at her desk when Mr. Johnston ducked his head into her cubical and motioned for her to follow him. Grace's stomach twisted into a knot for the third time this morning alone. A sense of impending doom settled over her like a heavy cloak as she woodenly followed her boss to his office and took a seat across from him at his immense mahogany desk.

She wasn't getting fired, was she? She'd clocked in with two minutes to spare today. Her mind spun wildly as she tried to remember if she'd recently done anything that would warrant being fired. There was nothing she could think of.

"I'm sure you're wondering why I asked you to come in here," he boomed.

Grace nodded, unable to untangle her tongue enough to speak.

"I have a special assignment for you."

A special assignment? That, she could handle.

She sagged against the back of the chair as tension fled her body.

"There's a PRCA roughstock rider who's been steadily climbing the ranks, thanks to the scores he's been pretty consistent about earning. He's a fan favorite and has been making enormous waves. We don't want to be left in the dust on this one. We've already reached out to him, and he's agreed to be interviewed."

Mr. Johnston paused long enough to give her a tight smile. "That's where you come in. He requested you specifically. I don't know why, and frankly, I don't care. All I know is that he said he won't talk to anyone but you. Your normal interviews have all been reassigned. This is the sole person you'll be interviewing for the next few months."

Who *was* this rider? And why did he only want to talk to her? It wasn't altogether unusual for someone to request a specific journalist, but nobody had ever demanded to be interviewed solely by her before. Usually, riders asked for one of her far more experienced coworkers. Most often, Bryan or Cindy.

"Okay. Still on the weekend, like normal?"

Mr. Johnston shook his head, his jowls jiggling slightly with the motion. Sometimes, the man really reminded her of an English bulldog. "No. You'll need to follow this rider around the circuit. This assignment is a bit more involved than what you're used to. You'll need to watch him ride at least two days a week, along with interviewing him every Friday. I know you're used to having more time to write and edit, but I'll expect your article to be in my inbox every Saturday by noon. By watching him ride, we're hoping it will provide you with more material to work with for your article."

He gave her a stern look, his steel-gray eyes intense. "Get to know this rider. I don't want to see some surface-skimming article highlighting what bulls he rode and how he scored. I want our readers to get to know who he really is. What makes him tick. How he thinks. What he likes and doesn't. You don't need to interact with him beyond your Friday interview, but we do encourage it if it will help your article."

Bulls. So this was a bull rider, then. That narrowed it down some, but so many cowboys were following the circuit at any given time, it was impossible to guess whom she'd be interviewing.

Grace nodded in acknowledgment. "Okay. When does this start?" It sounded like a fun assignment, but she already knew that Flint would be completely opposed to it. She hesitated, then asked, "Does this new position also come with a raise?" Flint would handle the news far better if it came with at least a modest pay increase.

"It does. Not much, but it's something. You'll start tonight. He's provided us with a schedule of rodeos he intends to attend for the next four months. It'll be in your email by the time your flight lands, along with more information about what this new assignment entails and what is expected of you." He reached into a folder and withdrew a plane ticket. "You fly out in two hours. A rental car will be waiting for you when you land. Any expenses—food, lodging, etcetera—can be put on your company credit card, as usual." He held the plane ticket out to her. "Any other questions?"

"Um, just one." She took the ticket from him. A flicker of excitement sprang to life, chasing away the last remnants of her earlier fears.

She'd seen several of her co-workers get similar assignments in the past and had heard how fun they were, but she never dreamed she'd get the chance herself. It didn't hurt that it would keep her away from home more too.

"Who am I interviewing?"

"Colt Boone," her boss stated breezily.

Oh no.

All at once, every bit of apprehension returned in a hurry, multiplied by a thousand.

"He was out of the game for a while and recently returned to the circuit," Mr. Johnston continued.

"Colt Boone?" Her voice came out like a squeak. She felt queasy all over again.

It wasn't that she didn't like Colt; she did, which was part of the problem. If Flint found out whom she was assigned to interview and figured out Colt was the cowboy from the cookout, this could be bad for her. Very bad. Unthinkably bad.

She swallowed hard.

Her boss frowned. "Yes. Is that a problem?"

She shook her head. "Um, no. It's no problem at all."

"Good. This is a big responsibility we're trusting you with. Massive. It's imperative that this goes well. Do well, and we'll talk about making the raise permanent."

"Thank you for this opportunity. I won't disappoint you." Grace forced a smile to her face and got to her feet. "I better get out of here and get packed."

Her boss gave her a curt nod that sent his jowls jiggling again and waved a meaty hand toward the door. She took that as permission to leave and hustled out of the room.

She stopped at her cubicle long enough to grab her purse, notepad, company-issued laptop, and voice recorder, then darted for the exit. Time was a wasting.

⚬

Grace stared into her closet blankly, her head whirling. She couldn't decide how many outfits to pack. Maybe it was her nerves blocking her ability to think.

On the way home, she'd figured it would be best to plan on being away for four days at a time to simplify her schedule. She could watch Colt ride on Wednesday and Thursday, do the interview on Friday, then fly home on Saturday after she submitted her article.

Crud, would it even be workable to come home in between at all? It wasn't like she had any experience with assignments of this nature. What would Flint do if she couldn't?

An icy chill skidded down her spine. What if he joined her on the road and saw the cowboy she was interviewing? Would he recognize Colt? Flint's memory wasn't the best, so maybe not—a small comfort. She would probably be safe enough through the week, but there was nothing stopping Flint from flying out to wherever she was after he got off work on Friday.

Her heart rate soared as her breaths came in fast, shallow gasps.

She sank onto the end of the bed and buried her face in her trembling hands.

Why couldn't she have gotten assigned to interview someone else? Why did it have to be Colt? Literally anyone else would be fine. Anyone but him. He was too dangerous, and not just because she'd be in a world of pain if Flint joined her and recognized him. It baffled her as to why Colt would request her specifically. They barely even knew each other. She did genuinely like Colt though—so far, anyway—despite not knowing him beyond their brief interaction and the information she'd found on him after a quick internet search. She couldn't deny that it'd been enjoyable chatting with him. It had felt great to laugh. Heaven knew it had been such a long time since she had.

That Colt was easy on the eyes and had a voice like good whiskey didn't hurt.

Maybe she'd imagined it, but she could have sworn Colt had been flirting with her during the short conversation they'd had after his friend's interview. While she was reasonably sure she could keep her own libido under control and keep this professional, could he? He knew she had a boyfriend, but what if that wasn't enough to keep him from making a pass at her? Would she be able to resist him if he did? With as long as it'd been since a man touched her with any sort of gentleness, she wasn't entirely sure.

She was fooling herself anyway by thinking Colt could possibly be interested in her. Flint never failed to remind her how nobody else would want her ugly ass. How lucky she was to have him. No doubt Colt was just being nice, and she was making something out of nothing.

Grace inhaled a deep breath and blew it out slowly then forced herself back to her feet. There was no time for this. Flint would be home for lunch in less than an hour. She needed to be gone before then.

She returned to the closet and withdrew several outfits, along with a few alternatives, then laid them out on the bed. Her hands were shaking so badly she had trouble unlocking the latch on her suitcase. Mumbling to herself, she tried again. This time, the latch popped open. Though tempted to simply toss her clothes into the suitcase and run out the door before Flint caught her packing, she forced herself to take the time to fold her clothes properly.

The prospect of embarrassing herself by showing up to the rodeo to conduct an interview in wrinkled clothing was enough to keep her from rushing. It wouldn't even be remotely professional. The fact that she wanted to look nice for Colt had nothing to do with it, or so she told herself.

She snapped her suitcase shut and walked out the door to load her truck.

Grace returned to the house long enough to scribble a quick note to Flint, telling him about the new job assignment and all of the details she knew he'd demand to know—except for the name of the cowboy she was interviewing, of course. She sent up a silent prayer that the raise would be enough to keep Flint from freaking out when he learned she was gone. She'd been sure to mention it twice.

As she backed out of the driveway, she wondered if this assignment would be a blessing in disguise. Despite her trepidation about it, she knew she needed the time away from the abuse. She was tired of walking on eggshells to keep from gaining more bruises. For the first time since she'd learned who she'd be spending the next several months interviewing, she felt a hint of optimism.

This could work out. Maybe this time away from Flint would even give her the opportunity to solidify her plan to escape safely.

A girl could hope.

Chapter 5

"Colt!"

Colt glanced around, trying to locate the woman who called to him. He recognized that voice, but for the life of him couldn't put a name to it. From the corner of his eye, he spotted a small, feminine hand waving to him as the woman called out again. He turned toward the sound, and his lips curled up at the corners.

It was Grace. She'd come.

Part of him had worried she might refuse once she learned he'd agreed to be interviewed by her, and only her, when her employer called to ask for a series of interviews over the coming months. Ordinarily, he would have immediately declined the request, as he had so many others. If it weren't for Grace, he would have, but it'd been too tempting to use it as an excuse to spend some time with her.

He wanted to see more of her. A whole lot more. On some level, he realized he was playing with a live grenade.

He ignored the other reporters and journalists vying for his attention and headed her direction.

"Grace." A crooked grin fitted itself to his lips. "You came."

"Of course I did," she said with a half-smile of her own. "You were amazing out there. The ride, anyway. Your dismount looked kinda rough."

His bull tonight had been tough. Named Earthquake, the yellow bull had definitely shaken him up. Though he'd ended up with a pleasingly high score of 89, the foul-tempered beast nearly messed him up good when his dismount after the buzzer left him flat on his back and gasping for air. The bullfighters had struggled to get Earthquake's attention pulled off of him. He'd caught a hoof to his shoulder before they'd managed it. His arm still felt a little numb, but he figured it'd be okay. At least it wasn't his riding arm.

"Thanks. It was alright. I got the air knocked out of me for a minute." His grin spread. "So, this interview. How about we do it over dinner?"

The hint of a smile that had been playing on Grace's face vanished in an instant, and her posture stiffened.

"I don't know," she said slowly. "Dinner isn't normally part of my interviews. It would be strictly business."

"Just business?" Colt made a face. "I don't know if I like the sound of that. It sounds so ... stodgy."

"You know I have a boyfriend, right?"

It hadn't been his intention to make her uncomfortable, but he obviously had. Shit, he hadn't considered how his words might be construed.

"I know you've got a boyfriend, Grace. How about dinner as friends instead? I wasn't hitting on you. I promise. I suggested dinner because I don't eat before I ride, and I'm about starving."

He took a small step back to give her some space. "I'll be able to answer your questions better without my stomach growling like an angry bear."

It wasn't a lie. After the adrenaline rush from riding faded, he was often ravenous—just as he was tonight. It'd been the only reason he'd brought up sharing a meal during the interview.

"Oh. I thought..." A rosy blush crept onto her cheeks. "I'm sorry for jumping to conclusions. I feel silly now."

He knew exactly what she'd thought. Colt chuckled. "You're fine. If you didn't have a boyfriend, you might be right about my motives."

That wasn't a lie either. He liked her and was far more attracted to her than was wise. He itched to touch her arm but refused to give in to the desire.

She seemed skittish. Even an innocent touch like that would probably have her scrambling to get away from him at the moment.

Grace didn't look like she quite believed him, but her pretty pink cheeks turned a deeper shade of red.

He ducked his head to meet her gaze. "So? Dinner as friends?"

To his relief, she blew out a breath and nodded. "Okay. Dinner as friends." She smiled shakily. "Sorry. I'm not normally so awkward. I don't know what's wrong with me today."

"You're fine. Seriously. Let me go stash my gear real quick, and we can get out of here. There's a pretty decent restaurant not too far away. It's usually quiet this time of night, so it should be perfect." He smiled. "Don't move. I'll be right back."

When he returned a few minutes later, it surprised him to see her still standing exactly where she'd been when he left her. He raised his eyebrows but made no comment. It didn't seem wise to say anything about it with as nervous as she was acting.

He wondered if she was always this jittery when interviewing someone or if it was just him. She hadn't appeared ready to bolt like a frightened rabbit when she'd interviewed Cash.

Maybe he shouldn't have insisted on dinner. He really *was* famished, though. There was no way in hell he'd be able to concentrate without some food, not with the way his stomach was grumbling.

Colt flashed a grin at her. "Come on. I'll drive." He took a step toward the parking lot then stopped short. His gaze swung back to her. "Unless you'd rather meet me there? I just realized I'm being a bit pushy. It's okay if you're not comfortable riding with me. It's not like you know me, or how well I drive."

She gave him a long look then smiled faintly. "Lead the way. There's no sense to both of us burning gas." She fell into step beside him when he nodded and continued on to the parking lot.

Once they reached his truck, he opened the passenger side door for her. She seemed taken aback by the action.

Did her boyfriend not open doors for her? It was basic manners. Colt's mother would have his hide if he forgot to.

A small, shy smile teased her lips. "Thanks." She ducked her head to tuck a strand of hair behind her ear while looking up at him from beneath her lashes, then turned away and settled herself on the bench seat of his truck.

Jesus fuck, the woman was breathtaking. His mouth went dry, and he cleared his throat. Her look, though innocent, had his body reacting in a rush. He hoped like hell she didn't notice.

"You're welcome," he murmured.

He stifled a groan and adjusted himself after shutting her door, then walked around the front of his truck to join her.

Maybe agreeing to these interviews had been a bad idea. Too late to back out now. He'd committed to this thing; he needed to see it through.

Colt slid behind the wheel and glanced over at Grace while starting the engine. "You're not a vegetarian or anything like that, are you? The place I was thinking of is a steakhouse. I don't think they'd have much to offer someone who doesn't eat meat."

She laughed and shook her head. "No. I'm more of a carnivore."

He tossed her a grin and backed the truck out of the parking spot.

"My kind of woman," he said before he could stop himself.

Grace said nothing in response to his comment, but she gave him one more of those little smiles as yet another blush colored her pretty face.

She was adorable. If he could keep his damn hands to himself and not scare her off, he was sure he would enjoy chatting with her.

Neither of them spoke further during the short drive to the steakhouse. That was fine by him. He wasn't really sure what to say to her anyway.

The whole being unable to come up with things to say to a woman was certainly new. Then again, he rarely found himself this attracted to one either. Especially one he'd already deemed completely off-limits. It wasn't as though he had dozens of female friends, platonic and otherwise—like Cash did.

Sometimes, he envied his best friend's ease when it came to women. Sure, Colt could flirt with the best of them, but flirting didn't always mean anything. It just came naturally. Shit, he could recall more than a handful of times he'd been told he'd been flirting without even realizing he'd been doing it. But when it came to a woman he was genuinely attracted to, that he really truly liked, his brain seemed to short out and often left him fumbling for words. It'd always been that way.

He was determined to figure out something to say. He wanted to become Grace's friend.

Once they arrived at the steakhouse, he hopped out of the truck and trotted around to help her down from the cab. He opened the door and offered her his hand. He couldn't help but notice the surprise that flashed on her face. Her boyfriend clearly needed a lesson in manners.

"Thanks," she murmured as she accepted his assistance. "Again."

Colt chuckled. "You're welcome. Again."

He ushered her into the restaurant ahead of him. After they were shown to a table, he pulled a chair out for her then seated himself. She still seemed way too tense for his liking. He didn't like it.

"I promise I don't bite," he joked, giving her a razz grin. "Let's order. Then, we can get this thing started. Sound okay?"

A little of the tension in her shoulders seemed to ease as she smiled in response. "Alright." She picked up the menu and stared at it for a long moment before glancing at him. "I assume you've eaten here before. What's good?"

He laughed. "I'm not sure I'm the best person to ask that. I'll eat about anything. I spend too much time on the road to be too terribly picky about my food." He thought for a moment. "I guess I'd say the sirloin and burgers are pretty good here. They've got pretty awesome all-day breakfast too if you're in the mood for that."

She returned her attention to the menu, looking thoughtful. "I guess I'll try one of their burgers. I'd love to get the steak, but the price is a bit too steep for me. The paper gives me a credit card for expenses, but I hate using it more than I need to. It makes me feel weird."

Colt frowned at her. "It's my treat. Get what you want. I'm the one who suggested dinner."

"Oh, no, I can't let you do that." She shook her head as if to emphasize her words.

"Sure you can. Get what you want, Grace. I insist."

She shook her head again.

He made a face but said nothing more about it.

He ordered himself a sirloin—cooked medium-rare with all the trimmings, just as he liked it. True to her word, Grace ordered a burger instead of the steak. She almost looked like she might change her order for a second, but in the end, she bit her lip and handed the waitress her menu instead.

Rather than begin the interview, they chatted about other things while they waited for their meals. Thank fuck Grace had been quick to start up a conversation; he hadn't had a clue where to start.

Being around her muddled his brain. She was so passionate when she talked about her journalism career. The way her eyes lit up was alluring. There was no doubt in Colt's mind that she loved her job.

Before long, she opened up and shared that she was adopted when she was just a baby, and that she very rarely uttered a curse word—something about her adoptive parents being firmly against swearing and it being a habit that stuck.

When the waitress returned to bring them their meals, Grace gave his steak a longing look and he almost smiled. Without a word, he snatched her plate away and pushed his in front of her. It was a risk, considering he didn't know how she'd react, but he wanted her to have what she truly craved. He wanted to make her happy.

"Hey, give that back!" She reached for her burger.

Colt picked it up and took a big bite. He chewed and swallowed, then smirked. "Nope. This burger is mine. If the steak isn't done enough for you, we'll send it back so they can cook it more."

She stared at him for a moment. So long, he worried he'd overstepped and upset her, but then he saw the faint twitch of her lips as they slowly curled into a smile. The tension drained from his muscles.

Grace picked up her knife and fork. "I like my steak the same way, actually." She shook her head. "You didn't need to do that, Colt. I was fine with the burger." She cut herself a bite of steak and popped it in her mouth.

Her little moan of pleasure made him glad the table hid his lap from view.

He flashed her a grin and took another bite of her burger. It was pretty damn good and exactly like he would have ordered it himself.

"Think you can eat and talk?" She pulled a voice recorder from her purse, sat it on the table, then delved back into her bag—plucking out a notepad and pen this time. As he watched, she flipped the notepad open to what appeared to be a lengthy list of questions.

"Sure, let's get this bull bucking." He settled back in his chair as she picked up her pen and pressed a button on the recorder.

Grace took another bite of the steak and looked up at him with a smile. "Ready?"

He snagged a fry from his plate before nodding, and she began rapid-firing questions while he did his best to keep up.

Chapter 6

THIS WAS THE MOST enjoyable assignment she'd ever been given, hands down.

Grace sat cross-legged on the hotel bed, staring into the screen of her laptop as she reviewed the notes she'd taken about Colt over the past month and a half. He was so refreshing to be around, and her boss seemed pleased with her work.

At first, she hadn't been sure what to make of Colt. He was undeniably flirtatious, but many of the cowboys she interviewed were. It didn't necessarily mean anything, and there was no way she was going to read into it. The first week, it'd made her more than a little nervous, but he'd never once taken things too far and was always respectful.

She liked him. Really liked him. She was willing to admit to that, though it hardly mattered how she felt. Until she got away from Flint, it couldn't go anywhere. While her jerk of a boyfriend undoubtedly didn't deserve her loyalty, being loyal was how she was built, no matter what.

Flint had taken the news of her assignment better than expected, though he'd demanded she call every hour to check in. It galled her, but the fear of what he'd do if she missed calling him kept her from saying no.

At least this assignment kept her away from home enough that she didn't have to deal with him in person much. She got home so late on Saturday that she rarely had to talk to him then. He worked 12-hour shifts at the factory Monday and Tuesday, so most of those days were also blissfully quiet. She flew out to wherever Colt was on Tuesday afternoon, leaving her with one full day with Flint each week. It was almost heaven.

Too bad the little time she did spend in his presence often left her with more bruises. Not having her home as often as he was used to agitated him. Her peaceful oasis doing these interviews seemed poised to crumble any time now. The past few days, he'd really ramped up his accusations of her fictitious wrongdoings, and threats to kill her if she ever tried to leave him. It worried her.

Grace shoved thoughts of Flint away, read over her notes one last time, then shut down her laptop and sat it on the nightstand.

It was Thursday. Too early in the week to start writing her article. She'd save that for Friday night after she got back to her hotel room.

If she was going to get to the rodeo in time to watch Colt ride, she needed to get her butt in gear. Grace crawled off the bed and padded to the bathroom for the fastest shower she'd ever taken. She needed to be at the rodeo grounds in thirty minutes. Barring any unforeseen delays, this rodeo had the roughstock events scheduled to begin then. She didn't want to be late.

The thought of talking to Colt tonight filled her with giddiness, just as it always did. Sometimes, she felt like a teenager with a crush. It was wrong feeling this way. Nothing could come of it, she knew that, but stopping her growing attraction to the man was nearly as impossible as stopping a runaway train. She'd already tried more than once.

Despite her boss telling her she didn't need to interact with Colt beyond the interview every Friday, three weeks ago, she'd begun occasionally meeting up with him after his ride on Wednesday or Thursday too. Sometimes she'd join him for dinner, or they would simply wander the rodeo grounds together and talk. A couple of times, she'd accompanied him to the afterparty.

For some inexplicable reason, she felt safe around him. It was crazy since they hadn't known each other long. Still, when they were together, she could be herself. Maybe that was part of the attraction. He seemed real, unlike most of the men she'd known in the past. She supposed he could be a fantastic liar, but she found that hard to believe. After living with Flint for so long, her ability to tell when someone was lying was pretty well honed. She and Colt spent so much of their time together laughing that she often forgot her woes, at least for the moment.

It was a pity she hadn't met him before Flint. What would life look like if she had? Happy, for sure, and full of laughter instead of bruises. Where would she be now? Would she still have ended up at the newspaper? Maybe. She'd always loved writing.

Hanging out with Colt was comfortable. Easy. Their conversations weren't always about the rodeo. They talked about life in general too. He told her a lot about his friends. So much so that she felt like she knew them too. She told him the more pleasant things going on in her life. The flea market Flint let her go to. The deer she'd seen playing in the back acreage at home. Her love of watching sunsets as often as she could.

The reverent way Colt would sometimes mention his late wife, and the life he'd had with her, made Grace almost jealous of the woman. He didn't speak of Sarah often, but it was obvious how much he loved her even still.

What would it be like to be loved that wholly, that intensely, even years after death claimed you? It seemed unlikely Grace would ever find out. Flint would never willingly let her go.

Sometimes, she felt tempted to tell Colt about the abuse she endured whenever she went home, but fear and shame made her hold her tongue. Flint had tricked her, manipulated her to get her right where he wanted her—trapped under his thumb. She felt stupid for letting it happen, like she should have seen through his act somehow. But his disguise had been so good, so believable.

What if Colt thought her cowardly, like she did, for not standing up for herself, for not finding some way to fight back? Flint knew just the right things to say or do to keep her too afraid to try.

It was too difficult to talk about. Besides, her friendship with Colt was too new for such a serious and deep subject. Not knowing how Colt would react made it a frightening prospect as well. She didn't have answers to the inevitable questions about why she stayed with Flint either. How could she explain in a way that made sense?

No, it was better to keep quiet about her suffering. For now, at least.

With ten minutes to spare, Grace ran her hairbrush through her still-damp hair, tossed on some clothes, and grabbed her purse from the little table tucked into the corner of the room. Grace peeked into her purse to ensure her notebook and pen were in the side pocket, then shouldered the strap. She snatched her rental car's keys off the dresser and walked out the door.

⸺◦⸺

Grace sat on a wooden bench outside the cowboy's locker room, waiting for Colt to reappear.

He'd had a great ride; she was definitely going to mention it in this week's article. His draw tonight was a big red bull known as Test Drive. If the animal athlete kept bucking the way he had been, he'd be headed for the National Finals. The bull bucked off about 84% of the cowboys who tried to ride him. He was tough. However, Colt had covered him tonight, earning himself a 90.3 score and a significant rise in the standings. It'd been a sight to see. She was glad she hadn't missed it.

He'd glanced at her and smiled after exiting the arena, but a vast group comprised of his friends, fans, and several reporters descended on him before she could even say hi. Before the crowd dissipated, he'd disappeared into the building she sat outside of now. There was no telling if he knew she was waiting for him. Probably not.

She wasn't sure how long she'd been sitting when the door to the locker room opened and Colt emerged. His clothes were dusty from the arena, and his eyes still had the wild look in their depths that all the roughstock riders got from the adrenaline coursing through their systems.

The sight of him took her breath away. He didn't seem to have noticed her yet.

She pushed to her feet. "Great ride, cowboy."

Colt's blue gaze jumped to her. His eyes widened a fraction before a smile split his face, making them crinkle at the outer edges. "Hey, you! Thanks." He moved toward her and tilted his head. "Since you're here, feel like grabbing a bite with me? I'm starving."

"You're not going to the afterparty after that ride?"

"Nope, not tonight. You're here." He ducked his head to meet her eyes. "I'd rather hang out with you than get swarmed by fans looking for autographs."

Colt's words made her stomach flutter as if he'd paid her some compliment. She was being silly.

"So, dinner?

Grace gave herself a mental shake and offered him a small smile. "Dinner sounds good. What did you have in mind?"

"I'm too hungry to care what I eat." He laughed. "How about you pick?"

She made a face. "This is my first time in this town. You probably have a better idea of the food choices here, don't you?"

"Nope. This is my first time at this stop too. Why don't you leave your car here and ride with me? We can drive around until you see something that looks appetizing to you."

For a second, the suggestion gave her pause. She'd ridden with him to the restaurant when she'd interviewed him for the very first time, but they always drove separately otherwise.

The prospect of spending the next little while with him in the confines of his truck was way too appealing to even attempt to resist. "Okay."

Colt grinned and offered her his arm. "Let's get on the road then, Princess."

Princess?

She gave him a quizzical look as she tucked her hand in the crook of his arm, far more delighted to have an excuse to touch him than she ought to be.

They'd entered the competitor's parking lot when she couldn't contain her curiosity any longer. "Alright, I have to ask... Princess?"

One corner of his mouth lifted as his shoulders rose and fell. He appeared a bit sheepish. It was endearing. "Yeah, uh, you kinda remind me of a fairytale princess. Do you mind me calling you that?"

Her heart stuttered. "No, I suppose not." She wanted to ask *how* she reminded him of a princess, but she wasn't entirely sure she wanted to know. Clearly, being around Flint for so long had her jaded because the first thing to come to mind was that he was mocking her somehow. "I hope I remind you of one in a good way."

"Of course! I wouldn't give you a nickname to make fun of you or anything." He gave her a strange look she couldn't quite interpret. "I've wanted to call you that ever since the auction, but I figured it'd be best to wait until we knew each other better." His lips quirked upward. "A stranger giving you a nickname would be a little odd, wouldn't it?"

She nodded but said nothing.

Nobody had ever given her a nickname before, unless she counted "bitch" as a nickname. Flint certainly called her that often enough. Her birth parents might have nicknamed her, but she'd been too young when they died to remember anything about them. She was one of the lucky orphans who'd been adopted by the first foster family they'd landed with. Her adoptive parents had been good people but rarely had time for her, far too busy working and fostering other kids. Now, they were gone too.

"I hope I didn't offend you. I promise I meant it in a good way. If you don't like it, I won't call you that. I know some people are weird about nicknames."

She glanced over at Colt. He was watching her with furrowed brows.

Grace swallowed past the lump in her throat and smiled, hoping to reassure him. "I'm okay with it. I feel like I should come up with one for you now."

"Go for it if you want." He chuckled as his handsome features relaxed. "As far as I'm aware, nobody has ever given me one."

That was a surprise. She'd have to think of a good one for him, then. It was only fair.

"I've never had one before either," she admitted softly.

He looked a bit perplexed by that.

They stopped at his truck, and she reluctantly released his arm.

Colt turned to face her. Something electric passed between them as their eyes met. Or maybe that was wishful thinking on her part.

"Well, you have one now, Princess." He bumped her arm playfully, then opened the passenger door for her and smirked. "Your carriage awaits."

Grace shook her head and hopped up on the bench seat of his black truck, ignoring the way her stomach fluttered.

His truck smelled like him, unsurprisingly. She inhaled, filling her lungs with his unique scent while she waited for him to join her. The smell was strangely comforting and invoked feelings of being safe and cared for. Too bad she couldn't bottle it up and take it home with her.

Once he slid behind the wheel, she looked over at him. "I'm kind of craving Mexican food. Does that sound good? I'm a sucker for the free chips and salsa."

"Sure, sounds good to me," he answered.

The rich baritone rumble of his voice did funny things to her insides.

She needed to get a grip. This was dinner with a friend, not a date or anything of the like. She sucked in a deep breath and exhaled slowly as he started the engine and backed out of his parking spot.

Grace gave Colt a good-natured shove as he escorted her back to her rental car. "Stop!" she joyfully cried. "My cheeks and ribs hurt. I can't laugh anymore!"

Laughter wasn't the only reason her ribs were sore at the moment, but it was certainly the far more pleasant cause.

She loved spending time with this man. It was so nice to relax and have fun.

He gave her an impish grin. "Nobody's making you keep laughing. You can stop any time."

"No, I can't. Not when you keep doing things that make me start right back up again." She shook her head and poked him in the stomach. His abs were so well-toned that she nearly hurt her finger in the process.

He stuck his tongue out at her but said nothing more.

The moment she unlocked the silver sedan she'd rented, Colt opened the door for her. She couldn't say she was quite ready for the evening to end. Time flew by far too quickly for her taste whenever they were together. It sucked.

Grace slid behind the wheel and turned to look at him. "Thanks for dinner, Eight." Eight for eight seconds. Since he was a bull rider, it seemed appropriate.

He grinned at her use of the nickname she'd given him.

"You're welcome." He still had his hand on the door as though preparing to shut it for her, but instead of moving, he gazed at her with a thoughtful expression.

She'd give anything to know what was on his mind. It seemed like he was hesitant to call the evening over too.

"It's still early. Maybe I'll go to the afterparty for a while, after all." Colt's throat worked for a moment. "Care to join me? You could follow me there."

The hope lurking in his eyes made her smile. He reminded her of a little boy who'd asked for a puppy for Christmas. How was she supposed to resist?

"Sure, lead the way."

A bright smile split his face and made his ocean eyes twinkle. "Give me five minutes, and I'll meet you by the gate." He closed her door, then full-on ran toward his truck.

Her laughter filled the car. That cowboy was trouble.

Chapter 7

Colt thought back over the past four months as he limped out of the arena.

It was Friday. Interview day. It had rapidly become his favorite day of the week. While they sometimes talked on Wednesday or Thursday—sometimes both—Friday was a sure thing. He still didn't like being interviewed, but he definitely liked the interviewer. Really liked her.

Shit, he was so fucking attracted to Grace that he could barely concentrate on anything else. He wasn't afraid to admit to that. There was no way he'd ever tell anyone how much he looked forward to seeing her, however. People would get the wrong idea about the nature of their friendship. She wasn't his and never would be.

Grace was great fun to hang out with, though. At first, she'd seemed nervous every time they were together, but after the first couple of weeks, she'd finally relaxed. Now, she laughed and joked around with him regularly, like they'd known each other for years. Sometimes, he had to remind himself that they hadn't.

Her laughter brightened the darkness he'd been living in since Sarah passed. Shit, Grace made *him* laugh again—like he meant it. After losing his wife, he'd believed it impossible to feel even remotely happy ever again, but Grace had proven him wrong. It was as if spending time with her was slowly mending some of the broken places within him.

The thought was sobering. He wasn't willing to examine it too closely, afraid of what he'd find.

A couple of weeks ago, Grace had joined him at a bar with a mechanical bull and shocked him by riding it. She'd seemed to have a blast despite going flying after barely half a second. That'd been one of the best afterparties he'd attended in a long while.

He was glad her boss had already called to extend the interviews through the rest of the season. There was no way Colt was ready to lose the excuse to talk to her any time soon.

This was a risky game he was playing. No matter how hard he tried not to get attached to her, he was losing the battle.

The fact that he hadn't so much as looked at another woman since he met her worried him some too. He wasn't interested. It figured that the sole woman he wanted was the one he would never let himself have, even if she suddenly became single. He liked her too much to risk ruining what they had. Besides, he'd gotten into too many fights and broken far too many hearts when he was younger to deserve someone like her.

He just hoped that when the interviews ended, she'd find some way to stay in touch. They hadn't exchanged numbers yet; maybe he should bring it up at tonight's interview.

Tonight had been a buck-off, his first in a while. Hotshot was a volatile bull with a crazy high buck-off percentage. He'd ridden him the full eight only once in the handful of times he'd drawn the animal, so his dismal ride tonight didn't quite surprise him. It still stung, though.

Colt shucked off his safety vest as he stepped behind the chutes and approached the spot he and Grace always met on Fridays. While the area looked a little different at every rodeo, it was always in the same location on the grounds.

His brows snapped together when he reached it. Tonight, she was nowhere to be seen. He scanned the crowd but saw no sign of her. She'd never been late to meet him before. Where was she?

He ignored the knot forming in his gut. These days, he found himself searching the stands for Grace before every ride. About a month and a half ago, he'd noticed her boyfriend in the stands with her one Friday night. Since, he'd spotted Flint with her there a handful of times.

Colt knew she was here tonight; he'd seen her sitting halfway up the bleachers just before his ride. Her boyfriend had been seated beside her, his arm looped around her shoulders.

So, where was she now?

Maybe Flint delayed her somehow. While the other man never had before, there was a first time for most things.

Colt didn't know why, but Grace's demeanor changed whenever her boyfriend was around. She'd seem about as skittish as a wild filly. Despite the fact that the other man never joined them at the interview, getting her to laugh or even smile was a hell of a challenge on those nights. She'd dash off the second the interview was over instead of hanging out for a while, like she normally did.

It concerned him, but he left it alone. They may have become pretty good friends over the past few months, but her relationship was her business. He didn't have the right to pry, no matter how much her abrupt behavior change worried him. Thankfully, Flint didn't join her often.

Colt hated seeing her so uneasy. He'd made it his personal goal to see how many times he could make her laugh while she was with him each week. It was somewhat selfish—she had the sweetest damn laughter he'd ever heard.

After tonight's disastrous ride, he was looking forward to hearing it. He was fully prepared to do whatever silly shit he had to in order to wring it from her.

With a frown, Colt leaned back against the railing to wait, sure she'd show up any moment. When Grace still hadn't arrived nearly twenty minutes later, he straightened and went to shove his gear into a locker so he could search for her unencumbered.

About to give up, he spotted her exiting the women's restroom next to the arena.

Thank fuck. He glanced to the sky as the tension holding his muscles tight eased in a rush.

Colt exhaled a deep breath and opened his mouth to call to her. It was then he noticed the stiff way she was moving. Warning bells began clanging in his mind. "Grace!"

She looked up, and those warning bells turned into a screaming air raid siren. For one, she didn't smile the way she always did whenever she saw him. For another, the rigidness of her body made her seem ready to bolt in the opposite direction. Something was going on, and he was pretty sure he wouldn't like whatever it was.

The knot in his stomach tightened down even further as he started toward her.

Once he was close enough to see her more clearly, his gaze homed in on her face, and his brow furrowed.

What the hell happened to her? Her lip was split, and her eyes were puffy and red as though she'd been crying. The faint shadowy area along her jaw worried him as well. It looked as though she had a bruise she'd attempted to cover with makeup.

A powerful surge of protectiveness rose in him.

Who the fuck hurt her? He'd kill them for it. She might not be his, but he'd be damned if he stood by and allowed someone he cared about to be harmed. Especially her.

"What happened?" He winced when his voice came out a harsh growl.

Her eyes widened, something that looked an awful lot like fear flashing in them.

Fuck, he didn't want her afraid of him. He'd sooner cut off his own hands with a dull knife than hurt her. At least she hadn't run.

Colt took a deep breath and slowly reached for her. He gently gripped her chin and tilted her face so he could get a better look at the shadowy spot bothering him so much. It darkened when he skimmed the pad of his thumb over it.

His jaw clenched so tight it was a miracle his molars didn't crack. Shit, he hadn't wanted to be right, but it was definitely a bruise she'd tried to hide.

Someone was dying tonight for hurting her. All he needed was a name.

She pulled her face from his grip, and he let her go.

He scrubbed his hand over his mouth, then met Grace's eyes.

She still hadn't said a word.

He forcibly gentled his voice as he tried again. "Who hurt you? Grace, talk to me."

"Nobody. I fell in the shower this morning." She crossed her arms in front of her, as if hugging herself, and looked away.

He didn't believe that. Not for a second. "You can talk to me; I hope you know that. Who hit you? I want to help."

Grace backed up a step and shook her head. "Nobody hit me. I fell. That's all that happened. Really. I'm fine." She sighed heavily. "We have an interview to do, don't we? Let's go. I need to head out early tonight, so I can't be too long."

Colt pressed his lips into a thin line.

Why was she lying? He thought he'd earned her trust over the past four months. What the hell was going on here?

"No. We're not doing the interview until you tell me what really happened." He took a small step toward her and dropped his voice an octave. "I've been in enough fights to know what it looks like when someone has been hit. Please, tell me what happened so I can help you."

Had Flint done this? That smarmy bastard had rubbed him wrong from the moment Tiffany dragged Colt over to talk to him at the cookout, and not because he was dating Grace. Something about him had set Colt on edge right from the start. The guy definitely seemed like the sort who'd hit a woman.

"Was it your boyfriend? Did he hit you?"

Her mouth opened as though words were perched on the tip of her tongue. For a moment, he thought she was going to tell him. Then something flickered in her eyes, and her expression shuttered.

His pulse kicked higher. She was going to run; he was sure of it.

She shook her head hard. "Stop! Nobody hit me. Leave it alone, Colt! Either let's do the interview, or I'm leaving."

Surprise slammed through his veins at the anger in her tone. His molars clamped together again. He shook his head.

She might be angry with him for pushing, but this wasn't something he could let go.

He took a half-step toward her and lightly touched her arm. "It's safe to tell me, Princess. I promise. Please let me help."

She recoiled from him. Whether it was because of his use of the nickname he'd given her, his touch, or both, he wasn't sure.

"Grace—"

"No. We're done here." Her chin wobbled, and moisture clung to her lashes.

Before he could do anything to stop her, she spun around and fled.

His heart dropped into his boots as she disappeared from view.

Everything in him wanted to go after her, but he forced himself to allow her to leave. She was a grown woman. If she didn't want his help, he couldn't force her to accept it.

He blew out a ragged breath. This night had gone to complete shit with record speed.

Damnit, he hadn't even had the chance to suggest they exchange phone numbers, so he couldn't even check in on her. There was no way for him to get it now without looking like a stalker.

Somehow, he suspected he would never see Grace again.

Fuck. The thought of that had him struggling not to break down and cry.

Chapter 8

GRACE PACKED THE MEAGER contents of her cubicle into the cardboard box on her desk. She would miss this job. Her boss was great, her coworkers were awesome, and the pay was excellent. It was unlikely she'd ever find another job she liked as much as this one.

Not that it mattered much since Flint wouldn't let her work anymore.

He hadn't even allowed her to give her boss a proper two-week notice. Instead, the moment they got home from yesterday's rodeo, he'd demanded that she quit immediately.

It'd been a challenge to come up with a plausible explanation as to why she was quitting so abruptly. Mr. Johnston hadn't seemed to buy her story, but he'd needed to leave for a meeting and had been forced to cut short his attempts to talk her into staying.

Her heart felt heavy, her movements stiff. How was she supposed to stay sane now without her job? Damn Flint and his absurd jealousy. How did he always know exactly which things to strip from her to wound her the most?

She should have known the glimpse of peace would never last. She'd gotten too complacent. Too used to feeling happy.

She'd been a fool.

Grace wished she knew how he'd figured out that the cowboy from the cookout and the rider she'd been interviewing were the same person. He'd never joined her down at the arena on the rare Fridays he showed up, and it wasn't often that he paid attention to anyone riding. More times than not, he spent the entire rodeo ogling buckle bunnies, and complaining about how boring the sport was and how he didn't understand the appeal.

The only explanation that made sense was that someone in town had told him. However it'd happened, it was every bit the disaster she'd worried it would be.

It hadn't been a lie when she told Colt she'd fallen in the shower. That really had happened. She'd been in the bathroom getting ready to head to the rodeo grounds when Flint came in, screaming at her. Before she could even figure out what had him so angry, he'd slapped her across the face so hard that she'd stumbled backward into the shower stall, where she'd promptly lost her balance and fell.

No matter how much she'd wanted to confide in Colt, she hadn't been able to bring herself to burden him with her mess. This was her problem to fix, not his. No doubt, the man had plenty of his own things to worry about. He didn't need to concern himself with her drama too. No, she'd either figure out a way to escape this hell on her own, or she'd die trying. With the ferocity Flint beat her with last night, dying was a distinct possibility.

Colt's concern had been touching, though. Nobody else in her life cared about her, not since her adoptive parents died. Her friends back in North Dakota had probably forgotten all about her by now. If they'd ever truly cared either; she wasn't sure they had. Sometimes, it hadn't seemed like it.

Now, she had nobody but Flint, and he didn't care about anyone but himself.

The worry she'd seen in Colt's eyes haunted her. As she had so many times before, she'd wanted to tell him everything. She almost had, but as usual, fear and shame stopped her. Seeing pity in his eyes—or worse, judgment—would have hurt worse than the thrashing she'd taken for talking to him.

Grace placed the last of her belongings into the box and hefted it into her arms. As much as she was going to miss this job, she was going to miss Colt even more—spending time with him, the long talks, the laughter. Since that first interview, she'd come to think of him as a genuine friend. Her *best* friend. She suspected he felt the same though he'd never said so.

It didn't matter now. Flint forbade her from so much as watching rodeo coverage, so there was little chance she'd ever see, much less talk to, Colt again. Since Flint had her locked out of the computer at home and her phone wasn't capable of browsing the internet, she wouldn't even be able to find out how Colt did at Finals in December. Not unless she found some way to get away from Flint before then, and that wasn't likely. She didn't even have a way to contact Colt. Grace wouldn't risk it, even if she did. Flint might go through her phone, like he had countless times in the past. It wasn't safe.

She stopped short of the doors and looked back. Her gaze moved over the rows of cubicles where her coworkers sat writing articles, editing, or planning interviews. All of them were blissfully unaware of her plight. She'd always been careful to keep conversations with her coworkers to small talk, even with the couple she'd become tentative work friends with.

Grace exhaled a weary breath and turned away. After using her hip to bump open the door, she left the building for the final time.

While she trudged slowly toward her truck, she wondered how many pieces of herself she'd have to give up before Flint was happy.

Chapter 9

As Grace washed dishes from dinner, her thoughts wandered back over the six months that'd passed since she'd been forced to resign from her job.

There was no winning with Flint. She'd quit her job at his demand, and he'd nearly sent her to the hospital later that night for it.

The number of bruises she was currently sporting was astounding. Flint had begun beating her daily, often multiple times. The only bright spot was that he'd kept the bulk of his abuse to the parts of her easily covered. Her face was glad for the reprieve. It was a welcome change from having to spend hours carefully applying makeup over bruises before grocery shopping.

Flint no longer allowed her to go anywhere else. This ranch had become her prison.

She supposed she should consider herself lucky he still let her grocery shop at all, but she couldn't drum up the energy to feel thankful for it. She just felt tired. The sort of tired sleep couldn't cure. That, and sore.

Nothing she did ever seemed to make him happy. Nothing prevented him from beating her again. No amount of begging or cajoling stopped him, and it was only getting worse. She could feel herself breaking. How long would it be before there was nothing left for him to destroy?

"Did you buy me more beer?"

She tensed at the sound of Flint's voice behind her.

When had he entered the kitchen? It wasn't often he could sneak up on her these days. Call it survival instinct, but she'd learned to keep tabs on his location and mood at all times.

"Yes. I put them in the refrigerator for you," Grace answered with an abundance of caution, her voice kept carefully neutral.

She didn't dare turn around or stop washing the dish she held. Anything could set him off, and she was still in serious pain from the pummeling she'd received this morning.

Flint grunted in acknowledgment, and then the fridge door opened.

"What the fuck is this shit? This isn't the brand I told you to buy!"

He slammed the refrigerator door shut.

Grace jumped. The plate she'd been scrubbing slipped from her fingers and sent a spray of soapy water up at her. Adrenaline shot through her veins, sending her heart rate soaring.

Not the right brand? It was the same brand she distinctly heard him tell her to get before she left to go grocery shopping earlier this afternoon.

Instead of arguing, she dropped her gaze to the sink. "I'm sorry," she whispered.

Flint wrapped his hand in her hair and yanked her head back. "What was that?"

Upside down, she saw his lips curl into a sneer.

She winced as pain shot through her scalp. "I said I'm sorry. I'll go back to the store right now."

To her dismay, he didn't release her. Instead, he transferred his punishing grip to her arm and spun her around to face him.

"Please, Flint!" A whimper escaped before she could stop it.

"Please, what?"

It was obvious from the euphoric gleam in his eyes that he was enjoying himself.

Tears burned her eyes, but she refused to cry. It would give him far too much pleasure to see her react that way. He was a monster. An absolute monster.

She dropped her gaze to the ground. Looking at him always made things so much worse.

"Please don't hit me." She wrapped her arms tightly around her belly as though the action would protect her. "Let me go back to the store and get the right beer for you. Please!"

"No."

That one word spoken so void of emotion let her know she was in for a night of torment. She squeezed her eyes shut and inhaled deeply, bracing for what she knew was coming.

His first punch sent her to the floor, and she automatically curled in on herself. Her mind slipped away to the peaceful glen it'd begun escaping to during times like this, disconnecting her from the agony her body was experiencing. She imagined herself surrounded by sunflowers, the sun bright above her. Nearby, a brook burbled over algae-covered rocks while a gentle breeze caressed her skin and teased her hair.

The beating seemed to go on for hours, though in reality, it likely only lasted a few minutes.

Grace cracked her eyes open once Flint finally stopped.

He stood next to her, breathing hard from his exertion but wearing a smug grin on his face.

She slowly moved to get up.

"Did I tell you to do that?"

She froze in place immediately, not even daring to breathe.

"You can't do anything right, can you? Stupid bitch. I don't know why I keep you around. You can't even buy the right damn beer, and you're too fucking ugly to look at without it!" Flint gave a long-suffering sigh and nudged her in the ribs with the toe of his boot. He stepped closer to where she lay and glared down at her. "I ought to kill you and be done with it. The world would be better off without you in it. Nobody would even miss you."

It was far from the first time he'd said something like that. Sometimes, she wished he'd do it already. She didn't want to die, but if he killed her, at least she wouldn't have to endure this anymore.

Would the world really be better off without her in it? She wasn't convinced of that.

"You're a monster." Her eyes widened in horror the moment the words left her lips. It would be an understatement to say she hadn't meant to let the thought on a loop in her mind slip out of her mouth.

Flint's face turned nearly purple, veins popping out along his neck and forehead. He dropped to his knees next to her, wrapped his hands around her neck, and squeezed.

A feral sort of panic gripped her as she struggled against him.

Was this it? Was this the day he finally made good on his threat?

The lack of oxygen made her head swim.

Her mind danced from one memory to another. Galloping through the fields on her old gelding. A father-daughter dance in elementary school that her adoptive father had insisted on taking her to.

Her nails dug into Flint's hands, his arms, and even his face as she bucked and writhed. This couldn't be happening. This couldn't be the way her story ended.

She couldn't get loose. Nothing was working.

No! She wasn't ready. It wasn't her time.

She fought with renewed vigor even as her vision dimmed.

Colt's face flashed in her mind, etched with worry and genuine concern, like it had been the last time she'd seen him.

She was going to die. She should have told him. Should have begged for his help. Now, it was too late. Flint was going to kill her. She'd taken too long to find a way to break free of his control.

Flint stopped as suddenly as he'd started. His fingers loosened a fraction, allowing her to suck a ragged breath into her aching lungs.

"Worthless slut. Next time, you won't be so lucky." He sat back on his heels and stared down at her. "Gonna call the cops on me again now? Bet they don't help you, just like they didn't any of the other times. Probably going to get yourself arrested if you keep wasting their time. They can see right through your bullshit lies. They don't care about you. Nobody cares about you!" He slammed her head against the hard tile floor, then released her.

Grace didn't move a muscle as he shoved back to his feet and stormed from the room. She lay there, trembling, her eyes locked on the clock on the wall next to the refrigerator. She watched the second hand move as time ticked steadily onward.

How was this her life? How had it come to this? More importantly, what did she do now?

Her gaze moved to the doorway. Where had Flint gone? She strained to hear him, but the steady ticking of the clock and the hum of the refrigerator were the only sounds.

Tonight, she'd come far too close to losing her life. A chill settled into her bones. She didn't want to die. There was so much she wanted to do yet. So much she wanted to experience. Places she wanted to go.

Moonlight was streaming in the window by the time she finally felt safe enough to get up. Flint hadn't come back, and the house seemed silent. Maybe he'd gone out. She hadn't heard the door, but that meant little.

Using the kitchen cabinets and counter closest to her, she levered herself to her feet with a soft groan.

She needed to get out of here. He could have killed her tonight. She wasn't sure why he hadn't. Maybe he'd been trying to scare her. To show her his power over her life. If that'd been his intent, he'd succeeded. She was downright terrified.

It'd been close. Too close. Tonight, she'd gotten lucky.

Adrenaline flooded her system all over again, mercifully dulling her pain. She didn't know where she was going to go, but anywhere had to be better than staying here. With her family all passed on, she was at a loss as to where to run. Flint kept her isolated, so she didn't have any friends to turn to. He'd even turned Sissy away from her with his lies. The woman lived too close anyway. It'd probably be the first place he'd look for her. Back to North Dakota? No. He'd expect her to head there.

Grace rushed to the bedroom as quickly as her battered body allowed. There was no time to waste, and she'd spent too much of it lying on the kitchen floor as it was. Flint might return at any moment. She yanked her clothes from the closet—along with the shoebox of money she'd hidden there—and emptied her dresser drawers, creating a pile in the middle of the bed. There was no time to fight with her suitcase, so she hurried back to the kitchen to grab a trash bag. It would have to do.

She hastily shoved her clothes into it, moved the paltry amount of cash she'd hidden away into her purse, then made a cursory search of the house for any belongings she couldn't bear to leave behind. She pushed what she could into the overstuffed black bag, grabbed her purse, and hauled it all out to her truck.

Headlights came around the bend in the road, and she froze in place, unable to breathe until the vehicle was close enough for her to see it wasn't Flint's car.

Her pulse kicked higher. She needed to get out of here. The next car could be him. If he caught her, it was over. He'd promised so many times to kill her if she ever tried to leave. After tonight, she knew it wasn't a bluff. He'd do it. She knew he would.

Not willing to delay any longer, she hopped into her truck and started the engine. She could figure out where she was going once she was far away from this town.

Grace glanced down at the fuel gauge with a groan. She'd filled the tank at the edge of town, but this truck was a gas guzzler. Had she been able to get it a tune-up regularly, maybe it wouldn't get as poor mileage as it did. Flint had only done the bare minimum to maintain it, like he did with everything he wasn't interested in doing.

She was going to have to stop for gas soon. There was no avoiding it. Considering she'd been driving as fast as was legal for hours now, it was probably safe to stop for a few minutes. It wasn't likely that Flint would be able to guess which direction she'd gone at the four-way stop by the ranch. At least, she hoped he couldn't.

Regardless, it was well past time for a quick stretch.

A huge sign to her right advertised that the upcoming exit had multiple gas stations and restaurants present. She swiftly switched lanes, took the next exit, and pulled in at the first 24-hour gas station she saw. The pump prices were outrageously high, but so were the surrounding stations'. This one was the cheapest of the three.

A pained grimace contorted her features as she climbed from the cab. Maybe driving non-stop hadn't been the smartest decision. Now that the adrenaline burst of earlier had faded, her battered body was complaining loudly—just as she'd predicted it would.

She set the pump to fill. While she hated to spend so much of her limited money, she was still far too close to the ranch. To Flint. He knew too many people in this state who'd undoubtably believe whatever story he told them and help him find her.

She couldn't stay here. It wasn't safe. She needed to get out of Kansas, at the least. Maybe then, she could relax a little.

Her gaze flicked back in the direction she'd been fleeing from. She half expected to see Flint roar around the slight bend in the road, intent on forcing her back to hell, but the road remained quiet beyond the traffic of a few semi-trucks. If Flint found her... A shudder rippled through her, and she forced her mind back to her current task, not wanting to think about what he'd do.

Grace leaned back against the truck's bed, inwardly cringing as the amount owed climbed higher and higher. It wasn't going to leave her with much. Enough for a handful or two of meals if she ate cheap. She could sleep in the truck to save some money. Food was more important than a pillow beneath her head.

When the pump finally shut off, she replaced the handle and wearily wandered indoors to pay. Before she left here, she was going to have to figure out where to head. There was no way she'd be able to afford to fill the tank a third time. This was it. Maybe when she ran out of gas next, she should abandon her truck at a bus station or something. There would probably be enough money left for a ticket to somewhere.

The low murmur of a television met her ears the second she walked into the small building. The clerk was so engrossed in watching it that he didn't seem to notice when she stepped up to the counter. She waited patiently—trying her best to keep from looking at the TV, out of habit—for several minutes before clearing her throat to gain the older man's attention.

The clerk jumped and whirled around in his seat to look at her. "Oh! So sorry, ma'am. I didn't notice you there. What can I do for you?" His rheumy gaze swept over her. "Are you okay?"

Crap. She probably did look pretty rough. It hadn't crossed her mind to look in a mirror. She'd been in too big of a rush to get out the door.

Grace produced a tired smile in hopes of reassuring the man. He had a friendly look about him, like he was somebody's grandfather. The corners of his eyes held the telltale crinkles of someone who'd spent the bulk of their life smiling.

"I'm fine, thanks. Um, I have pump number two." She held out her money.

He didn't look like he entirely believed her, but he nodded. "Pump two. Okay." He took the cash from her hand, rang her up, and handed back a pathetic amount of change.

She was officially broke now.

Grace mumbled her thanks to him and started for the door. She'd barely taken two steps when the announcer on the television said a familiar name—one that made her heart clench.

Colt.

She paused mid-step and swung her gaze up to the screen as he appeared on it. Her breath caught. According to the reporter interviewing him, the rodeo he'd ridden at tonight was only an hour and a half from here. Right over the state line. It sounded like the new rodeo season was going well for Colt too.

Her stomach fluttered as an idea began forming.

He'd seemed to care about her. Would he let her hide with him until she could get her feet back under her? The worry etched on his face the last time she'd seen him flashed in her mind and gave her a minute amount of confidence that he would. It was worth a shot. If he turned her away, it's not like she'd be any worse off than she was right now.

Dragging her eyes away from the screen, she hurried back to her truck. Her hands trembled as she grabbed the folding map from the glovebox and found the tiny town. If Colt wasn't there, she'd keep looking until she ran out of gas. What she'd do then was uncertain. That was a bridge to cross if she came to it.

She took a few moments to smooth her hair, change her shirt, and straighten her appearance as best as she was able. Her neck, though tender, didn't appear to have bruised as far as she could tell. There wasn't much she could do about her scratches and cuts, though.

As she tossed her truck into drive and turned back out onto the road, a flicker of hope bloomed within her for the first time in what felt like ages.

Chapter 10

A KNOCK ON THE door roused Colt from sleep. He squinted blearily at the motel alarm clock on the nightstand beside him. It was only three in the morning.

Who the hell was bothering him at this hour? More to the point, why was someone here this damn early in the first place?

He rolled out of bed with a groan and slipped into his jeans before shuffling toward the door as the person on the other side knocked again.

Jesus, his hip hurt. Last night's ride had been rough. He'd made the eight, but his dismount had been far from smooth. With as vigorously as Pure Chaos bucked, it was a miracle he wasn't more sore tonight. Riding that bull had felt like someone had tossed Colt into a giant cocktail shaker and shaken him up like a martini. He'd scored an 89 and jumped four spots in the standings, however. That was worth the bone-jarring ride.

"Yeah, yeah. Hold on," he said irritably as he undid the multiple locks and cracked open the door. Instantaneously, he was wide awake, every bit of his former annoyance vanished. "Grace?"

A myriad of emotions flowed through his veins, one after the other.

His eyes swept over her. She'd lost weight since he'd last seen her. Too much of it. Her bones seemed far too prominent, like she hadn't been getting enough to eat. Grace's bloodshot eyes seemed haunted, dark shadows beneath them. Her hair was tangled, and there was a small cut on her cheek and a few scrapes on her neck.

What happened to her? How had she found him? Why was she here at three in the morning? He had so many questions.

She gawked at him a moment, her gaze trained on his bare chest, before she swallowed hard and lifted her beautiful pale blue eyes to his. "Um, hi. I'm sure you're wondering what I'm doing here." While she spoke, her fingers fiddled with the hem of her shirt. "Can I come in?"

"Sure." Colt stepped back to allow her to enter the tiny motel room. He shut the door behind her then moved to his duffle bag to retrieve a t-shirt. After pulling it on, he turned to face her.

She'd seated herself on the edge of the bed, her gaze seemingly on her tightly clasped hands.

He sat down next to her. "What's going on, Grace?"

"It's a long story." Her voice was more subdued than he'd ever heard it. She took a shuddering breath before continuing. "I'm sorry for showing up at this hour. I didn't actually think about the time. My truck needed gas, and I saw your interview on the TV at the station, and—" Grace sighed. "I don't know why I'm here." She glanced at him then stared back down at her hands. "I guess I thought you could help me somehow." She grimaced and gave her head a small shake. "This was a stupid idea. I'm sorry for bothering you. I'll go." She surged upwards and started for the door.

"Hey, wait a minute." Colt bounced to his feet and snagged her hand, gently pulling her back. The way she flinched at his touch didn't escape him.

His heart clenched. Had he hurt her? Did she think he intended to harm her?

"Come sit back down and talk to me. What can I help you with? Are you in trouble?" With slow movements, he used a finger to tip her face up. The moisture clinging to her lashes alarmed him. "Don't run off and leave me worrying again. Talk to me, please?" He wasn't sure he could handle her vanishing again, leaving him fretting about her well-being. Especially not after seeing her like this.

Her throat worked for a moment, then she finally began speaking. "Flint and I had a fight, and I-I left him. I can't go home."

His jaw clenched as he realized his suspicions about Flint had been correct.

"I don't have any family left, and you're really my only friend. I can't afford to keep driving around. I didn't know where else to go." She visibly shuddered before meeting his eyes then shook her head. "I-I didn't think this through. I'm going to go. I'm sorry."

It moved him that she'd run to him, of all people. Despite what she said, surely a woman like her had others who cared about her. He couldn't quite believe he was all she had. The thought of it seemed impossible. Hadn't she once said something about being friends with some chick named Sissy or Misty or something like that? He could swear she had. Surely she could have run there.

Not that it mattered now. He would never turn Grace away. He couldn't. Not with how intensely disquieted he'd been about her since the interviews stopped.

The need to find and protect her had nearly made riding bulls impossible. He'd searched for her in every crowd, hoping to see her glossy black hair and ice-blue eyes. Hoping to at least have the assurance that she was alright, even if she no longer wanted to talk to him. But she'd been nowhere.

She pulled away from him and took a step toward the door, only to stop abruptly and cover her face with her hands. The muffled sound of her sobs filled the room.

"Ah, shit." Colt tentatively reached for her.

When she didn't resist, he pulled her against his chest and wrapped one arm around her. He rubbed soothing circles over her back with his free hand as she buried her face in his shirt and wept.

By the time her shoulders stopped shaking, his t-shirt was soaked through from her tears.

When she tugged away from him, he wordlessly released her, ignoring the way he instantly missed the contact. It was entirely the wrong time to be noticing how good it had felt to have her in his arms.

With quick strides, he grabbed a couple of tissues from the bathroom while she returned to her prior seat on the bed.

"Here," he said softly, offering her the tissues.

Grace took them from him, the ghost of a smile on her lips. "Thanks." She dabbed at the tears clinging to her cheeks, then looked up at him. "I'm sorry."

His brow furrowed. "Sorry for what?" He sat down next to her and angled his upper body her direction.

She gestured toward his shirt. "I know most guys don't handle tears very well."

"Don't worry about me. I'm fine. It's you I'm worried about."

"I don't want to talk about what happened. I can't. Not yet. Maybe not ever." She dropped her gaze to the room's parquet flooring. "I'll be okay. Eventually."

He rubbed a hand over his mouth, fighting the need to ask questions she wasn't ready to answer. "If you change your mind about talking about it, I'm here." He hesitated, then tentatively touched her knee in hopes she'd look back up at him.

Their eyes met.

'So, what is it you're needing from me?"

"I don't really know. A place to stay while I get my feet back under me? Some company while I lick my wounds?" She laughed, though the sound was void of humor. "I told you I didn't think this through."

A place to stay was something he could definitely offer her. "To be honest, I can't say I'd mind if you tagged along with me for as long as you like." He grinned, hoping to lighten the mood and maybe get her to smile if he was lucky. "You're good company." He gently bumped her leg with his own. "I've missed our interviews."

Grace smiled tremulously back at him. "I've missed our interviews too," she admitted softly. "I didn't want to quit. Flint made me."

The man had better hope that Colt never saw him again. Colt wasn't sure he'd be able to keep from going after him. It wasn't necessary to know exactly what Flint had done to Grace. The fact she'd been desperate enough to get away from the guy, to drive hours away to Colt's door—in the middle of the damn night—spoke volumes.

"Flint is a bastard," he said gruffly. "What was your plan if you didn't find me? How *did* you find me anyway?"

Grace shrugged. "There are only two motels in this town. I drove around until I spotted your truck, then hoped I picked the right room to knock on the door of." She tried for a smile, but it fell flat. "Thankfully, I got it right on the first try. As far as my plan, I didn't have one. I honestly don't know what I'd have done if you'd left town already or something."

He almost had. His next stop would take around eight hours to get to. Cash and Dusty left for it last night before the afterparty, but Colt had been hit by a strange feeling he should leave in the morning. Thank fuck he'd listened to his gut this time. He didn't want to even consider what would have happened to her had he not been here.

Colt scrubbed his hands over his face then turned to look at her more fully. She appeared understandably exhausted.

"Do you have anything you need to bring in?"

She gave him a vaguely baffled look. "Bring in?"

"Well, yeah. You've got to sleep somewhere. I'd get you a room, but the *No Vacancy* sign was lit when I turned in for the night. Was it still on when you pulled in?"

Grace nibbled at her lip. "I didn't notice. Um, I kind of left in a hurry, so I threw my clothes and a few other things into a trash bag and took off."

Jesus. If she'd left in that kind of rush, whatever happened had to have been even worse than anything he'd imagined. The mere idea of it made him want to crush her to his chest and fight off any demon that came for her, especially if that demon's name was Flint.

Colt stood and held his hand out to her, palm up. "Give me your keys. I'll go grab your bag. What's your car look like?"

"Um, it's the white truck. It was the only one out there like it when I got here." She hesitated, then dug her keys out of her pocket. "Are you sure you want to help? I don't want to cause trouble for you. Flint is going to come after me. He's told me he would if I ever left."

Let the fucker try. "I'm sure. Give me your keys."

Though she still seemed uncertain, she wordlessly placed them in his hand, and he offered her a tight smile.

"I'll be right back." He disappeared out the door.

Grace swung her gaze up to him the moment he walked back in with her bulging trash bag in tow.

"Thank you, Colt. For everything you're doing."

"Don't mention it."

For some reason, her thanks made him feel vaguely uncomfortable, though he couldn't put his finger on exactly why. Maybe it was because he was tired.

He sat her bag down next to the tiny table by the room's only window. "I think the first thing we ought to do tomorrow is get you something more appropriate to keep your clothes in. This bag will rip to shreds pretty fast while we're on the road."

Colt smiled as he handed her back her keys. "We can talk about things more in the morning. You look like you could use some sleep."

"I feel like I could sleep for a week," she admitted. "But, uh, where should I sleep?"

He looked around the small room and shrugged. One corner of his mouth twitched upward. "I suppose I could share my bed," he teased, hoping to see that pretty blush of hers again. It'd been far too long since he'd seen it last.

She didn't disappoint. Her face immediately turned a delicate shade of pink.

He chuckled. "I'll sleep on the floor, Princess. You can have the bed all to yourself."

She eyed the floor then shook her head. "No. You take the bed. I'll sleep... I don't know, in my truck."

He frowned at that. "You're not sleeping in your truck."

"We'll share the bed, then. It's big enough."

His eyebrows shot up as his gaze darted to her. Her face turned a slightly darker shade of pink as she bit her lip and looked away. What he wouldn't give to know what was going on in that pretty little head of hers right now.

Colt cleared his throat. "I'll be fine. Go get yourself ready for bed. I've slept worse places than this floor. Don't worry about me."

He was lying, but she didn't have to know that. The floor was hard as a rock. There wasn't even carpeting or any sort of rugs to use as a bit of cushioning. With the way his last few rides had left him so sore, he'd likely wake up barely able to move. He figured the pain would be worth it if she got some good rest. He'd survive.

For a few moments, it looked like she was going to argue, but then she got to her feet and moved to her bag. She dug around in its depths for a minute and came up with what appeared to be a pair of pajamas. He didn't get a good look before she ducked into the bathroom and clicked the door shut behind herself. That was probably for the best; after her offer to share the bed, he wasn't so sure he was ready to know what her pajamas looked like.

While he waited for her to return, he tossed together a makeshift bed on the floor and stretched out on it. Fuck, the floor was even more uncomfortable than he'd expected. He grimaced and shifted around, trying in vain to find a tolerable position. There was little doubt in his mind that he'd be regretting this decision in the morning. He exhaled a long breath and stared at the ceiling.

Colt eased up onto his elbows when he heard the bathroom door open, and wordlessly watched as Grace curled up beneath the remaining blanket on the bed, then reached over to turn off the light.

Even seeing her there, it was difficult for him to believe she was really in his motel room right now. In the bed he'd been asleep in a short time ago. It seemed more like a dream or something.

It sure wouldn't be the first time he'd dreamt of her. In the past six months, she'd never been far from his mind despite having disappeared completely. Nobody he'd asked had seen her or knew of a way to get in touch with her. He'd even given in and called her boss, but the only thing he'd been told was that she quit with no notice and that they couldn't give out her contact information. As time went on, he'd begun to lose hope of ever seeing or talking to her again.

And now she was here.

"Sleep well," he whispered, then turned his head to stare up at the ceiling again.

"Goodnight."

Colt remained as he was long into the night, listening to Grace's soft breathing.

He wasn't dreaming. She was really here, in his motel room, and most importantly, she was safe.

It was a long time before he sank into sleep himself.

Chapter 11

Colt groaned as he drifted back to wakefulness. His muscles stiffened even more than he'd predicted they would. There wasn't much of him that wasn't in complete agony right now.

He lay there for a long while, trying not to move too much, before he finally opened his eyes. Continuing to lie on the floor wasn't going to do him any favors. He pushed himself upright, wincing when his body protested loudly. Hopefully, a hot shower would reduce the pain enough for him to function today.

He used the edge of the bed to lever himself to his feet, trying his best to keep quiet so he didn't wake Grace. Finally standing, his gaze drifted to the bed.

She appeared to be sleeping peacefully now. She'd woke him twice in the night, whimpering and thrashing around. Though she'd remained sleeping through whatever nightmares she'd been having, it'd taken him a good long while to get back to sleep himself after doing what he could to calm her down.

Even with her hair all mussed up, she was undeniably beautiful. Her features were completely relaxed now, but no less regal. She really did remind him of a princess, and she deserved to be treated like one—not however Flint had been treating her.

The smile curling his lips while he watched her sleep turned into a grimace as he began limping his way to the bathroom. Some days, he felt like he was pushing ninety rather than being just shy of twenty-eight. This was going to be one hell of a long day if he kept feeling this rough. Would he even be able to ride tonight?

Steam from his shower billowed out into the room the moment he opened the bathroom door and stepped out with a towel wrapped securely around his waist. His gaze immediately landed on Grace.

She appeared to be just waking up, and he found her sleepy expression highly enticing.

"Good morning."

Her eyes darted to his then rolled down his body.

He stood still, letting her look, though he couldn't keep a smirk from creeping onto his face. The obvious feminine interest lurking in the pale depths of her eyes was nearly his undoing. Under her gaze, his body tightened, and he hoped like hell the thick towel hid his erection. He wasn't going there with her.

He chuckled, and her gaze jumped back to his while a rosy blush tinted her cheeks.

"You're allowed to look," he murmured huskily while fighting the desire to go to her.

Fuck. He wanted to kiss her.

Her blush deepened, and she bit down on her bottom lip. Grace shook her head, but her gaze slid over his chest again before she cleared her throat and abruptly tore her eyes away from him.

This was going to be a very interesting adventure—traveling with her—if she kept looking at him like that.

Grace turned to study the curtains as though she found them fascinating. "Did you sleep okay?"

Colt crossed the room, grabbed his duffle bag from its spot on the floor, and tossed it on the bed before answering, "I slept alright, I suppose." He unzipped his bag and dug through it in search of a clean pair of jeans. "I didn't wake you, did I?"

"No, I woke up while you were showering." She didn't take her eyes off the curtains. "I heard singing last night. I think. It may have been a dream. I don't know. Did you hear anything?"

Shit, she'd been awake enough to remember that?

He cleared his throat and rubbed one hand over the warmth creeping up the back of his neck. "You seemed to have a couple nightmares last night. You woke me up flailing around."

"I did?" She glanced back over her shoulder at him then resumed her study of the curtains. "I don't remember that. All I remember was hearing someone singing."

He hesitated. "Uh, yeah, that was me." Colt shrugged, even though she wasn't looking at him. "I didn't know what else to do to help. When I touched your shoulder, you got even more upset. My mom always used to sing to Cash and me when one of us had a bad dream, so I thought I'd try that. It seemed to work since you settled right down."

"Oh." She turned to glance at him again. "Thank you." She tossed him a smile as she pushed to her feet and headed for her bag.

He pulled a button-down shirt from his duffle bag then zipped it closed.

"It was no problem." He shrugged into his shirt and began buttoning it. "Sorry to have made you endure my awful singing. Until last night, I haven't sung in years."

"It's too bad I don't remember whether your singing was good."

"And it's probably better that you don't remember," he said with a laugh, then made the mistake of looking at her.

Her pajamas weren't anything overtly sexy, considering the snug-fitting, long-sleeved t-shirt and PJ pants didn't show even a hint of skin, but he couldn't drag his eyes away. She bent over to delve into her bag, giving him a magnificent view of her backside, and he momentarily forgot how to breathe as his body reacted to her for the second time this morning alone.

Frankly, he was pretty sure she could wear a burlap sack, and the sight of her would still send his blood rushing south. She was gorgeous and didn't seem to realize it. If she did, she'd given no hint of it in all the time they'd known each other.

His dick would never calm the hell down so he could finish getting dressed if he didn't stop looking at her. Even knowing that, his gaze followed her as she headed for the bathroom.

He waited until the door clicked shut behind her, and he heard the shower turn on, to drop his towel with a groan.

What the hell was wrong with him? Grace didn't need him sniffing around her. What she needed was for him to be her friend. *Just* her friend. Besides, she was fresh out of a terrible relationship. If these traveling arrangements were going to work, he needed to get control of himself and rein in his thoughts. She wasn't for him and never would be.

He muttered a curse and yanked on his boxers before jamming his feet into his jeans.

He was pulling on his boots when Grace stepped back out of the bathroom, fully dressed and towel-drying her hair. She smiled brightly at him and took his breath away all over again. He was glad to see her looking far more cheerful than she had been when he opened his door to her.

"Are you ready to tell me what brought you to my door last night?" He almost regretted his words when the smile fell from her face.

She shook her head, her posture stiffening. "No. I don't know if I'll ever be able to talk about it." She looked away from him, seeming to avoid his eyes.

He'd figured that would be her answer. "Okay."

As much as he wanted to know what happened, he'd already learned his lesson about pushing her for answers. That was a mistake he wouldn't be repeating.

"Are you hungry? I was thinking we would find a bite to eat before we stop by a store to get you a suitcase. Sound good?"

"Sure," she said, then frowned. "Um, on second thought, I can't afford all that. I spent most of what I had on me to get gas last night. I can afford food, but my trash bag will have to do for my clothes for now."

"You don't have any savings?"

Her shoulders slumped as she dropped her gaze to the floor. She shook her head, and her face flushed pink. "Uh, no. Flint wouldn't let me have a bank account. He said it was easier to share his. That it'd be best to let him control the finances. My paychecks were direct-deposited into his account. The only time he let me have any money was when he sent me grocery shopping. I guess letting it happen makes me seem like a bit of an idiot, but I swear the way he explained things when he talked me into it made sense."

It was clear from the way she refused to look at him that she was expecting to be judged for going along with Flint's bullshit manipulations. Colt would never do that to her.

Fuckin' Flint, man. Just when he thought he couldn't possibly hate the man any more, she had to tell him something that ramped up the feeling.

He took a deep breath in an attempt to cool his anger some before answering, "I understand. Don't worry about it. I've got you."

She shook her head again, harder this time. "No, Colt. You're being too accommodating. I can't ask you to bankroll me."

He pushed to his feet and crossed the small room to her, then met her eyes when she glanced up at him. "Listen to me, Princess. We're friends. Friends help friends; that's the way it is. So let me help you." His gaze dipped to her mouth of its own accord.

Friend? The thoughts that'd been running through his mind since he met her weren't the least platonic.

"Besides, you're not asking. I'm offering."

Grace sighed heavily. "Fine, but I don't need anything fancy."

She may not need anything grandiose, but she did need luggage that would hold up to the test of time and life on the road. Cheap wasn't likely to do that.

Rather than push her about it any further now, Colt decided to change the subject. "Are you sure you don't want to put on something cooler? It's supposed to be pretty warm today. You're going to melt in that top."

Grace tugged the hem of the long-sleeved shirt she wore. "I'll be okay. It's a pretty airy shirt."

He gave it a dubious look. "You're sure? It'll probably hit 90."

Her shoulders hunched for the second time this morning, and she returned her gaze to the floor as she nodded. "I don't want you to see my bruises," she said so quietly that he had to strain to hear her.

Colt sucked in a breath. He wasn't sure he wanted to see her bruises either. Somehow, he suspected even a glimpse of them would have him handing her off to Cash and hunting down that sorry sack of manure she'd been dating. He'd make that fucker pay for hurting her, even if it landed him in jail.

Shit, he didn't need much encouragement. He already wanted to do exactly that just knowing that Flint had put his hands on her in anger. He didn't want her feeling ashamed about what happened to her, or feeling as though she needed to hide from him, even more.

"I understand," he said softly. He gingerly tipped her face up and met her eyes. "I need you to know something, Princess," he said, his voice both fierce and gentle at once. "You didn't deserve anything he did to you. If you feel more comfortable hiding your bruises, you can if you want, but you don't need to. Not from me. Nothing you could show or tell me would make me think less of you, if that's what you're afraid of." He shook his head slightly. "I'm proud of you, Grace. You are brave and smart and beautiful. You got away. You survived."

She blinked, her lashes damp, but didn't say a word.

He spread his arms in offering. "Do you need a hug?"

One corner of his mouth lifted when she nodded and wordlessly stepped into his embrace. He wrapped his arms around her loosely, afraid he'd hurt her if he held her as tightly as he felt compelled to. She tucked her face against his chest, inhaling a shuddering breath.

Grace pulled out of his arms after a couple of minutes and gave him a shaky smile. "Thanks."

"Anytime," Colt said softly. "Are you sure you don't want to change into something cooler?"

"I'm sure. I'll be okay."

He gave her shirt another doubtful look but let the topic go with a quick nod. "Alright. Come on then, Princess, I can hear your stomach growling. Let me feed you."

***

He hated shopping with a passion, but it was necessary today. While Grace hadn't fought him when he'd bought her breakfast, they'd been arguing about the suitcases for the past hour. He didn't care if it took the rest of the day to talk her into it; he was determined to buy her a decent set. She was one hell of a stubborn woman, but he wasn't about to let her out-stubborn him on this. She needed the luggage. It wasn't a frivolous buy.

The suitcases he had his eye on weren't cheap, but he wasn't exactly broke either. He still had most of the money left from the sale of the ranch he'd shared with Sarah. Plus, he'd been on a winning streak.

He eyed Grace and shook his head as she pointed to a set of super cheap suitcases. While they'd probably do the trick for a time, they were likely to fall apart within a month. Maybe two, if they made it that long.

"Those wouldn't last a week on the road."

Grace studied them with a small frown. "Maybe, but they're cheap. The ones you want to get cost too much. I don't like owing people money, and it's worse now that I don't have a job. I'll never be able to pay you back."

He understood her position, but she wasn't making it easy to take care of her. Hopefully, she didn't intend to fight him like this the entire time she was with him, or he might go crazy. The last woman who'd made it this difficult to spoil her a bit was Sarah.

He shoved that thought away as soon as it popped into his head.

"You don't need to worry about paying me back. They're a gift. The set I want you to have is quality and should last you years. They're definitely the better bargain."

Grace's frown deepened, and she moved further down the aisle to look at another cheap set.

It took another hour to wear her down enough to let him buy the set he wanted for her. She still wasn't happy about it, however. He couldn't blame her. If he were in her place, it'd probably be stinging his pride to accept help too.

As he steered their cart toward the checkout, he glanced over at her. "Anything else?"

She gave him a weak smile. "You tell me, Eight. You're the one who keeps insisting on buying me things."

In addition to the suitcases, he'd talked her into letting him get her a cheap laptop in case she decided to do some freelance writing or something. He wanted her to have everything she needed.

He grinned at her use of the nickname she'd given him what seemed like ages ago. It'd been so long since she'd called him that. He hadn't realized how much he missed it.

"Learn to love it, Princess. I'm not planning on stopping anytime soon."

The look she gave him in response had him chuckling.

They stepped out of the store side by side, both blinking against the blinding sunshine baking the parking lot. Grace looked at something in the distance, and her expression turned thoughtful.

Colt followed her gaze to a *Buy Here, Pay Here* car dealership across the street. A huge banner hung above the building, proudly proclaiming that they were buying vehicles of all makes, models, and conditions.

"I think I'd like to go pick up my truck and see if that dealership over there will give me anything for it," Grace said. "If you don't mind ferrying me around everywhere, that is. It's not like I can afford to fill the tank again." She gestured toward the dealership as she spoke then turned a hopeful look on him. "It'd let me be able to pay you back for breakfast and the stuff you got me."

There was no way he'd take her money, but he didn't feel like arguing with her about it at the moment either.

He considered. They weren't going to make it to his next stop in time for him to ride, even with it being pretty early in the day yet. He'd have to skip it and go on to the next. It might cause him to drop a few spots in the standings, but a good ride or two could regain them if that happened. They had plenty of time for her to sell her truck before they needed to head out.

"Sure, we can do that. I don't need to be at my next stop until tomorrow afternoon at the latest, so we've got plenty of time. Let's check it out."

Colt glanced sideways at Grace while he drove.

She'd only gotten a thousand bucks for her truck. It had disappointed her, but she'd taken it. He'd offered to help her negotiate a better offer, but she'd predictably refused. She was clearly very determined to prove that she could take care of herself. He didn't doubt she could.

It was obvious she wasn't accustomed to being cared about by anyone. While it might make her uncomfortable, he didn't know how to make it easier for her to accept. She was important. He'd do about anything to help her out, no repayment necessary. He'd always been this way; it wasn't likely he could stop caring now. There wasn't much he wouldn't do for those in his inner circle.

She reached over and turned the radio to a different station. The sound of pop music filled the cab.

He made a face. "Sweetheart, I like you, but I'm not listening to this crap for the next six hours."

Grace laughed and changed the radio back to the country western station it had been on previously. "Fine." She stuck her tongue out at him.

He chuckled, the corners of his mouth twitching. "Is my music really that bad?"

"Hmm, I suppose not." The song changed, and her eyes brightened. "Hey, I know this one!"

He watched from the corner of his eye as she began tentatively singing along to the song, her soprano voice only breaking pitch twice. A small smile played on his lips. She had a beautiful singing voice. He could listen to her all day. His smile spread when her voice gained confidence and her volume rose.

The next song was a duet, and he joined in on the male parts. His own singing voice was quite rusty, but she didn't seem to mind. The grin she tossed him made warmth spread through him from the region of his heart.

Other than last night and now, when was the last time he'd sung anything? He couldn't remember, but he was enjoying himself.

The hours and miles seemed to pass faster than he could recall them ever passing before. Maybe it was the company. Colt took the next exit and pulled his truck into the parking lot of a tiny brick building with a gigantic sign out front proclaiming the place to be Millie's Diner.

He caught the questioning look Grace shot him and shrugged. "I'm hungry." They'd only made minimal stops, so he figured she had to be pretty damn hungry by now too. "Aren't you?"

She laughed. "I am, but aren't we only about ten minutes from the rodeo grounds? They probably have cheaper food there."

"You that eager to get away from me?" he teased. "Millie's is awesome! Way better than anything the rodeo offers. Besides, we're too early to eat at the rodeo grounds."

He threw open his door and stepped from the cab, then groaned while arching his back to stretch out his aching muscles. Sleeping on the floor last night had not been one of his better decisions. He was getting too old and beat up for that shit. It wasn't as though there had been any viable alternatives, though. His comfort hadn't been a priority.

Grace nudged his arm as she joined him. "I'm treating this time." She made a face when he shook his head. "Please, Colt. I'm not comfortable with you paying for everything. Let me pay. Just this once."

"Fine, but just this time. I want you to save your money."

On impulse, Colt moved to sling his arm over her shoulders companionably as they began walking toward the diner. The moment his arm raised, Grace flinched hard and ducked away from him. He froze mid-step as she dashed into the restaurant ahead of him.

The way she'd recoiled bothered the hell out of him. She didn't think he would ever hurt her, did she? Hell, he rarely ever raised his voice toward a woman. He'd never even yelled during his and Sarah's most heated arguments. Not that Grace had any way of knowing that.

Realizing he was standing alone in the middle of the parking lot now—staring after a woman who'd already disappeared into the building—he forced himself back into motion and joined her indoors.

He waited until after they'd ordered their lunch to address what happened outside.

Colt placed his forearms on the table and leaned forward. "Princess." Once she lifted her gaze from the placemat she was repetitively folding and unfolding the corner of, he continued. "I'm sorry if I scared you out there. I wasn't thinking." He paused for a second, considering his words. "I know you don't want to talk about what happened with Flint, and you don't have to, but I need you to know that you're safe here with me. I promise," he said with conviction.

Grace laid her hand on his forearm and gently squeezed as she leaned toward him. "I know. Out in the parking lot ... you took me by surprise, and I acted on instinct." She smiled tensely. "That's all."

Colt took a breath and angled toward her a bit more as he met her eyes. "I know we're still strangers in many ways, but I hope you know that I would never intentionally hurt you." He shook his head slowly. "Sometimes, I swear it feels like I've known you all my life. It's easy to forget that I haven't."

A shaky smile curled on her lips. "We may not have known each other for very long, but I know I'm safe with you. It's something I've known for a while now. It's why I ended up on your doorstep." She gave his arm another squeeze. "I can't promise I won't flinch occasionally, but I know you would never hurt me on purpose. You're nothing like him."

He smiled back at her, trying to ignore the heat coiling up his arm from where her hand rested on his bare skin. "I'm glad to hear that."

He settled back in his chair, easing his arm away from her fingers in the process. Her touch affected him too strongly, even as innocent as it was. It made him want things he had no business wanting with her. Things that couldn't happen between them.

Grace went back to fiddling with the corner of the placemat, her eyes following the movements of her fingers. "I'm sure you've probably been wondering why I stayed with him so long."

The question hadn't even crossed his mind.

Before he could formulate a reply, she sighed and said, "I guess the biggest reason was not having the money to leave." She cringed and curled in on herself as if trying to become smaller. "With him taking my paychecks, the only money I had was the little I could hide away where Flint wouldn't find it. If I had change left after grocery shopping, I stashed it away, but I hadn't managed to save up much. He never looked at the receipts, so I don't think he knew what I was doing." She folded the corner of the placemat with a bit more force but still didn't look up. "That money is what I used to get gas last night. There wasn't much; it was so slow to build up." Her voice trembled as she said, "I didn't have enough yet, but I couldn't wait any longer. Not after he—"

Her hand fluttered to her throat and her chin quivered. She didn't seem aware of the action. There was a faraway look in her eyes as though her mind had taken her somewhere other than this diner.

She took a deep, hitching breath. "Part of me kept clinging to the hope he'd go back to being the wonderfully sweet guy he'd been when we met," Grace continued, her voice regaining strength though it dropped in volume. A frown pulled at her lips as she resumed picking at the placemat—the corner was beginning to shred now. "I didn't want to admit he'd tricked me. That the sweetness was a lie. I still don't, not really. It makes me feel stupid, like I should have been able to see the monster he was hiding."

She was anything but stupid. Colt bit his tongue to hold back the words he wanted to say, determined not to interrupt.

"It took me a while to give up on the idea that what was happening was somehow my fault and that I could fix things. That if I tried harder and did everything he wanted me to, the Flint I fell for would come back." She gave her head a half-shake. "That was a lie I told myself. That version of Flint never existed. I know that now." She swallowed hard. "He used to tell me how lucky I was that he loved me," she said so quietly her voice was near a whisper. "That without him, I would have nothing and nobody. It made it even harder to leave. Part of me knows it's not true—or at least, hopes it isn't—but the rest of me ... still wonders if he's right."

"He's not." His gut roiled, and his heart hurt for her. Though he still didn't know the specifics of her life with Flint, he didn't need to. His imagination could fill in the gaps fine.

Grace finally lifted her troubled gaze to his, and her brow furrowed.

"Flint," Colt said softly. "He's not right. You have me. And you don't have to explain your reasons for anything, Princess."

The waitress returned with their meals, interrupting the conversation, and Colt felt vaguely thankful for it. He didn't know what to say to comfort Grace.

"Thank you," he said once they were alone again. At her bewildered look, he added, "For opening up to me. I know it can't be easy talking about it."

Rather than replying to his comment, she offered him a faint smile and picked up her fork.

"This looks great." She gestured to her plate containing a sizable portion of fried chicken, a heap of steamed broccoli, and a loaded baked potato.

"It's one of the best meals Millie's offers," he answered, taking her cue of needing a subject change. "I hope you like it."

Colt smiled, though he felt more like hunting Flint down and feeding him his fist repeatedly. Grace didn't need to see his anger, not after everything she'd been through.

"Think about what you want to do today. We're here really early, and I don't ride until tomorrow night, so unless you want to sit around the rest of the day, we'll need to figure out something to do." Hopefully, something that would distract him. "I think there might be a museum around here."

Grace nodded. "A museum sounds fun."

A comfortable silence settled between them as they both turned their attention to their food.

As he ate, Colt ruminated on Grace's words. She'd trusted him with part of her story. She felt safe with him. He hoped he never gave her cause not to.

Chapter 12

"How picky are you?" Colt asked, slanting a look at her.

The motel ahead of them seemed like it was barely holding together. Both the roof and siding were horribly worn. It was super cheap, but it probably had to be because of the dilapidated condition it was in. Who would stay here otherwise?

Grace gave the little ten-room roadside motel another critical look over and cringed. "It looks like it belongs in a slasher flick."

Colt laughed. "Get back in the truck. We'll stay at the hotel across town."

The hotel he spoke of was the only other option, and the price it advertised was five times more than this ramshackle motel. He'd already spent too much on her.

She gave her head a small shake. "No, I'll be okay. Let's just stay here."

Inwardly, she winced at the idea of sleeping in the dingy building in front of them. The place was a dump. It'd be a miracle if they didn't end up murdered, or pick up bed bugs or something equally as horrible.

He gave her a stern look, though it was ruined by the playfulness gleaming in the depths of his eyes. "Grace Parker, get your ass back in this truck before I come over there, toss you over my shoulder, and put you back in the truck myself."

She laughed but eyed him warily.

How serious was he? Would he really do it? Part of her wanted to find out. After Flint, the prospect of a man tossing her over his shoulder and forcing her to go somewhere should at least give her pause, but this was Colt. If he was serious about it, the feel of his hands on her body would make it worth it. So very worth it.

His lips twitched. "That doesn't really seem as threatening without your middle name. You do have one, right?"

When she made no move toward the truck, he stalked toward her with an impish grin plastered on his face.

Well, that answered her question about whether he'd do it. Grace chickened out. She hurried back to the truck and hopped onto the passenger seat once more. It wasn't like she really wanted to stay at this awful motel anyway.

"Victoria," she said with a smile once Colt seated himself behind the wheel. "My middle name. It's Victoria."

"Grace Victoria Parker, huh?" Colt asked as he started the engine. "I'll keep that in mind in case you decide to misbehave."

She looked sideways at him. The comment was light, nonchalant. What would he say if she told him how badly she'd love to misbehave? But only with him.

It'd been so long since a man touched her like she was a desirable woman. Maybe she wasn't one. She'd only had two boyfriends before Flint, and they hadn't stuck around long. Flint sure hadn't been interested in her in that way for a long time either. Not since well before the cookout. Maybe he'd been cheating on her, and that's why he'd been so insistent she was cheating on him—guilty conscience or something like that. Did Flint even have a conscience? She rather doubted it. Either way, it hadn't upset her that he hadn't wanted her. Honestly, she'd been thankful for it. She hadn't wanted him either, especially not once the abuse escalated. She'd been completely done with the relationship well before he'd thrown that first punch.

As if she'd summoned Flint by thinking about him, her phone buzzed in her pocket. Even without looking, she knew it was him.

There'd been twelve texts from him when she'd peeked at her phone at breakfast. Another six had arrived in the time since. She'd deleted them all without reading any. She would delete this one too later. It was a good thing she'd made the snap decision to silence the device when she'd stopped for gas last night. She'd probably be ready to toss her phone out the window by now otherwise. Tonight, she'd figure out how to block his number. She was done with him.

She wondered where he was right now. Was he on the road searching for her, like he'd promised he would if she ever left? Or maybe at a bar, picking up his next victim? She hated him. Hated him like she'd never hated anyone else in her life. Would he find her? She felt fairly confident he wouldn't—at least, not any time soon. There were too many directions she could have gone; it'd take him time to figure out which was correct. And she and Colt were even farther away now.

She gave herself a mental shake. Thinking about Flint only made her angry and afraid.

Grace arched a brow expectantly when Colt said nothing else while he pulled the truck back out onto the road. "Well? Aren't you going to tell me yours?"

He tossed her a crooked grin that made butterflies hatch in her stomach. "Nope."

"That's not even fair," she said while giving him the mockery of a scowl. "I told you mine; it's only right that you tell me yours."

"Nope."

She groaned, drawing a chuckle from him. He was teasing her, as he almost always had been during the interviews. She liked that about him. This man was nothing like Flint. Colt was easygoing and humorous. Steady. Around him, she could relax, knowing he'd shield her.

"My full name is Colt Montgomery Boone," he said a few minutes later. "Happy now, Princess?"

Her lips curled into a smile. "Yep." She turned her gaze out the passenger window, watching the buildings pass while they traveled back across town. "Colt Montgomery Boone." She tossed him a razz grin. "I'll keep that in mind in case *you* decide to misbehave."

He gave her a sidelong glance, and her breath caught. Very real heat smoldered in the depths of his beautiful eyes. It was gone an instant later, vanished as if it'd never been there at all. If she didn't know better, she'd almost think she'd imagined it. It left her reeling.

She swallowed, her mouth suddenly dry. They reached the hotel before she figured out something else to say, and he threw the truck into park by the office.

"Stay here. I'll go see if they have any rooms." He flashed her a smile, then hopped out of the truck and disappeared into the building.

She looked around the parking lot while she waited. There were an awful lot of vehicles here. Would there even be any rooms available? With the only other option being the seedy motel they'd been at, she would rather sleep in the truck if there wasn't a vacancy here.

"We're in luck!" Colt said when he returned to the truck, after what seemed like an eternity, and slid behind the wheel. "I got the last two rooms." He pocketed one key card and held the other out to her.

She took it while giving him a puzzled look. "You didn't have to get us separate rooms. As long as there was one with two beds, it would have been fine to get just one."

He raised an eyebrow and shrugged. "I figured you'd be most comfortable in your own room. Privacy and all that."

"Well, you aren't wrong there. Privacy is good, but I don't like you spending more on me than you absolutely have to."

He screwed up his face. "I wouldn't do it if I minded, Princess. Let me take care of you, maybe even spoil you a bit. If it makes you smile, I'm happy to do it."

Grace studied him for several beats, trying in vain to figure him out. She didn't know how to handle the kindness he kept showing her. What was his motivation? Why was he doing this for her? This was all far too unfamiliar.

"Fine, but the two rooms are this once. From now on, we get one room with two beds. Okay? There's no reason for you to spend more money on me than you need to. I'm fine with sharing with you." She stuck her tongue out at him. "Besides, you've been a gentleman so far. I don't think I have anything to worry about."

"A gentleman?" He burst into loud laughter.

Maybe "gentleman" had been the wrong word choice to describe him, but he had to have known what she meant.

It was several minutes before he reined himself back in. "I don't think anyone has ever accused me of being a gentleman before." He chuckled and shook his head. "Oh, Princess. If you only knew."

He turned to look at her. The heat she'd seen in his gaze earlier made a second appearance. Her stomach jumped. His eyes darkened as his pupils dilated. Maybe she'd been wrong about him not being interested in her. His look spoke of a hunger that astonished her. Nobody had ever looked at her like this, not as far as she could recall.

She nervously licked her lips. It was then he looked away and started the engine.

He cleared his throat. "Let's go find our rooms and see what we can find to do around here. There won't be much to see at the rodeo grounds until tomorrow, so that's out."

She arched a brow at him but nodded. "Okay," she said softly.

Grace always had been horrible with telling when a guy was attracted to her, especially if they were subtle about it. Most of her life, she'd doubted whether she was the sort of woman worthy of being wanted at all. She wasn't the girl guys flirted with. Maybe that's why it'd been so easy for Flint to hook her. He'd showered her with constant over-the-top attention from the start. It'd been overwhelming. A well-disguised trap.

It took a couple of laps around the parking lot before she spotted her room number and pointed it out to Colt. He pulled into an empty parking spot and shut off the engine.

Grace climbed from the truck and grabbed the suitcase containing her clothes from the backseat. Though she didn't want to admit it, the luggage set Colt had gotten her was way nicer than the set she'd been trying to talk him into. It rankled her to feel like she owed someone, though. No matter how many times he insisted they were gifts and that he wouldn't take her money, it made her feel weird accepting them.

"Nope, that's mine." Colt shouldered his duffle bag and took the suitcase from her before flashing a grin in her direction and leading the way to her room.

Grace unlocked and shoved the door open. She could feel Colt's eyes on her as she stepped in ahead of him. Her gaze swept over her temporary abode. It wasn't a big room, but it appeared clean and pretty well-kept. A faint perfumy scent lingered in the air. An air freshener maybe? It wasn't unpleasant, but it tickled her nose.

"Meet your approval?" He sat her luggage down on the small table next to the room's flatscreen TV, then looked around. He whistled. "This is way nicer than anything I've stayed in lately."

"It's definitely nicer than that first place you stopped at. I swear that place looked like the perfect setting for a scary movie." She laughed.

He chuckled. "Yeah, I guess it did." His broad shoulders rose and fell. "I guess I don't much care where I stay, as long as there is a clean bed and a working shower." He looked over at her. "While you're with me, I'll pick nicer places."

Grace smiled. "As long as they aren't too expensive."

Colt made a face at her and readjusted the strap of his duffle bag on his shoulder. "Let me check out my room, and we'll get out of here. Did you think about what you might want to do?"

"That museum you mentioned sounded pretty fun. I've never been to one before." When surprise filtered over Colt's face, she hastily explained, "The private school I went to didn't take field trips to things like that, and I've been too busy with life since I graduated to consider visiting one." She smiled and followed him out the door.

Colt's room was identical to her own, right down to the picture hanging on the wall behind the flatscreen television. Maybe the hotel had gotten a special deal on duplicate prints. She wasn't thrilled with how far away Colt's room was from her own, though not enough to say something. He couldn't do anything about it anyway. It was just... She felt safer having him close.

Colt pulled his phone from his pocket and opened an app while they walked side by side back to his truck. He typed something then frowned and typed something else. When they reached his truck, he used his free hand to open the passenger side door and gave her a smile.

"Hop in. May as well have a seat while I try to figure out where this museum is."

She ducked her head and smiled. It still threw her off whenever he opened doors for her. Flint would never have thought to do such a thing. If anything, he'd demand she open it for *him* instead.

Colt closed her door then crossed in front of the big vehicle before sliding behind the wheel beside her. The moment he was settled, his attention returned to the device in his hand.

Colt scrolled the screen of his phone, his brow bunching further the longer he thumbed through whatever he was reading.

She waited for the verdict in silence.

A few moments later, he finally looked up at her.

"Apparently, I was wrong about the museum," he grumbled before glancing back down at his phone. His gaze found her again a second later. "Do you like rollercoasters? There isn't much to do in this town, but there's an amusement park in the next town over. It's not too far away, maybe thirty minutes or so. If you feel up to it, do you want to go?"

"Rollercoasters? Um, I have no idea if I like them. I've never been to an amusement park."

"What? You haven't? Buckle up; we're going, then." He shook his head as he tossed the truck into reverse and carefully backed out of the parking spot.

She wasn't sure she really felt up to riding a rollercoaster with as stiff and sore as she still was, but she wanted to go. It wasn't as though it was likely to make her feel much worse. Not much could. At least the painkillers she took earlier had taken the edge off.

"Damn, woman, it's like you've lived under a rock all your life or something. Never been to a museum. Never been to an amusement park. Sheesh." He glanced sideways at her and smirked. "I promise I won't drag you on anything too wild since you're a rollercoaster virgin."

Grace choked on her spit as her gaze jumped to him. When she finally stopped coughing, she squeaked out, "I'm a what?"

"A rollercoaster virgin," he answered in a matter-of-fact tone as he turned the truck out onto the road.

She couldn't hold back her laughter. "A rollercoaster virgin." She laughed even harder. By the time she got control of herself, tears were streaming down her face and she was holding her aching ribs. Geez, they hurt, but it was a good hurt for once.

Colt looked over at her, his lips twitching as though he was fighting the urge to laugh too. "You going to live, or should I find a hospital?"

Unable to speak yet, she shoved at his arm and swiped at the moisture rolling down her cheeks.

"There are napkins in the glove box if you need a tissue."

She retrieved a small handful of the napkins and dabbed at her eyes. "Gosh, I haven't laughed like that in ages. Thank you."

"Hmm, my pleasure. I'm happy to make you laugh anytime." His expression sobered, and his voice seemed deeper when he said, "You have a great laugh, Princess. I love hearing it."

The truck's cab suddenly seemed too small.

"Thank you," she said, her voice barely above a whisper. She looked down at her hands, strangely uncomfortable.

"Did I say something wrong?"

She shook her head. "No. I'm sorry. I'm not great with compliments. I haven't gotten many in a very long time." In the past few years, genuine compliments came so far and few between that she no longer knew how to respond.

"I see. Well, I'll have to remedy that."

A not-quite-comfortable silence settled between them. She hated that her awkwardness had killed the lightheartedness of earlier. Why did she have to be this way?

Not knowing how to get it back, Grace turned her gaze out the window and watched the landscape pass.

———

To her joy, the tense mood faded pretty quickly once they arrived at the amusement park. They'd spent most of the time wandering around.

They'd deemed the lines of most of the rollercoasters to be too long to wait in, but they had gone on a few. She'd even surprised him by dragging him on one of the more intense ones. Twice.

"Well, what did you think?" Colt asked as he walked her toward her hotel room. "Did you have as much fun as I did?"

"You really have to ask that? I had a blast! If you didn't have a bull to ride, I'd ask if we could go back again tomorrow."

They stopped in front of her room, and Grace reached over to swipe her key card then pushed open the door.

She turned to beam up at Colt. "Seriously, that was the most fun I've had in many, many years." She cuddled the little plush horse he'd won her from one of the carnival games in the park. "And thanks again for Whinny too. I'll give him a wonderful home."

"Whinny? That's what you're naming it?" He shook his head, a slanted smile on his lips. "You're fun, Grace." His expression sobered as he gazed down at her. "I haven't been to an amusement park since I was a kid. I had a great time." He took a half-step closer. "Thanks for going with me today."

Was he about to kiss her?

Her lips parted, her tongue flicking out to moisten them. She wasn't sure if she was ready to take this step, but she'd been craving Colt's kiss since long before it was appropriate to want such things. Wondering how it'd feel. How he'd taste. But was this wise? What if they acted on their mutual attraction and it soured things between them somehow? What then? Even as she deliberated about it, she couldn't bring herself to back away.

The air between them crackled with electricity as they stared into each other's eyes. Somewhere in the parking lot, a cricket chirped. Her breath quickened as the moment stretched. His throat worked like he had words stuck in it, but he said nothing.

God, he smelled so good. She inhaled deeply, filling her lungs with his clean, masculine scent.

He skimmed his fingers down her arm, sending chills skittering over her skin. Her flesh prickled in the wake of the fleeting touch. She couldn't keep herself from swaying toward him.

To her disappointment, Colt cleared his throat and took a step back.

"Sleep well, Grace." His voice was a bit rough. Then, he turned and started for his room with long strides.

A rare impulsiveness she'd thought Flint had killed off rose within her.

"Colt, wait!"

Grace tossed the stuffed horse on her bed and sprinted after him.

He paused and looked back at her questioningly. When she reached him, she flung her arms around his middle, stepped in close, and rested her cheek against his chest. She felt him tense, but she didn't let it deter her.

"Thank you for today." After giving him a squeeze, she let go and retreated to her room before he could respond, though she felt his gaze following her. A smile played on her face as she clicked the door shut and engaged the locks.

Today had been amazing, far more fun than she'd expected it'd be. For the first time in ages, she found herself eager to find out what tomorrow would bring.

Chapter 13

Colt's brows pulled together as he glanced down at Grace. "Are you sure you don't want me to sit with you? I don't feel right leaving you alone all afternoon."

Especially not after she'd come running to his hotel room late last night, wide-eyed and shaking in the wake of another nightmare. It'd scared the shit out of him. His first thought had been that Flint had found her somehow and attacked her again.

"I don't normally watch the other events run, but I'd be happy to keep you company until I have to get ready to ride."

"I'm sure. I'll be fine. I've shaken up your life enough as it is. I don't want to disturb your normal routine any more than I already have."

He frowned. "Is that what you think you've done?" He grabbed her hand and pulled her around so she faced him as they stopped next to the arena.

They were early enough that the bleachers were still mostly empty. The bulk of the crowd would likely arrive closer to when the roughstock events began, considering they were typically the fan favorites at most rodeos. It was also the reason why most rodeo organizers scheduled them for last. It kept money flowing into the concession stand longer.

"Listen to me, Princess. I enjoy spending time with you. If you want me to hang out with you for a while today, say the word, and I will."

Grace shook her head. "I appreciate it, but I'm okay. Really. If it makes you feel better, I promise I'll come find you if I need some company."

"Or you could text me, and I'll come right back."

They'd finally exchanged numbers at breakfast. Long overdue, in his opinion. She'd seemed more than a little surprised when he'd unlocked his phone and handed it to her without hesitation. No doubt her asshole of an ex-boyfriend had been one of those guys who refused to let anyone touch his phone.

"Hmm, that would be easier than hunting all over the place for you, wouldn't it?" She laughed and placed her hand on his bicep as she gazed up at him. "I'll be fine, Eight. Seriously."

"As long as you're sure," he rumbled, once again doing his best to ignore the way her touch affected him.

"I am." She gave him a little push. "Now, go do whatever you normally do and forget that I'm here. Just don't forget to remember me before you go back to the hotel. I don't really want to be stranded here."

"Forget you?" His lips quirked upward. "That'll never happen."

If she only knew how many times he'd tried before she showed up at his motel the night before last. It'd been an impossible task. Every single time he'd thought he'd succeeded, he'd see something or someone who reminded him of her, and boom... There she was at the forefront of his thoughts all over again.

"Don't be afraid to text me. I'm serious."

She gave him a slightly exasperated look. "Go."

He grinned and held his hands up in surrender. "I'm going. I'm going."

Colt turned and walked away.

Once he was a short distance from her, he gave in to the need to look back.

She'd seated herself on a bench part-way up on the stands. Despite her assurances, he still didn't particularly like leaving her sitting alone. Maybe because this was the first rodeo since she started traveling with him. He didn't know, but the temptation to go back and sit down with her for a while was strong. She'd probably yell, but maybe it'd ease the knot in his gut.

"Dude, where have you been?"

Colt spun back around to see Cash rushing toward him.

"I had something to do." He hesitated. How did he explain the situation without telling more than he had the right to? "I was helping a friend." He jerked his head toward the bleachers, where Grace sat looking down at her phone with a slight frown on her face.

What was that frown about? He'd have to find out later.

Cash glanced in that direction, and his eyebrows shot toward his hat. He returned his green gaze to Colt moments later. "The reporter?"

"She's not a journalist anymore, but yeah. She had some shit happen and needed a friend." Colt hesitated then added, "She's traveling with me for a while."

"Really?" Cash turned to look at Grace with a speculative gleam in his eyes. "Traveling with you, huh?"

Colt gave him a hard shove. "It's not like that, asshole. She's just a friend."

"Uh-huh, sure she is." Cash smirked. "You? Just friends with a woman that looks like that? Yeah, right. I know you better than that, man."

Sure, in Colt's younger years, well before Sarah, he wouldn't have thought twice about attempting to seduce a woman like Grace. He wasn't proud of it, but his younger self had come by the title of heartbreaker honestly. He wasn't that man anymore. He didn't want to be. Sarah had changed him.

Rather than arguing, Colt tossed his arm over his friend's shoulders and guided him further away from the arena. "I'll explain what I can later. It's complicated."

Cash gave him a curious look but nodded. "Dusty got an 87 on Night Flight last night. You should have seen it; the kid was awesome!"

Even with the subject change, Colt knew that he'd be thoroughly questioned about Grace eventually. Cash was too damn nosey to let it go this easy.

"Night Flight? Damn! I hate that bull."

The black bull was a challenge even for him, and he'd been riding bulls since he was nine. He'd have to remember to congratulate Dusty when he saw him next.

The youngest of Colt's group of close friends, Dusty had only been riding on the pro-circuit for a little over three years. He was a damn good rider. He'd earned his first National Championship title his rookie year—a feat Colt, Cash, and Brody hadn't managed. The kid was going places. Dusty was already better than Colt and Cash combined.

Colt tried his best to pay attention as Cash filled him in on the rest of last night's rodeo while they sauntered toward the bull pens, but his mind was back in the bleachers with Grace.

Colt cautiously lowered himself onto his bull's black back while trying again to focus on his ride. There was no room for distraction when riding bulls, especially not ones like Seatbelt Required. His draw this evening was a demon. Not giving a draw your full concentration was a sure way for a roughstock rider to end up hurt, maybe even dead.

Tonight, Colt was so distracted he couldn't even remember if he'd done his usual pre-ride ritual. Shit, he was pretty sure he hadn't. His spotter slapped a hand to his chest less than a second before Seatbelt Required reared up in the chute. The back of the bull's head narrowly missed slamming into Colt's face. Fuck, not a great start. He needed to either get his head in the game or get off this bull. He would be no help at all to Grace if he got himself killed.

Flipping his chaps out of the way, he worked to get his legs into position then took a deep breath and forced his mind to clear. Again. He could continue thinking about Grace and pondering his feelings for her after he made the eight. Now was not the time. He swiftly tied in before the animal could act up again, double-checked his grip, then nodded to the cowboy manning the gate.

Seatbelt Required left the chute with an explosive leap that nearly unseated Colt right then. He cursed and tightened his muscles in an effort to stay centered on the animal's back as the bull settled into a spin. Success was his until the bull leaped high into the air and kicked out while twisting his hindquarters off to the side. There was no way any cowboy could stay on after a buck like that.

Colt slipped sideways but somehow managed to hang on.

The next powerful buck sent him flying. He slammed hard into the arena railing. A bullfighter yelled for him to get up as he dashed between Colt and the bull. He scrambled onto his hands and knees but wasn't able to gain his feet before the bull was back on him. The animal lowered his head and easily sent Colt into the air, despite the efforts the trio of bullfighters made to pull the ill-tempered bull's attention off him.

For a moment, the world was little more than a blur. The cloud of dust that rose when he collided with the ground next choked off his air as much as the impact. He forced himself to his feet, still gasping for breath, and darted for the fence as the pickup rider got the bull roped and turned toward the gate that would return him to his pen.

Cash and Brody met Colt behind the chutes moments later.

"You good, man?" Cash handed Colt his bull rope and hat.

Unable to speak yet, Colt answered with an affirmative jerk of his head. There was no doubt in his mind that he'd be hurting once the adrenaline wore off, but he'd worry about that later.

He slapped his hat against his leg and jammed it on his head. His gaze flicked toward the stands, but it was too crowded now to see Grace. Hopefully, she hadn't been watching. He didn't want her worried about him. He'd find her in a few minutes.

He ignored the reporters surrounding him and limped to the cowboy's locker room. The old injury to his hip was far from happy about the jarring it had received out there in the arena. He was going to have to ice it once he got his gear into a locker, or he probably wouldn't be able to walk in a couple of hours.

Colt hobbled out of the locker room after several minutes, holding an ice pack to his aching hip, and found himself nearly bowled over when Grace collided with him.

She looked scared out of her wits. Her face was ghostly white, her body tense and trembling. She flung her arms tightly around his waist.

His eyes shot wide, both her sudden appearance and her embrace taking him by surprise. "Woah there. Are you okay?"

Grace leaned away enough to look up at him, her face a mask of incredulity. "Am I okay? Are you being serious? Are *you* okay?" Her voice was overloud, almost shrill, but she seemed too shaken up to control it.

Colt dropped the ice pack and cradled her face in his hands, his thumbs unconsciously sweeping over the smooth skin of her cheeks in a gentle caress. "I'm fine, Princess. That was nothing compared to some of the close calls I've had. At least I didn't get stomped on this time."

She cringed, and he immediately regretted his choice of words.

He was supposed to be comforting her, not making things worse. It was true, though. Some of his rides had been way rougher than tonight's had been. Like that one wreck six years ago that nearly left him with a broken neck. He'd rather not repeat that one any time soon.

He met her eyes, his head dipping infinitesimally toward hers. "Don't worry about me, sweetheart. I'll be okay. I got the wind knocked out of me and have a minor scratch on my leg. I'm a little roughed up and I'll be sore later, but it's nothing I can't handle."

"But your hip! I saw you icing it."

He smiled slightly, more touched by her concern than he would let on. "It's an old injury. It didn't appreciate me getting myself tossed around." He shrugged. "It'll be okay."

She seemed to accept that. Her posture relaxed, though she caught her bottom lip between her teeth and nibbled at it.

His gaze focused on her mouth, drawn by the nervous action. The feel of her pressed against him rapidly overloaded his system. Hell, right now, even the ache in his hip was an afterthought.

How was it possible for her to feel so damn right against him like this? What would those lips of hers taste like? The desire to find out hit him hard.

His head moved a fraction closer to hers before he realized what he was doing.

This couldn't happen. It wouldn't be fair to her or to the memory of Sarah. His heart still belonged to his late wife.

He unwound Grace's arms from his waist and sat her away from him, badly needing some space between them before he completely lost his head and did something he'd undoubtably regret.

Grace's brow furrowed, her head tilting ever so slightly as she studied him. She looked as though she wanted to say something, but whatever it was, she didn't voice it.

Colt cleared his throat and bent to retrieve the ice pack. He returned it to his hip as he straightened. "What do you say to getting out of here? Maybe go find some dinner somewhere quiet?"

"Sure." Grace nodded at the door to the locker room behind him. "Do you need to grab your stuff before we leave?"

"Nah. It'll be fine. I can grab it in the morning before we hit the road." After a breath of hesitation, he looped his free arm around her shoulders and pulled her against his side, selfishly wanting the contact with her back. It was a bad idea, but he couldn't keep from doing it.

Not even two full days traveling with her, and here he was, already close to losing the battle to keep his hands, and lips, to himself. It didn't help that it was a battle he wasn't sure he even wanted to win.

Chapter 14

Colt was far from ready for this day to begin.

His dreams had been filled with things he'd rather not remember. The phone call from his mother-in-law. Sarah's graveside service. Those two workers lowering Sarah's casket into the ground.

Yanking on his boots, he heaved out a heavy sigh. Not even his shower had helped him wake up. He figured he would need about a gallon of strong black coffee for that. If he didn't have Grace to think of, he'd skip the next stop and find a bar instead. Drink himself into oblivion. Let the whiskey chase the memories away again.

Grace. Today marked the second week since she'd shown up at his motel, and last night marked probably the hundredth time he'd come dangerously close to kissing her since. It was getting increasingly difficult not to. No doubt, last night's near-kiss was what prompted the unpleasant memories to resurface and haunt him. It'd been the closest he'd come to giving in to his ever-growing attraction to her.

He didn't need to be kissing her. What he needed to do was keep his hands to himself from now on. Stop touching her. Stop letting her touch him. It would be more difficult than he was willing to admit. He wanted her, more than any woman before or after Sarah. Hell, probably more intensely than he'd ever wanted Sarah if he was being completely truthful with himself.

Guilt ran rough-shod over him as that realization settled in his mind. Wanting someone else more fiercely than he'd wanted his late wife seemed wrong as hell. Sarah had been his world, his everything. He owed her his loyalty, even with her irrevocably gone. His attraction to Grace left him feeling like he was betraying Sarah all on its own. He couldn't let this happen. This infatuation with Grace had to stop.

It wasn't like he did serious relationships anymore anyway. He had nothing to offer a woman like her. She needed more than a warm body in her bed every night and protecting her each day. She deserved a man who could give her his heart. His love. That man wasn't him. His heart lay in far too many pieces to give it to her. He needed to back off and regain some distance.

Colt broke from his morose thoughts when a knock sounded on the door, followed closely by Grace's soft voice drifting through the thin wood. She hadn't been happy that they'd had to get separate rooms again last night, but there hadn't been a choice. The only rooms that'd been left were two singles. The fact the motel manager had given him both rooms for the price of one had smoothed her ruffled feathers some, however.

Frankly, he'd found it a bit of a relief, needing the time apart from her to get his head back on straight. Unfortunately, he doubted it had worked.

"Just a second," he called to her as he shoved himself to his feet. He hoped he didn't look as haggard as he felt.

Colt crossed to the door and pulled it open. Despite his dreary mood, his spirits brightened at the sight of her. She was wearing a sundress today that matched her eyes and flowed over her curves attractively. The hem kissed her ankles. Her lips curled into a soft smile that reached her eyes, making them sparkle.

God, she was beautiful.

Her gaze swept over him, and her brows snapped together. "Are you okay?"

He scrubbed a hand over his face before answering, "Yeah, I'm good. I didn't sleep well." He threw her a tired smile. "Nothing a whole pot of coffee can't cure."

"Well, let's get going, then."

Colt made no move to join her outside. "Before we do, I have something I need to say." He stepped back and waved her into the room.

She sat her suitcase and stuffed horse down by the table, then turned to look expectantly up at him as he shut the door behind her. "Okay. What's up?"

He gestured for her to sit. She gave him a wary look but did. He paced the room with quick strides, chewing on his words in hopes of finding the right way to say what he felt he needed to.

After a couple of minutes, he finally turned to face her. "I owe you an apology for last night."

Grace blinked up at him, her brows pulling together. "An apology?" She rubbed at her forehead, frowning. "An apology for what exactly?"

He resumed pacing. "For nearly kissing you, for one." He shook his head. "I can't. That can't happen. You're fresh out of a bad relationship. I shouldn't even be thinking about kissing you." He felt like such a jerk springing this on her first thing in the morning. Shit, maybe he should have waited until later to talk to her about this.

She hopped to her feet and grabbed his hand, forcing him to stop.

Colt pulled his hand from her grasp but remained still. Hurt flashed in her eyes as she studied his face. That wounded look made him hate himself all the more. His gaze dropped to the worn carpeting beneath his feet.

"Yes," she began slowly. "I technically *am* just out of a relationship. But, emotionally, Flint and I were done ages ago. Well before I met you." She sighed heavily. "I'd have broken up with him a long time ago, but I was too afraid to. And then he threatened to kill me if I ever left. After that, I really couldn't do it. Honestly,

I'm still afraid he's going to come after me and make good on his threat. There's no way he'll let me go this easy."

He met her eyes. "As long as you're with me, I will do everything in my power to keep him from getting near you again."

"I know. I trust you." She tentatively touched his cheek.

Despite trying to persuade himself to, he couldn't move away again.

"I like you, Eight. Really like you. I have for a while now. I *want* you to kiss me."

Colt stifled a groan. "Don't tell me that." She was not making this easy in the slightest. "I like you too, but I'm not right for you. You deserve better than a two-bit rodeo cowboy and life on the road. I don't even own a ranch anymore to give you a home." He turned away from her. "I can't give you what you deserve."

"What can't you give me? What do I deserve?" She rubbed her temples. "Where is this even coming from?"

He reluctantly glanced at her again. "I'm sorry. I don't really know how to explain." Why couldn't he be better with words? With expressing his feelings? "I'm screwing this up. We can be friends. I want that. But it's all we can be." He picked up his duffle bag and shouldered the thick carry strap. "Come on, let's get going. I really need that coffee, and I can hear your stomach growling from here."

Before he could take even one step toward the door, she moved in front of him and placed both hands on his chest. "No, hold on. I want to know what you think I deserve that you can't give me."

He tensed beneath her touch. Her small hands scorched him through the thin flannel of his western shirt. He should have known she wouldn't let the subject drop so easily. She'd been a journalist. Back when she'd been interviewing him, if there'd been a question he'd been hesitant to answer, she'd kept asking it until he finally satisfied her with an answer. Her tenacity exasperated him at times.

Sighing deeply, he rubbed at the back of his neck with one hand. "Grace..." He mumbled a curse under his breath. "You deserve a relationship. You deserve love. A home with roots. Marriage. I can't give you any of it." He paused and looked at her. "I lost my wife, and I don't know how to move on from her. Shit, I don't know if I even want to attempt it. I'll never get married again. The only thing I could offer you is a fling, and you deserve more than that. It's better if we stay just friends."

Grace blinked, and her mouth fell open, then closed again. Her brows snapped together, and her gaze dropped to his shirt. She tapped a finger against his chest as though she was thinking.

When she finally looked back up at him, she swallowed hard and produced a nervous smile. "What if I'd be okay with what you could offer?" Her voice was quiet, tentative.

Colt's lips pressed into a flat line and he shook his head hard. "No. Not happening."

Grace stared at him for a long moment, then heaved out a deep sigh as she stepped out of his way. Her hands fell limply back to her sides, and she dropped her gaze to the floor.

"He was right," she whispered so quietly he had to strain to make out the words.

It was obvious she wasn't talking to him, but he couldn't let that statement go. He assumed she was referring to Flint, but Colt doubted that asshole had ever been right about anything in his life.

"Right about what?" he asked softly.

Her face flushed, and she shuffled on her feet. "You weren't supposed to hear that." Her eyes fluttered closed, shoulders hunching forward as though she was trying to shrink into herself.

For a long moment, she said nothing more.

"Right about me being too ugly to have sex with. He told me that so many times I lost count. He said he almost needed to put a bag over my head to be able to finish. That I was that disgusting to look at," she finally whispered, her voice just barely audible.

Her words floored him. Did she really believe Flint? Was that how she saw herself in the mirror? Disgusting? Ugly? It was the complete opposite of how Colt saw her. She was beautiful, and not just on the outside. Shit, it took Colt every scrap of self-control to turn her down at all.

Fuck, he'd hated Flint before, but this really put the nail into the figurative coffin. Screw that guy for putting such nonsense into her head. Flint was a goddamn psychopath. He'd better hope Colt never crossed paths with him.

"You're far from ugly, Princess. Don't believe anything that bastard said."

She didn't look up. Her chin wobbled, but her voice was steady when she said, "It's fine, Colt. I understand." Her eyes opened, and she picked up her suitcase and plush horse from where she'd dropped them. She straightened her posture, pulling her shoulders back and lifting her chin as she gathered herself. "Let's get going."

Nope. He wasn't willing to let the conversation end here. Not with her believing that bastard was right.

He took the suitcase from her hands and sat it back down before approaching her. Colt gently gripped her chin and tilted her face up, then met her eyes. "He's not right, Grace," he said softly. "Not even a little bit." He sighed and shifted restlessly on his feet. "I want you. I do. More than any woman I've ever met. If you only knew how many times I've almost kissed you..."

She searched his eyes then quietly asked, "Why haven't you?"

Colt rubbed the pad of his thumb over her bottom lip. Her lips parted, and his head dipped toward hers a fraction. "Because I can't," he whispered achingly. "Because I know already that one taste of your lips won't be enough. That if I kiss you, I won't want to stop there. I'll want more, Grace. More kisses. More of you."

He shook his head slightly and straightened. His hand fell to his side as he backed up a step. "A fling with you ... it'd be fun, sure, but it's not what I want. I want to keep you in my life."

Forever, if he was lucky enough for that. He wanted to keep hearing her laughter, seeing her smile. Giving in wasn't an option. He couldn't risk losing her too.

He wasn't about to say that to her, though, aware of how it'd sound. Giving in to this need for her would likely ruin all of that.

"It's better if we don't go there. If we just stay friends. I don't want to ruin what we have." He picked up her suitcase and opened the door. "Let's go get breakfast. I don't know about you, but I'm starving."

She sent him an unfathomable look that gave no hint of her thoughts, then nodded and silently preceded him through the door.

—◆—

Colt glanced sideways at Grace. They'd been on the road for an hour, and not one word had passed between them. Breakfast had been a tense and quiet affair. It had gotten no better since then.

Maybe he should have kept his mouth shut this morning, but he thought he needed to tell her. Showed what he knew. He always had sucked at talking to the women in his life who actually mattered.

She looked deep in thought now. He wished she would talk to him. Fuck, even yell at him. Anything to break this silence.

Taking a chance, he broke it himself. "What's on your mind, Princess?"

She swung her pale blue gaze over to him. "Us. You. Your wife. Will you tell me about her?"

He inhaled sharply. He wasn't sure what he'd expected her to say, but that definitely hadn't been it. "What?" he managed to get out.

"Your wife. I want to know more about her."

He still hated talking about Sarah. It always brought back the pain. The memories. The regrets. He avoided it at all costs, especially when reporters tried to pry. He didn't even talk about her with his own mother. Of course, his mom had a habit of prying as much as the reporters did.

He hesitated, then finally asked, "What do you want to know?" He hoped like hell he wasn't going to regret allowing this conversation. But at least Grace was talking to him. That was something.

She shrugged. "Whatever you're comfortable telling me. I want to know more about you, and since she was important to you, I want to know about her too. How did you meet?"

Colt's fingers flexed around the steering wheel. "She and two of her friends came to a rodeo I was competing at. One of her friends dared her to talk to me at the afterparty that night. I bought her a drink, and we spent the rest of the night talking. She started following me around the circuit after that. Before I knew it, she had me down on one knee, begging her to marry me."

He smiled at the memory and looked over at Grace. "Before meeting her, I was wild. Very wild. I was happy enough to chase the ladies around, but I had no desire to get serious with any of them. Ask anyone about my reputation, and they'll tell you some real horror stories about me."

He shrugged. "I know what's said about me even now. When I was younger, I broke a lot of hearts, drank too much too often, and got in a ton of fights. I was pretty crazy and just out for a good time. Settling down was not for me. No way, no how. Not until I met her. I've never pretended to be a good guy, but she made me want to be one."

He threw Grace a crooked grin. "I'm still pretty crazy. I mean, I ride bulls for a living. That's not for the sane, right?" His grin faded.

"Definitely not." She gave him a small, encouraging smile. "How long were you married?"

"We were together for four years and married for two. We were nearly to three when she di—" He swallowed hard. "We had a ranch together in Oklahoma. I sold it after."

Why was this conversation easier to handle than any other time he'd had to talk about Sarah? Where was the usual pain? All he felt was a dull ache. He eyed Grace, wondering if she might be the reason it was easier.

Colt took a deep breath. "Anything else you want to know?"

She nodded. "What was she like?"

"Um, well... she was a lot like you, actually. Beautiful and smart." He glanced over at her with a small smile. "Brave. Had an enormous heart. She was a bit shy but could talk your ear off once she warmed up to you. Sarah would do about anything to make the people she cared about happy." He tossed her a razz grin. "She used to fight my attempts to take care of her too." He thought for a moment before continuing. "Sarah had long brown hair that nearly reached her hips. I used to braid it for her before she rode her horse, Cupid."

He caught her look of surprise. "Yes, I can braid hair. I'm no hairdresser, but I can do a passable job. She never complained anyway. Anything else you want to know?"

Grace shook her head and lightly touched his knee. "No. Thank you for talking to me about her."

"Yeah." He flicked on the blinker, changing lanes to prepare for the upcoming exit. "Why'd you want to know about her?"

She turned her gaze out the window as she answered, "She had your heart. *Has* your heart. I wondered what sort of woman managed to rope you."

He glanced sideways at her. What did she mean by that?

When she said nothing more to expand on her statement, he let it go. He didn't have a clue how to even begin responding.

Silence fell between them yet again. Though it still wasn't comfortable, it didn't feel as oppressive as it had before. He'd take that as a win.

⚬

After the third lap around the parking lot of the rodeo grounds, Colt pulled up to the curb next to the entrance gate to let Grace out. He was going to have to figure out somewhere else to park. Maybe there would be a spot in the secondary competitor's parking lot. With as heavy and gray as the sky was—as though it may open up and pour any second—he really didn't want her having to hike who knew how far in the rain.

"I'm going to let you out here in case it starts raining. I'm not sure how far away I'll have to park. There's an umbrella in the glove box if you want to take it with you."

He unbuckled his seatbelt and reached across to open the door for her, but she covered his hand with her own before he could pull the door handle. Startled by the unexpected touch, he turned to look at her and lost the ability to breathe momentarily.

Hyperawareness of her flooded his senses and kicked his heart rate into high gear. With as hard as his heart was pounding, it wouldn't surprise him any if she heard it. He clearly hadn't thought this gesture out well enough. Her face was right there. Too close. He could smell her strawberry shampoo, feel the heat coming off her body.

"Thank you, Eight. For everything you've been doing for me. It really does mean a lot." Grace shifted to unbuckle her seatbelt, and her arm brushed against him.

He very nearly groaned.

She met his eyes and smiled softly, seeming unaware of how affected he was by their proximity.

"Uh, you're welcome," he choked out. His gaze dropped to her lips.

They parted, and the tip of her pink tongue darted out to moisten them. His breath caught yet again as temptation slugged him in the gut. He lifted his gaze to hers while he battled the impulse to give in. To kiss her.

She was right there. One little move, and he could finally find out what those lips tasted like. Turn that fantasy into a reality. Shit, he knew she'd welcome it; she'd told him so this morning. It'd be so easy.

Instead, he yanked the handle, shoved her door open, and quickly sat up. He sucked in air like a drowning man as she stepped out of the truck.

"Meet you by the arena?"

Colt gave her a sharp nod and she closed the door. He sat there, watching her retreating back until she disappeared from view.

It would be a better idea to keep away from her until after his ride. He was definitely in danger when it came to her. She made him feel too flustered to think straight. It was dangerous to ride that way. No, he would have to stay away from the bleachers until after his ride. She'd text if she needed him.

Decision made, he tossed his truck into drive and pulled away from the curb.

Chapter 15

GRACE'S GAZE DRIFTED OVER Colt as he knelt in front of his chute to talk to his bull, like he did before every ride. She hadn't seen him since this afternoon when he'd let her out of his truck. Honestly, she hadn't expected to.

He'd nearly kissed her again. She'd seen the hunger burning in his eyes. He'd been telling the truth about wanting her. That heat proved it. She knew him well enough now to know he wouldn't have said it if he hadn't meant it. That wasn't how he was built.

Oh, how she wished he had given in.

If she'd had more nerve, she'd have kissed him instead. There were times she caught Colt watching her with the most peculiar look in his eyes when he thought she wasn't paying attention. A soft expression she couldn't define. After everything he'd said this morning, it made her more than a little curious, but she was afraid to hope.

She did know she was falling for him. It was as frightening as much as it was exhilarating. There was a good chance he'd never feel the same. That wouldn't be an unfamiliar situation; it'd been that way most of her youth too. She'd fall fast and hard while they'd claim they thought of her like a sister. A sister! At least there was no chance that Colt thought of her like that.

Grace yawned and leaned back to stretch. When was the last time she'd felt so relaxed? So safe? She couldn't remember, but it had to have been a while.

It'd been days since the last text from Flint. Maybe he'd finally given up. No matter how many times she blocked his number, he kept coming back.

She hummed her favorite song while her eyes followed Colt as he stood and climbed the rail to get on his bull. His draw tonight was a tiny white beast with crooked horns named Popcorn, much to her amusement. What a name for a bull. Sometimes, she wondered how in the world they came up with the names for these animals.

A flicker of movement off to her left pulled her attention. She turned to look that way, and the air seized in her lungs as her blood ran cold.

How had he found her?

"Hey, babe. Miss me?" Flint smiled. To her, he resembled a feral dog snarling. He looked around the arena with an air of boredom. "I told you I'd find you. It took me forever to figure out where you might have gone. Should have known you'd run to the cowboy."

She straightened in her seat as she gaped at him, unable to believe he was really here. She tried to jump up, to run, but her muscles refused to respond to her demand. The sharp stab of fear paralyzed her.

Flint licked his lips and leaned toward her. "I've let you have your fun. It's time to come home now." He studied her face intently, making her want to squirm. "You still mad at me? You haven't answered my messages, so you must be."

Grace said nothing. Mad didn't really describe her feelings, but telling him that would only give him an excuse to hurt her some more. She was done being hurt by him. Her heart raced, thumping painfully against her breastbone. She needed to get away.

Flint's face fell as the silence stretched. If she didn't know better, she'd think she'd actually hurt him by leaving. "Aww, come on, babe. Don't be pissed at me. You know I didn't mean any of it; you just make me so mad sometimes. I promise it won't happen again. I love you so much; you know that. That cowboy you've been fuckin' around on me with will never love you like I can. You're nothin' to him. Come home, and I'll forgive you. We can move on like none of this happened."

She shook her head repeatedly, and Flint grasped her arm in a vice-like grip. She recognized it as a warning. If she survived long enough, she'd probably have a bruise there later. Based on what happened before she left him, she wasn't so sure she would.

A chill skidded down her spine. Why hadn't she sat closer to others? Only two people were in this section of the bleachers, both too far away from her seat to hear what was going on unless Flint began yelling. That wasn't likely. He never had been the sort to cause a public scene. Almost all of the abuse she'd endured at his hands occurred behind closed doors, and the rest had been veiled well enough to not be recognizable to strangers.

Shoot, the rodeo grounds were so loud right now between the cheers of the crowd, the announcer, and the lowing of cattle that she wasn't sure anyone would hear him even if he did start screaming at her right here in the bleachers.

She opened her mouth to yell for help regardless of how futile it seemed, but all that came out was a pathetic squawk. Grace licked her lips and inhaled in preparation of trying again, but Flint leaned closer.

"I wouldn't do that if I were you," Flint growled into her ear. "You wouldn't want me to have to hurt anybody, would you?"

Her eyes widened. Would he really do that? Hurt someone else because of her? Her throat locked up around the scream that'd been building in it. She swallowed hard.

He shook her slightly. "Last chance, Grace. Don't make this messy. You're coming home with me one way or another. I'll knock your ass out and carry you out of here if I have to."

Her entire body trembled as adrenaline surged. She needed to get away from him. Somehow.

Grace locked her eyes on the arena as Popcorn sprang free of the chute with Colt on his back. She was afraid to even look at Flint. Though her gaze tracked both bull and rider, she didn't really see either of them. She could feel the amusement radiating from Flint, along with his rage.

She fought to untangle her tongue. "How did you find me?" Her voice was barely above a whisper, to her dismay.

Colt thought her brave, yet here she sat quaking like a damn leaf in a windstorm and near paralyzed by fear. How was that for being brave?

She should have known Flint would find her. Should have kept her guard up. Her chin quivered as moisture sprang to her eyes, making them burn.

Flint's hand tightened even further around her arm and she fought to keep from crying out, determined to not give him the satisfaction of the reaction.

He rolled his eyes. "It wasn't really that difficult. Just a process of elimination." He cocked his head and sneered. "You really are a predictable little tramp."

The buzzer sounded, signaling the end of Colt's eight-second ride, and his gaze traveled to the arena as Colt dismounted and sprinted for the railing. "Looks like your new boyfriend made his ride. I'd let you go congratulate him and say goodbye, but it's a long drive back to Kansas."

"He's not my boyfriend," she said flatly, proud of herself when her voice only held a faint tremor.

"Good. He won't miss you, then. Come on; time to go." Flint stood, pulling her along with him. He started for the exit ramp.

She tried to pull her arm from Flint's grip, but he held on tight. She stumbled and nearly fell as he wrenched her arm, forcing her to follow.

Grace wrapped her free arm tightly around her middle. She dragged her feet to buy time, in hopes that Colt would come looking for her now that his ride was over. She might not have much of a choice about going with Flint, but she didn't have to make it easy on him. This might be her last chance to fight back, to resist the horrific fate he had no doubt already planned out for her.

"I'm not going back with you. That's not my home anymore."

"I'm pretty sure you are," Flint snarled as he yanked her down the ramp with him. Not one person glanced in their direction. "You're mine. You'll always be mine. I own you."

She bit down hard on her lip to keep the retort perched on the tip of her tongue from flying out of her mouth. Anything more she said would only anger him further. If she wanted to live, she needed to placate him somehow, at least long enough to figure out a way to escape again.

Her stomach roiled as she scanned the crowd while they walked, desperately wanting to call out for help but too terrified of what would happen if she did. What if he wasn't lying and actually did hurt someone else because of her? She would never be able to live with herself if that happened. Her blood froze. What if he had a knife or something on him right now? The rodeo grounds were supposedly weapon-free, but when had Flint ever followed the law? He thought he was above them. He'd often told her how stupid he thought most laws were.

She couldn't risk it.

Her wide eyes darted from side to side, looking for some other way to get away from Flint.

They were nearly to the gate that opened to the parking lot when an opportunity to get away presented itself. The crowd was thicker here, slowing them down considerably. A large man pushing a wheelchair stepped in front of Flint, causing him to mutter a curse and abruptly stop.

While Flint was distracted, Grace grabbed his pinky finger and twisted it violently. She both felt and heard it snap. The sound of it was absurdly loud despite the dull roar of the people surrounding them. Her stomach lurched, bile rising to singe the back of her throat.

Flint swore a blue streak and released her arm to cradle his injured hand.

She didn't hesitate. This was her one shot at freedom; she knew she'd never get another one. If she failed, she was dead for sure. Grace whirled around and ran, shoving her way past masses of people who shouted angrily after her.

It wasn't like she could stop to apologize. She couldn't stop at all. Her life was on the line. She didn't know these people. Would any of them get involved and help her? Nobody had so far, not even the two older women who'd given her concerned looks as Flint marched her past them. It seemed unwise to risk her life on a maybe. They couldn't be trusted to rescue her.

She could hear Flint following but didn't tempt fate by looking back to see how close he was to catching her. It was all over if he did. He'd kill her as soon as they left the rodeo grounds, or soon after. There was no doubt in her mind of that now. She'd broken his finger. He would be beyond furious.

She put on a burst of speed as the crowd thinned out, for once glad that her foster parents had forced her to try out for track. There was no way she could keep up this pace, however; her lungs were beginning to ache already. She always had been more of a sprinter.

Up ahead, the cowboy's locker room loomed. Had Colt already left it? Was she too late? Would one of the other cowboys save her if she dashed into the building and yelled for help?

As if to answer her first question, Colt stepped outside a second later. Relief exploded through her. She ran headlong toward him, colliding hard with his well-muscled frame. Grace clutched his shirt in a white-knuckled grip as she stared up at him, too out of breath to speak.

Colt stumbled back a step and blinked rapidly down at her as his eyebrows shot nearly to his hat. "Grace? What's wrong?"

She pointed to Flint, who had stopped a short distance away and now stood watching them with a scheming gleam in his eyes. She could only imagine the horrible things he was thinking right now. Her breaths still came in heavy pants, her lungs seriously burning.

Understanding dawned over Colt's face as he glanced in the direction she pointed. He slipped his arm around her waist and pulled her tight against his side.

His fingers were digging into her hip almost to the point of causing pain, but he didn't seem to notice. His eyes were locked on Flint, his jaw clenched so tightly it was a wonder she didn't hear his molars cracking. If she didn't know the fury swirling in his eyes wasn't directed at her, she might be terrified of him too. He looked near murderous.

She leaned into him, drawing comfort and strength from his closeness. He wouldn't let anything happen to her. She was safe now. Slowly, her breathing normalized and her heart rate slowed.

"Can we please go?" she asked. "He tried to kidnap me. I don't want to be anywhere near him."

"We should call the cops and let them deal with him," Colt growled without taking his eyes off Flint.

Grace shook her head, her eyes widening. "No! Please, no cops." They made everything worse, not better. She shook her head harder. "I just want to go. Please!" The need to run, to flee, was nearly overwhelming.

Flint took a step forward, tossing his arms out to the sides as he did. She hated the smugness on his face, the hatred glinting in his eyes.

"Hey, go ahead. Do it! Call the cops. They won't do shit! I got friends in high places." He laughed, the sound sending a shiver down her spine.

Colt looked down at her, his expression softening in an instant as he gentled his touch. "Okay. Let's get out of here. He's not worth the effort."

He kept her pressed against his side as he steered her toward the exit gate that opened to the competitor's parking lot.

They were halfway across the lot, nearly to the truck—according to Colt—when Flint stepped out from between two parked cars right beside them.

"Even if you get away now, Grace, I'll hunt you down again. That's a promise. I won't stop coming for you. Stupid bitch, you'll pay for breaking my finger! I'll fucking kill you! Just you wait."

Colt froze mid-step and turned to give Flint a hard stare. His body went rigid, as though preparing for a fight. "No," he growled menacingly. "You won't. If you want to get to her, you'll have to go through me first." He released his grip on her waist and pushed her behind him as he turned to face her ex-boyfriend more fully.

She began trembling all over again. This wasn't what she wanted, them fighting over her. All she really wanted right now was to get as far away from Flint as she could. Maybe into another universe, if possible.

She tugged on Colt's arm, trying to pull him further away from Flint, but he didn't budge. "Don't. Let's just go. Please!" To her dismay, he showed no signs of hearing her. He was too focused on Flint.

"Shit, I'm not scared of you, cowboy." Flint straightened to full height as he squared his shoulders. Even standing as tall as he could, Colt still towered over him. Flint's hands curled into fists at his sides. Despite his words, something vulnerable flashed in his eyes. Something she'd never seen before. It almost looked like fear.

"You don't seem too sure of that," Colt commented dryly.

He must have seen Flint's vulnerability too. It'd been a brief flicker, but it'd been there. Flint was afraid of Colt; she'd put money on it.

"What'd you come here for, Flint?" Colt asked. "She told me you were trying to force her to leave with you, but to what end? She broke up with you. You don't have any further business with her. It's pretty obvious to me she wants nothing to do with you."

"The shrew lied. She's mine, and I'm not letting her go."

Colt took a threatening step toward Flint. "You might want to stop calling her names." His lips curled into a sneer. "And she's not yours anymore."

"She yours, then? You two looked pretty cozy a moment ago. What are you, her guard dog?" Flint spat at him, but it failed to reach its mark and splatted harmlessly on the pavement.

"It's none of your business what we are. I'm someone who cares about her, and I won't let you hurt her any more than you already have. If that makes me her guard dog, then so be it." Colt imitated the sound of a large dog barking as he took another step forward.

Flint flinched but didn't back down. He gave a derisive laugh and took a step forward of his own. "Seems to me she got her hooks in you. What lies has she told you? Crazy whore lies all the time."

"Grace, come here for a second please." Colt dug into his pocket and withdrew his truck keys.

With reluctance, she stepped up next to him while keeping a wary eye on Flint. Her stomach twisted into knots. She had a feeling she knew what Colt wanted. "Yes?"

He held the keys out to her. "Go to the truck. I'll be there in a minute." When she hesitated, his gaze softened. He grabbed her hand and placed the keys in her palm, then curled her fingers around them. "Go on, Princess. I'll be there in a couple of minutes. You don't need to deal with this. I'll be okay. I promise. The truck is in aisle B, halfway down the row."

Her breath caught when he bent to press a brief kiss to her forehead before straightening to face Flint once more. Grace bit her lip but did as he'd asked. She'd only taken a couple of steps away when she heard Flint call her a whore again, followed by the solid sound of a fist colliding with flesh.

Who hit whom, she didn't want to know. She resisted the urge to glance back and hurried the rest of the way to the truck.

⊰•◦○◦•⊱

"You could have gotten in."

Grace jumped at the sound of Colt's voice and whirled around to face him. Her brows drew together as her gaze swept over him. He had a cut on his forehead and another on his cheek. A trickle of blood oozed from his nose, and his lip was split. It looked as though there was a bruise forming on his jaw too. He was a mess.

"Are you okay?" She asked as she rushed toward him.

"I'm fine." He dodged her hands when she tried to fuss over him. "Let's head back to the motel. I could use a shower before the afterparty."

"Let's go, then."

She handed him back his keys, then hopped up onto the passenger seat when he opened the door for her. He definitely needed a shower, though she wasn't sure that she wanted to go to the afterparty herself. What if Flint showed up there too? The sense of safety she'd gotten used to having at the rodeo had been shattered. After tonight, she doubted she'd be able to relax anywhere ever again. Damn Flint to hell.

Grace looked over at Colt as he slid behind the wheel. "What if he follows us?"

"He won't."

Her eyes widened. "How can you be so sure? He won't give up." Her chest felt tight, making it difficult to breathe easily.

Colt's lips pressed into a grim line and he looked away from her. "If you think I look rough, you should see him." He sighed. "He's not going to feel up to trying again any time soon. I couldn't let what he tried to do to you go. I'm not sorry, Princess. Someone should have done it sooner." He glanced sideways at her. "We'll call the police if he comes back, or I'll get rid of him myself. I've tangled with way tougher than him before. He's a coward."

Colt's gaze met with hers, his expression somber. "I won't allow him to hurt you again. While you're with me, you're as safe as I can keep you." He grimaced. "I'm sorry I wasn't there to keep him away from you today. Are you okay? Did he hurt you?"

She rubbed at her arm idly. It ached, but not as badly as she'd expected. "I'm scared, but I'm otherwise okay. I guess. I'll be alright."

He nodded and pulled out of the parking spot. "We should probably report this to the police anyway. Make a paper trail."

Grace stiffened and shook her head hard. "No. No cops. Every time I've talked to them, it's gotten worse for me. Why would this time be any different? Besides, what if he reports you for assault in retaliation? You can't protect me if you're in jail." She turned to him. "You shouldn't have hit him."

Colt made a face. "He hit me first, and there was a witness to it. He could file a report, but it wouldn't go anywhere. I just defended myself. Enthusiastically."

She cringed.

"Sorry, sweetheart, but he deserved it for what he did to you. Shit, he deserves worse. I'd do it again in a heartbeat. Are you sure you don't want to file a report? It might help if you get a restraining order against him."

She shook her head again. "There's no point. They won't help me. They've never helped me. He has friends on the force, Eight. Back in Kansas. They've always believed whatever he tells them, then he'd make me pay for calling them later." The beatings she'd get for daring to call for help had always been amongst the worst.

"This isn't Kansas. He doesn't have friends here."

"You don't know that." She sighed and looked down at her hands. "Flint knows just the right things to say and do to make me seem crazy, to discredit what I'm trying to tell them. He makes friends everywhere he goes. People think he's some wonderful person—and he can be, to them. It's all a trick. A ruse."

Colt frowned but said nothing more about it.

As they drove down the row toward the exit, she spotted Flint limping slowly toward an unfamiliar, beat-up pickup truck. It looked like he was leaving too. She would think he was intending to follow them, despite Colt's belief that he wouldn't, but he didn't even glance in their direction once. Maybe he was going home to lick his wounds and plan his next move. This wouldn't be the last she saw of him—that much she knew for certain. She shuddered and, from the corner of her eye, saw Colt shoot her a concerned look.

Once Flint disappeared from view, she studied Colt's handsome profile. He'd kissed her forehead earlier. Even as ticked off as he'd been, Flint had noticed. It had enraged him further. Maybe that was why Colt had done it, to goad Flint. With Colt's insistence that they couldn't be anything more than friends, she refused to read into it too far.

Colt had saved her, protected her. He'd done so much for her, and she didn't just mean in the obvious ways of ensuring she was fed and slept under a roof at night. He was her best friend and the one person she'd come to trust implicitly. It hadn't been an easy journey to get to that point, but he was patient, gentle, and kind. Everything Flint was not. By Colt's side, she'd been healing. She could feel it. Parts of herself she'd thought had been lost forever were returning. Confidence. Courage. Her sense of adventure. The ability to speak her mind without fear. She refused to allow Flint to ruin that.

Where would she be right now if she hadn't gotten away from Flint? If Colt hadn't been there to shield her from him? It was frightening to think about, but she couldn't help but wonder. Would she still be alive, or would he have snuffed out her life the moment they got away from the rodeo grounds? Before she'd broken his finger, he might have kept her alive for a time just to toy with her some more before killing her. That was a so much more horrifying possibility. She'd rather die straight away than be tortured first. Not that she wanted to die at all.

It had crossed her mind, when it seemed like Flint was going to drag her back to hell, that the last interaction she would have had with Colt was that almost-kiss in the truck this afternoon. Her time could have run out today, and that would have been it? What a shame.

She swore that if the opportunity ever arose again, she wouldn't squander it. She'd muster up every scrap of courage she could, and she'd kiss him. There was no way she was going to her grave without knowing what it felt like to be consumed by the passion she sensed lurked in him.

Chapter 16

COLT FELT CONSIDERABLY BETTER when he emerged from the bathroom fully dressed, save for his hat and boots. His jaw had bruised, but he couldn't say he cared. He'd had worse. Way worse.

His gaze immediately landed on Grace. She sat at the end of one bed with her face buried in her hands. Had she been like that the entire time he'd been showering? Fuck, he hoped not. His heart clenched at the thought of it and he felt a wave of now-familiar protectiveness crash over him.

He crossed the small room and sat down beside her.

Rather than speaking, he drew her into his arms, gratified when she came willingly. She curled herself against his chest with a soft sigh. He rested his cheek against the top of her head and pulled her scent deep into his lungs. There was no way he'd ever be able to smell strawberries again without thinking of her.

When the hell had he become so sentimental? Cash would probably tease him without mercy if he ever found out. Not that Colt truly cared.

All that mattered to him right now was the woman cuddled against his chest. The woman Flint could have taken away, without Colt even knowing until it was too late because he'd been being stupid and avoiding her. He never would have forgiven himself if something happened to her. As much as he would have loved to have really unleashed his temper on Flint, he'd been afraid Grace hadn't gone to the truck. He didn't want her to see his rage and end up fearing *him*.

Colt smoothed a hand over her hair, content to hold her for as long as she was willing to let him. He shouldn't have her in his arms right now—considering just this morning he'd decided he needed to back off—but she needed it. So did he.

When Grace pulled away, he immediately missed the contact with her. She began pacing the room.

"Are you okay, Princess?"

She turned her enchanting eyes in his direction, and his heart clenched all over again. Grace looked as though she was barely holding it together.

He shoved to his feet and offered her his hand. "Come on. Let's take a walk. You look like you could use it."

She placed her hand in his waiting palm, and he led her out the door and along the roadside. There was a park next to the motel. With any luck, there would be some hiking trails that they could explore there. All he knew was she looked like she needed to move. That was something he was familiar with. Often, when he got upset, taking a walk or a run helped him sort out his thoughts and pull himself back together.

His fingers flexed around hers as they walked. Her hand in his felt way too right. Too comfortable. He liked it. He liked *her*. Way more than he should. Definitely more than he wanted to. He had a feeling this thing developing between them was inevitable. Trying to prevent himself from getting attached to her, from being attracted to her, was like fighting to keep the tide from rolling onto the shore—an impossible task. That battle was already lost.

Today had spooked him probably about as much as it had her. It'd opened his eyes too. Why did this have to be temporary? If he asked her to, he knew she'd stay. He was tiring of battling back his need for her. The more he thought about it, the more he wondered if it was really worth the effort. After all, things with her might be different. It might not end in heartbreak.

Shit, if he let himself, he could fall for her so easily. Part of him wondered if he wasn't already in a free-fall; the rest of him refused to think about it. He was afraid to know.

If Sarah were able to put in her opinion, she'd encourage him to move on and start something with Grace. To be happy. He knew it, but also knew he couldn't—wouldn't—do it. He wasn't that selfish. No matter how much he wanted to give in and be what Grace needed, the guilt and fear that dogged him would never let up long enough to give her the relationship she deserved. He was too fucked up. He'd only hurt her. She had no reason to stay.

Eventually, this mess with Flint would end and she'd leave. That was inevitable too. This arrangement had always been meant to be temporary. She wouldn't be with him forever, no matter how much he might want her to be. Sure, they were friends and there was a good chance they'd remain in touch—if he didn't fuck things up between them—but it wouldn't be the same. He wouldn't see her every day, like he did now. Wouldn't be able to talk to her whenever he wanted.

Damn, he didn't want to think about her leaving right now. Not when she was still here, walking at his side with her hand in his.

Colt cleared his throat and shoved his thoughts away. "Feeling better?"

Grace glanced in his direction, her face far more relaxed than it had been. "Yeah, somewhat." She sighed. "He said he owns me. I'm not sure how he figures that. I'm not a piece of property, and it's not even like I owe him anything. The ranch is in his name, but every one of our other bills were in mine, including my cell phone. I'm in debt up past my eyeballs because of him."

Colt struggled to come up with something to say but came up dry. He settled for giving her hand a gentle squeeze. For a few minutes, silence stretched.

"He wasn't always like he is now," Grace finally said, her gaze locked on something far in the distance. "Things were great between us for the first year or so. It was perfect, a dream. But all that ended when we bought the ranch and I moved in with him to fix it up. That was when his mask began cracking, showing all the ugly beneath it. It was about the same time I started working for the paper." Her brow furrowed. "He told me he wanted to marry me one day. He said sharing a bank account would make budgeting our bills and such easier once we were." She shook her head. "I've never been so glad to not be proposed to."

She took a deep breath as though gathering herself.

"Things didn't get bad all at once," she continued. "At first, it was the occasional snide comment. To an outsider, they probably seemed pretty innocuous. But they hurt me, and he knew it. Then, he began breaking my things and screaming at me when he got angry. It gradually got worse, but it happened so slowly that I didn't really realize how bad it had gotten until the first time he hit me. That was when I truly knew the relationship wasn't able to be saved. Not long after he hit me that first time, during a huge fight, he screamed in my face that he'd kill me if I ever left him. I believed him. His face when he said it…"

A shudder racked her slim body, making Colt ache to hug her. He barely resisted, though he tightened his fingers around hers. Words perched on the tip of his tongue, but he held them back, determined to let her finish her story without interruption.

"It made me afraid to try but also even more determined to escape." Grace rubbed at her forehead with her free hand, then pinched the bridge of her nose before tossing an exasperated look to the heavens. "He's never going to leave me alone. This nightmare is never going to end."

Colt tugged her to a stop and turned her to face him. He couldn't take it anymore. White-hot fury churned in his gut. He wanted to find Flint and make him pay for the harm he'd caused her. Fuck, he'd have hit that bastard harder had he known all this. Even stronger than his wish to really teach Flint a lesson was the urge to pull Grace into his arms, and keep her close and protected.

"Hey, enough of that," he said softly. "It will end. Things will settle down, and you'll be able to go make a new life for yourself wherever you want, doing whatever you want. You were a talented journalist; maybe you can do that again. I loved what you wrote."

"Yeah, maybe. I wrote an article the other night while I was waiting for you to ride, but I don't know the first thing about submitting it anywhere." She tilted her head. "Wait. You read my articles?"

"Of course I did. How else would I know how talented you are?" Before Flint had turned her career topsy-turvy, Colt had bought copies of the paper she worked for to read her article. He knew she had loads of skill.

Grace shrugged, but a small smile crept onto her face.

Colt met her eyes. "I'm sorry you experienced what you did. Nobody deserves what you've gone through." He gently tucked a strand of hair behind her ear, his fingertips grazing her cheek. "Especially not you."

She didn't say anything, but another smile crossed her lips—a stronger one this time—as she grasped his hand and got them walking again.

Neither of them said anything more for a couple of minutes.

Her hand was warm in his. The impulse to kiss her whispered to him, tempting him, and he swallowed hard. "Think you feel up to going to the afterparty with me tonight? I scored 91; people will expect me to show up for at least a few minutes."

"I'm not sure. Let me think about it." She made a wry face. "You really scored a 91 on itty bitty Popcorn? I wouldn't have expected such a small bull to buck well enough to score so high." She laughed. "How do they come up with these names? Popcorn? Really?"

He chuckled. "I don't know how they come up with them, but he's a pretty nice bull. Not rank, like some of them, but he's got a great buck. He may be small, but he's got lots of power. He likes to do a lot of hopping around in between bucks. Between that and the fact he's white, that's probably how he got his name." He smiled. "I've thought about raising bulls myself once I retire from riding them. Bull riding is a young man's sport, and I'm getting old."

She raised her eyebrows at him. "Old? Are you being serious? You're only twenty-seven!"

"Yeah, and some days I wake up feeling ninety. The injuries pile up quick. Don't get me wrong; I still love riding and know that I'll miss it when I quit for good, but it's getting close to time to think beyond rodeo." He quieted for a moment, his mood sobering. "Sarah had been talking about wanting to start a family, but I wanted to try for one more championship first." He rubbed his free hand over his face, remembering things long in the past. "Had I retired when I first thought about it, Sarah would still be alive. She wouldn't have been driving home from the bar that night after watching me on their big screen. It's my fault she's dead."

He blew out a breath. "They might say that the hit-and-run killed her, but really it was me and my need to win another fucking title that did. It's because of me she's dead."

"Colt..." Grace shook her head, then pulled him to a stop and stepped around in front of him.

He jolted when she gently caressed his cheek, not expecting the tender touch. His gaze jumped to hers. Her eyes were soft on him, but he didn't see even an ounce of pity in their depths. He didn't think he could have handled seeing that from her.

"Please, don't blame yourself. It wasn't your fault." She shook her head again. "You don't know; you might have retired that year, and it still could have happened. She could have been on the way home from a friend's house or from getting groceries."

Her fingers smoothed over his skin and skimmed his jaw. He fought to not lean into her touch.

"You didn't kill her."

Colt caught her hand and pulled it away from his face but didn't release it. He unconsciously rubbed circles over her knuckles with his thumb. "I know you're right, but it doesn't stop me from thinking about how things could have been different had I made better decisions back then."

"It's possible things might have been," she allowed quietly. "You can't go back, though. Living in the past, playing what-if. It doesn't do any good. It won't bring her back." Her gaze roamed over his face before their eyes met once more. "I could have avoided the situation I'm in too if I had listened to my gut and said no from the start. If I'd made a different choice." Her voice dropped nearly to a whisper as she added, "But if I had, there is a good chance I might have never met you."

He smiled slightly, trying to ignore the way her words affected him and failing miserably. This was going to end badly for him; he just knew it.

"Look at you being all philosophical." He dropped her hand and took a step away before glancing back toward the motel. "We should probably get back if we're going to the afterparty."

"Colt?"

He turned back to Grace. "Yeah?"

She moved toward him, her hands landing on his chest, where they branded him with their heat. He sucked in a deep breath in surprise. His eyes locked with hers. The tender emotion he saw shining within her alluring gaze made his heart leap in his chest.

He was in trouble. So much trouble. He should put a stop to this. Back up and make her stop touching him. Make her stop looking at him like that.

But he couldn't. Instead, he stood still as a statue while she curled one hand around his nape and pressed up onto her toes. Her breath teased his skin as she leaned in. His body tensed, well aware of what was coming.

His stomach felt like thousands of butterflies were beating their wings within it. God, this woman made him feel like a damn teenage boy on his first date and about to get his very first kiss.

"I'm glad I met you," she whispered. "I wish what happened to us both hadn't happened, but I'm still happy to be here with you now."

He held his breath, waiting. The sweet smell of her shampoo curled around him. The birdsong surrounding them seemed to fade; it was just background noise—unimportant. All that mattered in this moment was this woman and his need for her.

She moved closer. His eyes fluttered shut.

He wanted this. He'd dreamed of this. His heart beat harder, and he fought the urge to lean in, to meet her partway as she moved closer still. So close that their lips nearly brushed.

Before their lips could meet, a yellow dog burst from the nearby trees, barking its head off. Startled, Grace jumped away from him.

A mixture of relief and disappointment raced through his veins as his breath rushed out of him.

"We should go back," he stammered.

Not waiting for a response, he turned and, with big strides, started back to the refuge of the motel.

When he noticed she was having trouble keeping up with him, he forced himself to slow his pace. His heart hammered in his chest like it was trying to escape. He both cursed and thanked that stupid dog for interrupting them.

This thing between him and Grace couldn't happen. It shouldn't. He knew that, but fuck, he wanted it to. He scrubbed his hands over his face and noticed they were shaking. Shit, what the hell was happening to him? He needed to get a grip.

Too bad what he really wanted to get a grip on was her.

He wanted to push her up against one of the trees lining the path and kiss her like it was the end of the world. Maybe lay her down in that patch of wildflowers they just passed and make love to her right there in the open.

Colt cursed under his breath and locked down his thoughts. He couldn't give in. He shouldn't. She deserved a relationship. Love. A man better than him. But his resolve was weakening, and the reasons why he couldn't be what she needed were starting to seem mighty stupid.

Once back in the motel room again, he turned to Grace. "Are you coming with me?"

She hadn't said a word since that moment between them in the park. Right now, it seemed like she was avoiding his eyes. He didn't like it.

"Is something wrong? Are you still worried about Flint? Did I do something?"

"No." She threw him a weak smile that did little to reassure him. "To all of those questions. I'm fine, just tired. It's been a rough day."

He wasn't sure he believed her, but he knew better than to push. "Why don't you get a shower and hit the bed early, then? I'll try my best to be quiet when I come back in."

With Flint's unexpected arrival earlier, he was glad for her insistence about sharing a room. If she'd had her own room tonight, he would only end up worrying about her all the more. He would sleep better knowing she was close and safe.

"Yeah, that sounds like a good plan. I'll do both."

The tone of her voice made him pause. Something was bothering her, and being tired was only part of it.

"Are you really okay, Princess? I can skip and stay here with you if you want. It's no big deal to me if I don't go."

"No, I'm good. I promise." She gave him a gentle shove toward the door. "Go. Have fun, and have a drink for me."

He nodded though he still wasn't sure he should go, then pulled his keys from his pocket. "I'm going to leave the truck here for you in case you need anything. The afterparty is at the bar two blocks away anyhow. I can walk." He handed her the keys and gave her a serious look. "Text or call if you need me, and I'll come straight back. I mean it."

He waited until she nodded, gave her one last lingering look, then walked out the door.

⸺◆⸺

Colt cursed as he staggered into the motel room and made a blind grab for the lamp he bumped into. He missed, and it clattered to the floor. Freezing in place, he squinted at the bed, hoping he hadn't woken Grace up. She seemed to be sleeping soundly still, to his relief.

He'd drank far more tonight than he'd planned to, but the fans had been out in force and who was he to turn down free liquor when they were offering to buy him a drink? Everybody knew that free alcohol tasted better.

After the events of the day, he'd really needed a drink anyhow. That near-kiss in the park was seared into his brain. Even as drunk as he was right now, he could feel her hands on his chest again, her breath fanning over his skin.

He groaned softly and eased deeper into the room.

He plopped onto a chair and yanked off his boots, then placed his hat on the table. From where he sat, he could see that Grace had curled up with the stuffed animal he'd won her—Whinny. She had it pressed tight against her chest.

A crooked grin crept onto Colt's face, warmth radiating through him from the center of his chest. God, she was so fucking endearing.

He couldn't recall a time he'd ever been jealous of a stuffed animal, but fuck, he sure was right now.

He got to his feet, using the table for balance when he wobbled for a moment. Man, he shouldn't have drank so much. He was going to have a hell of a hangover in the morning, but it was too late to worry about that now. Shedding his clothes, he then approached Grace's bed.

She wanted to cuddle the stuffed animal? Well, he wanted to cuddle her, so he was going to, dammit. Vaguely, he remembered he was supposed to be keeping his distance from her, but right now, he was too damn drunk to care. He wanted what he wanted.

Colt crawled into bed beside her and scooted up close. He slipped one arm over her hips and pulled her back flush up against his front. She moaned in her sleep and moved even closer.

A slow smile settled on his face as his eyes drifted shut.

This. This was what he'd been craving—her in his arms, her soft curves pressed against him. She fit against him perfectly, like they were two pieces of the very same puzzle. Her soft scent enveloped him, and he breathed her in deeply.

His whole body relaxed. It felt as though he was finally home.

More contented than he could recall being in a long time—maybe ever—it took next to no time for sleep to sweep in and carry him away.

Chapter 17

Something felt different. Strange. That was the first thing to come to mind as Grace slowly drifted back to wakefulness. There was a solid warmth against her back, and a strange weight draped over her waist.

It took her a moment to realize what she was feeling. When she did, her eyes snapped open. The weight across her hip was an arm. A familiar arm.

Colt was in bed with her.

Awareness of every spot their bodies touched rushed in. This felt far too delicious. What she wouldn't give to wake up this way every morning. But why was he in bed with her? How had she not woken up? She'd never been able to sleep deeply before. Apparently, that was one more thing that'd changed.

She could tell he was wearing boxers and she was still fully dressed herself, so it seemed innocent enough. Carefully, Grace eased onto her back and looked over at him. He frowned in his sleep and muttered something incomprehensible, then tightened his arm and drew her flush against him.

A smile curled on her lips.

She could smell alcohol on his breath. It made her want to wrinkle up her nose. Obviously, he'd gotten drunk last night. She sincerely doubted he would have climbed into bed with her otherwise. He was far too insistent that she deserved better than what he could give her. Whatever that meant.

After the relief she'd seen flash in his eyes yesterday, when the dog interrupted her attempt to kiss him, it would be an understatement to say she was surprised he'd climbed into bed with her last night, even if drunk. Still, alcohol didn't make people do things they didn't want to. It only lowered inhibitions and made people more inclined to do what they already desired—a fact her ex-boyfriend back in high school hadn't wanted to hear when she'd broken up with him after finding out he'd gotten drunk and jumped into bed with the prom queen.

Geez, she really had horrible taste in guys.

Her gaze drifted over Colt's handsome features, and she amended her previous assertion. She'd *had* terrible taste in guys. Past tense. The man in bed with her right now was one of the good ones, no matter what he thought to the contrary.

She tentatively smoothed a few stray strands of hair off his forehead. He needed a haircut. His hair was quite a bit longer now than it'd been when she'd interviewed him for the first time. That felt like forever ago. If she was being honest, she liked it better how it was now.

Grace reluctantly maneuvered out from under his arm and slid out of bed. As much as she would have loved to stay curled up with him until he woke up, her bladder was screaming. She gave him a long look, then tiptoed to her suitcase and retrieved some clean clothes before disappearing into the bathroom.

She emerged fifteen minutes later, fully dressed and ready to start the day.

Her gaze immediately fell on Colt, and an amused grin spread on her face. At some point while she'd been out of the room, he'd grabbed Whinny from her side of the bed and was now clutching the stuffed animal to his chest like a little boy. She did her best to smother the laugh that threatened to bubble up, but a soft snicker still escaped her lips. He looked so peaceful. So uncomplicated. It was endearing to see. What had he been like as a child? Somehow, she suspected he'd been a lot like now, only more playful, less serious. Warmth spread through her from the center of her chest.

Grace yanked her phone from her pocket. She snapped a quick picture to show him once he woke up. How long was he going to sleep anyway? It was getting pretty late, and she knew how much he liked to get an early start.

She nibbled her lip. Maybe she should go find them some breakfast to save time. Colt's next stop was nearly ten hours away as it was. They'd have to be leaving soon if they were going to make it.

Decision made, she grabbed her purse and the truck's keys, then scribbled a quick note for Colt so he wouldn't worry if he woke up before she returned. She placed the note on her pillow, where he'd hopefully see it, then headed out the door.

Colt was awake by the time she stepped back into the motel room. Her gaze swept over him. He'd showered and dressed, but he still looked like complete hell.

"Morning ... or nearly afternoon, actually." She nudged the door shut with her hip, offering him a smile when he peered up at her with bloodshot eyes. "Drink a bit too much last night?" She sat the drink carrier and bag on the small table near the window.

He groaned. "Yeah. Regretting it now too."

"I bet." She held out a cup to him. "Here, this may help some. It's the largest coffee they offer. I also got you a ham and cheese omelet if you feel up to eating."

"Thanks," he grumbled as he took the cup from her. "My head feels like it's splitting in two." He scrubbed a hand over his face then glanced down at the bed. "Um..." He cleared his throat. "I clearly climbed into bed with you last night. I didn't ... do ... anything inappropriate, did I?"

Grace's lips quirked up. "I woke up to you spooning me, but nothing else happened."

Colt visibly cringed, and she couldn't keep from chuckling.

"I can't say that I minded. You're a good snuggler. Way better than Whinny over there." She nodded toward the plush horse then smirked. "You cuddled with him too, after I got up. I even took a picture to show you. It's grainy, but my phone doesn't take the best pictures."

She laughed at the expression that crossed his face—equal parts horrified and embarrassed.

"Delete it. Please. God forbid anyone else sees it. I would never live it down. And stop laughing at me, woman."

"I'll delete the picture after we eat. What are you going to do if I don't? Stop laughing, that is."

He gave her an intense look that made her stomach jump. "Keep laughing and find out." That look held a threat but not of violence. More like the punishment he'd inflict would have her crying out with pleasure rather than pain.

"Promises, promises." She flashed him a grin in hopes of hiding her sudden case of nerves, then turned away to spread their breakfast out on the tiny table. "Come and eat. Then we should probably get going, or we'll never get to your stop in time."

"It's already too late. We'll have to go on to the next." He shoved to his feet with a grimace and joined her at the table. "Remind me never to drink again. Not that I'll listen." He smirked, and Grace burst out laughing all over again. "Ugh, don't laugh so loud," he groused and rubbed at his temples with one hand.

She tried to stop but only succeeded in laughing harder. "Sorry. I'm trying to quit," she chortled. Her statement ended with a soft snort.

His lips twitched, amusement making his eyes brighten. "Did you just snort?" He slowly shook his head. "You're adorable."

Their eyes met and held. She wanted to kiss him. What would he do if she leaned in and did so right now?

As if he could read her thoughts, his lips parted and he angled toward her near imperceptibly.

Her pulse jumped. Would he welcome it or push her away? After yesterday's failed attempt, she wasn't quite brave enough to find out. Would he kiss *her* instead? She couldn't interpret the look in his eyes.

His nostrils flared slightly when she wet her lips with a quick lick. He swallowed hard, then looked down at his plate while picking up his plastic fork. Just like that, the moment passed.

"This looks great." His voice seemed deeper than normal, almost husky.

"I hope it's as delicious as it looks." She tried in vain to calm her still racing heart.

They ate in silence for several minutes before she glanced back up at him. "Did I make a good choice with the omelet?"

He smiled. "You did. Thank you."

An answering smile curled on her lips. "You're welcome. I remembered you getting one when we went out to breakfast the other day, so I hoped it would work. Omelets are usually pretty easy on the stomach while hungover too."

Colt took his last bite then settled back in his chair to sip from his cup. "I notice you remembered how I take my coffee too."

"Yeah, um, I kind of had to learn to be observant when I lived with Flint. It was pretty disastrous if I got things wrong."

Damn, she didn't want to ruin the morning by thinking about that horrible man, but it was true. Living with Flint had taught her to pay close attention to even the tiniest details about pretty much everybody she came across.

Colt frowned, his brows snapping together as he leaned forward. "You know you don't have to do everything perfect now, while you're with me, right? I mean, I'm not going to yell if you forget I don't like pickles and get me a cheeseburger with pickles on it, for example. If you got it for me, I'd eat it anyway. Happily. I can always pick off the pickles."

She did know that. He was nothing like Flint. There was no way Flint would ever pick off the pickles if she were to forget he didn't like them. If it happened with him, he'd hurl the whole sandwich at her then beat her senseless while berating her, tearing her down.

"Wait. You don't like pickles?"

He shook his head. "Nope. Hate 'em. Let me guess; you love them?"

"Yep." She smiled. "I swear I could eat an entire jar in one sitting."

"Hmm, guess we're the perfect pair, then. I'll just give you all my unwanted pickles." He laughed and got to his feet. "Thanks for breakfast, Princess. I appreciate it." He gathered up their empty food containers and tossed them in the nearby trashcan.

"Are you going to be okay to drive? I can if you're not feeling up to it."

"I'm alright. I took some meds as soon as I woke up. Between them, the food, and the coffee, my headache is easing up some. I'll be fine." Colt grinned. "Grab your horse, and let's get on the road."

Grace turned to grab Whinny off the bed and tripped over her own feet.

Colt moved faster than she would have ever thought him capable of and caught her around the waist, narrowly keeping her from falling.

She gasped. Her fingers curled in his shirt as she clung to him for balance. Her body warmed and tingled under his hands, despite the innocent nature of the touch.

"Falling for me, Princess?"

Her eyes jumped to his. While the tone of his voice may have been teasing, his expression was not. The heat smoldering in his gaze stole any ability she may have had to respond as her pulse spiked.

He didn't smell like alcohol anymore. Now, he smelled of soap and the addictive masculine scent that was uniquely him. She inhaled deeply, filling her lungs with him. The urge to sway forward and press her body against his nearly overpowered her. Her fingers tightened in his shirt as she fought the impulse.

"Colt," she whispered, her voice both questioning and pleading at once.

Instead of releasing her, like she expected he would, he made a sound low in his throat and pulled her closer. It almost sounded like surrender. He buried his face in her hair, and she heard him mutter something about loving the smell of strawberries.

Her brow furrowed in confusion. Strawberries? Like her shampoo?

He lifted his head, and their eyes met once more—his dilated and stormy. Lust, mixed with some tender emotion she didn't dare name, swirled in their ocean blue depths. Her stomach fluttered.

This was new. The intensity. The emotion.

"Tell me you don't want this," he rasped as he crowded her, forcing her to back toward the closest wall while their gazes held. "Tell me you don't want me to kiss you," he begged.

She couldn't do that, no matter how much he asked her to. It wouldn't be true. First she'd woke up to find him in bed with her, and now this? Something had clearly shifted between them since that moment in the park. But what caused it? Not that she was complaining about this change in him.

"Why would I lie?" she answered with a gasp as her back hit the wall.

Her eyes widened at the light press of his body against hers as he caged her in with his arms. Not from fear but surprise, and no small measure of pleasure. How far would he take this? Her body ached for his touch.

"I *do* want you. I have for a long time."

"Don't tell me that," he said with a groan then shuddered hard.

Was he going to end this now? She braced for him to back away. Readied herself for the sting of rejection, of disappointment.

Rather than doing what she'd expected, Colt gently brushed her hair away from her neck and lowered his lips to the skin there.

A shiver cascaded over her. Her eyes slid closed while she tipped her head to the side to give him better access.

His mouth moved slowly over her skin, nibbling and kissing. "This shouldn't happen," he whispered, his breath teasing the shell of her ear and making her shiver all over again.

Pleasure skated through her veins. This was the most exquisite torture she'd ever experienced.

"Why not?" she asked with a small gasp as he nipped her earlobe.

She didn't see a reason for this not to happen. They were friends. Friends with a strong attraction to one another. And they were both single. Wasn't this the natural next step?

Colt didn't answer. Despite his assertion, one of his hands moved to her hip and pulled her lower half tight against him, while the fingers of his other hand tangled in the hair at her nape. She could swear she felt him tremble.

"Don't let me kiss you," he pleaded. "Tell me no, Princess." His breaths sawed in and out of him as he trailed hot, open-mouthed kisses along her jaw, drifting steadily toward her lips. "Please," he groaned before kissing the corner of her mouth. "Stop me."

Her body was on fire, aching for him. Grace tried to do as he'd asked—she really did—but she couldn't force herself to voice the words. She couldn't bring herself to stop him when she didn't want him to. What she wanted was to be closer to him, his mouth on hers.

"I can't do that." She arched against him. "Kiss me already. Stop teasing me."

He made a low, frustrated sound, then his lips brushed over hers. The tiniest taste. Before she could complain, he groaned, and then his mouth landed hard on hers.

It wasn't a gentle kiss, and she loved it. He kissed her as though he was starving and she was a banquet laid out just for him. It was scorching hot and unrestrained, as if some dam had burst within him.

She moaned and wrapped her arms around his neck as his tongue tangled with hers in a passionate dance. Nobody had ever kissed her like this. It felt like he was branding her soul, searing it. She couldn't get enough. She wanted more.

Her hands slid down his back and around to his abdomen. The moment her fingertips grazed his belt buckle, the spell shattered.

Colt yanked his mouth from hers and stepped away. "I can't. We can't," he panted, his chest heaving.

Her body wept for him. The throbbing between her legs was borderline painful. She squeezed her thighs together, hoping to relieve the ache.

He scrubbed his hands over his face and up into his hair. "I didn't mean to..." His gaze lifted to hers. The agony and conflict swirling in his eyes stole her breath as much as his kiss had. "Fuck, Princess." He grimaced. "I'm sorry. I lost control."

"I don't want or need your apology, Colt. What I want is more of you. That wasn't enough. I wasn't done," she answered breathlessly.

She hoped he realized she wasn't just talking about the kiss. Grace wanted a relationship with him. Something real and strong. She wanted his heart and his love, not just his body. How did she get him to give this thing between them a chance?

He clenched his eyes shut. Tension rolled off of him in near-tangible waves. For a moment, it seemed like he was going to give in and kiss her again, but then he shook his head and took another step away.

"This can't happen. I can't give you what you deserve." His eyes opened and locked with hers. Staggering pain clouded their ocean-blue depths. "I know you don't understand." He paced away from her and glanced at the ceiling before tugging at his hair. "Shit, Grace, I'm not sure I understand anymore either." He rubbed at the back of his neck and grimaced. "I'm pretty sure I'm broken. I don't want to hurt you." He sighed heavily and met her gaze once more. The look in his eyes was more intense than she'd ever seen it. "I can't lose you." His voice cracked on the final word.

Her heart squeezed. "I'm not planning on leaving. You're not going to lose me." She touched his arm and felt him shudder under her hand.

Grace stepped around him to retrieve her plush horse from the bed and inhaled a deep, steadying breath. "We need to talk about this, but I think we should probably get on the road. They're gonna charge you again if we don't check out soon."

"Yeah, you're right." He bent and grabbed both his duffle bag and her suitcase, then gave her a meaningful look. "I'm sorry again. I shouldn't have done that."

She nodded in acceptance of his repeated apology—though she still didn't want it—opened the door, snatched up Whinny, then followed Colt outside.

Grace pressed a shaky hand to her chest as she followed Colt through the crowd toward the arena.

While she'd waited for their breakfast yesterday morning, she'd gotten five more messages from Flint—some leaning toward almost amiable, others angry. In none of them had he mentioned where he was right now, or what he was doing. What if he had somehow followed them and was here right now—watching, waiting for the perfect opportunity to try to make her leave with him again? The thought sent her pulse skyrocketing.

She'd noted all the exits when they got here and planned an escape route. Just moments ago, she and Colt had stopped by the tent next to the concession stand to talk to the security guards and tell them to be on the lookout for Flint. Colt had promised not to leave her until he needed to ride, but what if it wasn't enough? What if despite her precautions Flint still got into the rodeo grounds and grabbed her?

Her eyes darted from face to face, searching for one in particular, as a cold sweat broke out all over her body. She didn't see him, but that meant little. So many people were here tonight. If he was here, she might not know until it was too late to flee.

She wasn't safe. This wasn't safe. She shouldn't be here.

Oh God, she couldn't catch her breath. Her body trembled from head to toe.

"Grace?"

She heard her name through a thick fog. The voice was familiar. Worried.

Colt.

She blinked, struggling to focus on him. "Can't. Breathe," she gasped, clawing at her throat.

Oh, God, why couldn't she breathe? Her head was spinning. She caught Colt's arm in an iron grip as she swayed on her feet.

Colt cursed under his breath. "You're having a panic attack." He glanced around the grounds then ducked to meet her eyes. "I need to get you somewhere quieter. This place is a madhouse. Can I carry you? You look like you might faint."

The moment she nodded, he scooped her off her feet, settled her against his chest, and started back the way they'd come from with long, quick strides.

Grace buried her face in the crook of his shoulder and struggled to regain control over both her racing thoughts and her breathing.

Colt settled her onto her feet next to his truck. Her legs wouldn't hold her. She sank to the ground and leaned back against the truck's tire.

Colt dropped to his knees beside her.

"Take deep breaths, Princess. Like this..." He demonstrated the technique—inhaling deeply through his nose, holding the breath for a count, then slowly exhaling through his mouth before doing it again.

She struggled to follow his instructions, but her chest felt heavy like some extraordinary weight was crushing her. Each breath was a challenge. It felt like an eternity before she could draw a deep breath easily again, and her heart stopped feeling as though it was trying to escape her ribcage.

Slowly, the tremors racking her body calmed.

"Better?" Colt asked at long last. His eyes moved over her face. "You've got your color back. You were pale as a ghost."

Grace focused her eyes on him. She might have her color back, but his normally tanned skin was washed out. His hat lay on the ground, and his hair stood up in disarray like he'd thrust his hand through it at some point. Maybe repeatedly.

"I think I'm okay now." She met Colt's concerned gaze and forced a faint smile. "Thank you."

His face relaxed. "No thanks necessary. I'm just glad you're feeling better." He glanced over his shoulder toward the rodeo grounds then returned his gaze to her. "Do you know what caused it?"

"Flint," she said with a small grimace.

"You saw him?"

Grace shook her head and looked down at her fingers where they fiddled with the hem of her shirt. "No. But I started thinking that he could have followed us here. That he could be here, waiting until I'm alone to try to grab me again." She glanced up at him. "I'm sorry."

Colt frowned. "You don't have anything to be sorry about. This is the first rodeo since he attempted to kidnap you; I should have thought about how it'd be for you." He yanked his hat up off the ground and slapped the dust from it as though he was angry with it, or himself. "I'm sorry, Princess, for not considering it."

"It's okay."

He shook his head. "No, it's not. You're more important than any rodeo." He stood then offered her his hand. Once she was standing, he nodded toward the truck. "Hop in. We'll go grab a bite to eat and head back to the motel. Call it an early night."

"But you need to ride. You'll drop in the standings if you don't. And what about your friends? Didn't you say you were meeting up with Cash and ... um, Brody, I think?"

"So I drop in the standings. And I'll text my friends to let them know where I am." He shrugged then ducked his head to meet her eyes. "*You* are more important. You need a break. My next stop is a hell of a lot smaller rodeo. It won't be as crowded." He hesitated, then dropped a kiss on her forehead before opening the passenger side door. "Get in, Princess. We'll find some Mexican food, then you can find us a movie on TV at the motel. I'll even spring for some microwave popcorn."

Her stomach quivered. Why was he so sweet to her? She still wasn't used to being treated so well. Maybe she'd never get used to it.

A warm sensation spread through her, chasing away the last remnants of her panic attack. She smiled. "Are you sure you want me picking the movie? It might be a rom com."

His grin crinkled the corners of his eyes. "I'm sure. Pick whatever you want."

She shook her head. He really was unlike any man she'd known before.

"If you insist," she said with a soft smile. "Alright, let's go."

Chapter 18

Colt glanced sideways at Grace. "I'm surprised you don't like barrel racing."

Grace laughed. "I do like barrel racing. I just think that the roping events are more exciting."

They'd been on the road for nearly an hour. Neither of them had mentioned Grace's panic attack at last night's rodeo. Colt was still beating himself up about it. He should have considered it might be difficult for her, especially with as crowded as that stop had been.

They hadn't talked about the kiss they'd shared a few days ago either. Rather than either topic, he and Grace had been having an enjoyable discussion about the pros and cons of each of the rodeo events. Frankly, Colt was good with it.

"Which one is your favorite?" Colt asked. "Team roping? Tie-down?"

"Breakaway." Grace smiled. "The others are fun to watch, but my favorite will always be breakaway." She looked over at him. "I used to do breakaway back in junior high and high school."

His gaze darted to her as his eyebrows shot nearly to his hat. "You competed?"

She laughed. "I did. I got pretty good at it back then too. There are times I really miss riding."

Something within him went still at that news.

Colt thought back to the auction and the weird feeling that'd come over him the moment he'd seen the little mare he'd ultimately purchased. His heart stuttered. He'd wondered why the hell he'd felt such a strong urge to buy a roping bred mare when he couldn't throw a loop to save his life. What if he'd somehow bought the horse for Grace? Sure, he hadn't even met her yet then, but still. They'd bumped into each other not twenty minutes later, and that brief encounter had jolted him to his core too.

Fuck, was it possible? The idea of it seemed crazy as hell. Colt knew if he were to ask Cash, his best friend would answer with a resounding 'hell yes'. Cash firmly believed in all that 'universe giving signs and fate being real' shit. Colt wasn't sure he believed in any of that nonsense. Still ... it seemed too big of a coincidence to dismiss out of hand.

"If you had a horse, would you want to compete again?" Colt tentatively asked, breaking the silence that'd fallen between them.

She scrunched up her face. "I can't exactly afford one right now." Her expression turned thoughtful. "But, I think..." She paused and nibbled her lip in silence for a moment before turning to look at him again. "I think if I *could* somehow get one, I might like to give it another try. Yes. I used to really love it. I'm not sure I would remember what I'm doing anymore, though. It's been so long."

She smiled wistfully. "Sometimes, I really miss my old horse. I had a grey gelding named Jinx. He was my best friend and only confidant for so many years. He saw me through so much." She sighed heavily, turning to stare blankly out the passenger side window. "My adoptive parents died a week after I turned seventeen. The foster family I got sent to for that last year lived in the city and wasn't willing to board him anywhere for me." She shook her head. "I don't even know what happened to him. I know they sold him, but I don't know to whom. I hope whoever got him loved him as much as I did."

Jesus, she just couldn't catch a break, could she? He marveled at her resilience, her strength. She'd endured hardship after hardship, and still she smiled. Laughed. Still, she was capable of optimism and hope. He wasn't sure he would be able to in her shoes.

His life had been smooth sailing in comparison to hers, and yet one single loss—Sarah—had brought him to his knees and nearly taken him out. Grace had lost so many, so much. Parts of herself even, and still she kept her chin up and took another step forward, determined to survive. Refusing to lay down and give up.

Without a doubt, this woman beside him was the strongest woman he'd ever met. He was wrong about her being a princess. She was a phoenix. A bright, beautiful, awe-inspiring phoenix.

He shifted his grip on the steering wheel and gently touched her knee. "I'm sorry."

She glanced at his hand before lifting her gaze to him, confusion written all over her expression. "Sorry for what?"

"About Jinx," Colt said softly. "It's shitty that your foster parents weren't willing to board him for you, even just until you turned eighteen.

She smiled, though a hint of sadness clung to it, then gave her shoulders a slight shrug. "They had so many other foster kids, they probably couldn't afford it." She shook her head as if shaking off the past. "Anyway, what brought on your question about my competing again?"

He returned his hand to the steering wheel. "Ah, well, I asked because I have a Quarter Horse mare. She's been trained to rope. I got her at the auction we, uh, ran into each other at. She doesn't even have a name yet beyond the one on her papers." His lips twitched then one corner of his mouth lifted. "This is going to sound really weird, but ... I think I may have bought her for you. I don't rope. Shit, *can't* rope. And I have no need for a horse. I had no reason to buy her." His shoulders lifted and fell. "I just felt like I needed to, like it was imperative that she was mine." He slanted a look at her. "Do you believe in fate?"

"Fate?" Her head tipped off to the side as she studied him. "I ... don't know," she answered. "Maybe." She rubbed at her chin then squinted at him. "You didn't even know me then. I don't know why you would have bought her, but I doubt it was for me. Maybe you just thought she was pretty."

Colt chuckled. "I told you it was going to sound weird. Cash believes in all that fate stuff. It's how he'd probably explain all of this." His gaze flicked over to Grace briefly. "She is pretty, though. Jet black with a huge star on her forehead and one white sock on her hind leg. If you think you might want to try competing again, I could call Cash and see if he'd be willing to take a break from the circuit for a few days so you can meet her. She's stabled at his place. It'd give you something more fun to do than sitting around waiting on me to ride."

Grace blinked. "You're serious?"

Colt flashed a smile. "I am. We'll be going right by Cash's place; it wouldn't even be out of the way. So? Want to?" He nudged on the blinker and changed lanes, anticipating a yes.

Grace nibbled at her thumbnail for a long moment, her expression contemplative, then finally nodded. "Alright. If you're really serious about it, I'll give it a shot. After all these years, I'm not sure I'll be able to ride, much less rope well enough to be competitive, but I'm willing to try. I really do miss it, and it might even be a good way to earn some money. I'm never going to get my feet back under me without that."

"True. I hadn't thought of that perk." He smiled and took the next exit, then pulled into the parking lot of the first truck stop they came across.

He threw the truck into park. Colt slipped his phone from his pocket and thumbed through his contacts, then offered Grace a smile while tapping the button to dial his best friend. "Okay. Let's see what Cash has to say about our plan," he said and lifted the phone to his ear.

⋅⋅⋅◦⋅⋅⋅

Colt spotted Cash's silver truck coming down the drive, sending up a cloud of dust behind it, as he led Grace from the barn for the second time. "Looks like he's finally here."

He'd already taken her on a tour of both the expansive barn and house while they were waiting. It was lucky that Cash still hadn't moved the spare key from where it'd been the last time Colt was here. It'd been so long he hadn't been sure where it'd be, if anywhere at all.

"I was beginning to wonder if he was ever going to show up," Grace said cheerfully as Cash parked not far from them.

"Now, why wouldn't I show up? I've never been one to leave a pretty lady waiting long," Cash said as he stepped from his truck and slammed the door shut behind himself before heading in their direction. "Traffic was horrible."

Grace smiled. "You have a beautiful ranch."

"It's even more beautiful now that you're here. Would you believe I won it in a hand of poker?"

The way Grace blushed at Cash's flirtatious comment rankled Colt, but he couldn't say why. Maybe because he'd kissed her. Or maybe because he wanted her himself. Either way, it wasn't an untrue statement, and it was highly unlikely that his friend meant anything by it. Cash was a flirt—always had been, probably always would be.

Colt rolled his eyes and stepped closer to Grace. He slid an arm around her waist and tugged her tight against his side. Cash raised an eyebrow as he watched, but Colt ignored him.

"Don't listen to him, Princess. He doesn't want anyone to know he bought it because he's thinking about settling down."

Cash gasped and theatrically acted horrified. "You take that back! Don't even joke about it." He faked a shudder, as though the mere idea of settling down was abhorrent.

"Whatever, man. I'm starved, and I'm sure Grace has to be too. Do you have any food here?"

"Nope. I'm never here. There's a good diner a couple of miles down the road, though." Cash waved a hand toward his truck. "Hop in. I'll drive. I'm about starved too."

"You treating too since we had to wait forever for your slow ass to get here?" Colt teasingly asked.

"Don't push it. You guys coming or not?"

Colt laughed. "Yeah, we're coming."

He helped Grace into Cash's truck, then climbed in himself.

⸺◈⸺

"She's beautiful." Grace stroked her hand along the mare's sleek neck. Her eyes lifted to Colt. "You really haven't named her yet?"

"Nope. The honor is all yours," he answered.

She turned back to the mare and murmured something he couldn't quite make out. It sounded like she may have told the horse that she was far too pretty to not have a name, but he couldn't be sure.

So far, the two seemed to be hitting it off, but she hadn't gotten on the mare's back yet. That would be the real test. He had every intention of gifting her the horse if they seemed like a good fit, even if it took him a year to talk her into accepting the animal.

The borrowed saddle he'd tacked the mare up with wasn't intended for roping, but it would have to do for now. He'd get Grace a proper set of roping tack before they got on the road if this all worked out.

"Need a leg up?" When she nodded, he moved in to give her a boost into the saddle. He crouched next to her left leg and gripped both her ankle and upper calf, then looked up at her. "Ready?"

"I think so," she said. "On the count of three?" She wobbled and leaned on his shoulder to regain her balance, then gave him a sheepish smile. "Or maybe not."

One corner of his mouth twisted up as their eyes met. "Guess you weren't." He chuckled. "Ready this time?"

She took a deep breath and nodded.

"Alright. On three. One. Two." He took a breath. "Three."

Grace bounced on her right leg then sprang upward. He straightened, taking her left leg with him. She swung her right leg over the horse's back and settled into the saddle.

"Good?"

Grace smiled, looking about as comfortable as someone who'd been riding all their life. "I'm good. It feels great to be back on a horse again. I didn't realize how much I've missed this until now. I hope I remember how to do this."

"I'm sure you'll be fine." He released her leg and moved to open the arena gate. "Why don't you put her through her paces? She rides pretty well. I tried her out when I got back to Crooked Creek after the auction."

She gave the mare a harder kick than she'd probably intended, and the horse jolted forward. "Oops, sorry girl." Grace shot him a sheepish look then tried again. This time, she gently nudged the horse into a walk and rode her into the arena.

Colt leaned against the fence.

Grace had a natural seat and light hands. The mare seemed to be responding to her cues nicely. This might work; he sure hoped it did. Maybe if she were actively competing too, she'd be more inclined to stay with him longer. To keep traveling with him even after she had her feet back.

He'd never be ready to say goodbye to her. Not even if it took years for that day to come. Keeping her with him wasn't the only reason he hoped she'd compete, though. There was a good chance it'd help head off any more panic attacks too. He wanted that for her. She deserved some fun, some joy, after everything she'd been through.

Cash came out of the barn and leaned against the fence next to him. They watched Grace and the mare move around the arena in silence for several minutes.

Cash gave Colt's arm a nudge and leaned closer to him. "You're acting weird. What's really going on between you two? You two dating?"

Colt gave his best friend a sharp look. "How am I acting weird? We're just friends, and I'm helping her out. Like I told you before."

"Still on that 'just friends' shit, huh?" Cash scoffed and rolled his eyes. "Tell me another one, man. That's bullshit, and you know it."

Colt glanced at Grace. She rode along the fence line at the far end of the arena, plenty far enough away to be unable to overhear this conversation. Her face was relaxed, happy. Warmth spread through his chest at the sight.

Colt straightened and turned to look at Cash more fully. His fingers curled into fists at his sides as his temper flared. "Why would you think it's bullshit? I want to hear your reasoning."

"My reasons? Fuck, man, where do I even start? You looked like you might murder me for calling her beautiful, for starters. You're always finding an excuse to touch her, even at dinner. Whenever you look at her, you get this strange look on your face. All dreamy or some shit. Should I continue? I can."

Colt made a face. He did not look at her all dreamy. Did he?

His gaze returned to Grace. Her attention was focused entirely on the mare. She leaned forward in the saddle and patted the animal's sleek neck, a joyful smile spreading on her face. A smile of his own crept onto his lips in response.

"You're doing it again!" Cash's eyes widened, realization dawning over his face. "Shit. You've gone and fallen in love with her, didn't you?" He barked out a laugh.

"What?" Colt vehemently shook his head. "I'm not in love with her."

He shoved away from the fence and stalked toward the barn.

To his annoyance, Cash followed right on his heels.

Cash was wrong. He had to be. There was no fucking way Colt was in love with Grace. Was he? Sure, he wanted her so badly it hurt and she made him feel things he hadn't in years—some of them stronger than he could ever remember feeling. But, love? The idea of it made him want to run for the hills.

"So much for you two just being friends!" Cash laughingly exclaimed from behind him.

"She *is* just a friend," Colt snapped.

Cash laughed harder. "Yeah, sure. Keep telling yourself that. Even if you haven't crossed the line with her yet, you want to. Admit it."

Colt's stomach twisted into a knot, making him feel like he might lose the burger he'd had for dinner. He shoved Cash's words into a mental box labeled *Nonsense*. The thought of being in love with Grace was too dangerous, too frightening to entertain. He refused to believe it.

"I'm not admitting to shit," Colt growled as he scowled at his friend. "Leave it alone, Cash. You're wrong."

Colt stopped in front of a stall and distractedly petted the chestnut horse it held.

Even if he did have serious feelings for her, it didn't change anything. His views about committed relationships and getting remarried remained the same. He was never doing any of it again. Not with her. Not with anyone. Period.

That was how it had to be for his heart's sake.

He'd barely made it through losing Sarah. If he let himself love Grace and he lost her too, he wasn't sure he'd survive it. He'd rather get trampled by two tons of pissed-off bull than go through that again.

"If you don't have feelings for her, why are you mad?"

Colt spun around to face Cash. "Who the fuck said I was mad?" he snapped.

"Um, well..." Cash gave a half-laugh, then raised his hands in mock surrender when Colt glared at him.

Colt shook his head angrily. "You have no idea what you're talking about. How the hell would you know anything about love anyway? You run away from commitment like it's something that might kill you. Stay the fuck out of my business. I'm serious."

"Yeah, about her," Cash mumbled under his breath. When Colt glowered at him again, he cleared his throat. "You may not be ready to admit it, but there's something there. I know you. This is the same way you acted with Sarah, but ... different somehow. You weren't so clingy with Sarah."

"Yeah, well, Sarah didn't have as much bullshit going on in her life either."

Cash reached out to pet the palomino horse the next stall over rather than answering.

For the next couple of minutes, the only sounds in the barn were horses munching on hay and shuffling around their stalls. Colt used the quiet to mull over Cash's words.

What if his best friend was right? Shit, hadn't Colt just suspected days ago that he might be falling for her? He gave himself an internal shake. Nope, he wasn't thinking about it. It wasn't true, and that's all there was to it.

"The horse seems to work well with her," Cash said, pulling Colt from his thoughts. "Think she'll agree to competing with her?"

Colt blew out a breath and tried to regain his calm. "I don't know. I hope so. She's not sure she'll remember how to rope well enough to be competitive. You don't happen to have a calf dummy sled she could practice on, do you?"

"Oh, I don't know, she sure seems to have roped you fine," Cash said with a smirk then sent Colt a knowing look.

Colt chose to pretend he hadn't heard or seen. Cash was wrong. His best friend was imagining things, seeing things between Colt and Grace that weren't really there. He had to be.

"I think there might be a roping dummy in the equipment shed. Whether it's in usable condition is another question. I hope she competes. It'd give her something to do besides sit around waiting on your ugly ass." Cash gave Colt a playful shove. "We should get back out there too. She's probably wondering where we are."

"Let's go then," Colt replied gruffly. He gave the horse one last pat, then followed Cash back outside.

Grace was still on horseback but was waiting next to the arena fence for them.

"Geez, I thought you guys abandoned me!" she called as he and Cash resumed their earlier positions against the fence.

Colt flashed her a grin. "Never, Princess."

As Grace urged the mare forward again, Colt wondered what she felt for him. He knew for certain that she liked him, but could she love him? He'd be damned if he was going to ask. He wasn't entirely sure he wanted to know the answer. The prospect of being in love with her was frightening enough, but the prospect of being the first to fall was almost worse.

Sarah had been the first to fall, and she'd let him know her feelings early and often. Loving her hadn't seemed so scary because of it.

He shoved away his thoughts as Grace pulled the mare to a stop in front of him and dismounted. "Well, what do you think?" he asked. "Want to give competing a try?"

She beamed. "She's great! I'll admit; I was more than a little worried. Until today, I haven't ridden since my junior year of high school."

"I would never have guessed from watching you ride. Cash said he might have a dummy sled you can use to get in some practice roping while we're here, if you want." He smiled and opened the gate for her. "You'll have to come up with a name for your mare now too. She can't go around without one."

He winked at her when she shot him a look. There was little doubt she'd try to dissuade him from giving her the mare later, but right now she seemed inclined to let his comment slide. With luck, she'd eventually warm to the idea of the mare being hers.

"I'm awful at naming animals, but I guess I could give it a try."

Cash pushed away from the fence and joined them. "I'd be happy to help you name her."

"Really? Okay. That would be great!" She laughed. "When I was a kid, one of my friends asked me to help her name her dog.

Yeah, that didn't go so well. That poor dog ended up with such an unfortunate name."

She shook her head and led the horse toward the barn. Colt and Cash trailed behind her until she glanced back at them with a smile. "I can cool her down and get her settled in her stall on my own. I remember that part of horse care fine. You boys don't need to babysit me."

Her eyes were twinkling, so Colt surmised she was joking around with them. He loved how she'd become so much surer of herself since she started traveling with him, even after the bullshit Flint pulled the other day. He fell back, content to let her have at it if she wanted to do it on her own.

When she finally reappeared, Cash approached her first.

"You really are a skilled rider." He winked at her. "Maybe you can teach me to ride better sometime? I'm a little rusty."

Grace's face skipped pink and went straight to bright red.

Colt's jaw clenched as he watched the interaction, but he said nothing. What could he say? It wasn't as though he had any sort of claim on her. She was free to make her own decisions, but what the hell was Cash doing?

He hadn't missed the sly look his best friend gave him before heading toward Grace. Was he purposely trying to provoke him? If so, why?

Grace's gaze shot over to him. Why was she looking at him? To see what he thought of his friend flirting with her? Cash was fucking pissing him off, but he wasn't going to let her know that. He kept his face carefully impassive until she turned to Cash again.

"I'm sure you ride fine," she said. "I doubt you need my help."

Cash seemed unperturbed by her response. He didn't back off either, however, to Colt's annoyance. Instead, he tucked a few flyaway strands of Grace's hair behind her ear. Her face turned an even darker shade of crimson.

"You really are cute when you blush. I can see why Colt's hooked on you."

Damn it. Colt scowled at Cash, but his friend ignored him completely.

Grace's eyes darted back to him, and her brow furrowed.

He knew exactly what she was wondering—whether he'd said something to Cash about his feelings for her. He could almost see the gears turning in her pretty journalist head.

"Uh, thanks." She stepped closer to him, putting more distance between herself and Cash. "I think."

Colt cleared his throat. Grace was practically radiating tension, her posture stiff.

He touched her arm lightly, leaning down to speak at her ear. "I need to talk to Cash about the horse trailer he's selling. Why don't you head into the house and we'll meet you there in a few minutes?"

Relief flickered in her eyes. "Okay." She gave him a tight-lipped smile then walked away.

Colt waited until she disappeared into the house, then finally exploded. He shoved Cash hard. "What the fuck was that?"

Cash staggered back a few steps but smiled placidly. "Chill out, man. I was testing a theory."

"Testing a theory? What fucking kind of theory were you testing that meant you needed to flirt with my—" Colt snapped his mouth shut and paced away.

Shit, he'd nearly called Grace his girlfriend. Cash was getting into his head. That's all it was.

Cash watched him with obvious amusement. It made Colt want to punch that damn smirk off his face.

"Flirt with your what? Finish your question. I want to know what you were going to say."

"My *friend*," Colt snapped. "She's my friend. *Just* my friend." He wasn't sure if he was answering Cash, reminding himself what Grace was to him, or both.

"Nah, she's not your friend, or at least, that's not all she is." Cash grinned. "I was right. You're so fucking lost to her. You look like you're about to put me six feet under, and I wasn't even flirting with her that hard. Shit, I barely even touched her. You might not want to admit it, but that girl is yours. You want her. Good news, bro; I'm pretty sure she wants you too." His grin only spread when Colt scowled at him. "Shit. I haven't seen you this bothered by a chick since Sarah. You fought your attraction to her too, remember? It took her months to wear you down."

Colt remembered. "This isn't the same. She's not Sarah."

That was certainly the truth. The two women had a few similarities, sure, but they were too different to be compared. Sarah met him when he'd been at his wildest, and while she'd tamed him in the end, there'd been times she'd been just as happy to run wild beside him. She'd been bubbly and bright, pure excitement and adventure. But Grace... Well, she was the quiet he hadn't known he craved. She brought peace, contentment. A warmth that chased away his demons and made him feel whole again.

He scrubbed his hands over his face. "She's different, man. I do like her. I *am* attracted to her. I'll admit to that. But we're friends, and that's all we can be." He felt guilty enough about having kissed her, like he'd betrayed Sarah somehow by doing it. It was stupid. He knew it, but he couldn't seem to get past it. He focused another glare on Cash. "You need to let this shit about me being in love with her go. You're wrong."

Cash shook his head and an almost sad look crossed his face. "Stay in denial, then. Have it your way." He tapped the center of Colt's chest with two fingers as he said, "There's room for both of them in there. You *can* love both. Sarah would want you to be happy."

Colt didn't need Cash, or anyone else, to tell him what she'd want. He already knew. It didn't mean he could do it, though. Not yet. Probably not ever.

"It's been years, dude. It's time." Cash started for the house then paused and looked back at Colt. "You can have that trailer too. I ain't taking your money for it."

"Alright. I appreciate it," Colt said, his voice gruff.

Cash slung his arm over Colt's shoulders. "Don't mention it. Come on. Let's get in the house before your woman worries. I assume you guys are staying the night since it's getting late?"

Colt shot Cash a warning look. Grace was not his woman. She never would be. His friend needed to knock it off. "Yeah. Hope your guest rooms are clean. We'll probably stay here a few days at least, so she can practice roping a bit."

Cash laughed. "Dude, I'm never here. You're the only guest I've had in ages. Well, and Grace now too, I guess. There might be a bit of dust, but they're probably cleaner than most of the motels you guys have been staying in." He cocked his head, giving Colt a sideways glance. "Speaking of, do you two share a room on the road?" He waggled his eyebrows suggestively.

Colt laughingly groaned and shoved Cash away from him. "Jesus, Cash, let it go!"

"Ha, so you do! I expect to be invited to the wedding!" He ducked the half-hearted punch Colt threw at him and ran ahead to the house.

Colt shook his head as he followed his friend indoors, knowing this wouldn't be the last time Cash would have something to say about him and Grace. His friend was far too stubborn to give up.

⊰•◦⊱

Colt walked with Grace down the hallway toward the guest rooms. She looked deep in thought while she worried her lip. It was making him want to kiss her, maybe nibble on that lip a little himself.

Their kiss days ago flashed in his mind, intensifying the desire. It hadn't been a lie when he'd told her one kiss would never be enough. He wanted more. So much more. Colt wanted her in his bed, sure, but he wanted her with him every day for the rest of his life too. He wanted to give her the relationship she deserved.

He cleared his throat. "What's on your mind, Princess?"

She looked over at him and shook her head. "Nothing much. I was wondering if I'll do well enough to make any of this worth it. I'm pretty intimidated by the whole idea of competing. Excited too. I've missed riding. I didn't know how much until I was on Summer's back today."

"You know you don't have to compete if you're uncomfortable with it, right? I won't force you to do anything you don't want to do."

"I know I don't have to compete, but I think I do want to try." She smiled.

He was happy that during the evening's lively discussion about what to name the horse, she'd only half-heartedly argued with him about the mare being hers. He'd hoped that might happen once she'd spent some time with the animal. Horses had a way of working their way into your heart at record speed, even when you tried to resist them. Women weren't so different there.

That thought gave him pause.

His gaze flitted over to Grace. First he nearly called her his girlfriend to Cash, and now this? As much as he was loath to admit it, Cash might actually be on to something.

They stopped next to the bedroom that would be Grace's while they were here.

Colt turned to face her. "I'm serious about Summer being yours. If you need help paying for her feed and care, I'm happy to pitch in for as long as you need, but I want you to have her."

"We'll see. I'm still not completely sold on you giving her to me. I don't get why you'd do that."

"Princess, I would give you the whole damn world if I thought you'd accept it." The words burst out of him unbidden, surprising even him.

It was true, though. He would. Anything at all.

She inhaled audibly and swayed on her feet. Her eyes shot wide, wonder sparking in their icy depths. It seemed he'd startled her with his statement too.

Heart thudding in his ears, Colt ducked his head to meet her eyes. "Anything to see you smile."

He swallowed hard, and his gaze dropped to her mouth. She was nibbling at her bottom lip again, and it was damn distracting.

He forcibly dragged his gaze away from her and locked it on the door to her room. "I was hoping to get an early start tomorrow. Think you can be up and ready to practice roping by 7 a.m.?" he asked, his voice rough.

"Sure." Grace stepped forward and slipped her arms around his waist, startling him. "Thank you, Eight."

His gaze jumped back to her. He sucked in a ragged breath, and his body tensed as she hesitantly pressed closer and leaned her cheek against his chest.

She was killing him. Why did she have to feel so damn good pressed up against him? It was too much to resist. Reluctantly, he slipped his arms around her in return.

"Thank you for what?" His brain was mush at the moment. He couldn't for the life of him think of anything she could be thanking him for.

"For the mare." She laughed against his chest. She tipped her head back to look up at him, her expression sobering. "For your friendship too. And for giving me a safe place to stay. For everything, I guess. I wanted you to know I appreciate what you're doing for me." She returned her cheek to his chest and sighed.

He smiled and rested his chin on the top of her head as he tightened his arms around her a fraction. She didn't need to thank him for anything. He enjoyed doing things for her, making her smile. She'd brought sunshine back to his life.

"Don't mention it. I'm happy to do it. Thank you for brightening my days."

They both fell silent, but neither of them made any effort to step away from the other.

An unfamiliar sense of utter contentment spread through him. He loved this. Her in his arms. It wasn't smart, but he loved it.

It wasn't until Colt heard Cash talking to someone at the end of the hall—probably one of his hired hands, from the sound of it—that he finally forced himself to release her and pulled away. The urge to draw her back into his arms and cover her mouth with his to kiss her goodnight was near unbearable.

He backed away another step. Cash seeing them there, hugging each other tight—or worse, kissing—was the last thing Colt needed. He'd never hear the end of it.

Colt rubbed the back of his neck with one hand and glanced warily at the end of the hall before returning his gaze to Grace. She was watching him with a soft look in her enchanting eyes.

He gave her a crooked grin and touched her arm. "Goodnight, Grace."

He dropped a kiss on her forehead and hurried down the hall to the sanctuary of his room.

Chapter 19

Colt nearly drank his weight in coffee—or at least it seemed like it—as he ate his breakfast while distractedly listening to Grace and Cash chat. After a week at the ranch, he and Grace were finally leaving. Not a moment too soon, in his opinion. He wasn't sure he could take much more of Cash.

This had been the roughest week he could recall having in a while. Definitely the most sleepless. Cash still hadn't let go of his theory and took every opportunity he could to razz Colt about it. The worst of it was that the more Colt considered things, the more he suspected his irritating best friend was right. Not that he'd ever admit it to anyone, especially not Cash. The asshole would never stop gloating.

This morning, Colt had whipped together a quick meal for them using the meager ingredients he'd rummaged up. With as often as they ate at diners, he figured Grace would probably enjoy having one last home-cooked meal before they got back to life on the road. Who knew when there would be another opportunity to cook for her.

He'd made pancakes, nothing too fancy, but he hadn't heard any complaints. They tasted pretty good to him, though he was far from the best judge of food—like he'd told Grace at that very first interview over dinner.

Man, that seemed like ages ago and yesterday simultaneously. She'd intrigued him even then. No, before then. When their eyes met at that damn auction was undoubtedly when he got hooked by her.

It was only when he reached for his coffee to take another long sip of the fortifying brew that he realized someone must have said something to him. Both Grace and Cash were staring expectantly, as though waiting for an answer to some question he hadn't heard.

"Huh?" His face warmed, and he resisted the urge to rub at it.

Grace smiled patiently. "I asked where we're headed from here."

"Oh. Sorry, I didn't sleep the best last night." Colt tried for a tired smile but wasn't sure if he succeeded.

Cash smirked. "So, why couldn't you sleep?"

Colt shot him a warning glare but shrugged. "Had a lot on my mind, I guess." Just like every single night since they'd shown up here and Cash started in on him about Grace.

She glanced between him and Cash several times, but she didn't ask any of the questions he saw lurking in her eyes, and he didn't volunteer any explanations.

Damn Cash. He was having far too much fun with this hypothesis of his.

Colt rubbed his forehead and tried to remember where the hell they were heading from here. Jesus, he needed more sleep. Trying to think was like trying to walk through waist-deep mud.

"Um, there's a rodeo about eight hours from here that Dusty and I talked about going to. I'm pretty sure he's still planning on going to it, but who knows. It's not as big as the one I had originally planned on, but it'll do. The food is worth it, plus it's closer. The light competition makes it a good choice for you to get your feet wet with getting back into breakaway too."

Colt focused his gaze on Cash. "Are you coming too?" He sure fucking hoped not; he needed a break.

"Nah." Cash grinned. "I'll meet up with you guys at the next stop. I know the one you're talking about. The food may be good, but it's too small beans for me. They need to spend less on the eats and boost the loot."

Colt nodded but said nothing more as Grace and Cash resumed their prior conversation. He vaguely wondered if he should worry about how chummy those two had gotten over this past week. At least they were getting along; that was something. He really did want her to like his friends. Even Cash. It seemed important that she did, though he wasn't sure he particularly wanted to examine why.

He turned his attention back to his meal. The sooner they finished eating, the sooner they could get Summer loaded and get out of here. Even after knowing Cash for the majority of his life, he'd never known the man could be such an opinionated busybody. He was over it.

◆

"Need any help with Summer?" Colt battled a yawn and lost while waiting for Grace to answer.

With the shoddy sleep he'd gotten this past week coupled with the long drive to the rodeo, he was well past ready for a nap. Thankfully, it was nearly sundown. He could hardly wait for bed. With any luck, he might be able to actually sleep tonight.

"I'm sure I could manage on my own, but I won't turn down your help," Grace said with a smile. She patted the little mare's neck, and led her down the trailer's ramp and into the rodeo's makeshift barn.

Colt fell into step beside them. "Nervous about competing tomorrow?"

"Hmm, a bit. I think it'd be more surprising if I wasn't, wouldn't it? I mean, I haven't done any roping beyond the practice at Cash's since I was seventeen." She laughed. "Damn, I feel old."

"You're not old, but you are beautiful." Damn it. Was he channeling Cash now or something? It was usually his best friend blurting things out without meaning to, not him.

Her eyes darted to his, a question shimmering in their depths.

He smiled and half-heartedly shrugged. "We may only be friends, but I'm male, and have eyes." He busied himself with filling Summer's water bucket and got it hung on the hook in the horse's temporary stall. "I was thinking we'd sleep in the trailer tonight if that's okay with you. Cash said it's clean and has fresh bedding. The area hotels are all booked up; I checked last night. The only place with any vacancies is about as bad as the horror flick motel from the other day, so I didn't think you'd want to stay there."

Grace made a face. "I'd rather not end up murdered in my sleep or something. No horror flick motels for me, thanks. The trailer will be fine." She put a flake of hay in the hay net hanging in Summer's stall, then glanced at him. "I guess if we're staying right here on the grounds, we won't have to get up so early in the morning too, right?" Her expression turned hopeful. "I'm not actually much of a morning person."

Colt chuckled. "Yeah, we can sleep in." He stepped from the stall and gave her a look. "Why haven't you said anything before now about not being a morning person? You wait until now to tell me that? I've probably been driving you nuts insisting on starting our days so early. I would have made sure you got to sleep in if I'd known."

"Flint." She cringed. "I guess I've gotten too used to not speaking up about things that bug me. Things got bad for me pretty quickly if I did with him, so I learned to keep my mouth shut and deal." She stepped from the stall and secured the door behind herself before turning to look up at him. "I know you wouldn't have gotten mad or anything, but it's a hard habit to unlearn."

He studied her for a moment, then snagged her hand and pulled her to him, wrapping both arms around her. She leaned into him as her arms snaked around him in return, her palms flattening against his back.

"I want you to tell me things like that from now on. At least, try to. Okay? Even if it seems like something silly." One corner of his mouth twitched upward.

She nodded against his chest. "I will." She gave him a squeeze then stepped out of his embrace. Her lips quirked up as she gestured between the two of them. "So, is this hugging thing something we're going to keep doing?"

He knew it probably wasn't the wisest, but he liked holding her too much to stop now. "Yeah, I think so. Unless you don't want to."

Grace laughed. "I'm not complaining. Not at all." Her pale eyes twinkled when she looked up at him.

Colt smiled.

"Hungry yet, Princess? This rodeo has some kickass chicken and noodles at the concession stand. They always start serving it the night before for early arrivals. I wish they'd share the recipe with every other rodeo. It's amazing!"

"Is that the reason you and Dusty chose this rodeo? The food?" she asked.

"Definitely. The prize money itself isn't worth it, but the food sure is. Once you try it, you'll understand."

"Well, that explains how this rodeo keeps people coming back despite the lack of money, then. Everybody knows the way to a man's heart is through his stomach." She fell quiet for a moment then smirked.

"Do I want to know what you're thinking now?" With the mischievous expression settling onto her face, he wasn't entirely sure he did.

"I was thinking that I should have cooked something for you while we were at Cash's place. Maybe then you'd stop thinking of me as just a friend," she teased, her eyes dancing with merriment, then stuck her tongue out at him.

"Ah, I don't know if that's necessary, but I sure won't turn down a homecooked meal. Not that you'll have much opportunity to cook out here on the road."

He could see the questions in her eyes, but she didn't voice them. Thankfully. There was no way he was ready to attempt to explain his confusing emotions to her.

He laughed, hoping to lighten the moment. "We could always get a grill," he offered with a wink.

"A grill might be nice." Grace slipped her arm around his waist and leaned lightly against his side as she steered him toward the concession stand. "For now, though, I think we need to go find that food you mentioned. I'm famished, and it's been forever since I last had chicken and noodles. You going on about it has me really wanting some now."

Colt grinned and slung his arm over her shoulders. "You're in for a real treat. I'll introduce you to Dusty too. I saw him headed that way when I was getting Summer some water."

◆◇◆

They stepped into the horse trailer together, laughing and jostling each other.

Colt felt like he was drunk despite having not drank a drop since his overindulgence at that last afterparty. Grace made him feel so ... light. Like all his troubles were so far away that they couldn't touch him as long as he was by her side. When was the last time he'd felt so carefree? He couldn't remember. It was probably when he was a kid.

Grace slammed to a stop in the middle of the trailer. "Uh... I don't think either of us are going to sleep comfortably on that couch, and there's only the one bed." She looked at him. "How are we sleeping in here?"

Colt shrugged. "I'll sleep on the couch or crash on the floor. You can have the bed." He toed the carpeting that covered the living quarters of the trailer. "The floor in here looks softer than the floor at that one motel was."

He hadn't even finished speaking before she began shaking her head. "No. You're not sleeping on the floor again. I'll take the couch. I'm shorter, so I'll fit better." She sat down on the couch and cringed. "Or maybe I won't. I think there may be a spring poking through the cushion." She jumped back to her feet.

If she wouldn't let him sleep on the floor and the couch was out of commission, what other options were there? He already knew she wouldn't be okay with him leaving the trailer to her and sleeping in his truck.

He eyed the bed. Could he sleep beside her and keep his hands to himself, knowing she'd welcome his touch? Fuck, he didn't know. His self-control was shaky at best when it came to her. He supposed he'd find out; there was no other choice but to give it a shot.

"We'll have to share the bed, then. The only other option is me sleeping in the truck." He turned to her.

She made a face. "You're not sleeping in your truck."

Yeah, he'd figured that would be her answer to that suggestion.

Grace gave the bed a dubious look. "That bed looks awfully small for the two of us, though, especially with the way you usually sprawl out when you sleep. That is only a full-sized mattress if I'm not mistaken."

One corner of his mouth lifted. "We could always spoon again." He got the reaction he was after when her gaze swung over to him and her eyes widened. "I was too drunk to remember if I liked it last time," he said teasingly. Her face flamed, and he chuckled softly. "Nah. I'll behave. I promise. There's plenty of space for both of us."

Grace trailed the fingertips of one hand over his chest, and he lost the ability to breathe as his body reacted in a rush. "What if I don't want you to behave?"

Sparks spread through him like wildfire despite her touch being brief. This woman was going to kill him yet. There were times he wondered if this need for her would ease up if he gave in to it. Gave in to her. His dick was definitely on board with that idea, but Colt wasn't so sure about the wisdom of it. It didn't help that Cash's stupid damn theory was probably right, though he still refused to acknowledge it.

"I don't think that'd be a great idea," he forced himself to say. "Even if you are seriously tempting me."

The smile she turned on him was one of pure female satisfaction. He shook his head at her. That look was trouble for sure.

"Maybe I should be telling you to keep your hands to yourself, huh, Trouble?"

"Trouble? I thought I was Princess." She smiled, clearly feigning innocence. "What did I do to earn a new nickname?"

"You're both, and you know exactly what you did," he grumbled. "This is going to be a rough night, isn't it?"

"It doesn't have to be. You could give in."

He swallowed hard and wondered what the hell was wrong with him to be turning her down. Again. "Yeah, it does. You're not a one-night stand, Grace. You deserve better than that."

She made a frustrated sound and looked away. "I don't see why it has to be a one-night stand. You like me, and I like you. We could have something more if you'd let us."

He didn't know why it had to be either. Not anymore. There was no point in attempting to explain. His reasons all sounded pretty lame, even to him.

When he didn't reply, she sighed and glanced at the bed again. "Fine. We'll share the bed, and we'll behave. But I still don't understand why we can't give this thing between us a try."

Fuck, if she only knew how much he wanted to. To find out where this thing between them might go. But the fear never left him alone. It kept him treading water and dreaming of something that could never be.

Colt seated himself on the couch to pull off his boots. "Geez, you're right. This couch sucks." He'd have to remember to replace it as soon as he had a chance.

He pushed back to his feet and hung his hat on the hook by the door meant for the purpose, then unfastened his belt. He felt her eyes on him as he stripped off his shirt and tossed it on the couch. Would he even be able to sleep tonight? He sincerely doubted it. Having her so close and not allowing himself to touch her was going to be torture.

He unbuttoned his jeans then hesitated. Maybe it would be safer if he slept in them.

Colt nearly snorted at the thought. Yeah, sure, as if having a layer of denim between them would keep him from wanting her.

He lifted an eyebrow at Grace. "You going to get ready for bed, or you gonna stand there gawking at me all night?"

She jolted into motion like she hadn't realized she'd been staring, and he bit back a laugh. Her face colored up all over again.

God, he loved making her blush. It was strangely appealing. He loved it as much as he loved making her smile and laugh.

Grace dug through her suitcase and came up empty-handed. Her gaze flicked over to him. "Do you have something I can wear? Apparently, all of my pajamas are dirty. I didn't even think about laundry while we were at Cash's."

"Sure." He rifled through his duffle bag a moment, then held up a black t-shirt with a bull riding joke printed on it in white. It was one of his favorite shirts. "Will this work? Shit, you'll probably swim in it with as tiny as you are." Especially considering the way he liked his t-shirts slightly oversized. The roominess made them more comfortable, and since his t-shirts were intended to be loungewear, well, comfort was king there.

A slightly tense smile crossed her face as she took it from him. "It'll work. Thank you."

He chuckled. "We'll swing by a laundromat on the way to the next stop."

She nodded then snapped her suitcase shut and ducked into the trailer's tiny bathroom.

Colt took advantage of her being out of the room to step free of his jeans and stretch out on the bed. Thank fuck, it was more comfortable than that damn couch. He folded his arms behind his head and stared up at the ceiling while he waited for Grace to join him.

When the bathroom door opened, he sat up. The moment his gaze landed on her, he knew he was in for another sleepless night. His eyes traced a slow path over her. Tonight was already going to be torture, so why not torment himself a bit further?

He liked seeing her standing there in his shirt. *Really* liked it. His heart rate kicked up as his groin tightened for the second time since they'd returned to the trailer. He shifted on the bed, trying to keep the blanket from making his reaction obvious. Shit, maybe he should have kept his jeans on after all. His boxers weren't going to hide much of anything. Not that his jeans would either, but the thick denim would do a hell of a lot better job of it than the thin cotton.

"I was right," he rumbled. "You're so small compared to me that you could practically use that shirt as a dress."

What was it about her? Over the years, many women had worn one of his shirts from time to time, but none of them had ever looked so damn irresistible in them. It made him want to pull her close and give her exactly what she claimed to want.

He cleared his throat, flipped back the covers on her side of the bed, and patted the mattress. "Coming to bed?" His voice was deeper than normal.

"Yeah." Grace gave him a slightly shy smile then crawled into bed beside him. Her eyes widened. "Oh! The bed is actually comfortable! After the couch, I was worried." She grinned, then snuggled beneath the blanket and rolled to face him, propping herself up on one elbow.

Colt rolled over and mirrored her position. "I was too. We'll replace the couch as soon as possible." His gaze traveled over her face, memorizing her features. For the first time, he noticed that her pale blue irises had a thin ring of darker blue at the outer edges. "You have beautiful eyes," he blurted.

Her eyes weren't the only beautiful thing about her. *Everything* about her was beautiful. Every single thing.

He sucked in a breath. This was such a bad idea, being in bed together, but it felt good. It felt right.

To his relief, she smiled instead of tensing up, like she often did whenever he complimented her.

He reached out and tenderly tucked a few errant strands of her silky hair behind her ear. "Thank you for this evening."

Confusion flickered over her face. "What? I didn't do anything."

"Yeah, you did." A soft smile played on his lips. "I don't know what it is about you, but when I'm with you, I feel… Hell, I don't even know how to explain it. Happy? Content? Alive? I don't know." His shoulder lifted and fell. "After my wife died, it felt like a big part of me had too. I've laughed with you more in the months we've been friends than I have in many years. Tonight especially."

Grace gave him a soft smile of her own. "I'm not sure what to say to that. You're welcome, I guess. Honestly, Colt, I've laughed with you more than I have in many, many years too." She lifted a hand and gently caressed his cheek.

He leaned into her touch, his resistance in tatters.

"You're a good man, Colt Montgomery Boone. No matter what you say." Her lips quirked up. "Maybe too good."

If she only knew how hard he was trying to be as good as she believed he was. To do right by her.

She pulled her hand away and laid her head on the pillow.

Colt rolled onto his back and laid his head down beside hers as he closed his eyes. "Goodnight, Princess."

"Goodnight," she whispered back.

⸺◆⸺

Something tickled Colt's nose, yanking him from sleep. With as long as it had taken him to relax enough to doze off, he was far from ready to be awake.

Annoyed, he rubbed at his nose without opening his eyes. His fingers encountered something soft, and his eyes popped open. It was her hair tickling his nose. He suddenly didn't mind at all. All of his irritation at being awakened faded in an instant.

A drowsy smile crept on his face. At some point in the night, Grace had curled against him. Her head rested on his chest, directly over his heart. He cautiously smoothed down her hair, successfully getting it out of his face before it caused him to sneeze and spoil the moment he was enjoying. He was far from ready to relinquish the contact with her. Holding her like this felt right. He wanted to wake up with her in his arms like this every morning for the rest of his life.

Grace sighed against his chest, her breath fanning out over his bare skin. Goosebumps prickled in its wake. He abruptly became aware that her leg was hooked over his hips when she shifted slightly. Her leg brushed against his rapidly hardening dick, and he barely stifled a groan.

Well, he was definitely awake now. Every single part of him was.

She shifted again, this time her arm, and he realized with regret that she was waking up too. He stroked his fingers up and down over the soft flesh of her arm as she slowly awakened.

"Morning, Trouble," he said huskily as she moved her head to his shoulder and blinked up at him. God, he loved that drowsy look on her.

"Um, good morning." A slow smile spread onto her lips. "Hmm, doesn't seem like I did so good keeping my hands to myself."

He chuckled. "Nope."

"You don't seem to mind."

"Nope." It was taking every bit of his self-control to resist rolling her onto her back to get another taste of her mouth. To not strip his shirt off of her and spend the morning buried deep inside her, making her cry out his name.

He sucked in a ragged breath as her fingers skimmed over his chest. This was hell. Complete hell.

She pulled her leg off of him, inadvertently brushing against his dick again in the process. This time, he couldn't hold back his groan.

She froze, her eyes darting to his. "Colt..." she breathed.

They stared at each other.

His breaths came faster as his heart pounded beneath her hand.

He needed to sit up and get the hell off the bed before his control snapped again, but he couldn't. Her pupils dilated, and her lips parted. There was no mistaking the hunger in her gaze.

Fuck, he wanted her. How was he supposed to keep resisting with her looking at him like that?

"We shouldn't," he grated out.

"So you've said." She smiled sweetly then pressed a kiss to his chest.

He knew right then that he'd lost not just the battle but the whole damn war. It was over. She was the victor. He'd do whatever she wanted.

Her fingers caressed his cheek then skimmed over the stubble covering his jaw. "Kiss me," she implored. "I dare you."

Colt tensed. The challenge shining in her eyes beckoned him closer, and he let it. He never had been able to resist a dare.

There were a million reasons he shouldn't, but right now, he couldn't think of even one. He let himself remember the kiss they'd shared. If it was like that between them every time their lips met, giving in to her now would be worth it.

Chapter 20

"You're playing with fire, Trouble," Colt rumbled as he rolled Grace onto her back and stretched his body over hers, propping himself up on one forearm to keep from crushing her. He enjoyed the surprise that cascaded over her face. "It's not a good idea to dare me."

"Are you sure? It seems like a good idea to me."

He gazed down at her, trying to formulate a response, but it was useless. The damn woman had turned his brain to mush again.

Rather than answering with words, he answered with the kiss she wanted. Unlike the one they'd shared in the motel, this one was tender. His heart hammered in his chest as he deepened the kiss. He was burning alive for her, had been since the day they met.

She flattened her palms against his back and pulled him closer with a soft moan. Her tongue slid against his in a sensual caress, stoking the flames higher.

Staying like this forever sounded pretty damn good to him. To hell with riding bulls. Kissing her was so much better.

She moaned, her fingers digging into his back as if she was trying to draw him even closer. This was dangerous. He knew it, but he couldn't bring himself to pull away from her. Not yet. The taste of her was addictive. He couldn't get enough. The kiss spun out.

Beneath the blanket, his hand moved to her hip. He knew he shouldn't let himself touch her like this, but he no longer cared. This had already gone too far. What was the point of stopping now? If they were going to do this, he intended to worship her body like she fucking deserved. He'd make her feel so good it obliterated any lingering doubts she had about him wanting her.

She gasped against his mouth when his fingers grazed the apex of her thighs, and a faintly crooked smile seated itself on his lips. He lifted his mouth away from hers and met her gaze.

"How far do you want to take this?" he asked, his voice so rough it was nearly a growl. "This is your rodeo."

"That depends on you." Grace tilted her head as she looked up at him. "You told me you'd give me the world if I'd accept it," she said. "I don't want the world, Colt. I just want you." A small smile curled on her lips. One of her hands skimmed his hip. "I don't just want *this*, though." As she spoke, she rubbed his erection through the thin fabric of his boxers.

He gasped and shuddered but didn't stop her. She slid her hand back up his body to rest over his pounding heart.

"I want *this* too." Her fingers tapped the center of his chest lightly.

Emotion surged, so sudden and strong it nearly overwhelmed him. The temptation to tell her he was hers perched on the tip of his tongue, but he couldn't force the words past his lips. It wouldn't be fair. It wouldn't be right.

How could he give her his heart if it still belonged to Sarah? Cash had said there was room to love them both, but Colt wasn't sure he could. He didn't know how to try.

"I don't think I can give you my heart," he rasped, though part of him wondered if she didn't already possess it.

He wanted her hand on him again, without his damn boxers in the way—even knowing it would be a mistake to let her touch him like that. There would be no turning back. He would be hers in every single way that mattered for as long as she wanted him. That wasn't something he was ready for. His dick threatened mutiny at his decision, far from happy about being denied.

"I'm broken, Princess. I don't think I can give you what you need from me."

"How are you ever going to know for sure if you don't try?" The look in her eyes was uncomfortably intense as she gazed up at him. " Try."

He wanted to. He really did, but the stubborn trepidation that hounded him still had too much power.

Instead of agreeing, he leaned down and nuzzled her neck, then nipped her ear. "Let's discuss this more when I can think of something other than burying my cock in you." He needed time to think. Time to consider things.

"So do it."

Colt chuckled and shook his head slightly. No matter how much he wanted to, that was a line he didn't intend to cross this morning. But that didn't mean he couldn't make her feel good.

He tugged the hem of her borrowed shirt. "You've got too many clothes on. I want to see you."

Grace pushed against his chest, and he eased back to give her space to sit up. She yanked the shirt up and over her head then tossed it blindly toward the couch.

She laid back down, trust shining bright in her siren eyes.

His heart squeezed.

"Damn," he murmured as his gaze raked down her body. His dreams had nothing on the reality of her. He swallowed hard.

This had been a bad idea. How the hell was he supposed to keep his dick away from her now? She lay bared to him, other than the pair of lacy dark blue panties that covered her mound. Her nipples pebbled under his gaze, and he smiled.

"You're breathtaking," he breathed, his voice colored with awe.

Her face flushed, but disbelief flashed in her eyes.

"I'm serious, Princess. You're gorgeous. Every fucking inch of you. You captivate me." He skimmed his fingers over her ribcage, enjoying the way her breathing hitched in reaction. It was damn near impossible for him to drag his eyes away from her.

She bit her lip. "Before we go any further, you should know that I'm not on the pill or anything. I quit taking it last year. It gave me horrible side effects and, I-I haven't been touched like this in a very long time. I didn't see a reason to keep suffering."

Colt lifted his gaze to meet her eyes. "Thank you for telling me."

He hooked a finger under the narrow waistband of her panties and tugged while lifting a brow questioningly. She lifted her hips in answer, and he pulled the scrap of fabric off of her. Fully bared to him now, he looked her over. Had Flint been blind along with stupid?

"Happy?" she asked, watching him intently again.

"Absolutely."

He resumed his prior position above her and caught her lips in a scorching kiss while his hand drifted down her body to briefly settle on her hip. With his mouth still on hers, he skimmed his fingers through the soft curls between her thighs, then lower to tease her entrance. She was already soaking wet. He loved it.

A moan escaped her as he eased two fingers into her core. He slowly thrust them a few times, then withdrew.

Grace whimpered. "Don't stop," she begged.

Colt smirked. "Who said I was stopping? I'm just getting started."

He had no intention of stopping until she was a boneless puddle of bliss in the middle of this bed. He'd go grab her breakfast from the concession stand after. If she could walk by the time he was done, he hadn't done right by her.

He trailed kisses along her jaw to her neck, then closed his mouth over her nipple.

She cried out, her back arching. The action pushed her breasts closer.

He loved that sound—her pleasure.

Colt spent a moment lavishing her other breast with attention too, not wanting it to feel left out, then kissed a path back up her body. "You're beautiful," he murmured reverently. "So beautiful." He tapped her chest over her heart. "Especially here."

Her eyes were luminous as she looked up at him. "Kiss me."

Unable to speak the words to express what he was feeling, Colt threw them into this kiss, hoping she'd be able to translate.

Without lifting his mouth from hers, he returned his fingers to the crux of her thighs. He skimmed a fingertip over her clit, drawing a needy moan from Grace. He smiled against her lips, and slowly pushed two fingers back inside her.

Colt had just begun thrusting them, intent on making her cry out his name, when there was a knock on the trailer's door.

They both froze, and their eyes met—Grace's shooting wide in an instant.

He cursed under his breath. For a moment, he contemplated ignoring whoever was out there and continuing. A second louder knock, followed by Dusty's voice, put an end to that notion.

Shit. Colt had forgotten they'd made plans to join him for breakfast this morning, and the kid wasn't likely to go away until he or Grace answered the door. Dusty was nothing if not persistent. Colt muttered another curse as the other cowboy knocked for a third time.

"Be right there," Colt called, annoyance lacing his voice.

While it was probably for the best that they'd been interrupted, it didn't make him—or his dick—any happier about it. He hadn't even had the chance to get her off.

"Sorry," Colt whispered to Grace. He leaned down to kiss her, then slipped his fingers from her body and lifted them to his lips. He wasn't about to give up this chance to taste her. He might not get another.

Their gazes met as he sucked her arousal from his fingers. The unique flavor of her pulled a moan from his throat as it exploded over his tongue. Her face flushed a darker shade of pink even as her gaze flared hotter.

"You'd better answer the door before he knocks again," she whispered.

"He can wait a bit longer," he grumbled. He didn't want to answer the damn door. What he wanted was another taste of her, to hear her cry out his name as he made her come. Too bad that wouldn't be happening. He kissed her again, harder, then reluctantly climbed off the bed and held a hand out to her. "I'll keep Dusty busy while you get dressed."

"Thanks." She accepted his assistance then crossed to her suitcase. After digging around in her remaining clothing a moment, she extracted a clean outfit and ducked into the bathroom.

Colt waited until the door clicked shut behind her, then yanked on his jeans and shoved his feet into his boots. He shrugged into a clean shirt as he headed for the door.

<hr>

Colt shifted on the banquette seat next to Grace. With her free hand resting innocently on his upper thigh, this meal was torture. No matter how much he liked Dusty, Colt would rather be back in the trailer, alone with her, than here in this crowded restaurant, feeding one hunger while the other grew steadily stronger.

It was probably better that they were here, however. He wanted her too much. Despite his plan to get her off this morning while simultaneously keeping his dick in his pants and away from her, he wasn't sure his self-control would have held up. Better to not put it to the test.

Grace waved her fork and tilted her head. Curiosity shined in her eyes as she focused them on Dusty. "What made you decide to start riding bulls, Dusty? I know Colt started because his grandpa rode, but how about you? Did your dad ride or something?"

"Nah. My dad had no interest in rodeo. I doubt he could have ridden a bull if he tried. After my older sister died, he was always too drunk to even think about it." A hint of bitterness laced

Dusty's voice. He paused to take a sip of his coffee. "When I was seven, he passed away too."

"Wow. I'm sorry about your sister and dad," Grace said quietly.

"Thanks. It was a long time ago," Dusty murmured then took a bite of his chicken fried steak.

Colt eyed his friend. How had he never known most of this? They'd been friends for years, and the only people he could remember Dusty ever mentioning were his mom and Levi. Sure, none of them really discussed their pasts much, but still.

"My mom and I moved to a tiny town in Colorado a few months later. Sunset Butte. I doubt you've ever heard of it. Most people haven't." Dusty chuckled. "I think the population was only about 600 people when I lived there. Probably still is. It's definitely a 'don't blink, or you'll miss it' type of place. Anyway, shortly after we moved in, I became friends with our new neighbors' kids, Levi and Destiny."

"I spent more time at Levi and Destiny's place than at home," Dusty continued after chewing and swallowing another bite of his breakfast. "Their dad rode bulls and bareback broncs when he was younger and often told us all stories about his time with the rodeo. It got me curious about the sport. I ate up every scrap of information he said about it. Probably drove him nuts asking questions too. He taught me most of what I know." His expression turned vaguely wistful. "I didn't actually start riding bulls until Destiny said she didn't think I could." His lips quirked upward on one side, making a dimple show itself. "I had to prove her wrong. Ended up joining high school rodeo and have been at it ever since."

Grace smiled. "Do you still talk to her? Destiny."

Dusty's expression shuttered. "No. We had a falling out right before I left for the circuit." He reached for his coffee and took a long sip, then flashed Grace a grin. "I'm still in contact with Levi, though. He's in the army, but we email back and forth a few times a month or whenever he's able. He hasn't been home since he left for boot camp. Unless he came home without telling me, but I doubt that. He's my best friend." He took another sip of coffee, his expression far more solemn than Colt had ever seen it. "Destiny used to be too ... until I screwed things up. We three did everything together."

Grace glanced sideways at Colt then turned her gaze back to Dusty. "That's too bad."

"Brody, Cash, and I ran into Dusty at Finals his second year on the circuit," Colt said, hoping to lighten the mood again. "He's followed us around like a lost little puppy ever since."

Dusty screwed up his face. "A puppy? What the hell, dude?" He picked up a grape from his fruit salad and whipped it at Colt.

Colt caught the fruit in mid-air and tossed it into his mouth. "You're not even twenty-one yet. That makes you the puppy of the group since you're the youngest."

Dusty threw a strawberry at him next. "Brody's only three years older than me. Does that make him a pup too?"

"Nope," Colt said laughingly. "He's a big dog, like Cash and me."

"That's not even fair, man," Dusty groused. His complaint was ruined when he laughed.

Grace looked between him and Dusty then giggled. "Colt's just jealous because he's an old man." She squeezed his thigh and threw him a razz grin. "I'm pretty sure I saw a few gray hairs when he had his hat off earlier."

"Guess that explains why he rarely takes it off," Dusty quipped, grinning.

"What is this, 'pick on Colt' time now?" Colt asked.

"Yep," Dusty and Grace answered in unison before looking at each other and dissolving into laughter.

The corner of Colt's mouth lifted. He shook his head and speared a bite of his omelet. "Eat your food. Both of you," he muttered then popped the bite in his mouth.

⎯⎯◦⎯⎯

Colt scanned the afterparty for familiar faces as he and Grace entered the dark bar. His ride tonight hadn't been as bad as he'd half-expected it would be, but as predicted, his score had been pretty lackluster. Mystic Corkscrew didn't buck well enough to give any rider a score higher than maybe an 83.

While his own ride may not have been awesome, he was proud as hell of Grace. With as out of practice as she claimed to be, her run had been damn good for her first official try in a long time. It had only taken her 3.7 seconds to rope her calf. One hell of a good time for as out of practice as she was. She and Summer were only bound to improve as they got to know each other better.

"Where's Dusty?"

He shrugged. "Doesn't look like he came."

That wasn't altogether surprising. Since Dusty wouldn't be of drinking age for another three months, he rarely showed up to the afterparty. No doubt if he were here, he'd be surrounded by a gaggle of buckle bunnies and female fans about now. He attracted them like flies to horseshit. The kid normally had a group of them following him around, hanging on his every word.

Maybe that was another reason he so infrequently showed up at the afterparty. Colt knew firsthand how the constant attention could cause you to feel smothered.

"That's too bad," Grace said.

Colt glanced down at her and chuckled. "Probably a good thing he's not here. I don't think I'm ready to have you two gang up on me again anyway."

After they'd gotten started, the duo hadn't let up until breakfast was over and it'd been time to head out. It was great to know she got along with at least two of his friends. The jury was still out about Brody. When he'd introduced them a while back, it'd been awkward to say the least.

The bar wasn't very crowded tonight. Colt could still hear country western music over the dull roar of the conversations going on around them. That was novel. It was often so loud at the afterparty that it was difficult to have any sort of conversation without having to yell.

He turned back to Grace. "What would you like to drink?"

"Uh, water with a slice of lemon, please. One of us has to stay sober to get us back to the trailer in one piece."

"I wasn't planning on getting drunk tonight. You can get whatever you want." She shook her head, and he shrugged. "Okay. If you change your mind, let me know." He nodded toward a collection of tables in the corner. "Why don't you see if you can find us a table while I get our drinks?"

Once she walked away, he headed for the bar.

"So, you're not much of a drinker?" Colt asked once he seated himself at the table she'd found them. He handed her both the water she'd requested, along with the truck's keys.

If it made her feel better, he would happily oblige her. He could swear she'd drank a time or two when she'd joined him at an afterparty while she'd been working, but maybe he was misremembering. His memory wasn't the greatest anymore. Too many concussions.

"I am. I'm not a fan of getting into vehicles with people who've been drinking the harder stuff, though, even if they don't seem drunk. And I hate riding in cabs," Grace answered with a laugh.

"I guess that makes sense." He grinned. "Are you one of those 'frilly, fruity drink' kinds of women, or do you like the harder stuff? Like this?" He held up his tumbler of whiskey then took a sip, waiting for her answer.

"Oh, I definitely like it hard." Mischief danced in her eyes.

Caught off-guard by her comment, Colt choked. He coughed and sputtered for a couple of minutes before he finally regained his ability to speak. "Damn, woman, are you trying to kill me?"

"Never." She smirked. "I would like to finish what we started this morning, however."

His brows lifted. "Alright, who are you and what have you done with the real Grace Parker?"

Her slim shoulders rose and sank as her expression sobered. "Maybe this is the real me. The me I was before Flint, or at least some version of her." She laughed, but there was no humor in the sound. "Before him, I was so confident. Not much scared me. Sometimes I really miss those days, you know? I get so tired of being afraid and lonely all the time. Life has gotten so complicated. I want to be me again."

He liked the current Grace Parker just fine. He couldn't blame her for missing the days before the abuse, however. In her shoes, he probably would long for them too.

She took a sip of water then looked back up at him. "I want you to stop being so darn complicated too. How do I get you to let me in and take a chance on me? Isn't it lonely there behind all your walls?"

Colt didn't have a clue how to respond to that. He stared blankly at her, trying in vain to come up with an answer. "Grace—" He chewed on his words some more. "I don't think I even remember how to let anyone new in." He paused to take a fortifying sip of his whiskey.

"Do I get lonely? Hell yeah, I do, but I can't go through what happened with her again. I can't open myself to the potential of experiencing that kind of pain again. I won't. Loving someone hurts." His gaze traveled to the people milling around the small bar. This was so not the place for this conversation.

"It doesn't always. Geez, Colt, I'm broken too! After everything that happened to me, shouldn't I be the one with the fortress around my heart, afraid to let anyone new in for fear they'll turn out like Flint, or worse? I should! But I'm not. That makes me either stupid or braver than you."

Her voice was rising. It was beginning to draw attention he really didn't want.

"Let's continue this conversation outside." He tossed back the remainder of his whiskey in one swallow and got to his feet. After this discussion, he might end up getting drunk after all.

He offered her his hand, but she ignored it as she stood and led the way out of the bar. Colt followed at a slower pace. Outside, he warily watched as Grace leaned back against the brick wall that made up the side of the building.

"You're not stupid, Princess," he finally said. "You're braver than me. I may be a bull rider, but I'm not immune to being scared. I'm afraid of more than I'll ever admit to. I don't have the luxury of showing it; I have a reputation of being fearless to uphold."

He yanked off his hat and shoved splayed fingers through his hair, then jammed it back down on his head before moving toward her. He locked eyes with her. "I shouldn't tell you this, but you scare me."

"Why?"

"Jesus, Grace, because I don't want to be just friends with you either, damn it!"

Her eyes widened, and her mouth fell open.

"I never have. Not from the first time I laid eyes on you at that auction. I want more with you. I want to be what you want me to be. What you need." He rubbed a hand roughly over his face and took a deep breath. "I'm pretty sure you could change everything, and it scares the hell out of me. This is somewhere I never thought I'd be again. Shit, it's nowhere I ever wanted to be. I'm not sure I'm ready for this. There's a good chance I never will be."

"Like I said this morning, how are you ever going to find out if you don't try?" Grace asked gently. Her pale eyes roamed over his face—soft, patient. She took a small step toward him. "What if your broken pieces and mine would fit together perfectly and make us both whole? What if this could be it? What if we don't give this thing between us a chance and we both miss out?"

He clenched his jaw and began pacing restlessly. He'd never tell her, but he'd wondered the same things himself more than once. If only she knew how badly he wanted to give her what she wanted from him. But he couldn't. He needed to pull things back, get some space. He didn't know how to explain his chaos to her. How to get her to understand.

"Colt."

He stopped and swung his gaze back to her. "What, Trouble?"

She caught his hand and pulled him toward her, then caressed his cheek as she gazed up at him.

Against his better judgement, he leaned into the gentle touch. The look in her eyes was killing him.

"Kiss me."

He tensed. "That's not a good idea." Despite his words, he moved closer. His chest rose and fell faster as he caged her against the wall with his arms and the press of his body.

"Kiss me," she repeated, firmer this time. Her eyes held him captive as she slid her hands up his chest. "Please?"

He groaned in surrender, lowering his mouth to hers. Why was he so weak for this woman? One hand landed on her hip and pulled her tight against him. "You're going to be the death of me," he whispered, then nipped her ear before kissing a path along the slim column of her neck. "Either that, or you're going to make me completely lose my mind. I'm a bull rider, baby. I don't have much mind left to lose."

"I said kiss me, Eight, not gab at me."

A crooked grin crossed his lips before he gave her what she wanted. Shit, what he wanted too.

He loved kissing this woman. Loved hearing her moans, her whimpers of pleasure.

Her fingers gripped his dusty western shirt tight as their lips collided again, harder this time.

Passion flowed from him with all the unrelenting power of a tsunami. Somewhere deep inside him, something cracked wide open. Something he'd fought hard to keep protected. He transferred his grip to her thighs and lifted her, demanding entrance to her mouth. She wrapped her legs around his waist with a muffled moan and parted her lips for his invasion.

How had a chance encounter at an auction led to this? Maybe fate was real, after all. If it was, he thanked its existence. He wouldn't want to miss this. No fucking way.

Colt groaned and ground his hips against her, letting her feel what she did to him. Her fingers curled around his nape, clutching him tightly to her while her tongue stroked against his in a sensual dance that stoked the flames higher. An inferno burned between them. Hot. Out of control.

He vaguely wondered how heated his blood could get before he spontaneously combusted. This kiss was likely to make him find out.

"Jesus," he muttered when they were forced to break apart to catch their breaths.

This kiss had been unlike any of the others they'd shared. Those had been admittedly mind-blowing, but this one ... this one was cataclysmic. With this kiss, she'd blown right through every single one of his walls, leaving him feeling raw and exposed.

He leaned his forehead against hers as he struggled to regain his breath, and at least a portion of his wits. After a few seconds, he eased her back to her feet, keeping hold of her hips as much to keep his own balance as to steady her. She looked about as stunned as he felt.

"Keep kissing me like that, Princess, and I might have to marry you." He froze, his eyes widening slightly as he realized what he'd said.

Where the fuck had that come from, and why the hell had he said it out loud?

His feelings for her hit him with stunning clarity.

Damn it. Cash was right. The truth was impossible to deny any longer. Colt was in love with this woman.

His stomach knotted as his heart rate picked back up all over again. A bubble of panic built within him. This was too much.

He dropped another kiss on her lips, hoping she'd let his remark go without comment.

"Geez, talking about marriage already?" Grace teased. "I think we should probably date first."

He laughed, but it sounded weird even to his ears. Colt released her hips and strode several steps away before turning to look back at her. His thoughts ran wild. The urge to bolt was overwhelming.

This morning he'd stepped over the line he'd drawn between them, and then he'd danced all over it with this kiss tonight. Now he was paying for it. He needed to get away from her for a while, get his head back on straight and his feelings locked down.

She frowned, seeming to realize something was wrong. "Are you okay?" She laid her hand on his arm, and he jumped like she'd electrocuted him. Her brow furrowed. "Colt?"

The bubble of panic burst. He felt too raw. Too full of conflicting emotions.

"I'm sorry. I need a moment." He dropped a kiss on her forehead as she stared at him with a mixture of confusion and concern. "Go back to the trailer whenever you're ready. I'll be back. I ... just need a minute."

He took off walking, uncertain where he was going and, frankly, not caring.

Chapter 21

GRACE GLANCED AT HER phone for the tenth time since she returned to the horse trailer. It was almost 1 a.m. now and Colt still hadn't come back. She had no idea what was happening, why he'd taken off the way he had, or where he'd gone. Though she probably had a right to be angry right now, she was more worried about him than anything else. He'd seemed upset about something, but she couldn't think of what it might have been.

She rubbed at her temples, hoping to relieve the stress headache that'd settled in since she returned to the trailer alone. Had it been the kiss? Their conversation?

She'd already texted him three times and had called once with no answer. Had she pushed him too hard tonight? Even if she had, she couldn't bring herself to regret it. This morning had been unexpected but wonderful. If Dusty hadn't interrupted them, she wondered how far Colt would have let it go. And tonight's kiss... Well, that had been unlike anything she'd ever experienced in her life. Not even their first kiss had been so intense. So hot. To her, it had been worth it.

Should she go out and look for him? She paced the trailer's small living quarters and tried to decide.

Her phone chirped from its spot on the nearby counter and Grace dove for it, slamming her shoulder on the edge of the kitchenette's cabinets in the process. She hissed out a breath and rubbed at it with one hand while opening the message with the other.

Colt

> Go to sleep Princess. I'll be back in the morning. I'm with Dusty.

Grace closed her eyes, her head falling forward as her muscles relaxed. She exhaled a big breath, then opened her eyes and tapped out a quick reply.

Grace

> Are you okay? What happened?

It took him so long to reply she almost thought he wasn't going to.

Colt

> I'm good. We'll talk in the morning. Sleep well.

At least she knew where he was now, and that he was safe. She tapped out one last reply.

Grace

> Goodnight

With a sigh, she sat her phone back on the counter then locked the door. She might as well go to bed if he wasn't returning tonight. Since they still hadn't done laundry, she stole another of Colt's t-shirts from his bag to wear to bed. If he didn't like it, too bad. Maybe he shouldn't have run off and left her worrying about him for hours on end.

Grace lifted the shirt to her nose and inhaled. Even clean, it smelled of him.

It was ridiculous how much she liked him. She hadn't expected to be here again, pining after a man. Maybe she was insanely stupid for it, but she couldn't bring herself to care.

She stripped off her clothes and tossed the shirt on over her head, relishing the way his scent enveloped her like a hug.

Flint had been a mistake from the very start. She'd been hesitant to date him at all, but he'd known all the right things to say to win her over and talk her into letting down her guard. She hadn't even liked him, not really. Thinking about it now, she was certain she had never loved him either. He certainly hadn't loved *her*. Between him flirting with other women and all the abuse, that was a pretty obvious fact. People who loved you didn't hurt you like that, and they definitely didn't attempt to kill you.

Colt was nothing like him. She trusted him explicitly, though she didn't entirely know why or how she knew it was safe to. That was something she couldn't explain; she just knew. The how and why weren't important. And at some point, she'd fallen in love with him. Her best friend.

She'd realized it the morning she woke up to him spooning her. Not that she'd tell him. Oh geez, that'd make him bolt for a place to hide like a spooked rabbit, for sure.

"Time for bed, Whinny," she muttered to her little plush horse as she snatched it off the couch. She snuggled it against her chest while she crawled into bed. If she couldn't snuggle with Colt, the stuffed animal would have to do. Not that it was even remotely close to being a suitable replacement. There was no substitute for him.

Perhaps it was a little odd for a twenty-five-year-old woman to still sleep with stuffed animals, but it'd always been a simple way to comfort herself in the messed-up world she'd grown up in. Her adoptive parents had been good people, but they'd fought constantly. The house had often been tense and chaotic. Cuddling a stuffed animal had helped. She'd kept up the habit for as long as she'd been allowed to have one.

Flint had thought it was childish and stupid. One day while she was at work, he'd taken her last two stuffed animals out into the yard and burned them. By that point, any money she managed to get her hands on was dog-eared for her escape, so replacing them hadn't exactly been a priority. At least that was something she never had to worry about with Colt. He respected her, for one. He thought her stuffed-critter habit was cute too.

Grace curled up beneath the blanket and let her mind drift over the events of the day. She wasn't sure where this thing with Colt was going, but she hoped it was somewhere good. She fell asleep with a smile on her face.

A faint beam of light was streaming in the window when her phone went off and woke her. Thinking it might be Colt, she yawned and slipped out of bed to grab it.

Geez, what time was it? The sun wasn't very high in the sky when she glanced out the window so it couldn't possibly be all that late yet. Ugh. She would never be a morning person.

She carried her phone back to bed with her and burrowed beneath the blanket before flipping open her phone. Eh, 7 a.m.; not as early as she'd thought. It was still far too early for her tastes, especially with as late as it'd been when she went to bed. She opened her text messages, and her heart nearly stopped.

It was Flint, not Colt. The first she'd heard from him in a couple of days.

His continued messages should probably scare her, but they didn't. Not anymore. Sure, they had at first, especially that first morning after she'd shown up at Colt's motel. But now, she'd started to expect to receive at least one text from Flint each day. He rarely disappointed there. He used to tell her she was nothing special, that she bored him. If that was true, why wouldn't he leave her alone?

She only read the first few words before deleting the message and tossing the phone on the bed beside her. He could apologize and swear he'd never do it again if she'd come back all he wanted, but she didn't buy it. It was more of his lies. He'd used the same tactic to keep her from leaving time and time again in the past for far less serious offenses. She wasn't stupid. It wouldn't work on her anymore. Never again.

He'd proven himself to be a monster. She wasn't foolish enough to think he wouldn't make her pay—probably with her life—for breaking his finger.

Grace flopped back against her pillow and closed her eyes. There was no chance she'd be able to doze back off now. How did she get Flint to leave her alone? She wished she knew. Though she felt horrible for it, she almost wished he'd find some other woman to take her place. While they'd been together, he'd flirted with every woman they came across. Why couldn't he take up with one of them and leave her the hell alone? She wanted to move on. Needed to.

No matter how many times she blocked his number, he kept finding a way to keep coming back, to keep harassing her. How did she get him to stop?

She groaned. Colt might believe this nightmare had an end, but she was far from convinced.

Grace wasn't sure how long she'd been laying there before she heard the door rattle, followed by familiar footsteps on the stairs.

"It's about time you came back," she muttered as she reluctantly opened her eyes and pushed up on her elbows to peer at Colt.

At least he looked contrite, and it smelled like the bag he carried in with him contained food. Good man. Food was a pretty good way to gain forgiveness from her. Unless your name was Flint.

Colt shuffled from foot to foot then scrubbed a hand over the back of his neck, fastening his gaze on the worn carpeting. "I'm sorry. I feel like a complete ass for running away last night. I just ... I panicked. I guess I felt overwhelmed." He lifted his gaze to hers. "You make me feel things I don't know how to handle, most of them stronger than I've ever experienced."

Her heart flipped. Was that why kissing him was so ... profound? As though he were unleashing a torrent of emotion each and every time their mouths met.

She knew how much he'd loved his wife. Correction, how much he loved his wife. Sarah might be gone, but his love for her remained. It'd been obvious from the very first time he'd mentioned her in their early conversations. If what he felt for Grace was stronger than anything he'd felt before, what did that mean? Did it mean he might love *her* too, or at least was leaning that way? The idea seemed preposterous, but a seed of hope sprouted in her heart nonetheless.

She scrambled off the bed, tugging down the hem of her borrowed shirt as she stood. "I won't say it's okay because it's not okay that you took off like that, but I forgive you. Yesterday was intense."

That was putting it lightly. When she'd dared him to kiss her, she'd half expected him to refuse. To back off. She hadn't thought he'd actually do it, or that he'd let things go as far as they had. It'd been delicious. It'd left her wanting more.

One corner of her mouth curved upward. "I wouldn't mind repeating it, minus the interruption."

"It can't. Yesterday was a mistake. It should never have happened." He grimaced and rocked from foot to foot again, then ripped off his hat and tossed it onto the couch. "I'm fucking this up. I'm supposed to be apologizing, not making things worse. I'm sorry."

"Why? I don't understand. Please, explain to me why we can't give this thing between us a try."

He plunged both hands through his hair then began pacing. Conflict swirled plain as day in his eyes.

"And don't cheapen what happened between us, Colt. It wasn't a mistake. I refuse to believe that."

He groaned. "You're right. It wasn't a mistake, but it still shouldn't have happened. I shouldn't have let things go that far. I'm sorry. What I need to do is keep my damn hands, lips, and every other part of me to myself from now on." He rubbed a hand over his face. "I don't know how to explain this mess in my head, Princess. I would if I knew how."

"Try. Please? Try to explain. I want to understand. What are you afraid of?"

Colt blew out a ragged breath but didn't answer.

Grace caught hold of his hand, stopping him from pacing. She stepped around in front of him and gazed up into his eyes. "Hey, talk to me. Please?" she softly urged.

He swallowed twice in rapid succession then nodded. "Losing my wife nearly killed me," he said quietly.

Her breath caught. She was glad it hadn't, that he was still here. That she'd had the opportunity to meet him even if this thing between them never went anywhere.

He pulled his hand from her grasp but didn't take his gaze from hers. His eyes seemed to plead with her as he continued, "Sarah was my world. She was my everything. I loved her so much." He shook his head slowly. "I-I can't do this again." His voice broke on the words. Colt cleared his throat. "The idea of letting anyone in like that ever again scares the hell out of me. No, terrifies me."

He inhaled a shuddering breath and resumed pacing.

The pain in his expression was killing her. She didn't know what to say, what to do.

"I can't. I want to let you in. I really do. But I just ... can't. I'm not sure I can love anyone new like they deserve to be. Like *you* deserve to be. I don't know that I want to try. Call me a coward, I guess." He cringed and stopped to look at her.

She ached to hug him, to wrap her arms around him tight and comfort him somehow. Only the uncertainty of how he'd react kept her from giving in to the impulse.

"If I let you in, if I open my heart to you, and then were to lose you too, I don't think I'd survive this time." He ducked his head and resumed pacing. "I like you, Grace. I really do, but I ... can't do this."

Her heart cracked in half. "Can't, or won't? It sounds more like won't to me."

"Both, I guess."

"What if we took things slow? Just one day at a time?" she couldn't keep from asking. "It's not all or nothing. We could ease into it."

He stopped and faced the kitchenette's countertop, bracing himself against it with both hands, and bowed his head. "Grace," he said, then groaned. "I can't." He sighed.

Her brow furrowed. She understood his fear, but she couldn't promise nothing would ever happen to her. Nobody could make a promise like that. Life was uncertain, unpredictable.

She moved toward him and tentatively laid a hand on his arm. His already rigid muscles tensed further under her touch.

"We're friends. Good friends. Don't they say friendship is the backbone of the best relationships? We could be happy. Nobody knows what life has in store for us. It's impossible to know. You're a bull rider, Eight. You could climb on a bull tomorrow, and I could lose *you*. The prospect of that scares the hell out of *me*, but being with you would be worth the risk. You're worth the risk!"

He closed his eyes and clenched his jaw but said nothing.

Her heart sank. She removed her hand from his arm and backed away. This conversation was going nowhere. She looked up at the ceiling in frustration, then pinned her gaze on Colt's back. "So, let me get this straight. You have feelings for me, stronger than anything you've felt before, but you're not going to do anything about it?"

Colt turned around and looked at her. "How the hell am I supposed to move on when wanting you makes me feel like I'm cheating on her?"

Her eyes widened as her mouth fell open. She rocked back on her heels as she struggled to come up with a response. All at once, she understood. The tortured look dimming his normally vivid eyes bothered her. She'd caused that by asking him for something he wasn't ready for. By wanting more when he'd already given her so much.

What the hell was wrong with her for pushing him how she had? She turned away, unable to stand seeing that look in his eyes any longer.

Grace wrapped her arms around her middle, her shoulders rounding forward. "I'm sorry," she whispered. "For making you feel that way." A band of tightness encircled her chest, and a lump rose in her throat. "I'm so sorry."

"You have nothing to apologize for."

But she did. She so did. It was her fault he was feeling this way. Hers. How could she have been so thoughtless? So selfish? She finally understood.

Her chin trembled.

She took a hitching breath, then jerked her head at the bag he'd brought with him. "What did you bring?"

"Nothing fancy. Some breakfast sandwiches."

She grabbed the bag off the stand where he'd sat it and withdrew both sandwiches, handing him one. They still felt warm. She unwrapped hers and took a small bite, though her stomach was roiling from their conversation and the agony she'd seen in his eyes. The ham, egg, and cheese sandwich was pretty good.

She offered Colt a tight smile. "Thanks for breakfast."

He unwrapped his own and took a bite. "It is pretty good. This is the first I've tried one. It seemed like the easiest option today, considering I didn't know if you'd be awake or even here at all."

Her eyes widened. "Why wouldn't I be here? Where else would I be?"

Colt lifted his shoulders in a half-hearted shrug. "I don't know, but I wouldn't have blamed you if you'd taken off. I really am sorry for last night. I'm an asshole. Another reason I don't deserve you."

She glanced over at him. His expression was shuttered now, his emotions hidden. Colt's gaze was on the nearby stand, his body still radiating near palpable waves of tension.

"Stop, Colt. I'm okay. Yeah, I'm disappointed, and more than a little frustrated, but I understand. Please, let it be."

His gaze flicked over to her, and he swallowed hard.

"I just ... don't want to lose you. I can't."

"You're going to lose your head if you don't stop it!" she snapped as the frustration simmering inside her boiled over. "I'm trying to drop the subject."

He held up his hands in mock surrender as a crooked grin crept onto his face. "You're adorable when you get mad."

She scowled. "You're so freaking aggravating!" She threw away her sandwich wrapper, stomped over to her suitcase and extracted a clean outfit, then darted into the tiny bathroom to change.

"I might be aggravating," he called through the door. "But you still like me."

She glared at the thin door separating them, even though he couldn't see it. Grace gave him a dirty look as she left the bathroom a moment later, then balled up her borrowed shirt and whipped it at his head.

Colt smirked and caught it effortlessly. "I like seeing you in my shirts."

"Yeah? Well, I kinda like wearing them," she said quietly. A small smile crept onto her lips. "They smell like you; it's like you're hugging me."

Their eyes met and held. An answering smile slowly curled his lips upward, and her stomach jumped. Something indefinable flickered in his eyes, making the atmosphere inside the trailer's small living quarters crackle.

He took a step toward her, and then another. She tipped her head up to gaze at him when he stopped directly in front of her. He was so close she could feel the warmth of his body. What was happening?

Her lashes fluttered shut as he stroked the back of his fingers across her cheek.

"I really am sorry about last night," he murmured.

She opened her eyes, and their gazes met once more. His was intense, some tender emotion swirling in the depths of his eyes. Those ocean blue depths were a whirlpool, threatening to pull her under their spell. She'd happily let them.

Her stomach quivered, and her pulse kicked up. "I know," she breathed, half-afraid to move for fear the spell would shatter.

His chest rose and fell faster as he shifted closer. He cupped her cheek and swept the calloused pad of his thumb across her bottom lip as his gaze homed in on them. He dropped his head toward hers a fraction, then paused.

Was he about to kiss her again despite claiming this thing between them couldn't happen?

She tensed, in agony, as she waited to see what he'd do. She mentally begged him to do it. To give in.

Grace leaned her face into his palm as her lips parted in invitation. Slowly, hesitantly, his lips lowered to hers—the barest sweeping contact at first, then again with more pressure.

He groaned. His free hand moved to her hip and dragged her lower half flush up against him.

The moment she tried to deepen the kiss, he backed away from her so suddenly it nearly upset her balance. She grabbed the nearby stand to keep from toppling over.

The look he gave her held a multitude of emotion all mixed together.

Colt rubbed a hand over his mouth, almost angrily. "I need to go grab my gear. Find me when you're ready to go," he said, his voice rough. Then he stomped out the door.

Grace stared after him long after he was gone.

What the hell was that?

She took a deep, shaky breath and shoved her feet into her boots before walking out the door herself. Summer still needed to be loaded before they could get on the road. There wasn't time to wonder about Colt right now.

◆

Grace stared down at the phone in her hand as despair spread through her veins and poisoned the happiness she'd found traveling with Colt.

How did Flint always seem to know when she was starting to relax again? It was as though he was watching her somehow. The thought made her shiver and glance around.

For a while he'd been mostly quiet, but not today. In the hour since Colt stormed out of the trailer, her phone had gone off no less than twenty times. The first couple, she'd thought it was Colt, but no. It was Flint. Always Flint.

Her phone buzzed as a new text came through, and she fought the urge to throw it. She didn't want to see anything more from him. Her text alert went off three more times in rapid succession. With reluctance, she glanced at the messages and her blood turned to ice.

Flint

> Got myself a gun today. It's a real beauty. You should see it. Maybe soon you will. Maybe your new boyfriend will too.

> You're mine, Grace. Mine! Maybe you need a reminder.

> Leave him, or I'll force you to leave him.

> Just imagine… Bang! One dead cowboy. Who will keep you from me then?

A cold sweat broke out all over her body and her legs gave out, landing her in a heap on the ground.

No. Oh, no. What was she going to do? She couldn't stay here. She couldn't risk Flint hurting Colt. These weren't the sort of messages she'd grown used to receiving long ago. These were different. His threats toward her were familiar, but he'd never aimed any at Colt before.

Her heartbeat thumped loudly in her ears. Grace covered her face with trembling hands, a small whimper escaping her. What was she going to do? She didn't want to go, but she couldn't stay either. She couldn't let anything happen to Colt. She couldn't.

Grace wrapped her arms around her middle and opened her eyes. Her gaze lifted to the horizon, toward the cowboy's locker room where Colt probably was right now. The thought of Flint following through on his threat was petrifying. There was a good chance it was a bluff, like so many of Flint's threats had been in the past, but she couldn't risk it. He was too unpredictable. She hadn't thought he'd ever raise his hand to her either, but he had, and it hadn't stopped there. Flint was a good shot. She remembered that from going to the range with him before their relationship turned sour. It was too risky. She was going to have to give in to his demands and leave.

Where was she going to go? She needed time to figure it out. Would she be safe on the circuit without Colt by her side? That was debatable.

Her heart broke into thousands of tiny pieces. She didn't want to leave. She couldn't lose Colt. When would this nightmare end? Would it ever?

Her phone went off twice more, and she bit down hard on her tongue to keep from screaming. She couldn't take any more of this. No more. Rather than opening the newest messages, she hit delete on all of them then shut her phone completely off. It was impossible to think about where she was going to go when Flint kept blowing up her phone.

Grace inhaled a ragged breath and forced herself to her feet. This was what Flint wanted, to make her afraid. Sitting in a heap on the ground would solve nothing.

She tucked the device into her pocket and glanced at the horse trailer. Summer would start making a fuss if they didn't get on the road soon. The horse wasn't a fan of being trailered for long, and they still needed to stop to do laundry at some point.

After taking a series of deep breaths in a futile effort to settle her nerves and hopefully conceal her fear, she headed for the cowboy's locker room in search of Colt.

Chapter 22

Colt leaned back in the flimsy plastic chair near the laundromat's huge front window, his gaze resting on Grace. She was frowning at her phone again, and he wondered why. He'd heard her text alert go off at least six times in the short time they'd been here. Each time, she'd seemed to become more tense.

The seat she'd chosen was on the opposite side of the seating area from him. It was as far away as she could get without sitting in the truck. After the shit he'd pulled last night and this morning, he didn't blame her. He was pretty pissed off at himself too. It bothered him that she was upset, but he didn't know how to go about setting things right. He'd fucked up in a big way. Simply saying sorry, again, wasn't going to cut it. Maybe it was a good thing that she wasn't talking to him right now. He didn't trust himself with her. Not anymore.

Her phone chimed yet again, and she jumped to her feet. As he watched, she headed for the exit with long, rapid strides.

He bounced to his feet to follow. Something more was clearly going wrong today than what happened this morning. He'd bet his life savings it had to do with Flint.

Colt found her outside the laundromat doors, looking on the verge of bursting into tears. His brows snapped together. "What's going on, Princess?"

She jolted and whirled around to face him. Her eyes were enormous, as though she'd been so pre-occupied with reading whatever was on that screen that she hadn't heard him approach.

"Woah. Easy. It's just me." He held his hand out to her, palm up. "Can I see, please?"

Grace nibbled her lip, her gaze dropping to the pavement at their feet. Just when he thought she was going to refuse, she sighed and handed her phone to him.

His heart sank as he read the texts. He'd been right about it being Flint. There were so many messages and all from today alone. Some of them had a friendly tone. Others were angry. Still more contained a variety of threats.

He couldn't care less about the threats against himself, but the ones toward her were unacceptable. Colt looked up. "How long has this been going on?"

She shrugged as though it didn't matter. "Since I left him. He never really stopped. This is the most in one day, but I've gotten at least one almost every day since I left him." Her shoulders hunched. "I normally delete them without reading any. I tried blocking his number, many times, but it didn't stop him. Nothing stops him."

Fuck. He hadn't known. How could he not have known? Thinking about it now, he remembered the times her phone would go off and she'd tense for a moment. He should have asked. She shouldn't have needed to deal with this nonsense all this time.

"You should have told me. I don't know how, but I'd have taken care of it." He clicked the button to delete the messages. "We need to change your number. We should have done that the morning after you showed up at my motel room. I didn't even think about it."

Grace was still staring at the ground. She looked so damn defeated, and it ate at him.

"I'm so sorry, Princess."

"It's not your problem to deal with," she said flatly. "I never should have dragged you into this. It was a mistake for me to come here. I've been nothing but a complication in your life."

Her words slammed into his gut like a freight train. Was that really what she believed? Fuck, had he done something to cause her to think that?

"That's not true. I enjoy having you here with me, and I care about you!" His stomach clenched.

What was happening? He didn't like this, at all. Did she really think she was a burden to him? He racked his brain trying to figure out what he'd done or said to cause her to feel that way.

"Your problems are my problems, Princess." Colt moved to give her the hug she seemed to need so badly, but she flinched and dodged his touch. The fingers of his unoccupied hand flexed as he dropped it back to his side with a frown. His eyes widened with surprise and his heart panged, warning bells going off in his head.

Something was seriously wrong. She never avoided his touch. Not in ages.

Something had clearly shifted between them since this morning, and not in an agreeable direction. The distance growing between them worried him. It didn't bode well.

Grace sighed heavily and shifted on her feet before holding her out for her phone. "I'll call and get my number changed soon. You're right that I probably should have changed it the moment I left him. I didn't think about it either," she said dispiritedly.

He handed her phone back while watching her warily. Everything about her demeanor was off, even her tone. The warning bells in his head clanged louder.

"Are you okay, Grace?"

"Yep. Fine." She flashed him a smile that didn't meet her eyes. "I'm sure the dryers are likely done by now. I'm sure Summer would like to get out of the trailer too. Let's get moving."

She turned and went back into the laundromat—leaving him standing outside alone, staring after her.

Colt absently applied rosin to his bull rope, his mind on Grace rather than his task. She had hardly spoken to him at all since their brief discussion about her phone at the laundromat a week ago. The silence between them since had been heavy, almost oppressive. The longer it stretched, the more it felt like it was going to crush him.

He wished he knew what was happening. She hadn't said anything about leaving him yet, but he suspected it was coming. It didn't seem like she wanted to be with him anymore. Gone was the laughter and conversations he'd come to love so much. These days, she was silent unless she absolutely needed to speak to him. When she did, it was curt though not unkind. There were no smiles. The teasing flirtation had evaporated. She actively avoided his touch, giving him a wide berth at all times to keep from even accidently brushing against him. It hurt and confounded him. She seemed to have pulled away from him completely, and he didn't know what the hell to do to fix it.

Was it his fault? He knew he'd upset her the morning it all started, but he hadn't thought this would be the result. He hadn't wanted this. She'd said she was fine, that things between them were okay. But they were anything but.

Could Flint's messages have caused this?

Colt inwardly groaned, unable to figure out what happened any more now than he'd been able to every single day of the past week. How the hell could he make her smile again? How could he set things right between them? He missed her. He really fucking missed her.

"Hey."

Colt glanced over at Brody as his friend stepped up next to him to rosin his own rope. "Hey. Who'd you draw tonight?" He needed to get his mind off of Grace and onto his ride. Being distracted tonight wasn't an option with the bull he'd drawn.

"Fly High," Brody said with a broad grin.

That brindle bull was sure money. He bucked well, and Brody had covered him multiple times in the past—once, to a 90 score. It was no wonder he was looking like the cat that ate the canary.

"I've got Copycat Illusion."

Brody made a face. "Oof, rough draw. Sorry, man."

It hadn't gone well the last time Colt drew this bull. He'd gotten bucked off at four seconds in, and the rank animal trampled him after. That wreck had left him with three broken ribs and a busted collarbone. He'd been lucky it hadn't been worse. That had been nearly five years ago, however; hopefully, tonight would go better. It might if he could focus.

"Hey, while you're here... I wanted to ask you something about that chick you've been traveling with."

Colt tensed. "What about her?"

"I was wondering, are you two, uh, together? I don't want to step on your toes or anything, but man, she's a beauty!"

Colt's first impulse was to say yes, to claim Grace as his own. The idea of her being with anyone else vexed him more than he was willing to admit. They weren't dating, though. He had no right to say that they were.

Did he want to be dating her? He wasn't entirely sure of that answer. Once upon a time, the answer would have been an immediate no, but now ... the answer wasn't so simple. Maybe.

Shit, considering the fact that they were barely even speaking anymore, it probably didn't matter. He had most likely already fucked up any chance he'd had to be with her.

His stomach churned. Grace could do way worse than Brody. He was a good friend, and to Colt's knowledge, had always treated women with the utmost respect.

Aware his friend was still waiting for an answer, he forced himself to reply. "No, we're not dating. She's just a friend." It felt like a lie, even as the words passed his lips.

"Cool. So, she's single?"

An irrational wave of anger slid its insidious fingers through his veins, but he fought to hide it. Regardless, his hands balled into fists at his sides. Brody didn't seem to notice. There was no way Colt would be able to explain. He couldn't even explain the reaction to himself. He'd already blown his chance. It was too late for him. He had no right to get angry about other guys taking notice of her.

He took a deep breath in an attempt to calm the hell back down. Brody would be good for her. He was closer to her age and, as far as Colt was aware, didn't have the emotional baggage that he did. Brody could give her the relationship he couldn't. The one she deserved.

"She's available," Colt choked out, the words tasting sour in his mouth. He snatched his rope down from where it hung and glanced at Brody. "See you out there, man. Good luck."

He didn't wait for a response before he stalked off to the chutes.

***

This was a disaster. Colt slipped sideways for the third time in two seconds as the bull beneath him abruptly changed directions again. His concentration was non-existent. He was going to get himself killed if this shit didn't stop.

The bull gave a powerful kick straight out behind him, and Colt felt himself lift off the animal's back. He cursed and tightened his grip. It wasn't likely he would be making it to the buzzer if he didn't get his brain to stop treating him to images of Grace in the arms of some nameless cowboy. His fucking mind seemed intent on torturing him at the worst possible time.

This ride was sloppy as hell. He cringed as the bull threw him into his riding hand. The sudden change in direction nearly unseated him yet again. After several more potent bucks, the buzzer finally sounded and Colt sprang off the bull's back. He landed neatly on his feet and sprinted for the railing. It wasn't necessary to look back to know that Copycat Illusion was right on his heels. Sure enough, the bull's horns hit the railing—right beneath his boots—with a resounding clang, just a breath after Colt scrambled to the top of the fence.

His eyes shifted to the scoreboard, though he didn't expect much from that trainwreck of a ride. 78.2. Not as bad as he'd expected but far from being one of his best. It was miracle enough that he'd made it to the buzzer.

The bullfighters distracted the bull, and Colt hopped back to the ground. As he left the arena, his gaze landed on Grace. Brody was talking to her. The pair tossed their heads back and laughed.

A pang of jealousy made his stomach cramp and his heart clench. Fuck. If they got together, he might have to stop hanging out with Brody. It would be too damn hard to see them together. He turned away and headed for the locker room with hasty steps.

Grace was waiting outside the locker room doors when he emerged a few minutes later. He stopped short. She seemed both tense and determined. Maybe a little sad.

Shit, this couldn't be good. He braced himself for whatever she had to say. "What's up, Princess?"

"We need to talk. In private." She gestured for him to follow and took off through the crowd toward where they'd parked the horse trailer.

Colt swallowed hard and followed at a slower pace, feeling a bit like she was leading him to his execution. His mind raced. Was she leaving him? Was this it? His stomach knotted tight.

Finally reaching the trailer, he reluctantly boarded the steps then clicked the door shut. "Alright, what do we need to talk about?" He inwardly begged her to not tell him. He didn't want to know.

Grace straightened, and her eyes locked on him while her fingers worried the hem of her shirt. She took a deep breath. "I think it would be best if I left."

Though he'd been expecting it, her words still punched every bit of air from his lungs. "Why?" he asked with a gasp. He wasn't ready, would never be ready. It wasn't time.

"Flint threatened to kill you if I stay. If he were to hurt you because of me, I would never forgive myself."

He didn't give a shit about Flint's threat. He dared the fucker to try.

Anger bubbled to the surface like lava, and he fought to hide it. Colt didn't want her thinking he was pissed at *her*.

"Besides, you don't need me hanging around all the time," Grace continued. "You had a life before I showed up at your door. It's time I let you get back to it. I appreciate everything you've done for me. I really do, but ... I need to go. I think I'd like to stay on the circuit, at least until the end of the season. I was planning on asking around if one of the barrel racers would let me and Summer hitch a ride. I can deliver her back to Cash's place after Finals."

He scrubbed a hand over his face then took a small step toward her. His fingers twitched as he fought the need to reach for her, to beg her to stay. "Grace—"

This couldn't be happening. His gaze traveled over her face. For the first time, he noticed the faint shadows beneath her eyes as though she hadn't been sleeping well. His heart squeezed hard. The words perched on the tip of his tongue, a plea for her not to go, but he swallowed them down. He couldn't do it. No matter how badly he didn't want to lose her, he couldn't ask her to stay.

"At least promise me you'll call if he gives you any more trouble. I'm not afraid of him, but I don't want him hurting you. Never again."

Sorrow passed over her face, clear as day, before she looked away. "I will. I promise. Thank you, Colt. For everything." Her gorgeous blue eyes shimmered as she looked up at him. The wetness clinging to her lashes made it even more difficult to resist pulling her into his arms. "Brody said he'd be my new guard dog, so you don't have to worry about me. He gave me his schedule for the next couple of months so I can make sure I'm at the same stop he is. I'll be okay," she said quietly.

"Brody?" Colt croaked. His stomach roiled. Maybe it was a good thing they were having this conversation in the trailer. He was pretty sure he might puke.

"Yeah, your friend, Brody. We talked today while you were riding. He asked me to go to dinner with him next stop."

No. Please, no. Her eyes were on him, so he schooled his features into a blank mask—or tried to. "Are you going to?" he forced himself to ask.

"I might. He seems like a good guy." Grace tilted her head. "Isn't he?"

He did not want to be talking up his buddy right now. The mental image of her in his friend's arms made him want to hunt Brody down and pummel his face to a pulp. Grace was his. Only, she wasn't. Fuck.

Colt swallowed hard and fastened his gaze on the stand, studying the grain of the wood while he struggled to regain control over his rioting emotions. "He is. He can give you what I can't."

Grace shifted closer. "Maybe," she said, her voice subdued. "But he's not you."

When he didn't look at her, she touched his cheek and forcibly turned his face toward her. He couldn't keep from leaning into her gentle touch. Their eyes met.

"You're not even going to ask me to stay?"

The tremble in her voice broke him. He pulled her into his arms so fast that she squeaked in surprise.

Colt buried his nose in her hair as he held her tight against his chest and filled his lungs with the sweet smell he'd forever associate with her. "It wouldn't be fair of me to ask you to stay." He pushed her away enough to be able to meet her eyes again. "I don't want you to go," he whispered hoarsely, thinly veiled anguish lacing his voice. "I want you to stay with me forever." He heard her inhale sharply and closed his eyes. "I can't ask that of you, Princess. You have no reason to stay."

He felt her cradle his face in her hands, and then her lips met his. Colt gasped, and she took advantage of his parted lips, her tongue darting in to slide sensuously against his. She backed toward the bed, taking him with her. The moment she stopped, her fingers began working the buttons of his shirt.

His eyes popped open.

"Grace—"

She placed a finger against his lips. "I know. I know we shouldn't, but I need this." She finished unbuttoning his shirt then looked up. Her spellbinding eyes seem to plead with him. "I'm leaving. Give me another memory before I go." She shifted back a step, grasped the hem of her shirt, and drew it up over her head. Grace tossed it away carelessly then reached behind herself and unclasped her bra, exposing her beautiful, full breasts to his view. She let it fall to her feet.

He sucked in a breath, tensing. His groin tightened as his gaze roamed over her. Fuck, she was glorious.

She reached for the button of her jeans. "Please?" she whispered.

He couldn't deny her. What little resistance he had left crumbled. If she wanted a memory, he'd give her one.

With a shrug of his shoulders, he finished removing his shirt then reached for his belt. He was going to hell for this. Colt hung his hat on the hook by the door, kicked off his boots, and stepped free of his boxers and jeans.

When he turned back to Grace—breathing hard and wondering what the hell he was doing—she was already fully stripped down and watching him while biting her lip. The hunger in her dilated eyes sent even more blood rushing south. He'd bet she was already dripping wet and ready for him.

Colt scooped her off her feet and placed her on the bed, then quickly joined her. "Why can't I resist you?" he asked with a groan. He knelt next to her and took in every glorious inch of her he could see, committing the image to memory. "You're so fucking beautiful," he murmured reverently, trailing his fingers across her belly, along the gentle curve of her hip, then down into the patch of curls between her thighs.

Her sharp intake of breath drew a grin to his lips despite the situation that had brought them here.

"I want to taste you," he murmured, teasing her entrance with the tip of his finger. As he figured she would be, her core was already slick with arousal.

Her breathing hitched. "I've never really liked that."

He sat back a bit. "We don't have to. Tonight is yours. Whatever you want." Colt leaned down to kiss her. Hard. Desperate. As though he'd perish without that contact with her. He threw the full depth of his feelings into it.

She responded with equal fervor, ramping up the desire already scorching him with its heat.

Her eyes were slightly unfocused by the time their mouths parted.

"I ... think I've changed my mind," she said, her voice strained.

Colt pushed upright and met her eyes. "About what?"

"About you, uh, tasting me. Do it."

"Are you sure?" He didn't want her doing anything she wasn't certain about. Not ever.

She let her legs fall farther apart, giving him access. "Yes." Her lips quirked upward. "I might like it this time. And..." Her smile faltered. "I-I don't want to regret not letting you."

His heart squeezed painfully at the reminder that tonight was all they had. If he had his way, she wouldn't just like it, she'd fucking love it. He would bet everything he had in the bank that she'd never been with somebody who'd put any real effort into pleasing her. He'd be all too happy to remedy that.

"I'll stop if you still don't like it." He positioned himself between her legs. "I mean it, Grace. Say the word, and I'll stop."

She nodded in acknowledgement but said nothing more.

Rather than immediately burying his face between her thighs like he wanted to, he trailed kisses down her neck to her collarbone, then lower. This was not a night to rush. This was a night to go slow, to savor. To stretch each moment as long as he could.

He paused at her breasts and glanced up at her. "Is this okay?" He closed his mouth over her nipple, drawing hard.

"Yes," she hissed. Her fingers clutched the sheet tight as her back arched, pushing her breasts closer. Offering them up.

He spent a few moments lavishing both of her breasts with attention, then lifted his head and looked at her. "What about this?" He coasted his hand back down her body and slipped two fingers into her center, thrusting them slowly.

"Oh," she said with a gasp. "Yes. Keep doing that."

Pleasure tightened her face as he moved his hand faster. He memorized the sight of her bliss and the sounds she made as he pleased her. He'd need them to get him through the loneliness sure to follow tonight.

There would be nobody else for him. Not after her. He hadn't even gotten inside her yet, and he already knew she'd ruined him. He was hers now, body and soul. And he would be forever.

After a few seconds, he added his thumb to the mix, using it to work her clit with practiced skill. Her moans were like music to his ears. Why the hell had he been denying himself this? Denying them both? If only he'd given in to her sooner.

When he figured she was ready, he moved down her body while continuing to work her with his fingers. Saliva pooled in his mouth in anticipation of her taste as he positioned himself. He kissed a path up her inner thigh before exhaling a breath on the curls covering her mound.

She gasped and shivered.

A faint smile tugged at his lips.

Colt pressed a kiss to her other thigh then replaced his thumb with his tongue. Her hips bucked as he took her by surprise, and he could swear he heard her mutter a curse under her breath. He set to work, determined to make her dream about his mouth on her. Determined to not stop until he had her screaming with bliss. Maybe it would bring her back to him.

It wasn't long before her thighs began quivering and soft whimpers escaped her lips. Her fingers were in his hair, clasping him to her while he deftly worked her with his lips and tongue. He thrust his fingers faster as he sucked down on her clit.

She came with a ragged cry, her thighs clamping around his head, but he didn't let up until her grip on his hair loosened and her body relaxed.

He lifted his head and raised one eyebrow. "Well? Still hate it?"

"Are you being serious?" she asked breathlessly. "That was amazing."

He smirked and settled onto his side next to her.

"What are you doing?" she complained. "I need you inside me."

From the look on her face, he could guess what she was thinking. Undoubtedly, she thought he was going to call this quits. That was far from his intention. He wanted a memory too, dammit.

"Giving you what you asked for." He rolled onto his back then pulled her partially on top of him. "Take what you want."

Understanding dawned over her beautiful face, and a faint smile curled on her lips. Grace straddled his waist, her core pressing against his lower belly. She leaned down to kiss him hard then positioned herself over him. Her eyes slid shut, and pleasure tightened her face all over again as she sheathed him with her body in one smooth movement.

Colt moaned. He couldn't help it. Her wet heat wrapped him in its snug embrace. They fit together so perfectly. It felt so right.

Then she began moving, and he about lost his mind. The rasp of her inner walls against him was exquisite. He skimmed his hands up her sides and teased the underside of her breasts with his thumbs as she rode him fast and hard.

Her rhythm faltered when he rolled her nipples between his thumb and forefinger. She threw her head back and moaned while her hips ground down against him harder, as though trying to drive him deeper.

God, he loved this woman. So fucking beautiful. He was going to miss her so damn much. Shit, he already missed her and he was still buried deep inside her.

To hide the sudden wave of grief that swamped him, he gripped her hips on her next downstroke and held her firm against his body while he rolled her beneath him, then picked back up the rapid pace she'd set. Her hands slid down his back to grip his buttocks, her fingers biting into his skin. Her eyes clenched shut, her face a mask of pleasure.

Colt slid his hands beneath her hips and lifted her to meet him as he pounded into her. Sweat rolled down his body, but he paid it no heed. Their moans mingled as he gave her what she wanted, what he'd been wanting too.

There wasn't a chance in hell he'd be able to last much longer, no matter how much he wished he could. She felt too fucking good, and it'd been far too long. He could already feel the telltale pressure building at the base of his spine.

"Touch yourself," he said, his voice nearly a growl.

Her eyes opened and met his, but she made no move to do as he'd directed. Her flushed face turned a darker shade of pink.

He committed that sight to memory too. He slowed his movements, reached for her hand, and guided it between her thighs. "Touch yourself, Trouble," he urged gently. "Come with me."

Grace caught her bottom lip between her teeth then began moving her hand. Her lashes fluttered, and she released the sweetest moan he'd ever heard.

"That's it, baby," he murmured while picking up speed again.

She whimpered and moved her hand faster. "Colt," she gasped. "Oh. I'm close." She locked eyes with him.

She had never looked more alluring than she did right now, with her face aglow and her eyes slightly dazed.

"Let go," he urged.

She exploded beneath him seconds later, with his name on her lips.

Colt plunged deep and followed her over the edge. He came hard enough to see stars. For a moment, his arms and legs felt tingly. Fucking hell, that was a first. He grunted and jerked with each hard spasm as Grace's body took everything he had to give.

When their mutual tremors finally slowed, he collapsed over her and tried futilely to catch his breath.

"Fuck, Grace," he groaned into the crook of her neck, his voice colored with awe. He trembled as aftershocks hit him, prompted by the continued flutters of her inner walls.

She kissed his shoulder then his neck. "I know."

He eased himself back up enough to capture her lips as he rocked his hips leisurely one last time. His cock was beginning to wilt now, but he wasn't ready to leave the warmth of her body yet. Wasn't ready to lose the feel of her around him. Fuck, he wasn't ready to lose *her*.

He shuddered as he reluctantly slipped free of her body and flopped onto his back beside her.

Colt held an arm out in offering. "Come here. Let me hold you a while."

His lips twitched upward when she complied immediately. She curled against his side and rested her head on his chest. He stroked his fingertips over the soft skin of her arm.

Neither of them spoke. He had thousands of things he wanted to say, but he didn't know where to even start.

Finally, he forced himself to break the silence. "I want you to keep Summer even after the season is over. I'll cut you a check to cover her feed and care through the end of the season. I want you to take the truck and trailer too. Before I leave here tonight, I'll sign them all over to you. If you don't want them, sell them and use the money to get back on your feet. I don't care. I want you to have them."

Grace moved her head to his shoulder and frowned. "No, Colt. I can't take your truck! Rodeo is your career! How will you get to the next stop if I have it?"

He brushed a kiss over her lips to shush her. "You can. Let me take care of you one more time. Brody and Dusty are here; I can ride with one of them to the next stop. From there, I'll catch a ride with one of the guys until Finals, then I'll buy a new truck. It won't be the first time I've done it." Colt shrugged slightly. "Don't worry about me, Princess. I'll figure it out." He hesitated. "About Brody—"

She laughed and shook her head. "I'm not going to date Brody." Grace turned her head and kissed his shoulder.

"You could do worse than him."

"I could do better too," she replied. "He seems like a great guy, but he's not you. It's you I want." She sighed dispiritedly. "I'm going to miss you." Her voice was barely audible.

"We can still hang out when we're at the same stop," he started, but she shook her head before he'd even gotten the last word out.

"No. I can't be your friend. If Flint found out we're still talking, he might come after you and that's not a risk I'm willing to take," she said, her voice shaky as though she might burst into tears at any moment. "Besides, I can't be around you and not want you. Not want this." She trailed her fingertips in random shapes over his chest as she spoke. "It'd be too difficult. I know you're not ready for anything, and I don't want to pressure you any more than I already have. I've pushed you too hard as it is." She took a tremulous breath. "When we part tonight, we can't talk again. I'm sorry."

His eyes slid shut as pain tightened his chest. "Unless you're harassed by him again. You promised you'd tell me." Colt felt her nod against his chest but didn't open his eyes. It felt like someone was carving his heart from his body with a rusty knife. All of his attempts to protect the organ, and here he was with it breaking anyway.

He pulled Grace closer and pressed a kiss to her forehead. To say he was going to miss her would be a massive understatement. A lump formed in his throat, and he swallowed hard around it. His fingers skimmed up and down over her arm. He concentrated on the softness of her skin, on the way she fit so perfectly against him. Anything to keep from thinking about what would happen the moment they left this bed.

They lay there together, wrapped in a not-quite-comfortable silence, for a time longer before Grace eased away from him and got to her feet. He opened his eyes and watched her.

She glanced over at him. "Can I steal one of your shirts?"

He took a deep breath. "Yeah. Take your pick."

Colt sat up and scrubbed both hands over his face. Fuck. He'd known this was coming one day. Her departure.

He wasn't ready. Would never be ready. How the hell had this woman gotten so deep under his skin with such ease? His heart ached. This wasn't how it was supposed to be. This wasn't how things between them were supposed to end.

He'd done his best to keep his distance, tried not to get attached to her. He'd failed miserably on both counts.

He loved her. He wanted her. But fear held his tongue hostage, and now he was going to lose her. He was being an idiot, and knew it, but didn't know how to stop this.

Grace slipped into the t-shirt she'd snagged from his bag.

Though he was loath to leave, he stood and began dressing. When he finished, he reached for her and pulled her into a tight hug. His feelings perched on the tip of his tongue, but he swallowed them down, too afraid to voice them even with the knowledge that confessing them might allow him to keep her. Instead, he muttered, "We forgot protection tonight."

Her face turned pink. "I know. I don't think the timing is right to have to worry." She glanced at him. "But I promise I'll tell you if ... you know."

Colt nodded. He wondered why the thought of her round with his child was strangely appealing. To his shock, he almost wished that it would happen. That he'd have that link with her.

When Sarah brought up starting a family, it had very nearly sent him into a panic. That night, they'd had the biggest fight they'd ever had. Why was the prospect of kids so vastly different with Grace when they weren't even dating?

Something to examine later maybe. Right now, he needed to sign the titles for the truck and trailer, along with the transfer of ownership for Summer, get her a bill of sale for them, then let her get on with her life. Without him.

His stomach knotted tight. "I'm sorry," he said quietly.

Her brows snapped together. "Sorry for what?"

"For not taking proper care of you. It's my responsibility to make sure you're safe." He shook his head. "I've never forgotten to use a condom before. Not even when I've been drunk off my ass. I wasn't thinking." He cringed and glanced at her. "I'm clean, at least. Until tonight, I've always used protection."

He wondered what she'd think if she knew she was only the second woman he'd ever slept with bare. And he'd slept with a lot of women over the course of his adult life. Sarah was the only other, but she'd been on the pill. This was different.

Hell, thinking about it, he wasn't sure he even had a condom to have used tonight. It wasn't as though he'd needed one in ages. He hadn't been interested in anyone since well before the auction, and the only woman he'd been wanting since was Grace. The one woman he'd been dead set on keeping his dick away from. Lot of good that had done him.

"I'm clean too," Grace said softly then touched his cheek. He met her eyes. "It slipped my mind too. You're not the only one who forgot."

Colt pulled away from her and dug through a drawer in the kitchenette, looking for a towel. Once he finally found a clean one, he dampened it with a bit of warm water from the sink and dropped to his knees in front of her.

"What are you doing?"

"I helped make this mess. The least I can do is clean you up." He gently nudged her thighs apart, then wiped their mingled mess from her skin as best as he could.

She had a soft look in her eyes that he didn't dare put a name to, as though his feelings were reciprocated. He pushed back to his feet and tossed the hand towel into the makeshift hamper nearby. For a moment, he wanted nothing more than to know what she was thinking but quickly decided it was probably better that he didn't.

Colt cleared his throat. "Let me go grab the paperwork for you." He jammed his hat on his head and dashed out the door before he did something stupid, like beg her to stay and tell her he loved her.

Grace was seated on the edge of the bed with a somber expression on her face when he returned to the living quarters of the trailer. He sat the signed paperwork on the stand and dropped the truck's keys beside them before stooping to pick up his duffle bag.

He wavered there, unable to bring himself to say goodbye. "Grace..."

She got to her feet, giving him a shaky smile and moved toward him. "This is harder than I expected it to be," she admitted as she wrapped her arms tightly around his middle.

A desperate sensation simmered within him as he slid his arms around her and tugged her closer. He didn't want to walk out that door. What he wanted to do was hold her tight and never let go.

This was killing him. The closer they got to saying goodbye, the more certain he was that he was making a mistake of epic proportions by not speaking up and putting a stop to this. A mistake bigger than any he'd ever made before. Why couldn't he open his fucking mouth and tell her?

Colt sucked in a ragged breath. "Take care of yourself, Princess. I know what you said, but if you need anything, call me. I'm serious."

She smiled weakly and stepped out of his embrace, then gave him a gentle nudge toward the door. He ran his fingers down her arm, needing to touch her one last time. His shoulders rounded as an empty sensation spread ice through his veins.

This was like losing Sarah all over again. No. Somehow worse. He hadn't had a choice about losing Sarah, but here, now, he had a choice. He could stop this.

He made it two steps toward the door before he froze. Though he tried, he couldn't force himself to leave the trailer. To leave Grace. His chest heaved in and out as he stood stock still where he was, his heart thudding in his ears.

"I can't," he said, so quietly he could barely hear his own voice.

"What?"

He turned to look at her. The anguish coursing through him made it difficult to draw air into his lungs. "I said, I can't. I can't do this."

In one long stride, he was back in front of her. He cupped her face with his hands and swept his thumbs over her cheeks. To his surprise, they were damp. When had she began crying?

His heart clenched. "I can't walk out that door, Princess. I can't leave here knowing I'll never talk to you again. Never hear your laughter, see your smile." He exhaled roughly and shook his head. "I can't. I can't handle losing you too."

She fell against his chest as her tears began in earnest. He wrapped his arms around her tightly, wishing he could hold her forever. Fuck, he never wanted to let go. Not now. Not ever.

Colt buried his face in her hair, inhaling her soft scent as his heart shattered. He'd thought he was broken when he lost Sarah, but he knew now that he hadn't even skimmed the surface of broken.

How did he get Grace to reconsider? How did he calm her fears and get her to stay? He couldn't do this. He couldn't leave this trailer knowing he was leaving his heart behind. Knowing there was a damn good chance he'd never have her in his life again. In his arms again.

A lump lodged itself in his throat, and it took everything in him to not cry with her. He held her until her tears slowed then finally stopped.

Once they did, she leaned away and looked up at him. "But what if Flint finds out?"

"Fuck him, and his opinions," he growled. "I don't care what he thinks about anything, and neither should you. I'm not afraid of him. Hell, I've dealt with far worse than him during some of the bar brawls I've been in." He searched her watery eyes. "Do you really want me to go?"

"No!"

"Then I'm not going anywhere, and neither are you."

"Colt…" Grace nibbled at her lip, trailing her fingertips along his jaw in a gentle caress. "This has to happen. I don't want him to hurt you. I-I can't risk it. I'm sorry. Maybe we can be friends again if this mess with Flint ever ends. I want that. To be friends again someday." She gave him a shaky smile. "Maybe you'll even change your mind and decide to give us a chance." From the look on her face as she said it, she didn't believe he would ever change his mind about being with her.

He wanted to tell her he already had, that he wanted to try with her, but he still couldn't get the words out. Until he was completely sure he meant it, he had no business speaking them anyway. Instead, he released her and scrubbed his hands over his face in frustration.

She wrapped her arms back around him and pressed close. "Stay with me tonight," she pleaded. "You can leave in the morning. I'm not ready for tonight to end. I'm not ready to say goodbye. Stay tonight, and hold me."

Colt was certain that would make walking away from her even more difficult, but he was powerless to deny her. Shit, he wasn't ready to walk out that door yet either. He never would be.

He smoothed his hand over the back of her head. "I'll stay tonight." He eased her back so he could meet her eyes. "This isn't the end, Princess. Flint doesn't get to win."

From the weak smile she gave him, it was obvious she didn't entirely believe his assertion, but a faint glimmer of hope shimmered in the depths of her eyes regardless.

He was determined to prove it. He'd give her some time, give her some space, but Flint didn't get to take her from him. He'd already lost one woman he loved; he would not lose another. He wouldn't fucking allow it.

Chapter 23

"THIS YOUNG LADY OUGHT to be mighty proud of herself tonight," the rodeo announcer enthusiastically chattered to the crowd as Grace rode Summer toward the exit gate where Brody waited. "That run will move her into second place and earn her a check! Let's hear it for her, folks! Grace Parker!"

Grace forced a smile and lifted a hand to wave to the crowd gathered at the arena as they clapped and cheered for her. She'd caught her calf in 2.8 seconds tonight. It'd been a good run, but it didn't bring her the joy it normally would have.

In the three weeks since she and Colt had separated, she felt like she was just going through the motions each day. There was little happiness. It was as though she was living in a world of grey. Everything was bland, monotone.

While the guys were often at the same stops together, they occasionally went separate directions. Like today. Dusty preferred the smaller rodeos while Brody and Cash favored the bigger ones. Colt went where Cash did, more often than not. Tonight, she and Brody were at a small stop together while the rest of the guys were at a huge rodeo a state away.

"Thought for sure that calf was going to duck off," Brody said the moment she pulled Summer to a halt next to him. "Glad he didn't."

Ideally, the calf ran in a straight line—and most of them did—but some turned to the left or the right, which made the run so much more difficult to complete, if not impossible. Tonight's calf had definitely thought about it. It wouldn't have been the first to do it to her.

"I did too," she replied while swinging off of Summer's back.

"Are you planning on going to the afterparty tonight?"

Grace shook her head. "Not tonight. Are you going?"

"Not if you're not." Brody took Summer's reins from her as they started walking together to cool the mare down. "Colt would kill me if I left you alone and something happened." He glanced over at her. "You guys might not be talking, but he still cares about you."

She inwardly winced at the mention of Colt. Most nights, it took everything in her to keep from calling him.

"I still care about him too," she said softly. Her shoulders slumped and she sighed heavily. "I miss him so much," she said around the lump in her throat.

Brody nodded and gave her a sympathetic look. "Are you sure any of this is even necessary? Have you heard anything from Flint?"

She shook her head. "Not since I changed my number."

She'd done that immediately after saying goodbye to Colt after their last night together in the horse trailer. He and Dusty probably hadn't even driven away yet. Since then, there'd been radio silence from Flint. No texts, no calls, no sightings. Nothing.

"It won't last. He hasn't given up; I know he hasn't." She turned to look at Brody. "I can't risk it. If Flint hurts him because I just couldn't stay away, I'd never forgive myself."

The eerie feeling that Flint was somehow watching her, keeping tabs on her, still hadn't gone away. No matter how much she missed Colt, she wouldn't risk his life. She couldn't. It was too dangerous.

Brody looked as though he wanted to say something, but he remained silent instead.

She didn't want to think about Flint or the danger he posed any more. Not tonight.

Grace sucked in a deep breath and let it out slowly. "Are you sure you don't want to go to the afterparty? I bet Andrea wouldn't mind hanging out with me."

Andrea McIntyre, or Rea as Brody called her, was a barrel racer he'd introduced her to a few days after Grace started following him around the circuit. He'd said he'd feel best about leaving her to ride his bull if he knew she was with someone he trusted. Apparently, his friend checked that box. Grace didn't know much about the woman, but Andrea was welcoming and friendly. Given enough time, maybe they would become friends. That would be nice.

"Rea is headed home after I ride tonight, so she won't be here for the afterparty. Her husband is a friend of mine from back in high school. He's been overseas for work the past six months and is heading home for a few days. She's gonna want to be there when he gets home." He flashed Grace a grin. "I've been keeping an eye on her for him while he's away. Gotta keep you women out of trouble."

A faint smile curled on her lips. "So you're a guard dog to two women then, huh?"

He laughed. "Yeah, guess so." Brody winked. "Getting pretty good at it, I think. Maybe I should have become a bodyguard instead of a bull rider." They reached the barn, and he led Summer into her stall. "I gotta go get ready for my ride. You need any help getting Summer settled?"

"No, I can manage."

From the corner of her eye, she spotted Andrea waving wildly to her from the other end of the barn, a huge smile on her face. Andrea's braided red hair bounced around behind her as she hurried down the barn aisle toward her and Brody.

Grace waved back, then turned her attention back to Brody. "Andrea is on her way. I'll be alright."

Brody smiled and waved at his friend. "Okay." He gave Grace a stern look as he backed toward the door. "Stay with Rea until I get back. No wandering off alone."

"Yes, sir," Grace said with a half-laugh. "Go. Score high and ride safe."

He nodded again, then ducked out of the barn just as Andrea skidded to a stop at Summer's stall.

Chapter 24

"This shit has to stop, Colt."

Colt looked up from his cup of coffee and focused his gritty eyes on Cash. His best friend stood off to his right, with Dusty by his side.

Was this another attempted intervention? It sure wasn't the first in the two and a half months since he and Grace parted ways. From the grimness written all over both his friends' faces, it sure seemed to be.

Great. Just what he needed right now.

"What shit would that be?" Colt asked.

His head was splitting. He sure hoped the combination of pain meds and caffeine worked their magic before he needed to ride tonight. Thank fuck he had four hours or so before then.

Cash glared. "You know exactly what shit. Stop being a dumbass. You're going to get yourself seriously hurt, maybe even killed. Is that what you want?"

His best friend didn't understand. Couldn't understand. Seeing Grace at the occasional stop but being unable to talk to her, hearing her voice from afar, catching a whiff of strawberries on the wind if he dared to get too close... It was too much. It was like getting kicked in the gut by a bronc each and every time. The only thing that numbed the pain any was the whiskey.

He shrugged. What did it matter what happened to him now? She had Brody keeping her safe. He trusted his friend to protect her.

Cash smacked him upside the head hard, sending Colt's hat to the ground and splinters of agony through his skull.

White-hot fury flared to life. "What the fuck, Cash?"

His best friend's green gaze flashed back at him. "Just trying to knock some damn sense into you," he snarled. "Someone needs to."

"What is it you want me to say? That you were right? Fine. You were fucking right, okay? And I fucking lost her." Colt staggered to his feet and stepped close to Cash. His hands balled into fists at his sides. "Since she left, I feel about as dead as I did when Sarah died! Happy now?"

"Why the fuck would that make me happy, asshole? You're my best friend and I fucking love you, dude. I don't want this shit for you!"

Colt's temper cooled in an instant. It was miracle enough any of his friends were still talking to him with as big of a jerk as he'd been being to them; he didn't need to be making things worse by getting into another fistfight with Cash now.

He snatched his hat from the ground, knocked the dust from it, and plopped it back on his head.

"Love you too, man," he muttered as he sat back down at the picnic table. His gaze flicked to Dusty. "Got nothing you want to add?"

Dusty shook his head and hooked a thumb at Cash. "Nope. He's got it covered. Just worried about you, dude. We all are."

Shit, he was worried about himself too. He was in a tailspin, and knew it, but didn't have a clue how to pull out of it.

"How the hell is drinking yourself to death fixing anything?" Cash asked, drawing Colt's attention back to him. "Go talk to her. Get her back. Jeezus, Colt, I thought I was the one who ran from commitment, but even I'm not this big of an idiot."

Colt's jaw clenched. He knew drinking the pain away was foolish, but it was the only thing that seemed to help. Shit, he'd spent more time inebriated this past week than sober. He was balancing on the edge of a slippery slope.

"I'm respecting her wishes," he replied flatly.

Not that it was easy. Last stop he'd seen her at, he'd come close to approaching her, talking to her. A couple of weeks ago he'd even tried calling, but a stranger picked up—a woman, thank fuck. His imagination didn't need the help having a man answer the phone would have caused. His dreams were haunted by far too many images of Grace in the arms of some faceless man as it was. He was glad she'd decided to change her number, however.

Cash shook his head. "This is stupid. You're both being idiots."

Colt shrugged and took a sip of coffee before looking back up at Cash. "Nobody told you to make any of this your business." His gaze shifted to Dusty. "Either of you."

"Man, fuck you!" Cash snapped. "I'm done watching you self-destruct. Get it together. I don't want to watch them bury you too." He shot Colt an exasperated look then turned and stomped away.

Dusty lingered, his throat working like he wanted to say something.

Colt waited, but his friend only shook his head before he too turned and walked away.

<hr>

"Don't ride tonight. You look like shit."

Colt glanced sideways at Cash as they approached the chutes. "I feel like shit too, but I'm good. Quit fussing over me like a mother hen."

"Can't. Somebody needs to," Cash said dryly.

Colt shook his head, instantly regretting the action when it made his headache intensify. His temples throbbed in time with his heartbeat. Fuck, that hurt. Maybe Cash was right and he shouldn't ride tonight, but he was determined to do it anyway. He'd ridden in worse condition a time or three in the past. He'd be fine.

After the confrontation earlier in the afternoon, he should probably be more surprised for Cash to be even talking to him right now. But he wasn't. It was just the nature of their friendship. Always had been. They fought and near immediately forgave.

His gaze flicked over to the stands automatically, though he knew Grace wasn't at this stop.

"She's not here." Cash gave him a knowing look.

Colt shot him a glare and made a face. "I know that. Brody texted me this morning." His friend and Grace were two states away tonight, at a stop Colt had originally planned on riding at too until Cash talked him into this one instead.

Cash shook his head. "Still not sure if it's a good thing he keeps you updated like that."

Colt grunted. He wasn't sure either, but he knew damn well that if Brody didn't, he'd be so busy worrying about her well-being that he wouldn't be able to concentrate long enough to ride at all. It was better to know, even if it made him want to talk to her all the more. Especially when Brody had news of her having a good run.

Cash bumped Colt with his arm. "I sure hope I don't end up having to tell her you've gotten yourself killed, dude. Don't ride tonight."

"I'll be fine," he growled and stomped up the steps ahead of Cash.

Cash gave a disbelieving grunt as he joined Colt at the top of the chutes. "Yeah. Sure. Just be careful out there, man." He leaned against the rail of a neighboring chute, his face pinched with worry. "I mean it. I ain't burying you."

Colt nodded but didn't otherwise answer. He had no intention of dying today, or any day soon for that matter. His bull tonight—a massive brindle bull known as Hostile Intent—was likely to give killing him a try, however. The big beast loved to go airborne, bucked unpredictably, and was well known to be just as mean as his name implied. He was also known to give a hell of a good ride and consistently scored high.

Colt's spotter for the night—a pockmarked young cowboy he didn't know—gripped the back of his vest as he climbed the railing and slowly lowered himself onto the broad back of his bull. The animal snorted and shifted restlessly while Colt got himself positioned and reached for the tail of his bull rope to tie in.

"You didn't talk to your ride," Cash mumbled half under his breath.

Colt paused and looked over at his best friend. "What?"

"You forgot to talk to your bull, like you usually do. Your pre-ride."

Shit. He had, hadn't he? Colt's stomach quivered, but he forced himself to shrug as though it didn't matter. "Guess I'm skipping it tonight."

It was just a superstition he'd picked up. This ride would go fine without it. Right? Right.

"Don't ride," Cash said, his expression a mask of worry. "Something feels off."

"I'm riding," Colt grumbled in response and double-checked his grip before raising his free hand into the air. He tucked his chin toward his chest, then nodded to the gateman before Cash could say anything more.

Hostile Intent exploded from the chute with an enraged bellow. Adrenaline pulsed in heady waves as Colt did his best to follow the bull's powerful movements.

Two seconds. Three. Four.

Despite his head feeling like it might split in two, this ride felt good. No, it felt great. This might just end up being one of his career bests. He hoped anyway.

The bull abruptly changed direction, throwing Colt onto his riding arm as he spun before giving a mighty leap high into the air.

Or maybe it wouldn't. Shit. Hostile Intent must have been holding back.

Colt slipped sideways as the huge animal landed. The bull's next explosive buck nearly sent him flying. By some miracle, he managed to hang on.

The buzzer sounded a second later, mercifully signaling the end of the ride, and Colt tugged the tail of his bull rope to release his hand while attempting to dismount. The rope didn't budge.

Shit. Fuck. He was hung up!

A red-hot poker of pain shot through his shoulder as the joint stretched to its limit. Colt struggled to stay on his feet as the trio of bullfighters rushed in to help him. He reached up with his free hand and pulled the end of his rope again, but it held tight. His hand remained wedged in the rope, holding him to the pissed-off bull.

Before the bullfighters could reach him, Hostile Intent leaped into the air again, taking Colt with him. Fear, more intense than any he'd ever known before, flared to life. This could be it. His last ride.

His breath sawed out of him as he fought to hold panic at bay. He needed a clear head if he was going to remain among the living. He wasn't ready to die. It wasn't time.

Colt lost his footing as the bull touched arena dirt once more. Sharp hooves pummeled him as the aggressive animal began dragging him around the arena. Dimly, Colt was aware of the bullfighters' shouts and the crowd's cries. Somewhere, he was pretty sure he could hear Cash and Dusty yelling too. What anyone was saying was a mystery. He was a little too busy trying to stay alive to listen.

Fuck, he was glad Grace wasn't here to see this. He didn't want that for her. She'd been through so much, survived so much trauma. She didn't need to see him have a wreck like this.

Grace.

Regret gripped him hard. He hadn't even told her he loved her. If he made it out of this, he swore right then he'd remedy that. He'd get down on his knees and beg her to take a chance on him if he needed to. But he couldn't do any of that if he died in this damn arena, though.

A fresh rush of determination coursed through his veins.

Colt gritted his teeth and used the last of his flagging strength to surge back to his feet. Success was his until Hostile Intent bellowed and went airborne yet again.

Shit. Not good.

He gasped for breath as he hit the dirt flat on his back. One of the bull's hooves landed on his chest. Pain was a living thing, and it was consuming him alive as it spread through him. The only bright spot was that the jolt had freed his hand.

He lay where he was, taking stock of his body as the bullfighters got Hostile Intent's attention and turned the bull toward the gate that would return him to the bull pens.

Colt could move, so he wasn't paralyzed. That was good. It was difficult to breathe, though. His breaths came in short, painful gasps. Something wasn't right. Why couldn't he catch his breath?

He rolled onto his hands and knees then slowly got to his feet, swaying unsteadily.

A pair of EMTs entered the arena, hurrying toward him at a jog, with Cash close behind. Colt managed two steps toward them before his vision grayed out.

Shit. His legs shook with the effort it took to remain standing. *Grace.*

He needed to live. He needed to see her, hold her in his arms. He needed to tell her he loved her.

Colt struggled to take another step forward, toward the EMTs, but the darkness pressed in, sending him back to the dirt.

Someone shouted. A familiar voice but too distorted, too far away, to make sense.

The darkness crept closer, promising peace. Too tired to resist any longer, Colt closed his eyes and let it carry him away.

Chapter 25

GRACE STOOD ON THE porch, nibbling her thumbnail, and stared at the front door. She'd already knocked twice with no answer. Should she look for the spare key Cash had mentioned and let herself in? Would that be too presumptuous? What if Colt had looked outside already, saw her, and was purposely refusing to answer?

She was still standing there, debating how to proceed, when the door suddenly opened and startled her. Her gaze jumped to the man on the doorstep, and her heart leaped in her chest.

Colt.

His arm was in a sling and his face was somewhat gaunt, but he looked pretty good otherwise.

"Hi," she squeaked as thousands of butterflies beat their tiny wings in her stomach.

Colt blinked rapidly at her, momentarily slack-jawed. It seemed to take him a few seconds to recover enough to speak. "What are you doing here? I thought maybe you were my parents back again."

His parents? Was he expecting them? She swallowed nervously. "Um, well, Cash told me where you were. Don't be mad at him, but he told me about your wreck."

He took a step toward her then paused. "Okay, but why are you here?"

Grace's brows pulled together. "I'm here because I care about you and I wanted to make sure you were okay. Had I known about your wreck sooner, I would have come to the hospital too." She blew out a shaky breath. "Why did you tell the guys not to tell me?"

"I didn't want you to know." His voice bordered on surly.

Her heart sank.

Why? Why wouldn't he have wanted her to know? Her shoulders drooped, and she backed up a step. Had she made a mistake coming here? Should she leave?

"It's okay that I'm here, right?" she asked cautiously.

He rubbed at his ear then shoved a hand through his hair. "Uh, yeah. Sorry, I'm surprised to see you after all this time is all." He gave her an unsteady smile and stepped back. "Come on in."

She followed him into the living room and took a seat on the couch. He sat in an overstuffed armchair opposite her. She nibbled at her lip as full minutes passed in silence.

Maybe this hadn't been a good idea. He hadn't seemed exactly excited to see her, and this was far from the reunion she'd envisioned on the way here. She clasped her hands together in her lap to keep from fidgeting nervously. Was this all that they were going to do, just sit here in silence?

"I've missed you," she said softly when she couldn't take the quiet any longer.

Colt pulled his gaze from the clock that sat on the mantle of the nearby fireplace and cleared his throat. He shifted in his chair to look over at her, his body stiff, tense. Unfortunately for her, his expression gave no hint to his thoughts. His gaze made a slow pass over her face before he cleared his throat again.

"I've missed you too," he finally said, his voice seeming almost hoarse. He swallowed hard and pursed his lips before leaning toward her. "So, how long of a drive did you have?"

"Almost twelve hours. I drove straight through, other than making a couple of bathroom breaks and to let Summer out to stretch her legs. I already gave her a stall in case you're wondering."

Colt turned to study her, his face still completely unreadable. "That's a hell of a drive. Did you at least stop to eat?" When she shook her head, he scowled. "Grace." Disapproval laced his voice.

Her face warmed under the weight of his gaze.

He pushed to his feet with a soft groan and approached her, then held his hand out. "Come on. Let me feed you."

She hesitated only a second before placing her hand in his. Her palm tingled where their skin touched. The sensation sent her heart rate soaring. The moment she was standing, he released her and rubbed his palm against his jeans as though he'd felt a tingle too.

Grace followed him into the kitchen. He grabbed a few items from the refrigerator, but she couldn't tell what they were.

"You don't have to cook for me." She came around the edge of the counter. "I can manage if you tell me where the pans and such are." She laid her hand on his forearm, keeping him from removing his sling.

He looked first at her hand, then up at her with a vaguely exasperated expression. "Why do you always have to fight me?" He jerked his head toward the kitchen table. "Take a seat, and let me take care of you." With that, he tugged his arm away from her, removed his sling, and moved to the sink to wash his hands.

She bit her lip and backed away. He'd never used that tone with her before. She wasn't sure what to make of it, but she seated herself at the table. While she wasn't sure exactly what sort of welcome she'd expected, this wasn't it. She rubbed at her forehead, feeling the beginnings of a headache taking root.

"Why are you really here?"

Her gaze darted back to him. She was sure her confusion was evident. "I told you why I'm here."

"You also told me you couldn't be my friend and that you couldn't talk to me again. I guess I don't see how my wreck changes anything. You could have just called me. It wasn't necessary for you to drive all the way out here."

Grace's breath caught, and her chin wobbled.

He didn't want her here. She should go. It was stupid to have come. He was right; she could have just called.

Her stomach clenched down. "I-I guess I wanted to see that you were really okay for myself." She shoved her chair away from the table and stood. "I'm sorry. I'm going to go. I made a mistake coming here. I didn't mean to upset you."

She only made it three steps toward the door before she heard him swear under his breath, and then he was at her side.

He grabbed her arm, and she instinctively flinched despite knowing without a doubt that he would never hurt her. Things between them may have changed, but that was something that never would. She still trusted him completely. He was still her safe place, even if he no longer wanted anything to do with her.

Colt's eyebrows snapped together, and he immediately released her. His hand fell to his side while he took a half-step back, giving her space.

"I'm sorry," he said. "I didn't mean to make you feel like you shouldn't have come. I know it probably doesn't seem like it, but I'm glad you did. Jesus, Grace, you have no idea how much I've wanted to see you, talk to you." He sighed as though the entire world rested on his shoulders. "My mood hasn't been great lately. I'm sorry. Please, don't go." He tentatively reached for her again. His fingers curled around hers with slow, deliberate movements. "Come eat."

She looked up at him from beneath her lashes then slowly nodded.

He led her back to her chair, and she sat. A delicious-looking sandwich appeared in front of her a couple of minutes later. Her stomach growled as the glorious smell of it drifted up at her. She eyed the food. It appeared he'd made her a grilled ham and cheese, heavy on the ham.

"This looks amazing."

His lips twitched like he was fighting a smile. "It's nothing much, but it'll stop your stomach from grumbling so you can get some sleep." He seated himself next to her at the table while she picked up the sandwich and began eating. No further words passed between them while she ate.

"Thank you," Grace said after swallowing her last bite. She stood to clean up. "I didn't even realize how hungry I was until I started eating. You make a mean grilled sandwich." Grace threw away the paper plate and washed her hands, then slowly approached Colt where he stood leaning against the wall, watching her.

She peered up at him with a shaky smile playing on her lips. For some reason, she found herself feeling uncharacteristically shy. Maybe because of everything that had happened between them. She wasn't entirely sure how to act now.

"Can I hug you?"

Something flared in his eyes. Something hot and hungry.

A frisson of excitement skittered through her body.

He'd put his sling back on, but he held his good arm out in offering. "Please do." His voice sounded deeper and more rumbly than normal, but maybe that was her imagination.

She stepped closer and wrapped her arms loosely around his waist. "I don't want to hurt you."

He slid his arm around her and pulled her closer. "I'm fine, Princess. Get over here." She felt him rest his cheek against the top of her head, then heard him make a small sound of pleasure. "God, I've missed you," he murmured as his arm tightened around her a bit more.

Grace leaned her head against his chest, closed her eyes, and inhaled—dragging his scent deep into her lungs. Warmth unfurled inside her then spread, chasing away the melancholy that'd been her near-constant companion while they were apart.

This was where she belonged. With him. In his arms.

Every bit of remnant tension fled as the sensation of finally being home again settled into her soul. They stood there, holding one another in silence, until a yawn snuck up on her. She felt Colt chuckle beneath her cheek.

"Let's get you to bed." He released her and started toward the hallway.

"Wait. I need to go grab my suitcase first."

He shook his head. "You can get it in the morning. I'll give you a shirt to sleep in."

That got her moving. She'd worn the one she'd stolen from him so many times that it no longer smelled like him. Maybe she should have stolen more than one. She'd have to steal another before she left here. If she left without him, that was. Honestly, she wasn't sure she could deal with being separated from him again. It'd been a mistake to let Flint scare her into leaving Colt in the first place. She knew that now.

"Okay." She followed him down the hall. "Which room should I sleep in?" She remembered that Cash had several guest rooms.

He paused and lifted an eyebrow as he looked back at her. One corner of his mouth curled upward. "Mine."

Her steps faltered as she gawked at him. "Yours?" Her stomach fluttered.

Colt nodded, watching her intently. "Yep, mine. Unless you really want your own. The others are clean and made up, but I can behave."

"I—Colt, you're injured. I don't want to bump you or something and hurt you. And you may be able to keep your hands to yourself, but you know I'm not so good at it."

"I'm aware." One corner of his mouth tilted upward. "I'll be okay. I promise. I've busted my ribs so many times they don't phase me much anymore, and most of my other injuries are pretty close to healed now. My shoulder still hurts, but not so much that I can't handle sharing a bed with you."

She couldn't even imagine that—breaking bones so often that the pain didn't bother you anymore. To her, it was unthinkable. But then, until the abuse started and she'd been forced to learn to function while in near-constant pain, her own pain tolerance had been pretty close to abysmal.

"Do you want your own room?"

She swallowed, her mouth feeling suspiciously dry. "No." She offered him a shaky smile. "I think I'm pretty over sleeping alone."

Colt grinned for the first time since she'd arrived and waved her ahead of him into the room closest to where they'd stopped. He followed her in and moved to the dresser, where he grabbed a t-shirt from one of the drawers.

She caught the shirt with ease when he balled it up and tossed it to her, but lost the ability to move or even breathe when he began undressing right after. There was no way she could pry her eyes off of him. It wasn't even an option. Her gaze was drawn to him like a magnet.

He caught her watching and smirked. "Like what you see, Trouble?"

"You know I do." It was a struggle to not give in to the desire to grab him and kiss him hard.

She sat the shirt at the end of the bed instead and kicked off her boots before stripping her shirt off over her head. She'd just let her bra hit the floor when she heard Colt make a somewhat strangled noise.

Her eyes cut over to him, and she smirked. "Like what you see, Eight?"

It wasn't necessary for him to reply. The heat smoldering in his gaze, along with the very obvious erection straining at the thin fabric of his boxers, made the answer quite clear.

"If you didn't look so damn tired right now..."

Her lips quirked upward, but she didn't reply. She really was bone-weary. It probably had been a mistake to drive straight through, but once she'd learned of his wreck, she hadn't been able to think about anything beyond getting to him as soon as possible. If it hadn't been for Summer, she might have flown instead.

Grace tossed the borrowed shirt on over her head before shimmying free of her jeans. Another yawn overtook her as she crawled into bed beside Colt a moment later. He switched off the light, and she found herself struggling to keep her eyes open. Maybe she was even more tired than she'd thought.

"I still don't think it's a good idea sharing a bed with you," she murmured as she rolled to face him.

"We're just sleeping, Trouble." Through the darkness, she saw his lips twitch. Then he added, "Tonight."

She arched a brow. "So, tomorrow might be a different story?"

"Maybe." He tucked a lock of hair behind her ear. His gaze was intense, but she was too exhausted to read the emotions lurking there. "Depends how the conversation I think we need to have goes." Colt leaned forward and pressed a kiss to her forehead, then rolled onto his back and closed his eyes. "For now, get some sleep."

Though she wanted to ask what conversation he thought they needed to have, she held her tongue. She supposed she would find out soon enough.

Instead of even attempting to keep her hands to herself, she slipped an arm over his stomach and curled as close to his side as she dared before closing her eyes. She was asleep in seconds.

⸺⸺◆⸺⸺

Grace woke alone. Well, alone other than the little stuffed horse that sat on Colt's pillow. She smiled as she snagged the toy animal and snuggled it against her chest for a moment.

He'd kept it. While he'd been busy loading Summer for her the morning after she'd announced she was leaving, she'd buried the stuffed animal in the bottom of his duffle bag with a note. It'd read that she was giving him Whinny to keep him from getting lonely behind all his walls. She wasn't sure what had possessed her to do it, but it slightly surprised her that he'd kept the stuffed animal all this time.

As she sat Whinny aside and climbed out of bed, she noticed her suitcase sitting next to the dresser. It probably hadn't been the best idea for Colt to carry it in for her, but she certainly appreciated it. Now, if she could manage to remember where exactly the bathrooms were at in this house.

Grace grabbed a clean outfit and stepped into the hall.

There was a bathroom directly across from the bedroom. She must have been too distracted, or tired, last night to have noticed it. Either way, it was definitely convenient.

From the clattering coming from the direction of the kitchen, she surmised that Colt was busy making breakfast. Her stomach grumbled at the idea of food. She hurried into the bathroom for a quick shower.

Grace sniffed at the air appreciatively as she entered the kitchen fifteen minutes later. It smelled absolutely incredible. She couldn't tell what he was cooking, but if it tasted as good as it smelled, it was sure to be delicious.

Her gaze landed on Colt as she walked around the end of the counter in hopes of a cup of coffee. The man looked pretty damn delicious too. His chest and feet were bare, his jeans low-slung on his hips.

"Good morning," she said softly when he looked up at her.

"Morning yourself. How'd you sleep?"

"Uh, I don't remember, so I'm going to say I must have slept well." She smiled. "I saw you kept Whinny." She poured herself a cup of coffee and took a small sip.

"Of course I did. What, did you think I would throw him away or something? Who would I have cuddled with if I'd done that? You sure weren't around."

Her lips lifted into a smile. "You did not snuggle with that stupid stuffed horse."

"I did, actually. More than once," he admitted softly. "I was drunk and missing you like mad. He was the closest thing I had to you." Colt gave her a sheepish grin then turned away to stir one of the pans on the stove. "He smells like you. It helped some."

Grace stared at him while a mixture of emotions cascaded one after the other through her. She'd done the same with his t-shirt. It'd brought her comfort on the long nights without him. Never in a million years would she have thought he'd do the same with the stuffed animal.

She still wasn't convinced he really had. "You're serious?"

He glanced over at her and chuckled. "I am." He turned off two of the burners then cocked his head as he met her eyes. "Why would I lie about something like that?"

There was no reason for him to lie, and he seemed completely serious. Rather than replying to his question, she decided to change the subject to something less uncomfortable.

She shifted closer to peer around his arm to see what he was cooking. "So, what's for breakfast?"

"Nothing fancy. Some scrambled eggs, bacon, and sausage. You woke up just in time." He tossed her a smile and clicked off the last of the burners. "Saves me from having to come wake you up." Colt nudged her arm playfully and dished up the food.

After they finished eating, Grace followed Colt back into the kitchen to help him clean up. "Okay, you're going to have to show me sometime how you got the scrambled eggs so fluffy. Mine turn out like mush compared to yours."

He flashed her a grin. "I'm glad you liked them."

"Where did you learn to cook?" Other than when he'd cooked while they were here together months ago, to pick up Summer, she couldn't remember the last time she'd had a man cook a meal for her. Not even her dad had.

"My mom. She taught Cash and me. According to her, knowing how to cook is a skill every man needs to know. Not just so he can feed himself, but also so he can cook for his lady one day." He shrugged. "I don't get the chance to cook very often. I kinda like it."

"Well, she was an excellent teacher. Everything you've made me has been great." She tilted her head. "There's something I've been curious about for a while."

"What's that?"

"Well, you and Cash. You've both said you're like brothers, and you said he grew up with you. Since your mom taught him to cook and your mom used to sing you both through your nightmares, I assume he was at your place a lot? I guess I've been curious how you guys became so close. You seem so different."

A look she couldn't quite interpret crossed his face. He almost seemed a bit uncomfortable.

"When we first met, I was ten and Cash was seven. We hit it off immediately and have been as close as brothers ever since. I was a lot like him before Sarah. No, probably worse." He smiled slightly. "You probably wouldn't have liked me much if you'd met me back then. Anyway, Cash and I, we were almost always together as kids. He spent way more time at my house than his own. Then, on his thirteenth birthday, he moved in with my family permanently."

"Why?"

Colt shook his head. "That's not my story to tell. All I'll say is that he had a really rough childhood."

She let the subject drop, sensing she was pretty close to a line that wasn't to be crossed. Grace touched his arm as she passed by on her way to the sink with the last of the dishes. "Thank you for breakfast."

"You're welcome," he murmured. "Hey, Grace?"

She turned to face him and startled at his nearness. When had he moved so close? Her pulse kicked higher as she lifted her gaze to his. "Yeah?"

He took a half-step closer. They were so close now that they were nearly touching. She could feel the warmth of his body radiating toward her.

"Thank you for coming out here. I know I was short with you, but I really am glad you're here. I've been told I'm no fun to hang out with when I'm hurt, however, so I'll understand if you decide to pack up Summer and go back to the circuit instead of hanging out with my grumpy ass."

"I like your ass, grumpy or otherwise." Grace smiled and laid her hand on his arm. She gave the firm muscles beneath her fingers a gentle squeeze. "Do you want me to leave?" She suspected the answer would be no, but she needed to hear him say it. She needed to know for sure.

"Hell no," he said immediately, his voice gruff. His throat worked as though he had more words stuck in it, but he didn't voice them.

She wondered why not.

He took a deep breath and backed away. "Come on, Trouble. Let's go to the living room. We can finish the dishes later. I think it's well past time that we talk about a few things." He didn't wait for a reply before striding out of the room.

That sounded more than a little ominous to her. A hint of trepidation flickered within her as she trailed behind him, uncertain if she wanted to know what he had on his mind.

Chapter 26

Colt studied the stonework of the fireplace as he tried to decide how to word what he needed to say to the woman seated on the couch, watching him warily. He could only guess what she was thinking right now.

"It feels strange being here without Cash around," he said without looking at Grace, in hopes the idle comment would somehow help dispel some of the tension flooding the room.

He'd been at the ranch for three days now—counting today—but the feeling he was trespassing or something still hadn't faded. Which was silly. There wasn't much he and Cash hadn't shared in the past. When they were younger—well before Sarah—they'd even shared a woman or two on the odd occasion. Those days were long gone now. He'd met Sarah and settled down while Cash had only grown wilder and more commitment-phobic. It seemed a touch curious to him that his friend had bought this ranch, however, all while continuing to swear that he would never settle down. Colt wasn't sure he bought the whole "investment opportunity" explanation Cash had given him.

With a sigh, Colt turned back to Grace and seated himself beside her. He didn't know how this conversation was going to go, but it was undeniably overdue and he'd delayed plenty long enough. Time to hope for the best and get it over with.

"I've been stupid," he began. "Really stupid. I realized the afternoon after we parted how big of a mistake letting you go was, but I figured it was too late to fix it. I was sure I had blown any chance I had with you. I'm still not convinced I haven't."

Her fingers began worrying the hem of her shirt, but she didn't speak, so he plunged on.

"I'm ashamed to admit that I went off the rails after we separated. I fell back on old coping habits and probably spent more time drunk than sober. I rode hungover more than once, despite the guys trying to talk me out of it. It was dangerous and I knew it, but I was caught in a tailspin and didn't know how to pull out of it." He shook his head. "I'm not proud of it, but I was hungover when I had my wreck too. That ride may have gone south even if that hadn't been a factor, but it probably didn't help anything."

He laid his hand over hers to stop the nervous fiddling of her fingers. "That's partly why I'm here. When the hospital released me, Cash convinced me to hole up here. I needed somewhere to heal anyway, and he figured the distance from you might help me get my head back on straight. Turns out, he was right. Seeing you but not being able to talk to you was too difficult."

Colt took a deep breath then spit out the rest in a rush. "When the wreck was happening and I was starting to wonder if that'd be my last ride, I realized I didn't want to die without finding out where this thing between us might go. I told myself if I survived and we crossed paths again, I'd tell you. Even if you yelled at me for talking to you. And now, here you are."

She inhaled deeply. "What are you saying?"

He could see the cautious hope lurking in her eyes. It made him want to smile despite the seriousness of the conversation.

"I'm saying that I want you to be mine," he said slowly. He hoped like fuck he wasn't too late. She was here, and she'd shared a bed with him last night; that seemed like a good sign. "I want to try. And I'm hoping that it's not too late." He angled his upper body toward her. "So, what do you say, Princess? Give a broken cowboy a chance?"

She blinked slowly, and the tip of her tongue darted out to moisten her lips.

The ornate clock sitting on the mantle ticked absurdly loud in the quiet room. Colt could almost hear his heart beating. Could she hear it too? For the love of everything good, would she say something? Anything.

The longer the silence stretched, the more tense he became. What if she said no? What then? Fuck, then he'd get down on his knees and beg. He'd grovel. He'd do whatever the hell he had to do to earn a chance.

Her eyes narrowed slightly as they roamed over his face. "You're serious right now?"

He nodded, praying she didn't leave him waiting for an answer long. His heart felt like it was going to beat right out of his chest with as hard as it was thudding against his ribs. So much rode on her decision.

A slow smile curled her lips upward, then she leaned closer and kissed him. Hard, greedy, desperate. Like she'd been holding back a tidal wave of emotion for a long time. Maybe she had. He knew he certainly had been. By the time she pulled back, he was breathless and aching to be inside her.

He smirked. "Is that a yes?"

Grace laughed and rolled her eyes. "Yes, that's a yes."

"Just checking." A mischievous grin pulled at his lips. He dropped a kiss on her mouth, resisting the urge to crush her to his chest and never let her go. "I have something else I need to ask."

Her shoulders stiffened, a bit of the earlier wariness returning to her gaze. "Okay?"

"What made you decide to leave when you did? Was it just Flint? I don't blame you, but it seemed... I don't know, like you were mad at me or something for a while before." He still felt the need to know if it'd been him. If he'd done something to cause her to shut him out so wholly. How could he keep from making the same mistake in the future if he didn't ask?

"It was mostly him. After everything he's done to me, I believed he would at least attempt to hurt you. I wouldn't have been able to live with myself if anything happened to you because of me. Fear got the better of me, I guess. That's why I left. I wasn't mad at you."

She glanced down at her hands then back up at him. "I haven't heard a peep out of Flint since you and I went our separate ways, but I'm still afraid he'll try. I'm determined to be as brave as you believe I am, though. When Cash told me about your wreck, I needed to see you. I guess the fear of losing you for good is stronger than the fear of what Flint will do if he finds out we're together."

She leaned toward him, the ghost of a smile playing on her lips. "I realized I'd made a horrible mistake the moment you and Dusty drove off, but I was too ashamed and afraid to call and ask you to come back. That's the reason I didn't try fixing things at any of the rodeos too. It was hard staying away from you. Cash said you needed me, so I didn't have much choice but to come here, even if I was terrified you'd tell me to get lost."

"I'd never tell you to get lost. Cash said I need you, huh?" One corner of his mouth tilted up. "Well, he wasn't wrong there. I do need you."

She smiled tenderly then her eyes swept over him. Her brow furrowed, and her smile turned into a small frown. "He said you might not be able to ride anymore because of your shoulder."

"He may have exaggerated some about my shoulder. It will be fine. It didn't even need surgery." He would have to remember to thank Cash for giving Grace a nudge the next time he saw him. "As far as riding goes, the doctors didn't say any of my injuries would keep me from continuing."

Not that he was entirely sure he wanted to ride again. He was beginning to wonder if it might be time to quit. This time, for good. There was no way he was ready to admit that to anyone else yet, however, not even Grace. Speaking those words made it too real, too open to influence. Until he'd made a decision one way or another, he wasn't saying a word about it.

"I've needed you too," Grace said softly.

Colt smiled and leaned over to kiss her. When he lifted his mouth from hers, he gave her a somewhat sheepish look. "I'm sure it's probably a bit too soon for the whole 'meet the parents' thing, but they're coming here for dinner tonight. I got a text from them this morning. Talking them out of it didn't go very far. I'm sorry." He sighed. "They've been a pain in the ass since my wreck. I've been here three days today, and so far, they've been here every day. They probably won't stay long. My mom hates being out after dark. They've been staying at a hotel a couple hours from here. There was nothing closer that met my mom's standards." One corner of his mouth lifted. "Maybe you being here will convince them I'm fine and they'll go back home."

Grace nibbled her lip. "I don't mind meeting them, but ... what if they don't like me?"

"It's impossible to not like you."

They'd love her for most of the reasons he did. She was brave, witty, and humorous. She had a way of putting you at ease. Shit, he couldn't even stay mad at her because the damn woman had such an uncanny knack of making him smile even when he didn't want to.

She didn't look convinced, but he didn't know how else to reassure her. She'd see for herself once they got here. He had no doubt they would be ecstatic to meet her. His mom especially.

He shoved to his feet and held out his hand. "Let me go grab a shirt and my boots, and we'll head outside to go get Summer exercised. She's probably wondering what's going on."

"Probably." She placed her hand in his and got to her feet.

He closed his fingers around hers and tugged her closer. "But first, I need something."

Her eyes sparkled as they met his. "Oh, yeah? What do you need?"

"This." Colt ducked his head and captured her lips.

All was right with the world again. She was here, and she was his. Some piece of him he hadn't realized was missing slid back into place.

—◆—

"That wasn't so bad, was it?" Colt asked as he pulled Grace in for a hug. "I told you my parents would love you."

If it hadn't started getting dark, his parents would most likely still be here visiting with Grace. His mother, especially, had been reluctant to leave. She had been both shocked and pleased to discover he had a girlfriend. He knew she'd worried about him after Sarah. She'd never liked how he'd sworn off relationships. His mom wanted to know he was happy and constantly bemoaned the fact she'd never have grand babies to spoil if he didn't date.

There'd never been a question in his mind about whether they'd like Grace. Still, he'd never planned on being here again. Definitely never wanted to be. It was funny how things could change when you least expected them to.

Grace smiled. "Your mom is sweet. I like her." She wrapped her arms around his middle and gazed up at him. "You are the spitting image of your dad too. You guys even have a similar sense of humor. There's definitely no denying he's your father; that's for sure."

He laughed. "Yeah, I've been told that before. He would never dream of riding a bull, though. I grew up a hell of a lot wilder than he ever was too. It's a miracle my parents don't have more grey hair with everything I've put them through."

This was the first time he could recall visiting with his parents and not ending up arguing with them about his career. They'd been so distracted by meeting his girlfriend that they'd spent the entire visit grilling her instead of trying to talk him out of riding bulls for a living. It'd been a relief. He tired of having to field their strongly worded opinions about his occupation. If they knew he was thinking about giving it up, they'd be overjoyed.

Each of these wrecks took more out of him. They were definitely taking their toll.

He dropped a kiss on the tip of Grace's nose then unwound her arms from his waist. "Let's go inside. I need to find my sling."

He hated the damn thing, but without it, the pull on his shoulder rapidly began testing the limits of his pain tolerance. There was no way he'd wanted to wear it around his parents, however. Even Grace's presence wouldn't have been able to distract them from the reminder of the danger he faced every time he climbed on a bull.

As they walked into the house and made their way to the living room, a faint blush crept onto Grace's face. "I'm embarrassed about having to ask, but I've forgotten your parents' names already. I was so nervous about meeting them that I wasn't really listening."

Colt chuckled. "My mom is Mary, and my dad is Clayton. Most people call him Clay."

"Mary and Clay," she parroted as she seated herself on the couch. "I'll try to remember that."

Her phone's text alert went off, and her shoulders tensed.

The thing had been obnoxious since early afternoon. She'd largely been ignoring it all day. He'd been wanting to ask about it, but with his parents around there hadn't been a good time. They didn't need to know about her troubles with Flint, and that's exactly who he suspected was texting her so often today.

He sank onto the couch beside her and nodded toward her phone as it went off for the second time in less than five minutes. "Is that Flint? I thought you changed your number?"

Grace sighed wearily. "It is, and I did—after I left. It has been quiet since then. Until today, that is. I don't know how he got my new number. One of his friends probably helped him figure it out. It's unlisted—or it's supposed to be, at least." She rubbed at her forehead. "I don't know what else to do. Do I change it again? Is there even a point to going through all that fuss if he can apparently find out my new number?"

"I could always put you on my service plan and you could drop yours. That should make it harder for him to reach you." He eyed her ancient phone and grinned. "You look like you could use a new phone anyway. How the hell old is that thing?"

She glanced at her phone. "Um, about six or seven years, I think. I had it before I met him. I couldn't afford a smartphone. This thing does everything I need it to anyway. I do wish it took better pictures, though." She cocked her head. "Let me guess; you're one of those tech geeks that have to have the latest and greatest."

Colt made a face. "Not hardly. I do like to update my tech at least every couple of years, but I thought everyone did." He kissed her. "Apparently, I was wrong. I couldn't live without my apps either. Dumb phones are not for me."

The phone chimed again, and his eyes narrowed on it. "Can I read his messages?"

She handed her phone to him. "Go ahead. You can delete them after too. I have no desire to read any more of them. I'm so completely over this whole thing." She growled in frustration. "It's been so quiet that I almost thought he'd finally given up." She threw an exasperated look at the ceiling. "It's like he's watching me somehow. How does he know I'm with you again?"

"I don't know, Princess. We'll go tomorrow to get you put on my plan. That should help."

He flipped open her phone, and his gaze dropped to the tiny screen. Every message he read made his jaw clench increasingly tighter. This was bullshit. Who the fuck did this man think he was? When Colt finished reading the last of them, he lifted his gaze back to Grace.

"What is he referring to here?" He turned the phone her way and pointed out one specific message. "Is that why you ran to me that night?" He remembered how frightened she'd looked, and his jaw clenched tight all over again.

She glanced at the screen, gulped, then looked away. "I still don't want to talk about that night, but ... I should, I think.

Someone needs to know what happened." Her gaze swept over his face before she locked her eyes elsewhere again. "Promise me you won't go after him."

If she wanted a promise like that, he already knew he wouldn't like what he heard. Still, it wasn't like he was in any sort of shape to go after Flint at the moment anyway. That didn't mean he couldn't send Cash or one of the other guys to deal with him, however. Maybe even all of them. While his friends might enjoy a bit of no-strings fun with willing women, none of them would tolerate anyone disrespecting or harming one.

"Colt. Promise me."

Shit, he was taking too long to answer. He sat her phone aside and took hold of her hand, then swept his thumb back and forth across her knuckles. "I promise."

Grace studied him for a few seconds then took a deep breath. "Let me start at the beginning of the worst of it. I think that might make it easier." She stared down at their joined hands. "The night of the cookout, he accused me of cheating on him because he caught me watching you. I recognized you from the auction, and I don't know, I guess I was drawn to you even then. I couldn't help but look, and it's not like it's a crime anyway. Flint used to hit on anything with tits right in front of me all the time. He had no right to get upset. That night was the first time he ever hit me."

Colt winced but bit down on his tongue to keep from saying anything. It pissed him off that she'd been hurt because of him. He'd been drawn to her too, though. Completely captivated. He remembered the moment he'd seen her there in her backyard, standing next to one of the coolers. She'd been so beautiful. It'd been difficult to pull his eyes away from her. Shit, he'd had trouble not going over to talk to her.

"When I got assigned to follow you around and interview you, it was like I'd won a vacation from hell. I loved spending time with you. At first, I felt guilty for enjoying it so much. I never expected you'd become my best friend."

She'd become his best friend too. Well, his best female friend, at least. He'd looked forward to spending time with her more than she'd ever know.

Grace flashed a tremulous smile up at him. "The job assignment let me start planning my escape, and spending time with you helped me keep my sanity through the nightmare my life at home had become."

Grace paused for a moment to take a couple of deep breaths.

Colt awkwardly pulled her into his lap, wrapping his good arm around her. It was tricky, but he managed. "I would have helped you if you had told me. You know that, right?"

"Of course!" she answered. "But our friendship was still so new, and I was too afraid. I didn't want to burden you with my issues."

Fuck. It wouldn't have been a burden. As much as he understood the feeling, he hated it. He wished she'd come to him sooner. Let him help her earlier. She'd suffered so much at Flint's hands. It killed him knowing he could have prevented at least some of it.

"I was embarrassed about being abused, and about not being able to leave. Ashamed too. I ... just couldn't." She shook her head. "I don't know when or how he figured out that the cowboy I'd been spending so much time with for work was you, but it really set him off when he did. If you'd been anyone else, I don't think he would have reacted like he did. I think you really make him feel threatened somehow." She glanced up at him. "I really did fall in the shower, like I told you. That night, while I was getting ready for our interview, he hit me so hard that I lost my balance and fell into the shower stall at the hotel I was staying at."

His arm tightened around her. Rage like he'd never known filled him, but he swallowed it down and tried his best to hide it. She didn't need to know how badly he wanted to hunt the bastard down, or how much he wanted to make him pay for every single wrong he'd ever done to her—to hell with the consequences. Maybe he'd look good in orange.

"I'm so sorry, Princess."

"I'm not done," she murmured without looking at him. "It gets worse." She squeezed his forearm. "As soon as we got home from that rodeo, he made me quit my job, then he told Sissy I was plotting to steal her husband. I wasn't; I barely even talked to the guy. But she believed him and blew up at me. She wouldn't listen to anything I had to say."

She frowned. "I miss her sometimes. I have such a hard time making friends, and I was really enjoying hanging out with her. Flint is great at getting people to believe anything he says, though, so I guess I'm not surprised she believed him. It still hurts she didn't even question what he was telling her."

Colt's heart hurt for her, his anger spreading to include Sissy—though to a lesser degree. Some friend she'd been if she hadn't even been willing to listen, to consider that Flint was lying.

Grace paused to take a shuddering breath. "Anyway, things escalated from there. Literally anything could set him off. Anything. I felt like I was walking on eggshells all the time. It was like I'd become his personal punching bag or something. Even things that couldn't possibly be my fault, like the weather, somehow were." She leaned against him harder.

His ribs protested the pressure, but he ignored it. He couldn't even imagine it, needing to tiptoe around someone else like that.

"The night I showed up at your motel, I accidentally called him a monster while he was beating on me. I really thought he was going to kill me. I still don't know why he didn't. He started choking me. I'm not sure what happened after that. I couldn't breathe, and I was panicking. The next thing I knew, he stopped and left the room. I was too terrified to move for a while, but when he didn't come back, I got up and ran. You know the rest."

Now *he* couldn't breathe, his chest tight. *She'd been strangled.* Fuck.

He remembered back to that night, to when she'd shown up on his doorstep. There hadn't been any bruises around her neck as far as he'd seen, but there'd been those scratches. Scratches from her fighting for her life.

His stomach lurched, and he swallowed hard in an effort to keep his dinner where it belonged. He thanked whatever deity might be listening that she'd survived. That Flint had stopped before he killed her. His arm tightened around her a bit more.

Colt closed his eyes and fought to regain his calm. Once he was reasonably sure the anger coursing through him wouldn't color his voice, he gazed down at her. "You didn't deserve any of that. He'll have to go through me to get to you if he's dumb enough to mess with you again. I will do everything in my power to protect you." He rested his cheek against the top of her head. "Thank you for trusting me. I know it had to be difficult to talk about." He dropped a kiss on the top of her head before she shifted around so she straddled his lap.

"I know you will." She cradled his face in her hands. "Thank *you* for being someone I can tell."

He didn't have a chance to reply before she leaned in and caught his lips in a tender kiss.

Colt tightened his arm a bit further and cursed his sling for the thousandth time today alone. Her tongue slid against his as she deepened her kiss, and the fury still coursing through his veins transformed to desire in an instant.

Chapter 27

Grace tipped her head to the side as Colt brushed her hair back and pressed his lips to her neck. Sparks flowed over her skin and heated her blood. It hadn't been her intention to start something tonight, but she couldn't say she was unhappy about the turn of events. He was growing hard beneath her.

Unable to keep herself from tempting him, she gave her hips a slow roll, eliciting a low groan from him, to her delight. "I want you," she whispered.

Regret flickered in the depths of his dilated eyes when he pulled back to gaze at her. "I don't have any condoms, Trouble. I didn't see a reason to get any after you left."

Her brows raised. "You haven't been with anyone since I left?"

She knew how popular he was with the buckle bunnies. It was impossible to spend any time around the rodeo grounds and not overhear gossip about him. Rumor had it that he was near insatiable, that he had such a high sex drive that many of the bunnies smugly complained he made it difficult for them to walk the next morning at times. She'd hated that talk. It'd always left her feeling jealous. Still, if all that was true about his drive, why hadn't he been with anyone? She found it difficult to comprehend.

Colt laughed. "No." He dropped a kiss on the tip of her nose, making her wrinkle it up. "There hasn't been anyone else for me but you. You're the only one I've wanted since we ran into each other at that auction."

What? Since the auction? A tiny smile lifted her lips as she digested that.

That was such a long time to have gone without. Such a long time to crave someone like he clearly had. Geez, and she'd had the audacity to think he hadn't wanted her. The notion was laughable now.

"I have some in my toiletry bag."

His expression shuttered.

She could guess his thoughts.

"I haven't been with anyone but you if you're wondering," she hurriedly explained. "I don't want anyone else." She shrugged. "I thought I should have some on hand in case you got tired of Flint keeping us apart and came after me. I ... was hoping. The box isn't even opened yet."

He lifted an eyebrow then one corner of his mouth twitched upward. "I would have come after you, but I figured you didn't want anything more to do with me. I thought I'd blown my chance."

She shook her head as her faint smile gained strength. "Well, you obviously didn't."

He grinned in answer. Colt nudged her off of his lap and got to his feet before offering his hand to her. "Come on. Let's go to bed."

Grace placed her hand in his and let him help her to her feet, then followed him down the hallway.

The moment they both stood in the bedroom together, he pulled her around to face him and bent to brush a kiss over her lips, then slipped his sling off his shoulder with a vague wince.

She stepped away from him and yanked her shirt off over her head while simultaneously toeing off her boots.

Colt didn't give her time to take off anything else before he closed the small space between them and skimmed his hands along her sides. "Your skin is so fucking soft."

Her gaze lifted to his. The hunger and promise burning in his eyes made her breaths quicken and her core ache. She remained motionless as he reached behind her to unclasp her bra before using his thumbs to push the straps off her shoulders. He lowered his mouth to her neck while her bra dropped to the ground.

She gasped and moved to give him better access as her eyes fluttered shut. "I love when you kiss my neck," she murmured.

She felt him smile against her skin before he continued kissing a trail down her neck and along her collarbone. When he reached her shoulder, he nipped the skin there, then lifted his head and stared down at her.

"I love kissing you." As if to emphasize his words, he ducked his head and caught her lips in a searing kiss. He kept his mouth on hers as he began walking her backward toward the closest wall. The gentle press of his body held her in place as his rough hands slid down to her hips. He flicked open the button on her jeans.

Her heart stuttered. A flood of desire pooled low in her belly, making her ache. Her body tingled, warmed, as he leaned forward to feather a kiss over her neck.

God, yes. He could keep doing that until the oceans dried up. She fought the need to press her thighs together in an attempt to ease the throbbing between them. No doubt her panties were soaked by now. She needed his touch. She wanted him inside her.

Colt pulled back and gave her a knowing smirk before dropping to his knees in front of her. He hooked his fingers under the waistband of her panties and in one fluid movement pulled them down along with her jeans.

She braced herself on his good shoulder as she stepped free of them, careful not to put much pressure on him, not wanting to hurt him and ruin this moment.

"I won't break, baby. You can lean on me harder than that if you need to." He leaned forward and brushed a gentle kiss over her lower belly, then nudged her thighs apart.

She could feel his breath on the damp curls between her legs. A shiver of pleasure raced through her veins.

She stared down at him. "What are you doing?" she asked with a gasp as he trailed a fingertip around her opening.

Colt glanced up at her with a wicked smile but didn't answer her question. "Hold on to me, Trouble."

When she hesitated, he grabbed her hands and placed them on his shoulders close to his neck. Then, he gently grasped her ankle and hooked her leg over his good shoulder.

It was suddenly quite clear to her what he intended to do.

Apprehension dimmed her desire some. With his other shoulder injured, she was afraid she'd accidentally put too much of her weight on him and cause him pain.

Maybe she should put a stop to this. "Colt, I don't think—"

He spread her open with his thumbs and gave her a long, hot lick with the flat of his tongue before sucking down on her clit.

The protest she'd been about to utter fled in an instant.

"Oh, God," she gasped.

It was a good thing he'd made her hold on to him, or the sudden sensation would have sent her to the floor. She slid the fingers of one hand into his hair and clasped him to her. He could keep doing what he was doing for the rest of eternity. She was absolutely fine with that.

"Sorry, what were you going to say?" He glanced up her body and lifted a brow.

She shook her head. "Not important. Don't stop."

Colt chuckled, then flicked his tongue against her clit before settling in to zealously work her body with his mouth, obviously intent on driving her mad.

Her head fell back against the wall with a dull thump as her eyes slid closed. She moaned and angled her hips toward him while her fingers tightened in his hair. Already, she could feel telltale pressure building in her core. Her cowboy was a wicked, wicked, wonderful man. Oh, God. So wonderful.

"Please," she breathlessly begged though she didn't know what it was she wanted. Just ... more.

He seemed to know what she needed. He redoubled his efforts, his tongue and lips working her without mercy.

Her legs began trembling, and her fingers dug into his good shoulder. It would be a miracle if she didn't end up on the floor before he was done with her. She felt him smile against her skin seconds before he sucked down hard on her clit, at the exact moment he plunged two fingers into her center.

The sudden fullness sent her soaring over the edge with a cry. Her body clamped down hard around him, but he didn't let up. He thrust his fingers in her while continuing to love her with his mouth until a second wave of intense pleasure crashed over her—this one so strong that she could do nothing more than shudder and gasp while her body tightened again.

She loosened her grip on his hair as he slipped his fingers free of her body and pulled back enough to look up at her with a smug smile on his lips.

Grace gazed back at him, unable to form words. It seemed pretty likely that her brain was short-circuiting at the moment. She slowly eased her leg off his shoulder while half wondering if it would even hold her up. Her legs felt like they'd turned to rubber.

"Got your balance?"

Grace nodded once she was reasonably sure she wouldn't end up in a heap on the hardwood floor, and he shoved back to his feet with a soft groan. His mouth crashed down on hers the moment he was standing. She could taste herself on his tongue—slightly sweet, vaguely salty. Her hands landed on his belt as the kiss spun out, but his buckle thwarted her efforts to unfasten it. She growled in frustration and tried again.

Colt released her lips and backed away. She watched as he toed off his boots and stripped off his clothes. A few faint bruises still marred parts of his chest. Once he stood naked before her, she stepped forward and feathered kisses over each of them, enjoying the way his muscles jumped and twitched beneath her touch.

Their eyes locked. His gaze was soft. His throat worked like he wanted to say something, but then he swallowed hard and snagged her hand.

He tugged her toward the bed. "Come on, Trouble. I'm not done with you yet."

Her lips quirked upward. "I would hope not. I'm not done with you either." She would never be done with him. This man was it for her. Forever and always.

She settled herself on the mattress when he tossed back the covers for her, and rolled onto her side to watch him prowl toward her toiletry bag. He retrieved a condom from the box and rolled it on before joining her on the bed.

Colt stretched out on his side beside her, mirroring her position, and stroked his fingertips along her ribcage. The look in his eyes as they roamed over her made her stomach quiver in anticipation.

He met her gaze, one corner of his mouth lifting. "You're too far away. Get over here."

She scooted closer, laying her head on his upper arm as he slipped it beneath her neck. "Better?"

His hard length was pressing against her belly. It was going to drive her mad.

In answer, he leaned in and kissed her. The hand of the arm beneath her head moved to her shoulder, kneading slightly as his mouth moved away from hers and traveled along her jaw to her neck. She hissed out a breath, shifting her head to give him more room.

She loved what he was doing to her, almost as much as she loved him.

One of his legs moved between hers. Instinctively, she wrapped her own leg over his hips, opening herself to him.

His hand delved between her thighs, and then the tip of him nudged the entrance to her core—so close to where she needed him but still too far away.

Her body throbbed, crying out to be filled by him. It was maddening. She needed him inside her. Now. Grace shifted her hips and he sank into her, stretching her deliciously. A satisfied sigh escaped her lips.

Colt moaned against the side of her neck, making her lips twitch into a gentle smile. His free hand grazed her side then gripped her hip as he moved slowly within her. Each stroke sent tendrils of pleasure skittering through her as his body rubbed against hers right where she needed it most. He pulled his head back and kissed her—tenderly, sweetly. As if he loved her too.

They made love as though they had all the time in the world. As though even eternity would be too short of a time together. Their soft gasps and moans intertwined as they steadily drove one another closer to the edge. It felt like he was making love to her soul, not just her body.

Grace gasped as Colt thrusted into her a fraction quicker.

She loved this man, with all her heart. Those three little words hovered at the tip of her tongue as they gazed at each other, but she held them back. She couldn't bring herself to speak them until he said them first, if that ever happened.

His fingers dug into the skin of her hip, but she didn't mind. He trembled as though fighting to keep his orgasm at bay.

"Let go," she whispered, then kissed his chest.

His body rumbled under her lips as he groaned.

"Not yet," he answered breathlessly. "You first."

He wouldn't have long to wait. Her climax shimmered there on the horizon. Close. So close.

She pulled her head back and met Colt's eyes. The impulse to tell him she loved him perched on the tip of her tongue once again, but still she held it back. His gaze was intense, his ocean eyes technicolor.

She caressed his cheek and pulled him in for a kiss.

They came together, gasping and shuddering as they clung to one another. It'd never been like this with anyone else. Nobody had ever made her feel this way.

Colt met her eyes again as he pulled his hips back and slipped from her body. His Adam's apple bobbed as though he had something to say, but instead of speaking, he kissed her hard.

What had he wanted to say? Why hadn't he said whatever it was? She wondered what he felt for her. Wondered if he could possibly feel the same way.

He lifted his head away from hers and murmured, "Stay here. I'll be right back." He climbed out of bed and, after giving her one last lingering look, left the bedroom.

Rather than staying put like he'd told her to, Grace slipped out of bed and wandered down the hall to the home's second bathroom. She needed to pee. A UTI would definitely dampen her and Colt's reunion. That would never do.

When she returned to the bedroom, Colt was already back in bed. He'd spread a bath towel out over the sheet on her side. She gave him a quizzical look as she approached.

A small smile crept onto his face. "Just in case. I didn't want you sleeping in a puddle."

Thoughtful.

Grace smiled. "Thanks."

She switched off the light before joining him, then curled comfortably against his side. She rested her cheek on his chest above his heart while he traced random patterns up and down her arm. Neither of them spoke for several minutes.

Finally, he asked, "What are your thoughts about kids?"

She blinked in surprise. "What?"

His chest vibrated under her cheek as he chuckled. "Do you want kids someday?"

This was definitely not a topic she'd expected to be discussing with him. At least, not at this point in their relationship.

"Um ... yes," she answered slowly. "I think I'd like at least two. If I'm blessed with any at all."

He made a small sound she couldn't quite interpret. She eased up onto her elbow. His eyes were closed, and his face was more relaxed than she could recall ever seeing it.

Unable to resist, she skimmed her fingertips over the rough stubble covering his jaw. "What about you? Do you want to have kids one day?" she asked softly.

His eyes opened, and he smiled. "I'll be honest; when Sarah brought up starting a family, the idea of it made me feel panicky. I think that's why I talked her into waiting to try until after I won another championship. Having babies was something we had never discussed before we got married. It probably would have saved us from having more than one argument if we had."

He fell silent as he skimmed his fingers over her side to her hip. "Now, though..." Colt lifted his gaze to hers, a half-smile creeping onto his lips. "Now, the idea of having kids doesn't seem so scary." He shrugged. "Maybe I just wasn't ready back then." He fell quiet, his fingers moving back and forth over her hip. "I think I'd like to have at least one someday."

What was different about now? Why had his thoughts on having kids changed? He still hadn't earned another championship title. He still was a bull rider too. His life seemed exactly the same ... except for the woman he was with.

Grace shoved that thought away immediately. He'd loved Sarah. Of course he'd have wanted to have babies with her someday. Maybe the change was as simple as him being older now, more mature.

She bit her lip, uncertain what to say. Finally, she tentatively asked, "Would you want a baby with me?"

Did he want one with her now? Is that why he'd brought up the subject? She wasn't sure she was ready for that step just yet, but one day, she could see it.

"Princess, I want everything with you." Colt pulled her back down, and touched his lips to the top of her head. "Does my wanting that with you eventually bother you?"

"No." She settled back in against his chest. "If anything, it's comforting to know that if something were to happen, I wouldn't have to worry about you bailing on me."

She could almost feel his frown.

"If I got you pregnant, you wouldn't be raising our baby alone. Even if we don't end up working out, I would never walk away from my kid. I won't lie, though; I think you'd be beautiful round with my baby. Even more beautiful than you already are." His fingers walked over her ribcage.

Grace nibbled at her lip as she digested that.

He pressed another kiss to her forehead. "I want you to know where I stand on the subject. Sarah and I never discussed it before we married, like I said. I don't want to make the same mistake twice."

Her eyes drifted closed as she nodded against him. A foreign feeling of utter contentment settled into her bones. "I can understand that."

"For now, let's get some sleep," he rumbled.

She smiled drowsily and turned her head enough to press a kiss to his chest. "Sounds good to me."

It wasn't long before sleep swept in and carried them both away.

⬦

The sun was just beginning to ease over the horizon when Grace woke. She rubbed a hand over her face and glanced at the window with a groan. It wasn't often that she was awake before Colt. She didn't even need to look at the clock to know it was too darn early for her taste.

With a soft huff, she snuggled deeper into the blanket and closed her eyes.

When it became apparent that sleep had no intention of returning, she reluctantly eased out of bed, trying her best not to disturb him.

She found the t-shirt she'd had on the night before last and tossed it on over her head before padding down the hall to the kitchen. They might be alone here in the house, but she wasn't certain that would remain the case, and she didn't cherish the thought of giving anyone a free show if one of Cash's hired hands unexpectedly entered the house. That would be absolutely mortifying.

She perused the contents of the refrigerator. What to make for breakfast? Colt wasn't exactly picky, but still. She'd never had the opportunity to cook for him before. She wanted to impress him.

At long last, she decided on french toast, scrambled eggs, bacon, and sausage. A hearty meal, but he had a lot of healing to do. His mom would undoubtably approve. When they'd had dinner with his parents yesterday, his mother had been quite insistent that he needed to be fed well so he could heal properly. That was something Grace could agree with. She gathered the necessary ingredients and set to work.

Colt was still sleeping soundly when she entered the bedroom next. Maybe she'd worn him out last night. He was usually awake by now. A cheerful smile lit her face as she crawled back into bed beside him and pressed a kiss to his forehead.

His eyes blinked open, and a sleepy smile formed on his lips.

"Morning." She leaned down to kiss him. "Hungry?"

"For you? Always." He tangled his fingers in her hair and gently tugged her back down for a lingering kiss that had her body humming by the time he released her.

"For food," she said with a grin. "I made breakfast. It's already out there on the table."

"Mmm, I think I'd rather have you for breakfast."

From the lustful gleam in his eyes, she certainly believed it.

Grace laughed and slapped at his hands as he made a grab for her. As tempting as it was to give in to him, she didn't want the meal she'd made him going to waste. "Later, cowboy. Get up."

He smirked. "I am up." He threw back the blanket, exposing the evidence that he was indeed up. "Or is that not what you meant?"

"You know exactly what I meant. Ass." She shook her head. Her lips twitched as she fought to keep from laughing. It wouldn't do to encourage him. The man was incorrigible enough as it was.

Colt chuckled and sat up with a groan. "You must have tired me out more than I thought last night." He glanced at his phone's screen. "It's late."

"Late for you maybe. It's still too darn early for me."

"Couldn't get back to sleep?" He swung his legs out of bed and got to his feet.

Her mouth went dry as her gaze feasted on him as he sauntered toward the dresser. "Nope."

He slipped into a clean pair of jeans and fastened them around his waist.

"I hope you like what I made us."

Colt flashed her a grin. "I'm sure I will. You made it." He ushered her out of the room ahead of him. "Lead the way, Princess."

Chapter 28

THE NEXT FOUR WEEKS passed without incident.

To Grace's joy, her new phone seemed to have bought her a reprieve from Flint's harassment. So far, there hadn't been anything more from him. She already knew that the peace wasn't likely to last. If Flint couldn't get to her on the phone, he'd find some other way to do it. It would be far more shocking to her if he didn't.

Things between her and Colt were phenomenal, however. He was nothing like any man she'd ever been with. Even their arguments were different. No matter how ticked off she made him, he didn't yell. He might growl and huff, but in all the time they'd been friends, he hadn't raised his voice at her even once. It was strange and wonderful. If this was all some sort of really intense, super intricate fantasy, she hoped that she never woke up. She never wanted this feeling to end. Not ever.

Grace rolled onto her back and stretched languidly. Her body felt sore in so many delightful ways. Colt seemed unable to keep his hands off of her for long, and she couldn't deny that she absolutely loved it. It wasn't as though she was any more successful at keeping her hands, or lips, off of him either.

Yesterday, they'd made love three times. Once in the shower, then on the kitchen table after lunch. The last had been in the barn, where to her utter embarrassment, they'd nearly been caught by Cash's ranch foreman. Regardless, she'd do it again in a heartbeat. Colt was far too irresistible not to. The sex was always amazing with him, hands down the best she'd ever had.

Colt groaned and rolled toward her. He threw one arm over her waist and pulled her to him. While not unusual in the mornings, what got her attention was the small whimpering sound he made next.

Her brow furrowed as she turned to look at him. He whimpered again, and his arm tightened around her. It was almost painful, but she was too concerned about him to care. He grimaced and thrashed his head from side to side. Tiny beads of sweat broke out all over what she could see of his body.

Should she wake him up? Didn't they say not to wake people during nightmares? That there was a chance they could lash out? The possibility made her hesitate.

When he began trembling, she couldn't take it anymore. Whatever his dream was about, it clearly wasn't good and only seemed to be getting worse.

Grace pried his arm off of her and sat up. "Colt," she whispered. She hesitantly touched his arm and shook gently. "Colt, wake up."

He flinched and came awake with a strangled yelp as he jolted upright in a hurry. His eyes were wild, and his chest heaved as he gasped for air.

"It's me. It's Grace."

His gaze darted to her and held there, but he didn't seem to really see her.

"It's okay. You're okay. You were having a nightmare." She hesitantly slipped her arms around him and pulled him against her, then smoothed one hand over his sweat-dampened hair. "I'm here. You're okay."

His breath shuddered out of him, but he slowly relaxed into her embrace.

What the hell had he been dreaming about? She wanted to ask, but first he needed to calm down. He was still trembling some, and she didn't like it.

When he finally pulled away from her, she ducked her head to meet his eyes. "What was it about? The nightmare."

He looked away. Was it that bad? He stared intently at the dresser across the room.

She'd nearly given up on him telling her when he took a deep breath and finally said, "It was my wreck. Sort of."

Colt shuddered, and Grace rubbed a hand in soothing circles over his back.

His gaze swung over to her. "I was hung up. Once I got free of my rope, the bull flung me into the air, then ran me over before whirling back around to come finish me off. I couldn't move. It was like I was paralyzed or something. I couldn't get out of his way." He scrubbed his hands over his face and up through his hair, sending the damp strands into disarray. "You woke me up as his head hit my chest. He was crushing me. I couldn't breathe. I could feel my bones breaking." He clenched his eyes shut and rubbed a hand over his still healing ribs. "I'm so fucking screwed if these don't go away."

This wasn't the first?

"How long have you been having them? I thought this was the first one."

He laughed, but there was no humor in it. "Ever since I woke up in the hospital. I've had at least one every night since. They're only getting worse."

How had she not known he'd been having nightmares? Sure, she was pretty worn out by the time they went to sleep between working with Summer during the day and all of her and Colt's sexual escapades, but she should have known he was having them before now. She wasn't that deep of a sleeper. At least, she never used to be.

Her eyebrows pinched together. "What do you mean you're screwed if they don't go away?"

He blew out a ragged breath. "I'm screwed because they make me afraid to ride again. I'm a bull rider; if I'm too afraid to climb back on a bull, who am I? What do I do next? Scared bull riders end up seriously hurt or dead. You have to be completely focused to ride. There's no place for fear."

"Didn't you say you wanted to raise bulls when you quit again? I think I remember you saying it was time to think beyond rodeo a while back. I assumed that meant you were thinking about retiring, or did I misunderstand you?"

He made a wry face at her. "You didn't misunderstand me. But there's a big difference between thinking about retiring and actually doing it. I still love riding. I still love traveling. There's no way I want to be forced out of my career by a bad dream. I want to go out on my own terms." He shook his head. "I don't expect you to be able to understand."

He shoved back the blanket and got to his feet, then came around to her side of the bed and extended a hand to her. "I don't want to talk about it anymore. Come shower with me, then I'll make us some breakfast."

She accepted his hand and followed him from the room while her mind churned.

Chapter 29

Colt propped his foot on the crossbeam of the practice arena next to the barn. One of Cash's boarders rode a pinto warmblood in the round pen behind her, but his gaze rested on his woman instead.

Grace let her loop fly toward the roping dummy he'd had a hired hand set up for her days ago. Her rope settled neatly around its plastic neck, and Summer sat back on her haunches, pulling her rope taut and breaking the connection.

Though his eyes followed the duo, his mind wandered. Maybe it really was time to consider hanging up his bull rope for good. Not because of the nightmares hounding him, but because his woman was making him think about things. Things he never thought he'd ever be considering doing again. Things he'd sworn he'd never do again, actually. Apparently, that was going to be a trend.

Cash would laugh his ass off if he knew Colt was considering proposing. For someone as opposed to committing to a woman as his best friend was, the asshole sure seemed to enjoy doing a bit of matchmaking. He knew Cash had his own reasons for avoiding relationships, but there had always been an unspoken agreement between them to not discuss it. With as painful as the other man's childhood had been before he'd moved in with Colt and his family, it wasn't altogether surprising he'd have a few issues.

When it came to Grace, Colt was glad Cash had meddled. Colt had needed the push; he knew that. He'd been being a complete idiot denying his feelings for her. She was a saint for putting up with his stubborn ass. Of course, her ass was pretty stubborn too.

She was so fucking gorgeous, and not just on the surface either. Her beauty was etched on her soul. It was who she was. She made him want to become a man worthy of her.

Without warning, a gunshot rang out, making him jump. Summer shied violently before rearing. To his horror, Grace lost her balance and fell, sending up a thick cloud of dust as she hit the dirt.

Adrenaline surged, sending his heart rate soaring.

Had she been hit? Had Summer?

Sweat beaded on his brow as he vaulted the fence. Every muscle stretched taut as he ran, praying she was unharmed—needing her to be.

Fuck, why was it taking so long to get to her? Dread spiraled through him.

Colt cursed as he slammed to his knees beside Grace and searched her for obvious injuries with wide eyes and shaking hands. "Grace! Are you okay? Baby, talk to me."

She grabbed his hand and squeezed. "I'm alright. I'm okay." Grace offered him a shaky smile. "Just shook up. Is Summer okay? What was that?"

"Gunshot." He gathered her against his chest and struggled to calm his racing heart.

Hearing that shot then seeing her hit the ground... Shit, he couldn't remember the last time he'd been so scared.

Where the fuck had the shot come from? He cradled her in his arms while his gaze swept over their surroundings.

A flicker of movement near the corner of the barn caught his attention. His eyes narrowed on the shadowy spot. The vague shape of a man lurked there, but he was too far away and the shadows too deep to make out any distinct features.

He tensed. It didn't seem like anyone who was supposed to be on the grounds. Hank, Cash's foreman, told him earlier that he'd be away until later tonight, and the shape was shorter than any of the hired hands. There was no reason anyone who belonged on the ranch would lurk in the shadows or fire a gun while Grace was on horseback either. That left only one possibility.

Flint.

Colt needed to get Grace somewhere safe. "Can you stand?"

"I think so. Why? What do you see?"

Colt pulled his gaze away from the figure in the shadows long enough to give her what he hoped resembled a reassuring smile. "I'm sure it's nothing, but I think I see someone by the barn. It doesn't look like one of Cash's hired hands."

He hated the fear that flashed in her eyes.

"Flint?"

He didn't answer. Instead, he pushed to his feet, taking Grace with him. "Go on to the house, Princess, and lock the door behind you. I'm going to check it out. I'll knock when I come up to the house." He pressed a kiss on the top of her head and nudged her toward the porch, then turned away.

She gripped his arm to stop him before he could take more than a single step toward the barn. His gaze swung back to her.

Grace stared at him with wide, frightened eyes. "Come back to the house with me. We'll call the cops and let them investigate."

"I thought you didn't want to involve the cops. Why call them now?"

"I still don't! But if calling them keeps you from getting hurt, so be it. If that really was a gunshot, that means someone's out there with a gun, and you're unarmed. What are you planning to do if you find them? What if it's Flint?" She shook her head vehemently. "No. Please don't. If it is Flint, he'll shoot you."

He caved. She was right. Even if he found whoever was lurking, there wasn't much he could do. If he ended up getting himself shot, it would leave Grace to their mercy.

"Fine. We'll call the cops, and I'll come back out later to take care of Summer once we're sure it's safe out here." He just hoped the scared animal didn't hurt herself before then. That was a chance he was going to have to take. Grace's wellbeing was more important.

"Let's go."

Colt tucked her under his arm, keeping himself between her and the barn as they headed for the house.

⸎

Colt growled in frustration as the last of the officers piled back into their squad cars. It'd been a complete waste of time calling them. Other than a note hung on Summer's stall, they'd found nothing else. No bullet, no prowler, not even a partial footprint where he'd seen the man. It didn't help that all of the hired hands they'd questioned claimed they hadn't seen anything, though they'd heard the shot too.

Even the note was lackluster proof. It'd been printed rather than handwritten, so Grace hadn't been able to confirm definitely that it was Flint who'd left it. They both knew it was him, though. Who else would have taped a note reading *Found you* on Summer's stall?

It pissed him off that the police hadn't seemed to take the situation seriously. They'd claimed they'd look into Flint, but Colt didn't have much faith they really would. The lead detective had seemed put out having to write up the report. He'd seemed bored. The cops had taken the note with them as evidence, at least. They claimed to be planning on checking it for prints, but Colt didn't hold out much hope of anything coming from it.

Flint was smart. Smarter than he'd given the man credit for. He'd probably worn gloves.

His gaze followed Grace as she paced the living room. How the hell was he going to protect her if that bastard came after her again? It was clear that the cops here weren't going to be much help. With no messages or voicemails to back up her story, there really wasn't much they could do anyway.

Maybe he should get a gun himself, hit a shooting range and brush up on his skills. The last time he'd shot at anything was when his dad took him and Cash hunting. They'd just been teenagers then.

Colt crossed the room and wrapped his arms around Grace as he continued pondering. He'd do whatever he had to in order to keep her safe. Anything at all. He dropped a kiss on her hair and tightened his arms around her as she leaned into his embrace. This woman was all that mattered. She was everything. He held her until she pulled away.

"I'm going to go start dinner." She tossed him a faint smile.

"While you do that, I'm going to go get Summer comfortable again. She's probably pretty annoyed about being left out there all tacked up."

She nodded and left the room. Colt watched her go with a frown. Everything about her was off. Tense. Subdued. He didn't like it. Not one bit.

As soon as he took care of her horse, he'd have to see what he could do to lighten the mood. There was no way in hell he was going to let Flint ruin even one more of her days. The bastard had stolen far too much of her happiness as it was.

Colt blew out a long breath and made his way back outside.

⸺◆⸺

"It smells good in here," Colt murmured as he entered the kitchen and headed toward Grace.

She stood at the sink with a thoughtful expression. It appeared she'd finished washing dishes.

"Your horse is back in her stall and was happily munching her hay when I left her." He encircled her slim waist with his arms and hugged her tight against him from behind. "What'd you decide to make for dinner?"

"Beef pot roast with potatoes and carrots. Sound good?" She reached for the nearby hand towel and dried her hands.

"Mmm, definitely. Can I have you for dessert?" He ducked his head to nuzzle her neck. "Or maybe as an appetizer instead?"

Grace pulled away and swatted his arm playfully. "You're insatiable!"

The smile on her face as she said it made warmth spread through him from the region of his heart.

Colt grinned. "Might be. You love it, though. Don't deny it."

"Never said I didn't."

He glanced at the kitchen timer on the stove. "Since it looks like we have a bit of time yet..."

He reached into his pocket and withdrew his phone. After a bit of fumbling, he got the radio app to cooperate and the soft tones of a croony country love song filled the kitchen. Grace gave him a curious look, but he said nothing. She'd find out soon enough.

He smiled and sat the phone on the counter before drawing her back into his arms. "Dance with me, Princess."

"You can dance?" She seemed surprised.

His lips quirked upward. "I can." He swayed them to the music. While he didn't dance often, he could slow dance and even two-step with the best of them.

A few minutes later, the song changed to Kane Brown's "What's Mine Is Yours", and Colt pulled her closer. He leaned his cheek against the top of her head and sang along. While he loved the song, the lyrics also said nearly everything he wanted to tell her. Music was great like that. If you searched hard enough, you could almost always find a song to express the things you wanted to say if only you knew how or had the courage to. He hoped she'd realize that he was singing to her.

He loved the feel of her in his arms. She fit so perfectly against him, like they were made for each other. Maybe they were. All he knew for certain was that this woman was it. No matter how he'd tried to fight it, she clasped his heart in her hands now. There was no doubt in his mind about that. He hoped she was gentle with it. What he felt for her was unlike anything he'd felt before. Not more or less than he'd felt for Sarah, just ... different. Cash had been right, after all. There *was* space in his heart to love both of them.

When the song ended, Colt slid his hands down to her hips and lifted her onto the kitchen counter before stepping between her legs. His gaze caressed her face. One corner of his mouth lifted.

"Do I want to know what you're thinking about?" she asked, arching one elegant brow.

"I don't know, do you?" When she nodded, his smirk spread into a full-fledged grin. He took a deep, steadying breath.

Fuck it. His wreck could have killed him. That fucking asshole, Flint, could have killed her. Life was too short to be holding back things that needed to be said.

Colt rested his forehead against hers, summoning every ounce of courage he had to whisper, "I was thinking that I love you."

To his surprise, her muscles tensed beneath his hands. He pulled back to look at her but couldn't read her expression to save his life.

"What?" Grace asked after a second, her voice little more than a squeak.

He chuckled, despite being more than a little concerned about her reaction. "I said I love you, Princess." He stroked his fingers over her cheek gently. "Is that okay?"

She swallowed and scrutinized his face for a moment with a faint tilt to her head, as though trying to discern if he was serious. Whatever she saw must have assured her that he meant every word as her body abruptly relaxed and she smiled.

"Yes, of course. You took me by surprise." She draped both arms around his neck and gently pulled him down to her for a brief kiss. "I never thought I'd hear those words from you."

The corners of his mouth curled upward. "I never thought I'd say them again," he admitted quietly. He locked eyes with her. "Those aren't words I throw around. I need you to know that. I only say them when I'm absolutely certain that I mean it."

"So you're absolutely certain about me, then?"

"I am." He brushed her hair away from her neck and lowered his mouth to the soft skin there. The way her breathing hitched when he gently sucked down made him grin.

There was silence for a moment, then Grace said in a vaguely strained tone, "Hey, Eight?"

"Hmm?" he queried without lifting his mouth from her neck, where he continued kissing and nipping a trail down to her collarbone. His jeans were uncomfortably tight now. If he didn't stop soon, he'd doubtless end up with the imprint of his zipper on his cock.

"I think I want that appetizer."

Or not. While he hadn't planned on taking things there right now, he was all too happy to oblige her. He couldn't get enough of her. Would *never* get enough.

Colt straightened as a wicked grin spread on his face. "Right here? In the kitchen?" It would hardly be the first time.

In answer, Grace caught her bottom lip between her teeth and pulled her shirt over her head. She tossed it somewhere over his shoulder.

Where it landed, he didn't know or care. He couldn't take his eyes away from her to look even if he'd wanted to.

"I'll take that as a yes," he grated.

She grabbed his shirt and made quick work of removing it as well. He reached behind her and released the clasp of her bra, then stepped back. Each breath panted out of him as he lifted her down from the countertop and flicked open the button on her jeans.

Colt's lips twitched into a smirk as he dropped to his knees and eased her jeans down over her hips. "Commando, huh? I like it."

"I thought you would," she shot back with a mischievous grin that took him by surprise. She gripped his shoulder and stepped free of her pants as he pulled them down her legs.

God, he loved seeing her smile. Especially after everything she'd been through.

He leaned forward and pressed his lips to her belly before pushing to his feet. She reached for him immediately. Colt stood still as her hands landed on his belt and her nimble fingers swiftly unfastened the buckle. His erection sprang proudly from its confinement the moment she shoved his jeans down enough to free it.

Her gaze flicked up to his as one corner of her mouth lifted. "No boxers, huh?"

Colt chuckled huskily. "I thought I'd give you faster access."

"Hmm, well, I like it," she answered.

He cradled her face in his hands and leaned down to kiss her. As the kiss spun on, her fingers skimmed his stomach before wrapping around his shaft. A groan vibrated from his throat when she began caressing him with agonizingly slow strokes. This woman would be the death of him yet.

He walked her backwards as he kissed her with renewed fervor, determined to make her burn as hot as he was. If he was going up in flames, he was determined to take her with him.

She gasped into his mouth when her bare backside came into contact with the cool marble of the countertop.

He straightened. "Better brace yourself, baby."

Lust made her dilated eyes shine as their gazes met. He skimmed one hand down her body and teased her core with a fingertip. She caught her bottom lip between her teeth and bit down gently.

Colt loved when she looked at him like that, with her eyes gleaming with the carnal hunger he'd put there. There was no way in hell he'd ever get his fill of this woman. That was a certainty.

He pressed two fingers into her already slippery core and thrust them slowly, wanting to feel her come apart around his fingers before he gave her what they were both craving.

She moaned loudly and immediately angled her hips toward him.

He circled her clit with his thumb as he dipped his head toward hers. Their mouths fused while he worked her body toward its pinnacle. A firestorm raged between them. He swallowed her moans, her pleasure only further igniting his blood.

Grace ripped her mouth away from his. "Please." Her plea ended in a small whimper.

He knew what she was asking for and was determined to get her there. Colt ramped up his efforts, moving faster.

She cried out seconds later, her body gripping his fingers tight as her orgasm crashed over her. He pulled his fingers from her body and spun her around to face the countertop, then stooped to retrieve the condom he had stashed in his jeans.

Grace leaned over the counter, gasping when her overheated skin came into contact with the cold surface. She glanced over her shoulder at him with a dazed expression on her flushed face while he ripped open the packet and rolled the condom on.

She hadn't said she loved him back, but right now, at this moment, he didn't care. He hadn't told her in hopes of her declaring her feelings too; he'd told her because she needed to know. It was important to him she knew, even if she never felt the same. This was enough, just being with her.

He gripped her hips and pushed into her with one quick movement. They moaned in unison. Her body hugged him with every deep stroke and stoked the flames in his blood higher. Sweat soon rolled down his back as he rocked into her hard and fast, determined to use his body to prove his words true.

His heart felt as though it might just explode from the sheer amount of love he had for this woman. He thanked the stars for her persistence, for her patience.

Far before he was ready, he felt his body gathering. His orgasm loomed right on the horizon. He ground his molars together, fighting to hold it off. Not yet. He needed to hear her orgasm first, feel her squeezing around him as she came.

Colt leaned forward and wrapped one arm around her. His fingers delved through the slickness between her thighs and rubbed her clit the way she liked. "Come for me, Princess," he panted.

Grace moaned at the added sensation and bucked her hips backwards, driving him deeper. "I don't think I can come again," she said breathlessly.

That wasn't something he was willing to accept. "One more, baby," he said through clenched teeth. He worked her body faster, determined to drive her over the edge ahead of him.

She whimpered, and her knees nearly buckled. The walls of her core fluttered, then clenched down hard around him as she came with a scream that left his ears ringing.

He loved it. He loved *her*.

Colt plunged deep one last time, then soared over the edge while her body still held him tight. He grunted and jerked as wave after wave of pleasure washed over him. Completely spent, he collapsed against Grace's back and tried to find the energy to move.

He needed this woman by his side forever, and not just because the sex was amazing. Sarah had been his soul mate—of that he was certain—but Grace, well, she was too. He wanted her in his arms until the universe ceased to exist.

"You're crushing me, Eight," Grace breathlessly complained while pushing back against him.

"Shit. Sorry." Colt straightened and backed away, slipping free of her body in the process.

She turned around to face him, a crooked grin on her lips. "I love you," she whispered.

His gaze jumped to hers. The tender look shining in the depths of her spellbinding eyes made his heart squeeze. *She loved him.*

A slow smile spread on his lips. "I love you too, Princess." He leaned in and caught her lips. "I love you so fucking much."

She smiled as he backed away to dispose of the condom then yanked his jeans back up.

It was as he fastened them that he noticed the kitchen was filling with smoke. *Shit.* The roast. He opened the oven and smoke billowed out into the room.

"Oh no!" Grace covered her mouth with one hand and looked over at him.

Colt's lips twitched as he met her gaze. Together, they dissolved into laughter. He wrapped his arm around her to hold her up when it looked like her mirth was going to send her to the floor. God, it felt good to laugh like this. To hear her laugh too.

His ribs were complaining loudly by the time they recovered enough to speak. He released her and grabbed a potholder. The beef roast was blackened and well beyond salvage by the time he yanked it out of the oven.

"Oops," he muttered and glanced back at Grace.

Laughter still danced in her eyes.

His lips twitched. "I'll clean this all up and make us something else. Feel free to go grab a shower if you want." He gestured toward the table. "Or you could take a seat over there and give me something beautiful to look at while I cook." He grabbed his shirt off the floor and handed it to her with a smirk. "Your choice."

"A shower sounds good, actually." She smiled and slipped into his shirt. "I seem to have worked up a bit of a sweat."

"Wonder how that happened." He grinned. "Don't use all the hot water. I get one next." He dropped a kiss on her forehead.

His gaze followed her as she walked from the room. The gentle sway of her hips mesmerized him. She was seductive without even trying. As soon as she disappeared from sight, he turned his attention to his task.

It only took a few minutes to clean the countertop with some disinfectant wipes he'd found under the sink, dispose of the ruined roast, and toss Grace's abandoned clothes into the laundry room. He washed his hands then inspected the contents of the fridge.

What to make? They hadn't gone shopping in several days. Something to remedy tomorrow.

Tacos checked all the right boxes for dinner tonight—fast, easy, and tasty. It looked as though they had everything necessary to make them too. He pulled out the ingredients he'd need for their meal and got to work.

He was in the process of dicing tomatoes while waiting for the ground beef to finish browning when Grace returned to the kitchen, wearing yet another of his t-shirts.

Her hair was still damp from her shower, longer now than when they'd first met. His fingers itched to braid it for her like he used to for Sarah.

Grace's ice blue eyes landed on him, and a soft smile curled on her lips. How the fuck had he been so lucky as to capture her heart?

"God, you're magnificent." His hands stilled as he drank her in. He was pretty sure he would never get enough of this woman. His dick seemed to agree as it stirred back to life as though it hadn't been buried deep inside her a short time ago.

Grace blushed while a shy smile curled on her lips. She wrapped her arms around him from behind and gave him a gentle squeeze as he returned to cutting up the tomatoes.

Though her hug made his busted ribs lament about the pressure, he didn't mention it. She pressed a kiss to his bare back, which did absolutely nothing to help calm back down his cock, then gave him another quick hug.

Grace shifted around to lean against the counter next to him. "Tacos?"

"Yep. That work for you?" he asked.

"Uh-huh, tacos are perfect. I could probably eat Mexican food every day of the week if I was able."

"I remember you telling me that." Colt transferred the tomatoes into the bowl he had waiting for them, then sat them on the table alongside the lettuce, shredded cheese, hard taco shells, black olives, and diced onion. "I need to finish seasoning the beef, and we'll be ready to eat."

"Is there anything I can help with?"

He thought for a second. "There are a couple of jars of salsa in the fridge if you want to grab one. I don't care what heat level you choose." He winked. "You already know I like it hot."

She blushed again, brighter red this time.

He chuckled. "I love that blush of yours, Princess."

She pressed up on her toes to kiss him then headed for the refrigerator.

While she chose a jar of salsa, he turned back to the ground beef and stirred in a few various spices. The recipe he was making tonight was one his mom had taught him when he was twelve. It had enough bite without being overwhelmingly spicy. In his opinion, it was perfect. Like the woman by his side.

He glanced at her before moving the finished taco meat to a bowl. "Ready to eat?"

Her stomach growled loudly in answer, and they both laughed.

"Does that answer your question?" she chortled.

"Sure does." He chuckled. "Come on, let's get you fed."

He carried the meat to the table and plopped down in a chair. They both made a couple of tacos each.

Grace moaned as she took her first bite. Her gaze flicked over to him. "This is amazing! Your mom is a great teacher. Remind me to beg her to teach me too when I see her next."

He grinned and took a huge bite of his own taco. It admittedly had turned out pretty good. "She'd probably be tickled to teach you."

He took another bite as he thought about his parents. It surprised him that they had gone back home to Montana after meeting Grace. He'd fully expected his mom to hang around and get to know his new girlfriend better. Instead, she'd declared she needed to get back to her garden now that she knew there was a woman here to keep him out of trouble.

A companionable silence settled between him and Grace as they ate.

After finishing his third taco, he looked up. "Hey, Grace?"

"Hmm?"

"I love you."

Grace turned a bright smile on him. Happiness shone in her eyes and softened her face. "I love you too, cowboy."

Damn if that didn't make him feel like a king.

Chapter 30

Grace patted Summer's neck and slipped out of the saddle. It'd been two weeks since the gunshot that had caused her to take a spill. They'd passed in a blur. She wasn't sure whether that shot had been Flint toying with them or if he'd been trying to make good on his threat against Colt. If it'd been the latter, she was overjoyed that he'd missed.

So far, Flint hadn't done anything else, but she was certain it was coming. She knew him too well to believe otherwise. It was probable that he was waiting for an opportune time to strike. He always had liked to do that. It certainly wouldn't be the first time he'd waited around for her to relax a bit before springing his trap and attacking. She wasn't falling for it this time. There was no way this horror story was over yet. Sooner or later, Flint would pounce. It was a matter of when, not if. Still, she refused to let the inevitability of another conflict with him send her into hiding.

This morning, she and Summer had a productive training session, although the little mare was extremely frolicsome. It was a beautiful day, so it wasn't altogether surprising. Maybe it was the fresh air or maybe it was spending time with Summer, but she felt less jumpy—more grounded—here at Cash's ranch, even after the incident with the gunshot and the note.

The stationary roping dummy Colt had found in the equipment shed had come in handy this morning. While it wasn't the same as tossing her loop at a running calf, it was still helpful. She was pretty sure she was getting better. Whenever they returned to the circuit, she might end up scoring well enough to move up a couple of ranks. There was a long way to the top of the standings, but she was really competing more for fun than anything else anyway.

It still shocked her that Colt had given her his horse. It surprised her even more that she'd actually accepted the animal as her own. Of course, the fact that Summer was endearingly sweet-natured had something to do with it. How was she supposed to resist? It was no less of an impossibility as resisting her attraction to Colt had been.

While she'd given him back the title to the truck and trailer, she'd gone ahead with finishing the paperwork to transfer ownership of her mare to herself.

She led Summer from the arena. They'd worked long enough for today. The pretty mare deserved a couple of treats, a flake of hay, and a rest. First though, Grace needed to get her cooled down and comfortable.

Colt stepped from the house as she and Summer started for the barn. He wore the blue western shirt she'd bought for him. It was the exact shade of his eyes. The moment she'd seen it at a shop in town yesterday, she'd known he had to have it. It looked even better on him than she'd expected.

Her gorgeous cowboy. A happy smile lit her face as she stopped to wait for him.

He planted a kiss on her lips the moment he reached her. "Have a nice ride, Princess?"

"We did. Summer was feeling pretty rambunctious; it took some time to get her to focus. Thank you again for braiding my hair for me this morning. It was so much easier to focus on what I'm doing without my hair blowing into my face all the time."

"It was my pleasure, Princess. I'll braid your hair any time you want." Colt smiled. "If you'd let me ride, we could go on a trail ride tonight. That'd help Summer burn off some of that extra energy so she can concentrate on your practice sessions better. Cash told me his mares are both pretty quiet. I'd even pick the calmer of the two. She'd be plenty safe for me to ride."

Grace made a face. "Nice try. Like I told you before—not until you're officially cleared. I heard what the doctor told you at your last appointment."

He groaned. "Never in my life have I waited to be cleared before climbing on a horse's back. If you were anyone else..." He shook his head. "Fine. I guess I can wait a bit longer."

She gave his arm a sympathetic pat and rose on her toes to kiss him. "Soon. It's only two more weeks. You can make it."

Colt grunted again. "I guess." He sighed heavily and ran a hand over Summer's ebony neck. "I've got some plans for us this evening, so you'll need to stay out of the house for a while." He lifted one brow. "Think you can manage that, Trouble?" he asked teasingly.

She laughed. "Yeah, I can do that. I'll get Summer groomed and put away, then I'll run to the store. I heard one of Cash's boarders talking about a new shipment the tack shop got in recently. It might be fun to have a look, even if I can't afford anything." She canted her head at him and narrowed her eyes. "What do you have planned, Mr. Boone?"

Some sort of a gift maybe? No, he wouldn't need her out of the house for that. Geez, why did he have to be so good at surprises? It was always so difficult to guess. His birthday was a week ago and hers wasn't for quite a few months yet, so a surprise party of some manner didn't seem likely. Gah, what could it be?

His lips tipped into a slanted smile. "You'll see." He dropped a kiss on the top of her head and swatted her behind playfully. "Go on. Get."

She laughed and led her horse away.

Grace had just finished grooming Summer when she felt eyes on her. Her skin crawled at the sensation, and her body went rigid. She knew exactly who it was without even turning around.

"What are you doing here, Flint?" She double-checked the latch of Summer's stall. It wouldn't do for her horse to get out because her ex had her distracted.

"I'm taking you home. Where you belong."

"I'm not going anywhere." She turned around to face him.

Her chin lifted ever so slightly as she glared at him in defiance. Until this moment, she hadn't realized how much being with Colt had helped her regain her confidence. She felt more like herself. Like the woman she'd been before Flint broke her down and turned her into some timid stranger she didn't even recognize.

She refused to be that woman anymore. "You have no say over what I do."

"Pretty sure I do." He grabbed her arm and jerked her toward him. "You're mine."

She bit her tongue and shook her head hard. Adrenaline pulsed her veins, and her heart raced. This was a dangerous game she was playing by defying him, but she'd be damned if she'd go along with him without a fight. There was no way.

Should she scream for Colt? Would he even hear her? He'd been heading back to the house the last time she'd seen him, so she doubted it.

She forced herself to straighten and gave Flint a hard stare. "We broke up, Flint. I've moved on. Let me go!"

He laughed. The maniacal sound of it sent a shiver down her spine.

"Nope. That's where you got it wrong, babe. You tried to break up with me. I don't accept it. You're mine, you cheating whore! You'll always be mine." He slapped her across the face hard enough to leave her with the taste of blood in her mouth. "Come on, we're going home, and then you're going to pay for that stunt you pulled at that rodeo. You didn't really think I'd let you go after that, did you?" He leaned toward her with a sneer. "Scream, and I'll fucking gut you like a deer."

Gut her? She watched in wordless horror as he pulled a knife from his pocket and flicked it open. The blade gleamed under the barn lights. He gave her a venomous grin, closed the blade, and slipped it back into his pocket.

She had one too, in her boot, but could she get to it before he used his? With the way her hands were shaking despite her bravado, she wasn't sure about that.

Flint yanked her along with him down the aisle toward the rear doors.

Colt would never see them leave that way. Her gaze bounced around the barn as she tried to stem the tide of panic threatening to overtake her. There had to be a way to stop Flint, or at the very least, to buy some time. This was a working ranch; someone was bound to come by soon. Hopefully. She dug in her heels and tried her best to resist as her mind spun.

Flint growled something incomprehensible under his breath and viciously twisted her arm before yanking her after him harder.

Grace cried out and stumbled over her own feet. She lost her balance and fell. She automatically curled in on herself, pulling her knees up to protect her belly while raising her hands to protect her head as Flint's heavy fists began raining down on her.

Grace tried to scream, but the toe of Flint's boot caught her in the ribs, sending the air from her lungs in a rush. She squeezed her eyes shut. Her mind drifted back to the peaceful oasis it'd created to shelter her. The haven it hadn't needed to visit in so long. She hid there, shutting out what Flint was doing to her until the punches stopped falling.

The faint sound of a man's voice drifted through the barn. Probably Hank, Cash's foreman. That must be why Flint had stopped. It'd ruin all of his plans—whatever they were—if he got caught.

Where *was* Flint? Had he left? She hadn't heard him leave, but then, she hadn't heard his approach either. She wanted to open her eyes and look, but fear kept her from doing so.

The voice became louder as though Hank was walking toward where she lay. Though she couldn't make out exactly what he was saying, it seemed like he was talking to the horses as he passed each stall. Relief surged through her. She was safe now. Hopefully. The blows had stopped and though Hank was older—at least in his early seventies—he was far from a little man. Flint wouldn't want to tangle with him.

"Grace?"

A calloused hand touched her arm, and she flinched hard. Her eyes popped open, her gaze darting wildly around what she could see of the barn before landing on Hank.

His weathered face was pinched, his dark green eyes filled with concern.

"What happened, darlin'? Are you okay? Can you stand?"

"It was my ex-boyfriend. I-I think I'm alright." Slowly but surely, she uncurled and sat up with a soft groan. Her gaze lifted to Hank's. "Can you go get Colt, please? He's in the house, I think."

The older man seemed reluctant to leave her side, but he eventually nodded and stood. With one last worried look in her direction, he left the barn.

Grace remained right where she was. Standing up was unthinkable right now. With the adrenaline beginning to fade, her body was starting to quake. With as shaky as she was already, it was likely she'd end up right back in a heap on the ground if she got up yet.

She pulled her knife from her boot and opened it, holding it at the ready as her eyes moved restlessly around the barn, searching the shadows.

How had Flint snuck not only onto the ranch but into the barn in broad daylight? Sure, Cash didn't have as many hired hands as some ranches this size would have, but the few he had employed had all been informed to keep an eye out for Flint. There was no way he should have been able to get in here without being seen. How had he found her?

Would anyone have spotted them and stopped him if he'd succeeded in getting her out the door? Was he even gone, or was he lurking somewhere and watching her even now, waiting for another opportunity to grab her?

Chills skittered down her spine at the thought.

The sense of relative safety she'd grown used to having at Cash's place evaporated in that instant. She'd gotten too relaxed. Too used to the peace.

This was no longer a safe haven. She should have known better after the gunshot, but she'd convinced herself it'd just been someone trying to frighten an animal off of their land or something equally innocent. She'd convinced herself that the note had been meant for someone else too. Cash had dozens of boarders, and Summer was hardly the only black horse with a big white star.

How could she have been so foolish? She felt the urge to run, but where to? The circuit wasn't safe either. Flint had already found her at a rodeo once before as it was. Was anywhere safe? No matter where she went, he always found her.

She closed her knife and tucked it back into her boot, then used the stall closest to her to lever herself back to her feet. She leaned hard against the wood. Though she felt a bit steadier now, she was still trembling and couldn't seem to stop.

"Grace?"

The sound of Colt's deep voice made her want to cry. Her head swiveled toward him. "Flint was here."

She threw herself against his chest. Her eyes slid closed as his strong arms came around her. He held her close, like she was the most precious thing in his world. Maybe she was. All she knew for certain was that his arms made her feel protected. Secure. Safe.

"He had a knife and said he'd use it if I screamed."

Grace blew out a ragged breath. Rivers of tears rolled down her cheeks, but she was helpless to stop them. The gentle breeze flowing down the barn aisle made the dampness feel cool on her skin despite the warmth of the day.

Colt leaned his chin against the top of her head. "It's okay now, Princess. I have you." His arms tightened a fraction. "What happened? Tell me everything."

"I had just gotten Summer settled in her stall after grooming her, when he showed up. I think he got in through the rear doors. That's where he was trying to pull me. He said he doesn't accept our breakup. That I'm still his and he was going to take me home. That I was going to pay for breaking his finger. I tripped and fell while I was trying to keep him from getting me out the door. That was when he started beating on me."

Colt sat her away from him. His worried gaze swept over her as his jaw clenched tighter.

"I'm sore, and I know I'll have bruises later, but I'm okay. I'm not sure I would be if he hadn't heard Hank and ran off."

She glanced at the older man, who was leaning against a stall nearby. He didn't look any happier about what'd transpired than Colt did. Her breathing hitched.

She turned her gaze back to Colt. Though she didn't want to voice it, she needed to. "What if he's still here? What if he's waiting for another shot to grab me?"

"If he is, he'd better be ready to take me on. I'll kill him if he tries to get to you again."

Colt said it so matter-of-factly, with that determined gleam in his eyes he so often got.

It left no doubt in her mind that he would do exactly what he said if it came down to it. She wasn't sure how she felt about it.

Colt shared a look with Hank, who nodded as though the two men were having some sort of silent conversation. Maybe they were. Hank shoved away from the stall he was leaning on and headed for the rear doors without a word.

Colt slid his arm over her shoulders with excruciating gentleness, pulled her against his side, and led her toward the main door. "We're going to the hospital. I want you checked over."

Grace stopped abruptly and vehemently shook her head. "No. I'm fine. No hospital."

He gave her an exasperated look. "You're not fine! Your ex-boyfriend attacked you. Please don't fight me on this, Princess." He grimaced. "I'll toss you over my shoulder and put you in the truck myself if I have to, but you're getting checked out."

She took in the stubborn set of his jaw and the steel in his eyes. There was no way she'd win this argument. He really would toss her over his shoulder if she didn't go along willingly. That, she already knew from experience. It wouldn't be the first time he'd done so.

She hated that she loved the way he was so protective of her, even if he reminded her of a caveman at times.

Grace sighed heavily and relented. "Fine. Let's get it over with."

Chapter 31

Colt paced the tiny waiting room while he waited for Grace to return.

He truly hated hospitals. The antiseptic smell and overly white everything made him unsettled. The suspicious looks the nurses had given him before they led Grace away and directed him to the waiting room bothered him too, but he understood them. He knew how it probably looked. In their profession, they probably saw battered women brought in by the very man who'd caused them injuries far more often than he wanted to think about.

He knew Grace didn't want to be here any more than he did, but it looked like Flint had been really hammering on her. It had Colt scared shitless. Sure, she seemed alright at the moment, but he wasn't going to be able to relax until he was sure that she was truly okay. He was all too aware that internal bleeding didn't always have obvious signs right away. He'd seen it before. It happened from time to time on the circuit, especially amongst the roughstock riders. She was so petite. Flint might not be a big man, but he still could have really hurt her.

The thought of losing her made it difficult to breathe. Chills prickled Colt's skin despite beads of sweat popping out all over him. He stopped pacing. His heart hammered against his ribs, feeling as though it was trying to break out. It felt like he had a bull sitting on his chest. He rubbed at his breastbone, willing the heavy sensation to ease.

"Sir?" The nurse who approached sounded worried, but he couldn't reply. The woman laid her hand on his arm, making him jump. "Sir! Are you alright?"

His wide-eyed gaze snapped to her. "My girlfriend..."

"Take deep breaths. Like this." She took several herself to demonstrate.

He focused on her and tried his best to follow her instruction. Gradually, his panic eased. "Thanks," he murmured sheepishly as his heart rate and breathing normalized once again.

She gave him a friendly smile. "What is your girlfriend's name? I can check in on her for you."

"I'd appreciate that. Her name is Grace Parker. Her ex-boyfriend attacked her."

The nurse gave him an odd look but nodded and hurried away.

Colt resumed pacing while he waited for the nurse to return.

Several minutes later, a grey-haired man wearing a white coat approached.

The man smiled kindly. "Colt Boone?"

Colt stopped and turned to face him. "That's me."

"I'm Dr. Andrews. I appreciate your patience. This sort of situation can be delicate. We like to speak with the patient alone while we assess what happened." Another smile crossed his face. "If you'd like to follow me, she's been asking for you."

Colt nodded. "I understand." The beginnings of a headache throbbed in his temples. He absently rubbed at them while he followed the doctor down the hallway to an exam room.

Both Grace and the nurse with her looked up at him when he entered. It appeared that the nurse was dressing a cut on Grace's arm that he hadn't noticed earlier. He stood silently off to one side, waiting.

"I'm roughed up but okay," Grace said after the nurse left the room, leaving them alone. "Like I told you I was." She poked him in the belly and gave him a tight smile.

He shook his head then brushed a kiss over her forehead. "I needed to make sure. You haven't seen yourself in a mirror yet, Princess. If you saw how you look, you'd understand why I insisted on getting you checked out." He flopped into the chair closest to her. "After Sarah's accident, I swore off relationships. I didn't do it because I wanted to be alone. I did it because the thought of letting in someone new, *loving* someone new, and having them get ripped away from me too was too terrifying to contemplate."

She slipped off the exam table and moved toward him. He reached for her hand and pulled her into his lap, then wrapped his arms around her and inhaled her scent.

Some of his tension eased. "He could have really hurt you. Flint could have taken you from me, and there's not a damn thing I would have been able to do to stop it."

"But he didn't," Grace said softly.

Not this time, but would she be so lucky the next time her ex came after her? He'd underestimated the other man. Again. Not taken the threat as seriously as he should have. It could have cost not just her life but his. If anything happened to Grace, he was done for too. He knew that already.

This was exactly why he hadn't wanted to get involved with anyone. Loving someone was dangerous. In his opinion, it was riskier than climbing on a pissed-off bull's back. Not that it mattered now. He was well and truly roped and tied. The best he could hope for was that this ride would end differently than the last.

"If you swore off relationships, what made you decide to take a chance on me?"

Her question brought a wry smile to his lips despite the seriousness of the conversation. "We kissed at the afterparty, and you blew my walls to smithereens. There was no resisting you after that. It scared the shit out of me. Then you left and I nearly died, and I could no longer deny how much I wanted you. How much I loved you."

Her lips quirked upward. "Well, I'm glad you gave in."

He gave her a gentle hug. "I am too."

Grace was silent for a moment. Slowly, her smile faded and her expression turned solemn. "I don't feel safe at Cash's place anymore, but I don't know where else we could go." Her gaze met his. "I'm not sure it's truly safe anywhere. Every time I think I can finally relax, he finds me again."

His heart clenched as her quiet words registered. That's not how he wanted her to feel. Not ever. "We'll go back to the circuit then."

The sadness clouding her eyes troubled him.

"The other guys will help me keep you safe."

She shook her head. "I don't feel safe there either. Not really. He found me there once already. What's to stop him from finding me there again? I've been fooling myself thinking it was safe. You guys can't keep watch all the time. Besides, you've got at least two more weeks before they'll clear you, don't you? Is it really a good idea for you to ride again yet?"

Colt gave her a wry look. "I'm sure I could get them to clear me early."

She gave him a hard look in response to that, and he sighed heavily.

"How about this? I'll get a doctor to clear me now, but we'll stay at Cash's for another week if you feel okay with that. There's a bull ranch a few miles down the road. I know the guy who owns it. I could probably talk him into letting me hop on a couple practice bulls before we go back to the circuit."

He gave her a small squeeze, mindful of bruises. "The practice bulls are a heck of a lot safer for me to ride right now than jumping right back on the pro bulls."

"That's true," she allowed softly. "But what if Flint comes back?"

"He'd be wise not to. After what he did to you today, I'm not the only one wanting to make him pay. Hank called while I was waiting for them to let me back here. Flint's got Hank and several of Cash's men pissed too. They'll be watching for him. They fully understand the threat he poses to you now."

"That ... strangely makes me feel better." She nibbled her lip for a moment then slowly nodded. "Fine. If you can somehow get cleared early, we'll go with your plan. I really doubt you'll find a doctor willing to clear you now, though."

His lips turned up at the corners. "Wanna bet?" He kissed her then nudged her off of his lap and got to his feet. "If you get your discharge paperwork before I get back, I'll meet you in the lobby, then we'll get the hell out of here."

She rubbed a hand over her face, wincing when a finger came in contact with a small scrape on her cheek. "I'm still waiting on the social worker they want me to talk to, so I might be a bit yet."

"That's fine. Just meet me in the lobby when you're done, then." He dug out the truck keys and handed them to her. "Think about what you want for lunch. I was thinking we'd pick up some takeaway on the way home." He gave her a gentle kiss then met her eyes. "I love you."

A small smile crept onto her lips. "I love you too."

⸺◆⸺

Finding a doctor and demanding they do whatever tests they needed in order to clear him to ride hadn't taken long. Grace had been less than pleased that they had, however. She'd spent nearly the entire ride back to the ranch trying to talk him out of riding the practice bulls he'd mentioned.

It hadn't helped things that he'd insisted on stopping in at the police station to report the assault, like she'd said the social worker recommended. While he'd won the battle and she'd talked to the cops, she wasn't happy with him. She was still so afraid to talk to them, believing it would make things worse for her. The product of Flint's gaslighting, no doubt, but Colt couldn't say he understood it.

Figuring out why she had so much trepidation about him climbing back on a bull was far easier. The other night, he'd caught her watching a video clip of his wreck. He really wished she hadn't seen it. That wreck hadn't been pretty. It was a miracle he hadn't been hurt worse, or killed. According to the doctors, dying from his injuries had been a distinct possibility. There was no way he'd be telling that to Grace, though, and he'd kick Cash's ass if he ever told her too. That wreck had largely been Colt's own damn fault.

If he was being completely honest, the idea of riding again scared him more than he'd admit. The nightmares still hadn't stopped. If anything, they'd only grown worse. Not that he'd be admitting that to Grace. She didn't need anything else to worry about. This wasn't the first time in his career that a nasty wreck had left him with twisted dreams. He'd get through it the same as he had all the others.

He knew from experience that the easiest way to get over the fear was to face it head-on. To climb back on a bull and ride. He'd either sink or swim. Either way, he'd know whether he could still ride or if he was done. Tomorrow, he intended to contact the ranch down the road and see if they'd let him on their bulls.

At the moment, though, returning to the circuit was the last thing on his mind. The gorgeous woman with jet-black hair and enchanting ice-blue eyes who'd stolen his heart—and what remained of his sanity—was at the forefront. This morning, he'd begun planning a romantic evening for her, and he'd be damned if he would let her asshole of an ex-boyfriend ruin his plans. No fucking way. Tonight was happening. He hoped he could pull it off. Romance wasn't exactly his forte.

Colt wandered down the hallway to the bathroom. While not part of his original plans, setting Grace up with a nice soak in the tub would serve two purposes—soothing her battered body and keeping her out of the kitchen while he prepared dinner. He ran the bath and added a heaping scoop of Epsom salt, then sauntered back out to the living room where she waited on the couch.

He held a hand out to her with a crooked smile. "Come on, Princess, let's get you soaking."

She gave him a small, bemused smile as she placed her hand in his and pushed to her feet. "Why are you so good to me?"

"You know why. I love you."

She made a face at him. "You were good to me even before you loved me."

He gave his head a small shake. "I think I fell in love with you the moment our eyes met at the auction." That seemed like so long ago now, especially with as much as had happened since then.

One corner of her mouth lifted. "You did not."

"Do I look like I'm joking?" he asked as they stopped in front of the bathroom. "I couldn't get you off my mind, no matter how hard I tried."

Grace turned to look up at him, disbelief shining in her eyes. "You're being serious?"

"Of course I am." A tender smile curled his lips as he jerked his head toward the bathroom door. "Go soak in the tub before your water gets cold. I've got food to cook." He brushed a kiss over her lips and left her to bathe.

Back in the kitchen, Colt washed his hands while contemplating his original plans for the evening. While parts wouldn't work out now—considering how roughed up Grace was—most of it would. He normally would have preferred to grill the steaks he intended to make tonight, but Cash's grill had been completely out of propane when he checked it earlier. The broiler would do an acceptable job. He'd have to keep a closer eye on them to keep them from overcooking. At least, they should be nicely marinated by now.

He placed the broiler pan into the oven to pre-heat, then turned back to the fridge to retrieve the ingredients he needed for the rest of their meal. Before long, he had dinner well underway. While he waited for the potatoes he'd peeled and diced to finish boiling, he scrutinized the dining table. He needed flowers ... and candles. The candles were easy, but the flowers would take more work.

Colt checked on the contents of the pans on the stovetop, then hustled outside to cut a few blooms from the rosebushes growing at the corner of the house. He returned to the kitchen with half a dozen scarlet red roses. Unsurprisingly, Cash didn't seem to have any vases, so Colt haphazardly arranged the flowers in the tallest glass he could find and placed his makeshift vase in the middle of the table. He added a pair of tall, tapered candles on either side of the flowers.

Did it give off romantic vibes? He wasn't too sure about that, but he'd tried.

With a slight shrug, he returned to the kitchen to finish their meal before Grace got her curiosity up and came sniffing around to see what he was up to. She'd promised to stay out of the kitchen until he came to get her, but he knew how she got. He'd better hurry.

———◦○◦———

"I hope you're hungry," he said as he stepped into the bedroom to fetch Grace.

She was reclined back against a pile of pillows on the bed with a book in her hands. Where she'd found the book, he wasn't sure. Cash had dozens of them stashed in various places throughout the house, so it could have come from anywhere.

Grace's face brightened when she glanced up at him. She sat her book aside and climbed off the bed. "I'm starving," she admitted. "Is dinner ready? It smells amazing." She crossed to him, wrapped one arm around his waist, and leaned into him. "What are we having anyway?"

"You'll see." Colt grinned mischievously and slid his arm around her shoulders, then led her from the room.

His nerves were shot. This was almost as bad as waiting for his ride on a tough bull. He felt reasonably sure she'd find tonight romantic, but he was admittedly pretty hopeless in that regard. He wanted to do better for Grace. Be better.

He glanced down at her as they entered the dining room. Before going to get her, he'd shut off the kitchen lights and used the dimmer in the dining room to set the mood, then lit the two tapers. He hoped the way her eyes widened was a good sign.

He pulled out her chair and waited for her to sit before joining her at the table.

Grace studied the food, flowers, and candles, then looked over at him. She seemed on the verge of tears. He sure hoped they were happy ones.

"This is amazing," she said at long last, a smile in her tone. "You didn't have to do all this! It looks great. Where did you get the roses? I didn't see you grab them at the store."

"I know I didn't have to, but you're special to me so I wanted to do something for you. You deserve it." He smiled wryly. "I cut the roses from the bushes outside. Don't tell Cash in case he's partial to them." Even with as many years as he'd known Cash, it was impossible to get a full read on what the other man found important. Things Colt wouldn't have thought would upset his friend often did, and vice versa.

"The secret is safe with me." She made a motion like she was zipping her lips and throwing away the key, then laughed. "You're full of surprises, aren't you? I wasn't expecting this."

He chuckled. "Yeah, I guess so." He gestured toward her steak. "My memory isn't as good as yours, though. I forgot how you like your steak, so I cooked yours the same as I like mine. Medium-rare. If you like it more done, I can put it back on."

"Medium-rare is fine." She gave him a wide smile that warmed his heart then picked up her utensils and cut into it. "It's a crime for steak to be cooked any more than that." Grace popped a bite into her mouth and moaned. "Oh geez, I think I'm having a foodgasm. This is seriously delicious." She shook her head and leveled a mock glare on him. "You're going to make me fat if you keep feeding me this well."

"Does that mean you don't want the chocolate cake I made for dessert?"

She sat up a little straighter and gave him an eager look. "Chocolate cake? I take it back. The cake is mine. All mine."

A loud laugh burst from him. "Yeah, that's what I thought. It's homemade even, not that boxed mix crap. My great-grandma's recipe." He grinned and stabbed a chunk of his own steak. "You'll love it."

"Homemade?" Grace made a small sound that seemed like a cross between a moan and a groan. "I might have to marry you."

He nearly choked on the bite of steak he'd just swallowed. His gaze darted over to her, and she laughed. He could only guess what the look on his face was.

"Why is that?" His voice still sounded a bit strangled.

She was joking—he could tell that from her teasing tone—but he wondered what she'd say if she knew he'd been tossing around taking that step with her.

"Because homemade chocolate cake is the best and this steak is amazing. I'm not sure what you marinated it in, but it's the best I've ever had." She smiled. "If that cake is as delicious as this steak, you're definite marriage material."

He laughed. "Should I propose with cake, then?"

Her eyes twinkled as she nodded emphatically. "You definitely should. I'd be forced to say yes; I wouldn't have any choice."

"I'll have to keep that in mind," he rumbled, giving her a wide grin. Colt nodded toward her salad. "If it helps to seal the deal, I made the dressing for the salad, and the mashed potatoes from scratch too. In case you were wondering." He winked at her when she blinked at him. "I'm glad you like it, Princess."

"Like it? I love it! I sure hope you're serious about us 'cause I'm keeping you."

He smiled at that. "I sure hope so. I'm planning on keeping you too."

Forever if she'd let him.

"Come on, Summer. Get on in there!" Colt growled, trying yet again to get the little black mare up the ramp and into the horse trailer. He'd lost count of the number of times he'd attempted to get the animal loaded in the past hour. Every single time he thought he was getting close to success, she'd put up a fuss and they'd end up right back at square one. His patience was nearing its breaking point.

It was evident that Summer was as reluctant to go back to the circuit as her mistress was. Colt wished he could come up with a better option, but there wasn't anywhere else they could go unless they holed up with his parents or at a hotel. Neither option held much appeal. At least, back on the circuit, his friends would be able to help him keep Grace safe. He hoped anyway. It was the best way he could think of to protect her.

He glanced over at Grace. She stood a distance away, leaning lightly against the barn, watching as he struggled to load her mare. It looked as though she were struggling not to laugh.

She caught him looking and gave him a small, roguish smile. "See? We should stay here."

Colt narrowed his eyes. "You could always help me instead of standing around, you know? She's your horse. You're more likely to get her in the trailer than I am." He frowned. "She didn't give me this much trouble any other time I've loaded her."

Grace looked away. "She doesn't want to go, and neither do I."

He rubbed a hand roughly over his face. "Why?" Exasperation colored his voice, but he was powerless to hide it. "Give me one good reason why you don't want to go, and maybe I'll reconsider."

She shoved away from the barn wall and took Summer's lead rope from him. "I don't know what to tell you. I have a feeling it's a bad idea. Flint could show up again and make more trouble, for one." She sighed heavily. "I don't know. Maybe I'm afraid of you having another wreck. The last one could have killed you. I could have lost you."

"I'll be fine. The doctor wouldn't have cleared me if he wasn't sure it was safe for me to ride again."

A sizable part of him worried about her bad feeling, though he'd never let her know it. It was a well-known fact that women had superior intuitions. Now that he thought about it, Sarah had tried to talk him out of leaving the weekend before her accident too. Maybe she had somehow suspected that something was going to happen.

He shoved that thought away the moment it popped into his mind. This was different. Everything would be fine.

Grace made a face. "That's not entirely true, and you know it. Didn't that rookie bronc rider, Billy somebody, ride with his leg in a cast a few months ago?"

He flattened his lips but said nothing. What was there to say when she was right? It was far from uncommon for an injured cowboy to be cleared to resume riding well before their injuries were fully healed. It was crazy, but it happened. Roughstock riders were a different breed.

She looked as though she wanted to say something else but instead shook her head and quietly led her mare up the ramp and into the trailer. Summer didn't put up even one tiny ounce of trouble.

He screwed up his face as he stepped in to help her close the trailer doors. She glanced over at him and dissolved into laughter.

"Yeah, yeah, so funny," he said dryly though his lips twitched. "She's definitely your horse." He snagged her hand and pulled her toward him. "I promise I'll be as careful as I can. I'll even wear a helmet if it'll make you feel any better."

He slid an arm over her shoulders and steered her toward the house. "Come on, let's go double-check that we have everything, and then we can get out of here." He tossed her a slanted grin. "I don't want to have to turn around because you discover you've left something once we get halfway there. Again."

He couldn't resist teasing her about the time she'd forgotten her little stuffed horse at a hotel and had begged him to turn around to get it. Though he'd half-heartedly moaned about it, he'd driven the two hours back to the hotel. Anything for her. The woman had him wrapped around her finger, and he suspected she knew it.

"Hey, that only happened one time!" Once they reached the porch, she smiled sweetly up at him then lifted onto her toes to press a kiss to his cheek. "You know you love me."

"You know I do." He ducked his head and dropped a kiss on the tip of her nose, then opened the door and ushered her in.

Chapter 32

Grace sat on horseback, waiting for the previous competitor to leave the arena so she could have her turn. Her stomach flip-flopped. While she really did enjoy competing again, today felt weird, like something ominous was creeping closer. It was the same eerie feeling she'd had since she and Colt returned to the circuit a week ago. No matter how hard she tried, she couldn't shake it. She wished she knew what was causing it.

Summer danced beneath her, and Grace fought to get her back under control. There was little doubt in her mind that the animal was picking up on her stress.

She needed to get past this feeling. It wasn't as though anything bad had happened to explain it. Maybe she was worrying over nothing. Each of Colt's rides this week had gone well, and since the incident in Cash's barn, there had been no trace of Flint. Not even a whisper. There was nothing that stood out to explain her anxiety.

Grace took a couple of deep breaths before urging Summer forward into the box next to her calf's chute, then turned the excited mare to face the rear of the box to keep her from jumping the start. Once Summer was standing relatively quiet, Grace nodded to the cowboy in charge of freeing her calf. The mare whirled immediately and charged after the mustard yellow calf as it bolted into the arena ahead of them.

Grace whirled her rope above their heads. Her gaze narrowed on the calf as she loosed her loop toward it. She prayed she'd judged the distance correctly. To her relief, the rope settled neatly around the animal's neck and Summer immediately sat back on her haunches, pulling the rope taut. The rope broke away, stopping the clock.

Grace's eyes flicked up to the scoreboard as it lit up with their time. 2.3 seconds. As far as she could remember, that was one of her fastest times ever. Her heart beat a rapid staccato as excitement spread through her. A little of her unease fell away. Maybe today was going to be a good day, after all.

She patted Summer's neck then nudged her back into motion.

Colt met her at the gate with a huge grin on his face and Brody at his side. She allowed him to drag her from her mare's back and into his arms.

Brody grabbed Summer's reins. He was smiling too, but she didn't have a chance to say anything before Colt spun her around in a circle and planted a congratulatory kiss on her lips.

"That was a great time, baby! I knew you could do it."

Colt's grin was infectious.

Her lips curled upward. "That was the second fastest time I've ever gotten. As far as I can remember, that is."

"We'll celebrate tonight. I'm proud of you! You and Summer make a great team; I'm glad I talked you into taking her."

"Talked me into it? You didn't give me much of a choice but to take her."

Brody chuckled, and her gaze flitted over to him. The cowboy had been good company while she and Colt were apart. As promised, he'd kept a close eye out for Flint for her. Though they hadn't spoken often, she counted him as a friend now.

It'd surprised her when he'd approached her for a date. He'd taken her rejection far better than any other guy she'd ever known, which had surprised her as well. Maybe he'd half expected what her answer would be, or maybe he hadn't really been all that interested in the first place. Perhaps he'd only flirted to gauge her interest in Colt, like Cash had told her *he* had. Whatever the reason, while Brody was handsome, with his short brown hair and dark green eyes, he didn't hold a candle to Colt. She liked Brody, just not like that.

She offered him a smile then returned her gaze to Colt.

"You and I make a pretty good team too." She lifted onto her toes to give Colt a brief kiss, feeling her face heat. No doubt she was blushing again. Before meeting him, she couldn't recall a time she'd ever blushed so much. She found it rather annoying.

Colt grinned. "Yes, we do." He touched his lips to her forehead, seconds before he dipped his head closer to her ear and whispered, "I love you, Princess."

The loudspeaker blared, telling the roughstock riders to prepare for their rides before she could even open her mouth to reply. Her stomach twisted as her nerves rioted all over again.

Watching him ride was torturous. Would it ever get any easier? Watching the other guys didn't bother her any, but it was different when it was the bull rider your heart belonged to.

Once the man on the loudspeaker finally shut up, she smiled up at Colt. "I love you too, cowboy." She stepped out of his embrace and took the reins back from Brody. "You boys go. I can get Summer cooled down on my own." She gave Colt's arm a gentle shove. "Ride safe and score high."

Neither man moved. Colt and Brody exchanged a look.

"Actually, I thought I'd keep you company tonight." Brody moved toward her a step. One corner of his mouth lifted as he raised his arm to show off the cast she hadn't noticed earlier. "Busted my riding arm two stops ago, so I'm on bodyguard duty for the next little while." He tilted his head. "If you don't mind hanging out with me, at least."

"Oh." Her gaze traveled to Colt.

A small smile played on his face. She should have known he wouldn't leave her alone. He'd made sure there was someone with her at all times this past week, though this was the first that one of his friends offered to guard her. Even with as much of a comfort it was, it was an annoyance too. She could hardly wait for the day that it was no longer necessary. If that day ever actually came.

She offered Brody a smile. "I don't mind. It'll be nice to have company."

Maybe she could get him to open up a little while Colt was riding. Of all of Colt's friends, Brody was the one she knew the least, even with him having acted as her bodyguard while she and Colt had been apart. Brody was so quiet, like he held all of his cards close to his chest and refused to let anyone get a glimpse of who he really was. The journalist in her craved to find a way past his walls so she could learn why he kept to himself so much. There had to be a reason.

"Now, I can go," Colt murmured. "I need to know you're safe while I ride. I know it bugs you, but I promised I'd protect you." He bent to kiss her, nodded to Brody, then walked away.

"That woman was flirting with you." Grace gave Brody a sidelong glance as they led Summer toward the barn.

The woman who'd stopped them a few minutes ago to get an autograph from Brody had been very clearly trying to provoke his interest, but he hadn't seemed to notice.

Brody shrugged. "I know. She wasn't exactly subtle." Though his gaze was on something off in the distance, a small smile tugged at his lips. "I don't date, and I don't fool around with fans or fellow competitors."

Grace's brow furrowed. "You don't? Then why did you ask me out to dinner a few months back?"

He laughed. "Because Cash said Colt needed a push. Seems to have done the trick too. Besides, where's the harm in going to dinner? Everybody needs to eat, and it would have been a good time to get to know you better. Just ... not *that* much better. You're beautiful, that's no lie, but it was obvious you were already Colt's, even if he was still being a dummy about it."

Grace's face grew warm. "Oh." She said nothing more until after she'd led Summer into her stall and relieved her of her halter. "Why don't you date?"

Brody's shoulders rose and fell. He filled Summer's water bucket with the nearby hose. "Present company excluded, women are full of shit. One minute they're claiming to love you, and the next they're gone like you were nothing." Bitterness colored his voice. "I'm not interested in playing that game. It's easier to be alone."

"I see." Grace waited, but he said nothing more.

It was obvious someone had hurt him. Badly. Sensing she was treading far too close to something painful, she let the subject drop and focused on getting Summer settled in. Silence fell between them while she filled the hay rack attached to the interior of the stall.

"Sorry I wasn't much help," Brody said after she finished grooming her horse and stepped from the stall.

"You helped plenty." Grace smiled.

"If you say so." Brody laughed. "If we hurry, we might be able to watch your man ride. That bull he drew for tonight is rough. Fucker has tossed me every time I've climbed on him." He glanced at her as they started for the door of the barn, and his lips twitched upward. "When I got started with rodeo, climbing onto the back of homicidal bulls wasn't exactly what I'd planned on doing."

Grace lifted an eyebrow. "What did you want to do?"

"Team roping and bareback broncs." He gestured for her to precede him through the barn's side door. "I didn't try bulls until senior year of high school. After that first bull, I was hooked. I forgot all about broncs and roping. From then on, I was all about the bulls. Shit, I wish I ha—"

She turned to look back at him when he quit speaking mid-sentence, at the same time as she heard a strange thump. Alarm sent her heart rate skyrocketing when her gaze landed on him. He lay unmoving on the ground, blood pouring from a gash on his forehead.

What the hell? Her blood turned to ice.

Was he alive? With the way he'd fallen, she couldn't tell if he was breathing. He had to be unconscious. She didn't even want to consider the alternative; it was unthinkable.

Her gaze lifted to the horizon, trying to find help. This had to be Flint.

She tried to scream, but the fear flaring to life within her made it come out more like a strangled squeak.

A hand clamped over her mouth before she could try again. A familiar arm wrapped around her waist and yanked her back against an equally familiar solid chest. Spicy cologne made her nose wrinkle in disgust. Flint always had practically bathed in the stuff. Some things never changed.

Her heart hammered against her ribs. It became horribly obvious what was happening.

"Hello again," Flint said at her ear before kissing her cheek. "Watched your run. Nice time. Pretty horse too." His voice was deceptively light, seeming almost amicable.

She wasn't fooled by his act. The pressure of his hand over her mouth betrayed his intentions. He wasn't here for a friendly chat.

Her stomach knotted into such a tight ball she thought she might be sick. He'd found her again, like she'd worried that he would.

Colt had been so confident that she'd be safe back on the circuit. That too many eyes were watching for Flint for him to get close to her. She'd wanted to believe Colt, but at gut level, she'd known better. Flint would keep coming for her until he either finally killed her or he found someone else to victimize. Even having one of Colt's friends with her hadn't kept Flint away. Now, because of her, Brody was hurt ... or worse.

She'd known she would never be safe. Not at Cash's, not on the circuit, not anywhere. It was disheartening to be right.

"No screaming."

Flint's hand lifted away from her mouth, and she fought the urge to do exactly that. She bit down hard on her tongue and focused on the pain in an attempt to calm herself. Panicking wasn't going to get her out of this mess. Screaming would be pointless anyway; it was unlikely anyone would hear her over the noise and excitement in the rodeo grounds. Tonight was chaos. Kids were shouting as they played somewhere, and cheers echoed elsewhere. There didn't even seem to be anyone looking in their direction. Plenty of people were in the barn, but it was debatable if they'd hear her either. It wasn't worth the risk.

"What do you want, Flint?" It impressed her that she'd managed to keep her voice steady despite the fear roiling through her. Colt would be proud of her.

Thinking of him made her want to cry. Would she ever see him again? At least she'd told him she loved him; she wouldn't die without him knowing how she felt.

From the corner of her eye, she saw Flint smile. If you wanted to call it that. To her, it appeared more like the snarl of a rabid dog than anything else.

He transferred his grip to her upper arm. His fingers bit into her skin, making her wince.

"You're going to come with me. We're going to go somewhere quieter to have a little talk. Somewhere I don't have to worry about the cowboy you're fucking showing up and spoiling things." His fingers dug in deeper as he gave her a little shake. "Don't try anything, or I'll knock your whore ass out and haul you out of here over my shoulder. We clear?"

She gulped in a breath of air and nodded. What choice did she have at the moment? Her knife was in the glovebox of the truck, and while Colt had taught her a few self-defense moves, she had little faith that she could outmaneuver Flint. He was bigger, stronger, and definitely meaner. Even if she could somehow get someone's attention, he'd threatened to hurt people at the stop she'd broke Flint's finger at. He'd already hurt Brody; she couldn't stand the idea of anyone else getting hurt because of her.

"I'll go quietly," she answered, thankful that her voice remained steady. She didn't want to give him the pleasure of knowing she was afraid.

"Good." He started forward, pulling her along with him.

Grace struggled to pay attention to where they were going as Flint led her away from the crowds. Her phone was still in her pocket. If Flint didn't notice it, maybe she'd get the opportunity to send Colt, Cash, or someone else a message. There was little chance she could get out of this without help. Flint was too strong. He overpowered her too easily.

Would he kill her now, like he'd threatened to so often? Was Brody okay? There'd been so much blood.

"Where are you taking me?"

He sneered at her in response but didn't answer. Of course, he wasn't going to tell her. That would be far too easy.

She glanced longingly over her shoulder at the arena as Flint steered her out the gate and away from the rodeo grounds. They crossed the street then turned a corner. It felt like they'd been walking forever before he finally pulled her down a narrow alley toward what appeared to be a warehouse, or maybe some sort of factory.

While Flint fumbled with a padlock one-handed, she glanced around in search of some sort of clue she could give Colt to help him find her. There was no signage outside the building they were at as far as she could see. This was looking worse with every minute that passed.

Flint yanked her into an immense room. Row upon row of towering metal shelves cluttered the space, each filled with plastic-wrapped pallets loaded with boxes of various shapes and sizes. A thick layer of dust covered everything. If this was a warehouse, it clearly wasn't frequented very often. Even the air smelled stale.

He jerked her down an aisle to a small room that looked like it'd been an office at some point.

"Sit," he commanded with a growl and shoved her toward the chair next to a nearby heavy-looking wooden desk.

The moment she was free, Grace turned on her heel and ran for the door. She'd barely reached the doorway when Flint snagged her by the hair and dragged her back to him. A scream escaped her as pain shot through her scalp.

"Did you really think you could get away again?" Flint laughingly taunted. He wrapped his hand tighter in her hair and sneered.

She could hardly see him through her tears.

"You won't get away with this," she flung at him.

"Bet I do," he said with a confident grin.

In a desperate bid for freedom, Grace twisted as much as possible—ignoring the searing sting in her scalp—and sank her teeth into Flint's arm.

He roared and released her hair, as she'd been hoping he would.

She swiveled around but didn't have time to flee before Flint grabbed her arm and spun her back around. His fist connected with her stomach and drove the air from her lungs. Each furious blow hammered more of the fight from her. Agony wrapped her in its fiery embrace.

After the third strike, Flint shoved her toward the chair again. "Sit," he ordered.

This time she obeyed, unable to find the air or energy to fight him any further. The rusty metal chair groaned under her weight as she sat heavily. A cloud of dust rose up around her and sent her headlong into a coughing fit.

With watery eyes, she watched as Flint rummaged through a backpack on the floor nearby. It seemed out of place, considering it was the only thing that didn't look long abandoned. Flint moved toward her with something in his hands, and she tensed. He wordlessly kneeled next to her and secured her ankles to the chair's legs with two of the four zip-ties he held.

She caught her lip between her teeth and scanned the room. There was no signage in this room either. The desk held papers, but nothing visible on them gave any hint as to what this place was. Not that much could be read at all, considering how dim the room was. The single bulb above them did little to offer light. It hardly mattered. If he zip-tied her hands to the arms of the chair too, she wouldn't be able to contact anyone anyway, even if he gave her opportunity to.

He'd finished with her ankles when his phone rang. Flint mumbled a curse and pushed to his feet as he pulled his phone from his jeans' pocket. He didn't even spare her a glance before stepping from the room while talking.

She waited only until his footsteps faded then burst into motion. This was it. The only chance she was likely to have.

Grace hastily shifted around, ignoring the excruciating pain the action caused, and grabbed her phone from her back pocket. She thumbed it open, keeping a wary eye on the office doorway. Colt was the first person in her recent calls list, thankfully. Without knowing how long she had before Flint returned, she'd take any way she could to save time. She rapidly typed out a message to Colt, hit send, then deleted the text to hide the evidence.

Flint returned before she could slip her phone back into her pocket. His eyes narrowed on the device. The blank expression on his face as he stalked toward her gave away no hints as to his thoughts or intentions.

Her stomach clenched. The closer he got, the louder her heartbeat pounded in her ears. She braced herself for a blow when he stopped in front of her, but to her surprise, it didn't come.

Without a word, he snatched the phone from her hand, swiped it open, and looked through it. She was glad she'd deleted the text to hide what she'd done. This situation would have gotten worse for her with lightning speed if she hadn't. That much, she knew for certain.

"Looks like I caught you in time." He gave her a smug smile. "Were you planning on calling for help?"

She didn't respond. It was unlikely he expected her to anyway. She hoped—prayed—her message had gone through.

"How about we remove the temptation, hmm?" He whipped the phone at the concrete wall. On impact, it splintered apart with a loud crunch. "There we go," he said, his voice strangely cheerful.

Grace flinched as he turned back to her and stroked the back of his hand along her cheek. His touch sent her stomach swirling. She swallowed hard, hoping to calm the nausea. Despite the light tone of his voice and the gentleness in his touch, she could tell he was well beyond livid. His eyes always gave him away. Even with the darkness cloaking the tiny room, she could see the wrath glittering in the depths of his brown eyes.

He snatched the remaining two zip-ties from the floor where he'd left them and hastily secured her wrists to the arms of the heavy metal chair, her palms up.

"I thought you said we were going to talk, Flint. Let's talk," she said with more confidence than she felt. "How did you find me?"

"I've got my ways. Got my friends too, or did you forget about them?"

She hadn't. How could she when he took every opportunity he could to remind her of all of his connections, of how invincible he believed they made him.

He tugged the final zip-tie tight enough to make her wince and glanced up at her.

The grin he gave her sent a chill skidding down her spine.

"I've changed my mind about our chat. I can't trust anything that comes out of your mouth."

He shoved to his feet then pulled back his fist and drove it into her stomach. Every bit of air left her lungs with a whoosh.

"I don't think I want your used-up ass back anymore either. Think I'll teach you a lesson. Maybe use you to send a message to that asshole you left me for. Show him what happens when he steals someone else's girl." He slapped her across the face hard enough to turn her vision red.

She struggled to draw much needed air back into her lungs. "Please," she gasped. "Don't."

He looked down at her scornfully and laughed, then grabbed something from the backpack. It wasn't until he turned to face her again that she realized he was holding a knife.

Her blood ran cold. She struggled against her binds as he prowled toward her, but he'd tightened them down too much for her to do anything more than abrade the skin from her wrists.

She wasn't getting loose. There was no way out of this. Even if her message to Colt had gone through, he'd never find her in time.

Hopelessness settled into her bones as she stared up at Flint with wide eyes. His intentions were written openly on his face.

She was going to die. Flint was going to kill her.

Chapter 33

COLT'S RIDE COULD HAVE gone better. It could have gone worse too, he supposed. At least he'd made the eight seconds and had come away with a score of 83. It was far from a bad score, considering he was still getting back into the swing of things after a major wreck, but it didn't thrill him. Still, Smooth Voodoo was far too predictable and lazy to buck well enough to give much higher of a score anyway.

At least he could still fucking ride. He hadn't been able to ride any practice bulls before he and Grace left Cash's place, so he hadn't known for sure if he'd still have the nerve it took to climb on a bull's back. Tonight proved that he did. Thank fuck. He still wasn't sure if he was completely ready to retire for good, and he sure as hell hadn't wanted to be forced from the sport by bad dreams.

Cash came up behind him and clapped a hand to his shoulder. "Decent ride, dude."

Colt made a face at him. "If you say so. It was sloppy." He grabbed his phone from his locker and tucked it into his back pocket without looking at it. "I've got better draws for the next three stops." He worked his shoulder; it was sore after being jerked around tonight.

"How's that shoulder feeling? He had you on your arm most of that ride."

"It's fine," Colt muttered.

"Sure it is." Cash rolled his eyes then gave him a knowing grin. "Don't let your girl know it hurts. She'll probably tie you up with that rope of hers so you can't ride next stop."

Colt snorted. "It's a breakaway rope. I'll break loose and ride anyway."

Cash laughed and shook his head. "Are you guys still wanting to hit that new Italian joint with me and Dusty tonight?"

"I think so. Let me double-check with her." As he exited the locker room with Cash on his heels, Colt pulled his phone from his pocket and swiped it open.

A new message notification was waiting for him. Probably Grace. When the rodeo grounds were as teeming with people as they were tonight, it was often easier to text than hunt for each other. He tapped open the message and stopped cold in his tracks.

Cash bounced off of his back, but he hardly noticed. Ice was spreading through his veins as insidious as a wildfire during a drought.

Grace

> Flint. Warehouse? Help

Fuck. Fuck! Not again. Not fucking again. How had Flint gotten to her? Brody was with her. Where the hell was Brody?

"What the hell, man?" Cash stepped around his side and studied him with narrowed eyes. "What's wrong? You look like someone told you you'll never ride again."

Colt glanced up at his best friend but didn't really see him. His heart was racing, his mind spinning faster than an amusement park ride.

"Grace. Her ex," he gasped.

Was he hyperventilating? He felt like he was. He couldn't seem to slow his breathing, and his head was getting fuzzy.

A chill settled into his bones, followed by a blast of anger so red-hot he turned and slammed his fist into the side of the wooden wall of the locker room. Blood dripped from his split knuckles, but he was far from caring. His entire world, his heart, was in a warehouse somewhere. He had to find her.

First, he needed to calm down. He needed a clear head. Panic wouldn't help him. Or her.

His gaze darted to their surroundings, moving from one building in the distance to the next as he forced his mind to clear and sucked in deep breath after deep breath. She could be anywhere.

He'd only been to this rodeo twice. How the fuck was he going to find her when he wasn't even familiar with this town? She was in a warehouse? That helped, but this whole town was pretty industrial. They'd passed multiple buildings that could be factories or warehouses on their way to the rodeo grounds from their hotel.

"Her ex? That Flint asshole?"

Colt jerked his head affirmatively. "He has her." He inhaled another deep breath as a fresh wave of panic rose up to consume him. He handed Cash his phone and pointed at the message. Colt's throat felt far too thick to say anything else. He needed to find her.

He shifted on his feet, trying to decide where to search first.

Cash read it, and his eyes shot wide. "A warehouse." His gaze jumped to the horizon then back to Colt. He thrust the phone at Colt then rubbed a hand over his mouth. "There aren't that many warehouses near here, assuming they walked. We'll find her."

Colt didn't respond and Cash grabbed his shirt, getting up into his face. "Stay here, Colt. I know you want to go find her, but stay here. Let me get the guys. Five minutes. Stay put."

Colt swallowed hard but nodded, and Cash disappeared back into the locker room.

Colt could hear his blood rushing in his ears. It was so loud it was almost deafening. It felt like he was teetering on the edge of a breakdown.

He couldn't lose her. Not when he'd just let her in, let himself love her. Damnit, she'd had a bad feeling about heading back to the rodeo, and he'd brushed it off. Like he had Sarah's concerns so long ago. He hadn't fucking listened. Again. Flint had her because of him.

Where was she?

He lifted his eyes to the horizon and studied the few buildings he could see from where he stood while concentrating on his breathing, trying to keep his terror at bay. Movement off to his left caught his attention. Someone approaching.

Brody was limping toward him. A cut above his eye dripped blood steadily. His normally mild-mannered friend looked absolutely incensed.

"The bastard knocked me out. I was following Grace from the barn when he snuck up on us," Brody growled. His dark green eyes searched the few people milling near the locker room. "Where's Grace? Please tell me she's here."

Colt's lips flattened into a tense line. "Can't tell you what's not true." Unable to speak the words, he held his phone up for his friend to see Grace's message.

The hope that'd lurked in Brody's expression vanished in an instant. "I'm sorry, man. We'll find her." Brody straightened with a groan and studied the surrounding buildings. "I'm going to hit the medic tent and get them to stop this fucking bleeding, then I'm helping to look." He pulled his gaze from the buildings in the distance and turned his gaze onto Colt. "Have you called the cops?"

What was the point? They hadn't been much help. If they had been, Flint wouldn't have still been walking around free to grab Grace again.

Colt shook his head. "Maybe you should have them check you over first."

"Fuck that. They can check me out after we find your girl," Brody snapped. "And I'll call the cops for you." Determination glinted in his eyes.

Colt knew better than to argue. He didn't have time to anyway.

Cash exited the locker room with ten bull riders and six bronc riders in tow.

Colt glanced at Brody. "Text Cash when you're done with the medics."

Brody nodded and took off at a jog.

Colt turned back to Cash and the large group of fellow roughstock riders. "Let's go."

He didn't wait for an answer. He clenched his jaw and started for the closest of the warehouse-looking buildings.

—◇—

"Grace!" Colt called as he and Cash combed through yet another of the buildings that surrounded the rodeo grounds. They'd been through three others already. Dusty, Brody, and the other guys were searching elsewhere.

Every muscle stretched taut as he strained to hear any sort of reply. A groan. A whisper. Anything. All he heard was his own ragged breathing and Cash's heavy footsteps.

Shit. They were running out of places to search. What if they hadn't walked? What if Flint had driven her somewhere else? What if they didn't find her?

"Colt! Over here! There's an office. I found her."

His heart jumped into his throat. He half ran in the direction he'd heard Cash's voice come from while cursing the pallets and boxes that prevented him from moving as quickly as he wanted to. From the tone of his best friend's voice, it didn't sound good. He braced himself for what he might see.

His heart clenched the moment his gaze landed on Grace as he entered the small room. She was slumped over in a chair. The metallic tang of blood hung heavily in the still air.

Was she alive? He couldn't tell.

His gaze darted to Cash, who hovered nearby with his phone in his hand. "Call an ambulance, and tell the cops where we are. Tell the rest of the guys we found her too."

"Already done," Cash growled in answer.

Colt fell to his knees at Grace's side and tentatively touched her arm. Her skin was warm, which was vaguely reassuring, but she didn't even twitch. That didn't seem like a good sign. His fingers came away sticky with blood, and his breath caught in his chest. He glanced down and, for the first time, saw the trio of horizontal slices up her arm as though Flint had slit her wrist. One still oozed, but the other two seemed to have clotted. Colt glanced at her other arm. It had suffered the same.

He sucked in a shaky breath. Her head hung forward limply, causing her hair to obscure her face from view like a curtain. It seemed like she was unconscious ... or dead.

He didn't want to think it, but she was so still, so silent.

Colt leaned forward, squinting at her in hopes of seeing even a tiny flicker of movement, but there was none. He touched two fingers to her neck, but felt no pulse. Was he even doing it right? Fuck, he didn't know; He'd never had to check anyone for a pulse, until now. He shifted his fingers to another spot, holding his breath as he concentrated on the skin beneath his fingertips.

Nothing. His stomach lurched as hope evaporated.

Fuck, they'd been too late. He'd lost her. Just like Sarah.

His head dropped forward as he ripped off his hat and pulled at his hair. His eyes snagged on the blood on her legs, on the floor. So much blood.

He'd failed her. He'd fucking failed her. He should have listened. Just like with Sarah.

"Colt," Cash said.

Grace had died in this fucking dark, dusty room all alone. He hadn't listened, and now she was gone. Dead.

He gasped for breath. Why couldn't he breathe? The room was pressing in on him, crushing him.

"Fuck, dude. Snap out of it!" Cash yelled and shook Colt's shoulder. "Colt!"

Colt couldn't take his eyes off Grace. His heart ached. "She's dead," he whispered hoarsely.

"No, she's not," Cash snapped. "She's breathing, bro. She's breathing. Look!"

Breathing. Not dead. Alive.

He didn't move. Couldn't move.

Colt swallowed hard.

Was she really breathing? He hadn't lost her?

With the way she was slumped in the chair, it was impossible to tell if her chest was rising and falling. He stared hard at her, and a puff of air stirred her hair.

"Grace," he breathed.

He closed his eyes and bowed his head for a moment. She was alive. Breathing. He hadn't lost her. A trembly laugh left his lips as he reached for her hand with his own shaking. *Alive.* He tipped his head toward the ceiling as emotion swamped him. Silent tears streamed down his face. He swiped them away and ducked his head to inspect what he could see of her face from his position at her side.

"Oh, Princess," he breathed as his gaze drifted over the visible damage. A gash above her eye was dripping blood steadily, and a trail of red trickled from her nose. Her lips were split in several places. There were so many bruises, and he couldn't even see her full face yet.

He'd thought he'd felt rage before, while she'd been recounting her story to him back at Cash's, but what he felt now made that seem like a minor annoyance.

What the fuck had Flint done to her? The bastard had better hope the cops found him before Colt did. He would kill him for doing this to her. There would be no saving that asshole by the time he was through with him. Grace didn't deserve this. No woman did.

Colt pushed to his feet and stalked through the office in search of anything he could use to free her from the zip-ties. Why the hell hadn't he stopped by the truck to grab his knife from the glovebox? If he'd been thinking clearly, he would have. He found a utility knife in the drawer of the nearby desk. It wasn't ideal, but it would do.

He grabbed it and returned to her side. After carefully slicing through the ties around her ankles, he eyed the ones securing her wrists to the chair. They appeared to be the only thing keeping her upright at the moment. The second he released her wrists, she would likely topple forward and end up on the floor.

He looked up at Cash. "Can you get the ties on her wrists? She's going to hit the floor if I do it. I can't cut them and catch her at the same time."

From the savage expression on Cash's face, it was obvious to Colt that he wouldn't be the only one sitting in a prison cell for murder if they caught up to Flint before the cops did. At least he'd be in good company. Cash might not know Grace well, but he didn't need to. She was female, and someone had hurt her. That was more than enough to get his best friend riled and ready to pulverize whoever did it.

"Are you sure we should move her? What if she has injuries we can't see and moving her makes them worse?"

Cash's questions echoed Colt's worries. "Hell fucking no, I'm not sure, but I can't let her keep sitting there like that until help gets here. I can't. Please, man, help me." He needed to hold her. He needed to assure himself that she was truly alive. That he hadn't lost her.

"Give it here." Cash shoved his phone into his back pocket then held his hand out for the utility knife.

Colt muttered a thanks and handed it over before focusing on Grace. He gripped her shoulders as gently as possible to keep her in her seat while Cash released her wrists. The skin beneath the zip-ties was raw and bleeding, as though she'd struggled to get free.

She groaned softly as he carefully eased her out of the chair and into his arms. It was the first sound she'd made since Cash found her. While Colt hated her pain, the small sound was wonderful to hear. It was proof she was still with him.

"Hurts," she whispered hoarsely.

He seated himself on the ground and gingerly cradled her against his chest. Her lashes fluttered, but her face was too swollen and bruised to allow her to open her eyes.

"Shh, I've got you. You're safe now. Help is coming. Rest."

She sighed heavily and shuddered. "Hurts," she repeated, then relaxed against him as though she'd fallen unconscious again. Maybe she had.

While he wasn't much of a religious man, Colt closed his eyes and tipped his face toward the ceiling while whispering a fevered prayer that she'd survive this.

Chapter 34

Colt paced the waiting room. They'd been at the hospital for nearly six hours already. What the hell was taking so long?

The endless scenarios racing through his head wouldn't stop and kept getting worse the longer it took for them to bring him news about Grace's condition. A nurse had been by to inform him that a doctor would be out to talk to him as soon as they finished examining her.

"Sit down. You're going to wear a groove in the floor."

He tossed a glare at Cash. "Don't fucking care."

Colt scrubbed a hand over his face and up through his hair. Where the hell his hat was, he didn't know. It was his favorite, but right now it wasn't important. It could be replaced; his girlfriend couldn't.

"I'll sit down once I know how she is. She's my whole damn everything."

Maybe Cash would understand someday. He doubted his friend could dodge love forever. No matter how careful you thought you were being, it had a way of sneaking up on you. By the time you knew your heart was in danger, it was already lost and it was too late to run. Shit, he'd found that one out firsthand. *Twice.*

Cash wisely shut his mouth.

From the corner of his eye, Colt saw Dusty and Brody exchange a look, but he didn't have the energy to analyze it.

He glanced around at the collection of cowboys dominating the large room. It didn't matter that the majority of the men had never met Grace; they'd still come to offer their support. That's how it was in the rodeo world. They were one big family.

When the doctor finally entered the crowded waiting room a time later, Colt nearly bowled the man over. Why wasn't the doctor speaking yet? Damn it, he needed to know how she was, if she'd live.

"How is she? Can I see her?"

Cash stepped up next to him but remained silent.

The doctor's expression gave away nothing. "She's stable. The injuries she has sustained were considerable. She has experienced significant trauma, and we're not quite out of the woods yet, but I'm cautiously optimistic." His gaze skimmed the occupants of the room before settling on Colt once more. "Does she have family here? Husband? Parents? Siblings? It would be best if we kept her visitors to immediate family members only for now."

Immediate family members. To hell with their rules.

Colt wasn't waiting any longer to see her. He couldn't care less what he had to do; he was going to see her right this damn moment. "I'm her husband."

From the corner of his eye, he caught the startled look Cash shot him. His jaw tightened. He hoped Cash kept his damn mouth shut.

The doctor smiled slightly. "Alright. If you want to follow me, I'll take you to her." He started toward the doors leading to a nearby hallway.

Cash grabbed Colt's arm before he could even take a single step after the doctor. "I'll get Summer back to my place. You guys can hole up there once she's released if you need to. Call me if you need anything. I'll fly back if I have to. You guys are more important than standings."

Colt nodded. "Thanks, man. I appreciate it." He gave Cash a one-armed hug, slapped his back, then steeled himself and followed the doctor.

As the doctor led Colt down the overly bright hallway, he said, "Your wife is a very lucky woman to have escaped worse injury. She does have evidence of having a concussion, but both her head CT and MRI were clear. She has two broken ribs, a bruised sternum, and her right orbital socket has been fractured. There is a hairline fracture to her right cheekbone, and her nose is broken. The cuts on her arms are mostly superficial. Two were deep enough to require suturing. More concerning is the Grade II liver laceration she sustained, but I'm cautiously optimistic that it will heal fine without surgery. We'll be keeping her here in the ICU for at least five to seven days to keep a close eye on it. After that, we'll re-evaluate."

Colt couldn't find the words to respond. The knowledge of how close he'd come to losing her settled into his mind and made his stomach churn. By the time they got to Grace's room, the headache that'd begun when he arrived at the hospital had his head throbbing in earnest.

He hesitated in the doorway and glanced back at the doctor. "She's going to be okay?"

The man gave him a tight smile. "Like I said, we're not quite out of the woods, but I'm cautiously optimistic. Right now, things are looking pretty promising. We'll be doing some more testing over the next few days and should know more then."

Colt nodded and took a deep, steadying breath as he faced the room again. The moment his gaze landed on Grace, his chest constricted, making it hard to breathe.

Her bruises stood out in stark contrast with the white sheets she lay on. While she was a petite woman to begin with, she seemed even tinier laying there in that bed.

Seeing her like this was tearing him apart. A wave of some emotion he couldn't quite identify washed over him. The urge to turn around and run surged to life, and he nearly gave in to it. His worse fear had nearly come true. Could still come true.

Rather than running, he clenched his jaw, steeled himself, and entered the surprisingly spacious room. The doctor pulled the door shut behind him, giving them privacy. She appeared to be sleeping, but Colt still appreciated the gesture.

As he slowly approached her bedside, his gaze drifted over the various monitors clustered around the head of her bed. He didn't recognize most of them. Despite his numerous serious wrecks while bull riding, he'd been fortunate to not get hurt badly enough to land in the ICU himself. That was probably a miracle all in itself.

Colt sat on the thinly upholstered chair to the left of Grace's bed. For a couple of minutes, all he could do was watch the rhythmic rise and fall of her chest. His throat felt thick, and his eyes burned.

He swallowed hard, struggling to regain control over his emotions. She didn't need to see him breaking down when she woke up. What she needed was for him to be strong for her. He inhaled a ragged breath and reached for her hand.

The moment his fingers touched hers, she jerked and opened her eyes as much as her puffy skin would allow.

"Colt," she whispered, turning her head to look at him. "I'm really alive." From her tone of voice, she seemed surprised by the fact.

His heart clenched. "Yeah, baby, you are. Thank fuck. The police are looking for him. There's an officer floating around the hospital somewhere too. She said she needs a statement from you when you feel up to it. He won't get away with doing this to you."

"Brody. Is he—is he okay?"

Colt nodded. "He has a pretty nasty cut on his head and a mild concussion, but he's fine, other than being worried about you and pissed at Flint."

"Good. There was so much blood." Grace shuddered. "As far as the police, I don't want to talk about what happened. I want this nightmare to end." She shifted on the bed with a grimace and closed her eyes. "I want to forget."

He wanted to forget too. The sight of her in that office with her wrists slit, blood everywhere, and her body bruised and beaten was seared into his mind. He had a feeling he'd never shake it loose.

"I know, Princess. One way or another, he'll get what's coming to him and this mess will end. I swear it to you."

His free hand balled into a fist as he thought about what he'd like to do to Flint. He didn't tell her that the police were struggling to find the asshole. It was like Flint had vanished. "I know you don't want to talk about it, but the police need to know. I'll be right beside you while you talk to them."

She gave him a vague semblance of a nod but didn't reopen her eyes. "I'll need you with me. I don't think I'm strong enough to do it on my own."

He frowned. "Princess, you're the strongest woman I know. I'm serious. You're so fucking brave, and beautiful too. We'll get through this." He pushed to his feet and brushed a featherlight kiss over her forehead. "I love you."

The barest hint of a smile twitched at the corners of her lips. "I love you too." She sighed heavily. "I'm sorry, I can't stay awake. They gave me something for the pain, and it's kicking my butt."

"Get some rest," he said softly as he sat back down.

Her fingers tightened around his. "Don't leave me."

"Never," he replied gruffly. He pressed his lips to the back of her hand. "I'm not going anywhere. They'll have to drag me away. Go to sleep. I'll be right here when you wake up. I promise."

She didn't reply.

Colt rubbed his temples with his free hand and settled back in the chair. A nurse entered the room before he could even attempt to relax any. She gave him an apologetic look. He knew what was coming before she even opened her mouth.

"I'm sorry, sir, but you're going to have to leave now. I'm afraid visiting hours are over. You can come back at 6 a.m."

"I'm not leaving," he returned firmly.

The nurse's expression turned anxious. She fiddled with the clip of the clipboard she held. It didn't look as though she knew how to handle his refusal. From her very obvious case of nerves, it seemed to him that she was either new or simply uncomfortable with someone pushing back. His vote was for new. She looked young, like she was fresh out of med school.

"I'm sorry, sir, but you have to. Visiting hours are over. It's against hospital policy to have overnight guests in the ICU."

Colt sighed and turned to look at the woman more fully. "Look, I'm not trying to get you in trouble or anything, but I'm not leaving. I'll stay out of the way and let you guys do your job, but unless you call security to force me to leave, I'm not budging from this chair. You may as well bring me a bed so I can stay with her. I made a promise, and I intend to keep it."

"We don't really do—"

His expression hardened. "I'm. Not. Leaving. Get me a bed, or call security. It makes no difference to me which you do, but you won't get me to leave her side quietly."

The nurse backed toward the door, still fidgeting with the clipboard. She seemed to finally realize how serious he was. She wavered there in the doorway, as though deliberating on a course of action.

He turned away, uncaring of her decision. Unless security came and forced him to leave, he wasn't going to willingly do so. He'd made a promise to Grace, and he'd be damned if he was going to break it because of some bullshit rule the hospital had. When he glanced at the doorway next, the nurse had gone.

Colt leaned his forehead against Grace's bed and shut his eyes. He was exhausted. With everything that'd gone on today, it was little wonder.

The temptation to join the hunt for Flint was strong. He needed to know that fucker wasn't going to get away with this. Grace needed it too. Somehow, he didn't think he'd be able to keep himself from killing the man, however.

He wasn't sure how long he sat there, dozing, before he heard a noise at the door. He lifted his head in time to see an empty hospital bed being wheeled into the room by a gangly male orderly. The man said nothing as he moved the bed into position on the other side of Grace's and engaged the wheel lock before leaving the room. Evidently, the nurse had chosen not to call security, then. Good choice.

He pried his hand out of Grace's grasp and slipped his phone from his pocket. There was shit reception in this room, but the signal seemed strong enough to toss a quick text to the guys to update them about Grace. He tapped out a group text and hit send, then pushed to his feet to shut off the overhead light and close the door. She'd get far better rest without that overly bright light glaring in her face the whole night. He knew that from personal experience. God knew he'd spent more than his fair share of time in the hospital himself.

Colt stretched out on the extra bed wearily. It seemed unlikely to him that he'd even be able to sleep. Every time he shut his eyes and let himself drift, he saw her in that damned office all over again. Felt the terror of not knowing if she was alive.

He'd come far too close to losing her. He'd probably be locked up in a psych ward right now if he had. It was impossible to think of life without her. Of a world without her in it.

He stared up at the ceiling tiles and exhaled a tired breath. This was going to be a long night.

◆○◆

Colt idly scrolled through his phone rather than attempting to sleep any further. This past week had been hell. He hated hospitals—the smells, the sounds. It all made him twitchy. It was quieter on this floor than it had been in the ICU, but he still couldn't relax.

Grace, on the other hand, had been sleeping since they moved her to this room a couple of hours ago. She needed it more than him. He'd catch up on sleep when they released her. Earlier, the doctor had said that might happen in a few more days if Grace's repeat scans were satisfactory.

Grace shifted on her hospital bed, drawing his attention. She rolled on to her side with a soft whimper. Her brow furrowed, though her eyes remained closed. "Colt," she murmured.

He shoved himself to his feet and was at her bedside in one big stride. She'd been having nightmares every night since they'd been here. This looked to be yet another one of them.

He picked up her hand. "I'm right here, Princess," he whispered. "You're safe. Go back to sleep."

"I'm scared." The tremble in her voice about broke his heart. "Hold me," she pleaded.

Colt hesitated. The bed was barely big enough for her alone. While he didn't want to deny her, he didn't want to cause her pain either.

"Please? Hold me."

He couldn't bring himself to say no. It would be a tight squeeze, but he'd figure it out. She needed him.

He released her hand and carefully eased onto the bed behind her.

"I'm here," he whispered as he laid his head beside hers and gently pulled her back against his front. "I've got you. You're safe now."

He buried his face against her neck and inhaled deeply, drawing the familiar scent of her deep into his lungs.

Some of his tension eased. This was the first he'd held her since the night before Flint had turned their world upside down. She was in his arms, where she belonged. He hadn't lost her. She was alive. Breathing.

"You're safe," he repeated then brushed his lips against her neck.

She shuddered against him in reaction then laced her fingers with his where his hand rested against her stomach.

His lips curled upward for the first time since they arrived at the hospital. Mere moments later, he followed her into sleep.

Chapter 35

Awareness of her surroundings trickled in slowly as Grace awakened. The disinfectant smell of the hospital room tickled her nose, nearly making her sneeze. She clenched her eyes shut and reached for the dream she'd been having, but it'd already slipped too far away.

After talking with a police officer last night—for the second time since her admission to the hospital—she wouldn't have expected to have such a pleasant dream. But she had. She was still wary about talking to the cops, but Colt was right—they needed her testimony in order to help. *If* they helped. She still couldn't bring herself to believe they would.

Flint didn't know anyone in this particular precinct, though. It'd be more difficult for him to talk his way out of trouble this time. He'd tried to kill her. Again. And there was plenty of evidence for a change.

The female officer who kept visiting seemed sympathetic and determined to catch Flint. No matter how friendly the officer was, Grace still doubted they'd actually find him and put him behind bars.

He'd tried to slit her wrists. That was attempted homicide, wasn't it? She wasn't sure, but she was certainly glad he'd failed to cut deeply enough to do more than leave her with some gnarly scars. She supposed he wasn't as smart as he thought he was.

With a sigh, Grace opened her eyes. Today was hopefully the day she'd be getting out of this place. At least, that's what she'd been told last night after the doctors and nurses finished poking and prodding her for what felt like the millionth time.

This room was bigger than the one she'd had in the ICU, but it was still too small. It made her feel twitchy, borderline claustrophobic. She wanted to get far, far away from this town too.

What if Flint was still lurking somewhere around here? Everyone knew hospitals didn't have the world's best security, and Flint was so persuasive that she didn't doubt he could find a way in if he wanted to. It surprised her that he hadn't tried. As far as she knew anyway.

She felt like a sitting duck stuck in here, even with Colt by her side.

After nearly two weeks in this place, she was ready to get out of here. Hospitals gave her the heebie-jeebies as it was; they always had.

Her gaze drifted to the wall clock. The doctor should be here any time with the verdict.

"You're awake."

She turned to Colt and tried for a small smile. "Yeah."

He was sitting in his usual spot next to her bed, looking as rough as she felt. True to his word, he hadn't left her side for longer than it took for him to grab some food from the cafeteria. He'd insisted on helping her shower, so they hadn't even parted then. The scruffy beard covering his jaw was evidence of it.

She still thought he was the most handsome man she'd ever laid eyes on. And he was hers.

"Morning."

"Good morning, yourself." He smiled slightly. "How are you feeling today?"

She wrinkled up her nose. "Ugh, don't ask. I thought the pain was supposed to get better, not worse."

Thankfully, the swelling had gone down enough to see more clearly, even if her right eye still refused to open fully. That was progress, though every movement she made still made her want to scream.

Grace slowly eased herself upright, swallowing the whimper that tried to surface when her body protested loudly. When would the pain fade? She'd asked the doctor last night, but he hadn't been able to give her an answer.

"Gimme that," she demanded, reaching for the coffee Colt had taken a sip of.

He pulled it out of her reach. "It's not fixed up how you like. I can go get you one."

She shook her head. "Give it here. I don't care what it tastes like; I need the caffeine."

"Are you even supposed to be having caffeine yet?" He chuckled and handed it over after taking another drink.

"I don't know. Probably not, but I need it." She took a tentative sip of the fortifying brew and hummed in satisfaction. While it wasn't at all how she normally took it, it didn't matter. After all this time without it, it tasted amazing to her regardless.

"Now that you're awake, there's something I would like to talk to you about. I've been thinking about it for a while."

Something about the way he said it made her stomach quiver. "Should I be worried?"

He smiled and shook his head. "No, it's nothing bad. I've been thinking about things and realized we haven't discussed the future much. This seemed like as good a time as any to bring it up."

The future? Well, he wasn't wrong there. That was something they hadn't exactly discussed beyond whether or not each of them wanted to have kids.

"Okay, what about it?" she asked.

"I'm curious, where do you see yourself in ten years?"

The question momentarily took her aback. "Um, I don't really know." Her brow wrinkled as she thought it over. "I guess I'd like to be married and hopefully have a couple of kids by then. Maybe have a ranch, kinda like Cash's, with an enormous garden. I could become one of those women who go to flea and farmer's markets on the weekends. I think I'd like to be living the simple life with my family. I've had more than enough excitement for one lifetime."

"Do you see us still being together?"

She studied him. His expression was unreadable, but there'd been something distinctly vulnerable in his voice as he'd asked the question.

Had he changed his mind about being together? He'd been so afraid to open up and love again in fear of that person being ripped away from him, like Sarah had been. Flint had nearly taken *her* from him too.

"I'd like to think so," she said carefully then offered him a cautious smile. "What about you? Where are you in ten years?"

He didn't even hesitate. "Married to you. Raising our kids and probably some bulls." He flashed her an easy grin. "Like I told you before, I'd like to raise bucking stock once I retire for good. I'm getting too old for this riding shit. I've actually been thinking this may be my last season."

Her eyes widened. Though she heard the rest of his words, her brain homed in on one statement in particular. "Married to me?"

He nodded slowly. "Would that be okay with you?"

A truckload of butterflies hatched in her stomach. Something about the intensity of his gaze sent her nerves haywire. What had prompted this conversation all of a sudden?

"I thought you said you would never get married again. Why would you want to marry me? I'm nothing special."

Inexplicably, he laughed—the sound rich and deep.

"You most certainly are special." He leaned forward and dropped a kiss on the tip of her nose. "Trust me on that. I said I'd never be in a serious relationship again too, and here we are. Things change." His expression sobered as he took the paper coffee cup from her hand and sat it on the small table by the bed, then clasped her hand with both of his. "You've changed everything for me, Princess. Everything. As to why I'd want to marry you, well,

I'd want to because I love you and I want to be the man by your side for the rest of your life."

Her breath caught in her chest. What? Had she heard him right?

Grace's mouth fell open, but words failed to come to her. To say she was shocked would be an understatement. She could do little more than stare with wide eyes as he stood.

He truly wanted to marry her someday?

"I'll be right back," he murmured before darting out the door.

Grace's brow furrowed as she waited for him to return. What was this all about? Where had he gone? She idly picked at the blanket draped over her legs.

Colt wore a smirk when he stepped back into the room after several minutes. "I know it's not homemade, but I hope it'll still work."

He placed a delicious-looking slice of chocolate cake on her bedside table, then seated himself at the end of her bed.

Cake? He'd left to get cake? Why?

Confusion knit her brow as he took hold of her hand. His thumb swept back and forth across her knuckles.

His gaze drifted around the small room before resting on her. "This isn't how I wanted to do this," he murmured. "But I don't want to wait any longer."

"Do what?" she asked.

Her heart began racing as his throat worked as though his next words were stuck in it. He seemed more nervous than she'd ever seen him. Grace had a feeling she knew what was coming.

He swallowed hard and met her eyes. She held her breath, waiting for him to spit out whatever words he was chewing on.

"Grace Victoria Parker, would you be my wife?"

Despite the fact they'd been talking about marriage and the future, her mouth fell open. This couldn't be real. Maybe she'd fallen asleep again and this conversation was all a dream. It wouldn't be the first time she'd dreamt of him proposing. She pinched her arm and winced. Nope, not dreaming.

"What?" she squeaked. She needed to hear it again to believe this was truly happening. That he'd really asked what she thought he had.

One corner of his mouth lifted. "Will you marry me, Princess? I know the cake isn't homemade, but I tried, so I'm hoping you'll say yes anyway. Be my wife, and I'll make you a cake any damn time you want."

The cake. That's why he'd gone to get it.

A laugh threatened to bubble up. She inhaled a lungful of much-needed oxygen as her gaze roamed over his face. He appeared completely serious. Was he sweating? It seemed that he was.

"Hmm, well … I did say you should propose with cake." She laughed. "I suppose it's okay that it isn't homemade. It's still chocolate and looks delicious." She smiled and skimmed the fingers of her free hand over his cheek. "Yes. Of course I'll marry you."

He let go of her hand and jumped to his feet with a joyous whoop, then ran into the hallway and shouted, "She said yes!"

Grace laughed. It hurt, but she couldn't stop. She held her ribs and tried in vain to regain control of herself as he returned to the bed and sat back down. If his grin got any wider, it would split his face in two.

"I love your crazy ass," she chortled.

His lips quirked upward. "Just my ass? Not the rest of me?"

She acted as though she had to think about it, and he made a face at her. "I mean, you do have a really nice butt."

He barked out a laugh and shook his head. "I love you too, Princess." He leaned in to kiss her. It was excruciatingly gentle—a soft brush of his lips against hers.

She looped her arms around his neck before he could withdraw and tugged him closer. "I won't break, you know. Kiss me like you mean it."

He hesitated a moment then gave her what she wanted. Grace made a small sound of satisfaction as he pressed her back against the bed. Even as sore as she was, her body was humming with need by the time he sat back up. From the bulge in his jeans, she wasn't alone in that regard. A joyful smile curled on her lips.

He smiled back. "Since this was spur of the moment, how about we stop by a jeweler on the way to Cash's place and you can pick out a ring?"

"That sounds fine to me. We could pick out wedding bands too if you want."

Colt lifted an eyebrow in question.

"I think long engagements are kind of silly. Since we'll need to shop for them eventually, it'd save time to get them now."

"I can work with that. We should probably stop and get you a new phone too, but that can wait until after we get to the ranch." He leaned in to capture her lips again just as the doctor entered the room.

They turned to look at him together.

"Sorry to interrupt," he said with a smile. "The results of the repeat tests we did yesterday are in, and I have good news. I don't see any reason you can't go home today."

An elated grin spread on her face at that. "That sounds great! You all have been wonderful, but I can't wait to get out of here."

The doctor chuckled. "I'm sure. A nurse will be in shortly to go over the paperwork. I would recommend visiting your own doctor within the next few days, but I'm not anticipating any problems."

Colt straightened more fully and gave the doctor a steady look. "Thank you."

The man smiled in answer and left the room.

Before long, a harried-looking nurse hurried into the room with a stack of papers in her hand.

"I hear you're ready to head home." She offered them both a friendly smile, handed Grace one portion of the papers, then clipped the others to a clipboard. "Those papers have information about at-home treatments for any lingering swelling or pain you may have. There's also a paper on things you'll need to watch for that mean you need to come back in. The last one has a few recommendations for therapists with specialty in helping women in your situation. It can be healing talking to someone."

She handed Grace the clipboard and a pen. "I need your signature on these, and then you're free to go." She pointed out the areas that needed to be signed.

Grace quickly scrawled her name where the nurse had indicated, then handed them back.

The perky woman smiled broadly. "Alright. You're good to go." Her gaze swept over Grace and Colt. "Congratulations on the engagement too!" She smirked at Colt knowingly. "Guess she really will be your wife soon, huh? Don't worry, it happens a lot." She winked, then her smirk spread into a full smile. Her eyes focused on Grace. "We heard your mister here from the nurse's station." She ducked out of the room before either of them could reply.

Really will be his wife?

Grace arched an eyebrow at Colt. "What was her comment about?"

Colt turned to her, his face tinting an adorable shade of pink. He shrugged. "They weren't going to let me see you because boyfriends aren't considered immediate family members, so I stretched the truth a little." A crooked grin settled onto his face. "I've been planning on proposing for a while, so I figured it'd be the truth eventually."

He had? How long had he been thinking about it?

"While you get dressed, I'm going to step into the hall to call Cash," he continued. "He said we can stay at his place while you heal up, but I want to make sure we're still good to head there. Dusty hauled Summer over there already since Cash doesn't have a hitch." He grabbed the plastic bag containing her clothes from beneath a chair and sat it on the bed beside her before bending to brush a kiss over her forehead.

"Don't tell any of them we're getting married yet. I think I'd rather tell them together."

"Okay." He dropped another kiss on her forehead, then swiped open his phone while leaving the room.

Grace looked over at Colt once they'd been on the highway for some time. "We'll be going right by the guys, won't we? Do you want to stop in and say hi? We could get a room and then continue to Cash's in the morning."

Colt glanced sideways. "Are you sure you're feeling up to that?"

She smiled. "I'm feeling pretty good now that I'm up and moving around. Aren't you entered at this stop too? Do you want to ride?"

"I'm entered; I drew Cry Uncle. But no, I'm not wanting to ride. You're more important." He flicked on the turn signal and took the next exit. "We won't stay long. I don't want you to get worn out."

"I can think of better ways to get tired out than wandering around a rodeo," she agreed, tossing him a smirk.

He grinned and shook his head. "When you're feeling better."

Once they arrived at the rodeo grounds and parked, Colt helped her from the cab. As they walked hand in hand toward the entrance gate, he said, "I've made a decision about riding."

She arched an eyebrow. "Huh? You already said you weren't wanting to ride tonight."

He shook his head. "I don't mean tonight. I've decided that I'm going to permanently retire after Finals this year."

She slammed to a stop and stepped around in front of him. "What? Why? You love riding!"

His shoulders lifted and fell as if it were unimportant. "I haven't told you or anyone else, but I've been thinking about it since my last wreck. I do still love it, but my body can't take it much longer. My next wreck could leave me too torn up to chase any kids we have around, or worse, leave you a widow. I don't want that. You've been through too much at it is. You don't need that kind of pain, Princess." He took a deep breath and let it out slowly. "Besides, I won't be leaving the rodeo world entirely anyway. Switching from riding bulls to raising them lets me stay in. I just won't be risking my life every damn day."

She wasn't sure how she felt about what he was saying. "How about we discuss this more later on when we're back at the motel?"

He nodded and got them walking again. "Yeah, that's fine. I'm not sure I want any of the guys knowing yet anyway. They'll probably try to talk me out of it."

Without a doubt, they probably would. She'd heard they'd tried to stop him from quitting the first time, after Sarah's funeral. Neither she nor Colt said anything more as they wound their way through the crowd.

They spotted Cash outside the cowboy's locker room at the same time he looked up and saw them.

A huge smile spread over his face as he ran over and skidded to a stop in front of them.

Cash's green gaze swept over her, seeming to take in every bump, scrape, and bruise still visible. "You're looking way better than the last time I saw you. How are you feeling?"

A small smile curled on her lips. "I'm doing alright. Tired. Still a bit sore. But good. Thanks for taking care of Summer for me."

"That was all Dusty and Brody. I'm boarding her at my place for you. That horse is a pain in the ass to load. It took all three of us almost an hour and a half to get her in that damn trailer. I just about gave up on it."

"She's as big of a brat as her owner," Colt muttered, tossing a razz grin in her direction while giving her fingers a gentle squeeze.

Grace made a face. "Yeah, yeah, I hear you. Keep it up, and you'll owe me more cake. Maybe a cherry chip this time."

Colt winked. "I can keep it up. You know that."

"Ugh. Get a room, you two! Nobody needs to see or hear that lovey-dovey shit around here. You two make me sick," Cash grumbled. The playful gleam in his eyes ruined the impact of his complaint.

"You're just jealous, Cash. Admit it. Who knows, maybe you'll find your own lady one of these days, and then you can stop whining so much," Grace teased then laughed when his expression turned horrified.

"God forbid. I'm quite happy running wild and sowing my oats. Thanks."

Grace shook her head. "If you say so. I'm not sure I believe you, though." No matter what he said, that man was lonely. The more he insisted otherwise, the more certain she was of it. She hoped he found his someone too someday. He deserved it.

A sudden wave of fatigue hit her hard, making her sway on her feet slightly. She glanced at Colt. "I think I may have overestimated how much energy I have. I need to lay down."

Colt wrapped his arm around her waist, and she gratefully leaned against him.

"We'll get going, then." He looked at Cash. "Sorry to cut this short, man."

Cash's gaze bounced to Colt, surprise flooding his expression. "You're not staying to ride?"

"Nope, not tonight. I've got to take care of my lady." Colt clapped his free hand on Cash's shoulder. "We stopped in to say hi. Tell Brody, Dusty, and the other guys that we'll see them whenever we return to the circuit."

"Or you guys could meet up with us for breakfast tomorrow morning before we get back on the road," Grace suggested.

"Breakfast sounds good to me. I'll run it by the other guys and see what everyone says." Cash focused on Grace again, his expression turning somber. "I'm glad you're feeling better. You scared the living shit out of all of us. I'd really love to find that asshole and teach him a lesson."

"You and me both," Colt grumbled.

Grace ignored both comments. She pulled away from Colt's side and stepped in to give Cash a quick hug. He stiffened in surprise the second her arms slipped around him, but she didn't let it deter her.

"Thank you for everything you've done to help me," she told him softly. "I really appreciate it." She rose on her toes and pressed a kiss to his cheek before releasing him and returning to Colt's side.

"Uh, you're welcome," Cash mumbled as his face turned beet red.

She'd never seen him blush before. Maybe there really was a first time for most everything, like Colt liked to say.

Colt laughed and slipped his arm back around her waist. "Alright, we're out of here. Tell the other guys we say hi, and let us know about breakfast. Good luck tonight too. Your bull is a jerk."

"Thanks. I might need it." Cash slapped Colt on the back and winked at Grace. "Have fun with your nap. I'll text Colt when I know about breakfast." With that, he swaggered away.

Chapter 36

Colt yawned and seated himself on the bed to pull his boots off. It was a good thing Grace had insisted on them stopping for dinner before returning to the motel; he was having trouble staying awake despite it being early yet. Now that he was sitting, he sure didn't feel like going back out any time soon.

"I think I'm about ready for bed. These past two weeks have been hell. Worse for you than me, but man I'm exhausted."

Even calling the past couple of weeks hell was an understatement. After Flint's latest stunt, Colt's stress level was through the roof. It bugged him not knowing where the asshole was. It was as though he'd vanished, like a fucking ghost or something. Had he gone back to Kansas? Or was he lurking somewhere nearby, watching everyone run around looking for him? Did Flint know Grace had survived his attempt to slit her wrists? If so, was he planning to try again?

Colt didn't have a fucking clue about any of it. The only thing he knew for certain was that there wasn't a snowball's chance in the fiery pits of hell that he'd be leaving Grace's side until Flint was behind bars or dead. Either one was fine by him.

"I'm definitely good with going to bed early."

Grace looked asleep on her feet. Maybe stopping at the rodeo hadn't been the best idea. She needed to rest.

"How about I run you a bath first so you can unwind a bit?"

A tired smile crept onto her face. "That sounds fantastic, actually. You spoil me."

"Nah. I'd be a pretty lousy fiancé if I didn't take care of you, wouldn't I? Besides, I love doing things for you." He flashed her a grin. "Be right back."

He hustled into the bathroom to fill the tub. It was too bad he didn't have any of the Epsom salt he'd added when she'd needed to soak at Cash's. That had really seemed to help last time.

Grace was standing in front of the room's large window, staring out into the rapidly darkening parking lot, when he stepped from the bathroom.

"Your bath is ready," he said as he approached.

She turned to face him with a tight smile. A man didn't need to be a mind reader to know what she'd been thinking about. Her worry was written all over her face.

"They'll catch him, Princess."

She didn't look convinced. Shit, he wasn't convinced they would either, but she needed the hope. Rather than saying anything more, knowing words couldn't soothe her concerns, he gripped her by the waist and bent to give her a lingering kiss.

"You'd better get before your water gets cold. Go relax," he said when he finally lifted his lips from hers.

She pulled him down for another kiss then padded to the bathroom while stripping her clothes off.

Colt waited until he heard the tell-tale sound of sloshing water to peel his own clothes off and stretch out on the bed. He really wanted a shower himself, but that could wait for morning. Grace's comfort was more important at the moment. The hot bath would do more to ease her aches and help her heal than laying down would on its own. He knew that from experience.

He yanked the blanket up to his chest and reached for the remote. After a few minutes of idly flipping channels, he settled on an old black-and-white movie. There was nothing quite like a classic to pass the time. He folded his arms behind his head and settled in to watch it. Before long, his eyes drifted closed.

"Did you fall asleep?"

"Hmm?" He cracked open his eyes and rolled his head to look over at Grace.

She stood next to the bed, fully nude and still slightly damp.

A drowsy smile crept onto his face. "I guess I must have dozed off."

"Just couldn't wait for me, huh?" She slid into bed beside him and burrowed beneath the covers.

"I guess not." He chuckled. "I tried." He clicked off the TV and sat the remote on the nightstand before rolling to face her. "How was your bath?"

"Good. I'm still pretty sore, but I feel a little better. Thank you."

"Anytime, Princess. I'm glad it helped some." He held out his arm in offering. "Come here and let me hold you."

Rather than snuggling against him, like he'd thought she would, Grace rolled away from him then wiggled backwards to fit her back against his front. He draped his arm over her hip and flattened his palm over her lower belly. A faint smile tugged at his lips.

"I was curious what your thoughts are about a ranch for us. What do you think you want as far as looks, number of rooms, and all that?" He pressed a kiss to her shoulder then nuzzled her neck. "I was thinking a ranch-style would be best. I don't know how well my hip would hold up to stairs. It's an old injury, but it acts up from time to time."

He hesitated a moment. "I'd love to have a place somewhere near my parents, but we don't have to if you've got somewhere else in mind."

Sarah had balked when he'd suggested it to her. She'd wanted to live closer to her own family instead. It'd been a surprise to him, considering she'd gotten along better with his mother than her own, but he'd gone along with her wishes in the end. Anything to make her happy.

Grace was quiet for a long moment. Long enough that he almost wondered if she'd fallen asleep.

"I like your parents," she finally said. "I think I would like to live somewhere near them so they can see their grandbabies frequently once we have kids."

Their kids. Fuck, he could imagine them. A little girl with long black hair and bright blue eyes, on a Shetland pony, laughing hysterically as she bounced along the trail. A boy, fishing pole in hand, sitting beside him on the bank of the creek Colt fished at for all his youth.

Grace's hand moved to her lower belly and covered his. He wondered if she was thinking about their potential children, like he was.

"When I was a kid, I would have loved to have grandparents close enough to see them more than once a year," she continued. "Montana is beautiful too. I could be happy there."

"Alright, so Montana works then, but what about the rest?

She went silent again then rolled over to face him. He moved onto his back and gathered her against his chest. After brushing her lips over the skin above his heart, she began telling him about the ranch she'd dreamed of having since she was a young kid.

They discussed the specifics of their future home until she finally fell asleep. Colt followed soon after, lulled to sleep by the contentment and love warming his heart.

The ringing of his phone woke Colt. He eased out from under Grace, trying his best not to wake her while he fumbled for the noisy device. By some miracle, she didn't even twitch. Maybe she'd been more exhausted than she'd let on.

He cursed under his breath when he realized he'd left his phone in his jeans' pocket. With a soft groan, he sat up and swung his feet out of bed. He yanked his phone from its place and glanced down at the screen.

Geez, it was only three in the morning. Who the hell had the audacity to call at this hour?

It wasn't a number he recognized. For a moment, he was tempted to silence the ringer and get some more sleep. Instead, he answered the call and ducked into the bathroom to keep from disturbing Grace. This had better be important and not some telemarketer or something of that sort.

"Hello?" he mumbled, his voice rough from sleep.

"Hey, man, it's Cameron Steele. Cash's friend. Don't know if you remember me from when we were looking for your girl."

Yeah, Colt remembered him. Short, stocky cowboy. Cocky attitude, but likable. Pretty damn good with the bulls but not so much with the bareback broncs he'd started riding this year. While they'd never talked before the situation with Grace, Colt had seen him a time or three in the locker room, and Cash had mentioned him from time to time. He seemed like a good guy.

"Cash gave me your number," Cameron continued. "Sorry to have waked you, but I have a police scanner app on my phone. Couldn't sleep worth a damn, so I was listening to it. I'm pretty sure they found Flint next town over. Only about ten minutes from here."

Colt tensed, wide awake in an instant. "What?"

"I don't know it for fact, but the description of the guy the dispatcher mentioned sounded an awful lot like how you described Flint. Guess the guy is parked behind a store and got into an altercation with an employee when they told him he couldn't sleep there. Pointed a gun at the employee and all, so they called the cops."

Yeah, that sounded like something Flint would do.

Colt heard the vague sound of an engine starting, then Cameron growled, "I'm heading over there to check it out. After what that fucker did to your girl, I'd love to get my hands on him, but I'll settle for watching the cops haul him away."

Yeah, him too. Colt peeked out of the bathroom at Grace. Should he wake her up or let her sleep? He needed to go. He needed the closure watching them arrest that bastard would provide. Grace probably did too, but she needed her rest even more. It was better to let her sleep. If the police really had found Flint, it would be safe enough to leave her for a little bit. He'd call Cash, just in case. Have him come and stay with her while he was gone.

"Pick me up, man. I'm coming too," Colt said into the phone. "Blue Moon Inn and Suites. Give me five minutes, and I'll meet you outside the lobby."

"It'll take me about that long to get to you. See you in a few, dude."

Colt hung up then immediately dialed Cash.

Moments later, he hung up the phone. There'd never been a question in Colt's mind as to whether his best friend would be willing to sit with Grace, but it was a relief to know Cash would be here. Colt sat the phone on the nightstand and quickly tossed back on yesterday's clothes before hunting through the nightstand for the pad of paper and pen most hotels put there for guests.

He scrawled out a note to Grace, letting her know he'd needed to step out but that he left the truck in case she wanted to join him, that he'd tell her what was going on when he got back otherwise, and that Cash would be sitting outside the door if she needed anything or didn't feel safe. Colt sat it on his pillow where she'd be sure to spot it and bent to brush a kiss over her forehead.

Then he placed the keys to the truck on the nightstand, tucked his phone into his pocket, and silently made his way outside to meet Cameron.

◆

Colt climbed from Cameron's truck and crossed around front. The parking lot they'd decided to park in was on a slight hill. From this height, it gave a good view of the drama unfolding in the back lot of the grocery store below. It'd been impossible to get any closer even if they'd wanted to, considering the police had blocked the entrances of the grocery store's lot. It was probably for the best anyway. He and Cameron sure didn't need to be getting in the way. Not with Flint having a gun.

Colt pulled out his cellphone, opened the camera, then adjusted the zoom feature to give him a closer image. He felt Cameron's eyes on him and glanced over. "Easier than using binoculars, which we don't have."

"Actually, I do have a pair. I use 'em when I go hunting when I'm at home." Cameron dug around in the backseat of his truck then held up a pair. He grinned. "Glad I remembered to put them back now. I'd probably miss half the show without 'em."

Two police cars sat a good distance from a beat-up pickup truck, their doors hanging wide open and their lightbars still flashing. Four officers stood behind the doors with guns drawn and aimed at the bed of the truck.

At first Colt thought the truck was empty, but then he spotted a flicker of movement seconds before a man's head and shoulders became visible over the edge of the bed.

Ah. There the bastard was. To Colt's eyes, Flint looked more pissed off than scared.

As four more police cars pulled into the parking lot and positioned themselves in a half-circle around the truck, it appeared like Flint yelled something to the officers already out of their cars. From this distance, it was impossible to hear what was said, but from Flint's stormy expression it couldn't have been good.

Shit, what Colt wouldn't give to know what had been said. For the first time in his life, he wished he could read lips.

The atmosphere was heavy, charged, like the air before a thunderstorm. Even from the neighboring parking lot on the hill, the sense of it enveloped Colt, accelerating his pulse.

A short, heavyset officer shouted something back as Flint got to his feet and stood up in the truck's bed. No doubt, he'd probably told Flint to put his hands up. Wasn't that what they usually did first in situations like this? Colt was pretty sure they did.

"Is he laughing?" Cameron asked, his voice incredulous. "What the fuck, man? There's twelve officers with their guns pointed at him, and he's fucking laughing?"

Colt nodded. "Yep, looks like it." Flint's shoulders were definitely shaking. Somehow, it didn't surprise Colt any. The man was deranged.

"Jesus," Cameron muttered. He rubbed his hand over his mouth, his blue eyes wide, then lifted the binoculars back up.

Flint yelled something back to the police and shifted on his feet.

Not one but two different officers adjusted their stances in response. Shit, they looked like they might fire on him. Would they do that? He hadn't pulled a gun. Yet.

The tension in the air skyrocketed.

Colt tensed. He wasn't sure how he'd expected this to go down, but this wasn't it. This was intense. His heartbeat thudded in his ears as three different officers shouted orders at Flint.

Flint's expression shifted, and then he smiled. He fucking *smiled*. It was the creepiest thing Colt had ever seen in his life. A chill skittered down his spine, and the skin on the back of his neck prickled.

Time seemed to slow to a crawl as Flint reached behind his back and withdrew a handgun. He leveled it at the officer closest while saying something.

Colt nearly dropped his phone as the night abruptly erupted into chaos. The thunderous sound of gunfire ricocheted off the buildings, echoing from every direction all at once.

Oh, shit. They were shooting him.

Flint's body jerked and shuddered as a volley of bullets found their mark.

Colt's stomach lurched. He yanked his gaze away and emptied the meager contents of his stomach on the grass beside him. As much as he hated the man, he hadn't expected to witness Flint's death. He spat into the grass, then tugged up the end of his shirt and wiped his mouth.

The reverberant gunfire stopped as rapidly as it had started, leaving Colt's ears ringing.

He didn't dare look back down at the parking lot. His stomach was threatening to upend itself again as it was. Instead, he met eyes with Cameron.

"Fuck." He couldn't seem to find any other words.

Cameron chuckled dryly. "You can say that again." He glanced at the grocery store's parking lot. "Kinda wish I hadn't seen that shit. Never gonna get that out of my head now." One corner of his mouth lifted. "Couldn't have happened to a better asshole, though. Least your girl will be able to sleep well at night, knowing he won't be sneaking up on her ever again. You too."

That was true enough. "Not sure I'll be getting much sleep for a while after seeing that." Colt waved a hand toward where Flint lay then sucked in a ragged breath.

How should he tell Grace? Before breakfast? After? Odds were good that he'd earn her ire if he sat on the information too long. Maybe it'd be best if he told her as soon as she was awake enough to comprehend what he was saying.

The wail of sirens split the night.

"We should probably get out of here," he told Cameron. His mind was swirling. He wanted to be back in the hotel room with Grace. Now.

Cameron nodded and gestured at his truck. "Hop in. Think I'm done looking at the mess down there anyway."

Colt still hadn't decided how to best break the news to Grace when Cameron dropped him off at the hotel. He continued mulling it over as he walked back to their room.

"So, what's going on?" Cash asked as he stood from where he'd been sitting on the ground outside the room's door.

Colt shook his head. "I'll tell you later." He scrubbed a hand over his face. "Pretty sure I'm still processing."

"Alright," Cash answered. "If you don't need anything else, I need my bed. It's too early, dude."

"Go get some sleep." Colt slapped his best friend on the shoulder. "Thanks. For coming to guard the door."

"Of course." Cash flashed a grin. "Talk to you later, then. Goodnight." With that, he wandered toward his truck.

Colt let himself into the hotel room.

There was no way in hell he was going to get any more rest. Not after what he'd seen. Today was going to be a long day; he could tell that already. Colt sunk into the armchair in the corner of the room.

His gaze rested lightly on Grace. Her nightmare was over. Flint would never hurt her again.

The first rays of sun were just beginning to stream into the room through the space between the curtains when Colt finally hauled himself up from the chair. He took a deep breath and let it out slowly, then stripped off his clothes and padded to the bathroom for a quick shower.

Grace was beginning to stir when he emerged. He yanked on a clean pair of jeans and fastened his belt before crossing the room to seat himself on the bed beside her.

"Morning, Princess," he murmured, leaning down to kiss her gently. He felt her smile against his lips. Her eyes blinked open as he straightened. "How are you feeling this morning?"

Her small smile faded. "I wish everyone would stop asking that." She pushed herself upright with a wince. "I'm pretty sure every muscle in my body stiffened up overnight."

"How about I run you another bath before we get going?"

"Mmm, yeah, that sounds great. The ride to Cash's will seem a lot longer if I keep feeling this rough." She scrubbed her hands over her face then looked at him. Her eyes narrowed. "What's wrong? You look tense."

Shit. How was she always so perceptive? Was it a skill all abused women acquired or something? He'd been hoping to give her time to wake up before giving her the news. Apparently, that wasn't going to be happening. "I got a phone call this morning."

Grace straightened and grabbed his hand. "About Flint? Did they find him?"

Colt hesitated. "They did," he began slowly. "They found him sleeping in the bed of his truck in the parking lot of a store in the next town over from here." He squeezed her fingers gently. "He pulled a gun on them, and they were forced to fire on him to protect themselves."

She inhaled sharply and locked her eyes on him. "Is he dead?"

"Yes," he said quietly. "I saw it happen with my own eyes. You don't know him, but one of Cash's buddies has a police scanner. He heard what was happening on it and called me. We went to watch them arrest him." He shook his head then met her eyes. "I'd have woke you, but you need your rest. Besides, you didn't need to see that." He swallowed hard. "I'm glad you didn't see that. You've been traumatized by him enough."

Colt tried for a faint smile and gave her fingers another gentle squeeze. "It's over, baby. He won't ever hurt you again."

She blinked and looked away, seeming to be struggling to figure out how to react.

Unsure of how to help her process her feelings, he gently drew her into his arms. She sank against him and buried her face against his still-bare chest. She released a shuddering breath over his skin.

Words were failing him. What could he say? He rubbed his hand over her back in soothing circles while the silence stretched.

Finally, he asked, "Are you okay, Princess? Do you want to talk about it? Tell me how I can help you."

Grace pulled away enough to look up at him. "I don't even know how I'm feeling right now. Relieved, maybe? A little sad? I ... don't know. Does it make me a horrible person to be happy he's gone for good?"

"No. You couldn't be a horrible person if you tried. You're not built that way. It's not who you are. I'd be a bit worried if you didn't feel at least a little relieved. Hell, I'm relieved that me and Cash won't have to hunt him down and kill him ourselves." He touched his lips to hers and gave her a faint smile. "I'm not sure orange is really my color."

Her lips twitched. "Probably not. I've heard conjugal visits can be difficult to arrange too." She trailed her fingertips over his jaw then cupped his cheek. "Thank you."

"For what?" he asked before turning his head to press a kiss to her palm.

Grace shrugged. "For loving me, for rescuing me from him, for being my rock. For everything."

"There's nothing you need to thank me for. I need to thank you, though."

She tilted her head. "Why would you need to thank me? I haven't done anything."

He laughed. "Princess, you've done more than you know. Ask Cash. After Sarah died, I was on the fast track to getting myself killed. If the drinking and fighting didn't take me out, my bad habit of climbing on the backs of homicidal bulls most of the other guys won't even try would have." He looked away. "It's not that I wanted to die; I just no longer cared what happened to me. My life was already over, as far as I saw it."

His gaze moved back to hers. "When I met you, everything changed. You turned my life upside down in all the best ways. I'm pretty sure you saved me, Grace. You made me look forward to each day again, especially when I knew you'd be at the stop I was at. Even if we didn't talk, it was enough to see you. You brought laughter and light back to my life."

"We saved each other," she said. "So much has changed since you tried to turn me into a pancake at that auction."

"You're never going to let that go, are you?"

She smiled. "No. What fun would it be if I did?"

Colt shook his head. "I love you," he whispered, leaning in to kiss her tenderly.

"I love you too." She pulled him in for another kiss then slowly climbed off the bed. "We should probably get going if we're meeting the guys for breakfast." She glanced back at him. "That is still the plan, right?"

"As far as I know, it is." He hadn't thought to ask when he'd talked to Cash earlier. It hadn't exactly been a priority. "I'll call Cash while you're in the bath."

"Alright." She selected a clean outfit from her suitcase, then paused in the doorway of the bathroom and looked back at him with a smile. "I can't wait to be your wife."

Chapter 37

"We're meeting some people," Colt told the hostess at the restaurant they were meeting his friends at. "Should be seven or eight rowdy cowboys, I think."

Grace glanced sideways at Colt in surprise. Seven or eight? She hadn't expected anyone other than Dusty, Cash, and Brody at breakfast. Who else was joining them?

The woman smiled and gestured toward a room separated from the main dining room. Raucous male laughter drifted through the arched doorway. "They're right through there."

Colt thanked the woman then grabbed Grace's hand and led her toward the room.

"About time you guys showed up," Brody said as they approached the table.

"We hurried as fast as traffic would let us. For a small town, this place has way too many cars on the road," Colt answered while pulling a chair out for her.

Grace sat, and he plopped into the chair at her side.

"Yeah, tell me about it," Dusty groused. "I thought I would never get here, and my motel was closer than the one Cash said you guys stayed at."

Her gaze traveled around the table. She only recognized Cash, Brody, and Dusty. The other four men were a complete mystery.

A couple of them looked vaguely familiar, but for the life of her, she couldn't come up with names to go with their faces. Maybe she'd interviewed them at some point, but she couldn't be sure. She tossed a questioning look at Colt in hopes of an introduction.

He caught her look and grinned. "You know these idiots, Princess," he said while gesturing toward Cash, Dusty, and Brody. "But these other guys are Garrett Harding, Stetson Dalton, Tate McKinney, and Cameron Steele. They helped with looking for you too." He pointed out each cowboy as he said their names. "Guys, this is my fiancée, Grace Parker."

They murmured greetings, and Grace offered them a smile as Cash's eyes shot wide. Dusty and Brody wore similar expressions on their faces. It made her smile widen.

She and Colt had decided this morning, before leaving the hotel, that they'd announce their engagement today at breakfast. He'd wanted to be the one to break the news, and she'd been happy to let him. They'd been his friends first, after all.

"Fiancée? When the hell did that happen?" Cash shook his head. "Where the hell did Mister 'I'm never getting married again because love sucks' go?" He looked over at Grace and quirked an eyebrow while hooking his thumb at Colt. "You sure you really want to marry that guy?"

She laughed. "It's recent, and yes. He asked me at the hospital before they discharged me."

"He did what?" Cash shot Colt a disgusted look. "The hospital? That's not even romantic, man. What the fuck is wrong with you? Proposing in the hospital. You're lucky she said yes."

Colt grinned, not the least perturbed by his best friend's outrage. "What would you know about romance? When was the last time you even had a girlfriend?"

Cash screwed up his face. "I know more than you, apparently," he said dryly. "You know I've never done that relationship shit, but if I did, I sure as hell wouldn't propose in a fucking hospital, dumbass. Did you at least get her a ring? I don't see one on her hand, so probably not," he scoffed.

"No ring yet." Colt chuckled. "We're planning on stopping at a jeweler somewhere on the way to your place. Is that acceptable, Mr. Romance?"

"No, but at least you're getting her a ring. Proposing in a hospital. Shit."

The other men at the table burst into boisterous laughter, and a couple razzed Cash for his ranting. He scowled back at them.

Grace shook her head and decided to change the subject. She had no idea Cash was so passionate about romance. Colt's proposal had been perfect in her eyes. He'd even remembered the cake. It seemed like every time she was around Cash, she learned something new about him. He wasn't the wild playboy everyone seemed to think he was. Or at least, that's not all there was to him. She would bet on it.

"Thank you guys for everything you did to help find me," she said softly, addressing all of the men gathered around the table. Her words didn't feel like enough. If it weren't for everyone here, would she have been found before it was too late? She sure didn't trust that the police would have found her in time if it'd been left to them alone.

"Thanks aren't necessary. We were happy to help," Garrett said.

"What he said. I'm glad you're okay," Dusty added. "Have you guys heard anything? Did the cops find your ex yet?"

Colt raised an eyebrow and glanced at Cameron. "You didn't tell them?"

"Nah, man," Cameron answered. "That's your news to share."

Grace glanced between the two men. So Cameron was Cash's friend, then, the one who'd had the police scanner. She offered him a shaky smile then flicked her gaze over to Colt. Beneath the table, he reached for her hand. She tangled their fingers together and tossed him a grateful smile. She wasn't sure she was ready to talk about it just yet.

Colt cleared his throat. "Cameron called me last night, saying he heard something on his police scanner about Flint being spotted. He and I went to watch them arrest him, but..." She sucked in a breath, and Colt squeezed her fingers gently. "Well, let's just say it went south. Grace won't have to worry about Flint ever again. He's dead."

Cash grunted. "Good," he growled.

"Are you okay?" Brody asked her quietly.

Grace nodded. "I think so. My feelings about it all are complicated."

He gave her a sympathetic look, his dark green eyes full of compassion.

"Understandable," Garrett murmured.

She could see the curiosity lurking in the eyes of most of the men. They wanted to know what happened. She knew they did, but she needed a subject change. She still wasn't sure how she felt about Flint being dead. He'd made her life hell and tried to kill her, but there had been good times between them too. It was confusing.

"Colt can tell you more about what happened later." She reached for her glass of water and took a small sip.

The waiter arrived to take their orders, preventing anyone else from commenting. As soon as the waiter walked away, she let her gaze drift between the four men she hadn't met before tonight. "So, are you all bull riders too?"

The others at the table eagerly jumped on the subject, and the conversation shifted to rodeo for the remainder of the meal.

<hr>

Grace held her hand out in front of her and admired the ring on her finger. It was perfect. While it wasn't a conventional engagement ring, she loved it. The primary stone was a gorgeous princess cut blue sapphire set in an elegant white gold band. It was surrounded by tiny white sapphires sparkling with a fire that dwarfed that of any diamond. At least, in her opinion. She'd never really been a fan of diamonds.

"Is that the one you want?" Colt asked.

She looked over at him with a massive smile and nodded enthusiastically before turning her gaze back on the ring. "Yes, I want this one."

Colt turned to address the sales clerk hovering nearby. "You heard the lady. We'll take the one on her finger and the two bands we picked out earlier."

She still couldn't believe they were really getting married. It seemed so surreal. She was equal parts excited and scared. Part of her still figured he'd change his mind before they actually made it to the altar; he'd been so insistent that he'd never get married again. Until they'd made it to the altar and they'd said their vows, she wasn't sure she'd be able to believe he was completely serious.

"Have you thought about when you might want to get married?" he asked while they waited for their purchases to be rung up. He slipped his arm around her waist and pulled her snugly against his side.

She looked up at him. "Not really. Maybe once we have our own place? It might be nice to have a backyard wedding or something. I know I don't want the whole white gown and church thing. That's too much fuss. I've never been big on the idea of it."

"Small wedding or large?" He grabbed the bag the clerk handed him and steered Grace toward the door.

She waited until they reached the truck to answer. "Small, I think. I don't have any family to invite, and I don't really have any friends beyond yours. We could invite your family and a few of the guys? Their families too."

"Brave inviting a bunch of bull riders." He opened her door.

"Well, I'm marrying one too, so..."

Colt laughed. "True."

"Oh, Brody's friend, Andrea, and her husband as well. She was good company when you and I were apart."

"Sounds good." Colt grinned and helped her into the truck. As he started the engine and pulled the big vehicle away from the curb a moment later, he glanced over at her. "So, talk to me about your dream wedding and reception. I can't guarantee I'll be able to make it all happen, but I'll do my best."

Her dream wedding. She took a deep breath. "Well, when I was a little girl, I'd always wanted to get married outside at sunset. Maybe in a pasture or something." She closed her eyes, seeing it in her mind. "Hay bales on either side of the aisle with twinkling fairy lights wrapped around them. LED, of course; we don't need any fires. At the end of the aisle, there'd be a wooden arch with some sort of blue and white flowers growing on it, with more fairy lights there too." She opened her eyes and smiled at him. "I always envisioned getting married under an arch like that. If the weather cooperates, it might be lovely to have a bonfire at the reception."

"Okay, so a country wedding, then," he murmured, looking thoughtful. "I can work with that. What else?"

Grace smiled brightly and told him the rest of her hopes and wishes for their wedding and the reception after. Together, they spent the remainder of the drive to Cash's place discussing and planning.

Chapter 38

Seven Months Later...

Grace stood in front of the full-length mirror, studying her reflection. She and Colt designated this guest room as her bridal chamber days ago. It looked the part right now.

The simple gown Amy, Garrett's wife, had helped her pick out was almost the exact shade of Grace's eyes—a pretty pale blue—and flattered her figure. It was exactly what she'd hoped for. Simple, but sophisticated. She loved it. Her hair, however, seemed to be missing something. She couldn't seem to figure out what. Amy had helped her put it into an elegant up-do before disappearing to check in with the baker about the cake. Her hair admittedly did look nice, but something wasn't right.

She was interrupted from her contemplation by a knock on the door. She glanced back over her shoulder to see Colt's mom, Mary, standing in the doorway with a huge smile on her face. The older woman's bright blue eyes twinkled as they swept over Grace from head to toe.

"Well, look at you! That dress is absolutely perfect for you. Amy has a good eye." Mary moved into the room and circled Grace, looking her over more thoroughly. "You look beautiful!"

A hint of warmth crept on to Grace's cheeks. "Thanks, Mary."

"Mary." The older woman tsked and waved a hand dismissively. "No need for such formality. You can call me Mom if you want, dear. You're going to be my daughter-in-law in less than ten minutes, after all."

Tears sprang to Grace's eyes, and she swallowed thickly. "Okay." A shaky smile lifted her lips upward. "Thanks, Mom."

"That's more like it." Mary dug into the oversized tote bag she'd brought in with her. "I brought you something to finish your outfit."

She withdrew what appeared to be a small decorative hair comb. "This can be your something borrowed and old. It could be your something blue too, I suppose, but your pretty dress has that covered." She beamed as she held the comb out for Grace to inspect. "This comb has been worn by nearly every bride in our family six generations back. Now, it's your turn."

It was gorgeous, clearly antique from the tasteful patina covering it. The open work swirls of the silver hair comb were encrusted with a combination of blue and white sapphires that glittered even in the dim lighting of the bedroom.

"It's beautiful," Grace said. "Thank you. You've been so wonderful to me." She waved a hand at her face as she fought back tears again.

"Ah, no crying. You'll smudge your makeup." Mary grabbed a tissue from the nightstand and carefully dabbed at the few tears that'd escaped to roll down Grace's cheeks.

"Would you mind helping me put it in my hair?"

The older woman's face lit up. "Well, of course, dear! I'd be happy to."

She took the comb back from Grace and, after taking a moment to contemplate, slid it into Grace's hair. Mary stood back then clasped her hands over her heart. "Oh! It looks even better than I thought it would!"

Grace turned to gaze back into the mirror and gasped. This was it, the thing that her hairstyle had been missing. A smile spread on her face as she reached up to touch the comb carefully. "It really does."

Had Sarah been given this comb too? She couldn't help but wonder.

As though she could read Grace's mind, Mary said, "I couldn't find it when Colt married the first time. I searched the whole house, high and low, but it never showed itself. It popped right out and said, 'Here I am,' this time, however. Maybe it was meant to be yours. I'm happy my son has you now. After Sarah's death—God rest her sweet soul—I worried about him. He was so lost without her. And now... Well, now, he doesn't seem to stop smiling. Thank you for that."

"If you keep saying stuff like that, I really will cry," Grace warned with a shaky laugh.

Mary patted her arm and smiled. "That wasn't my intention, dear." She grimaced and touched a hand to her back. "If you don't need any help getting ready, I think I'm going to go take a seat."

Grace's eyes slipped to the wall clock above the dresser, and her stomach flipped. She glanced at Mary. "I think I'll be alright. I'm pretty much done; I'm just waiting for it to be time now." She gave Mary a quick hug. "Thank you again."

"Of course," Mary said with a joyful smile. She touched Grace's arm once more then left the room.

Several minutes later, another knock on the door interrupted her contemplation. Grace looked up as Cash stepped inside.

He blew out a whistle as he looked her over.

In his hand, he held a small bag. "Before we go, I got you something." He passed her the gift bag.

She gave him a curious look as she took it. He looked slightly uncomfortable as she withdrew the bag's contents—a small black velvet box and an actual sixpence.

Her gaze shot to him as her eyes widened.

"Where in the world did you find a 1952 sixpence? Aren't those the rarest ones?"

She was pretty sure she remembered reading that somewhere when she was looking up wedding traditions while deciding which ones she wanted to incorporate and which she didn't.

Cash shrugged. "I have no idea, but I know somebody who knows somebody who knew somebody who had one. Took forever, but now you've got one for your shoe." His lips curled upward. "Had to make sure you guys had a lucky marriage. You both deserve it."

He nodded toward the box. "And that's your something new. I hope you don't mind me getting it for you." He rubbed his hand over the back of his neck.

Grace opened the box and gasped. Inside lay a white gold necklace with a dainty teardrop-cut blue sapphire pendant with a small diamond above the primary stone. It matched her engagement ring and the antique hair comb nicely.

"It's gorgeous!" She waved her hand at her face, once again trying hard not to cry. "You didn't have to get me anything, but thank you!"

Cash shuffled awkwardly on his feet. "I know I didn't, but Colt's pretty much my brother. That makes you kinda like my sister-in-law. I wanted to get you something to, I don't know, welcome you to the family or something. I guess."

He held out his hand. "I can help you put it on, then we should probably get that sixpence in your shoe and you outside. I think it's about time."

"Thanks." She smiled and gave the box to him, then turned around so he could fasten the chain around her neck. Once he was finished, she crouched down and tucked the sixpence into her shoe. As she straightened again, she took a deep breath and glanced at the clock.

Cash was right. It was time to go.

"Last chance to save yourself. You sure you really want to marry that idiot?" Cash asked as he offered her his arm. "You look beautiful, by the way."

"Thanks, and yes."

She placed her hand in the crook of his elbow while a nervous smile played on her face. It had surprised her when he'd offered to walk her down the aisle despite also being Colt's best man. Colt's father had tried to get him to let him have the honor, but Cash had been insistent on being the one to do it. She found it sweet, especially considering his alleged disdain for relationships.

She glanced up at him. "Someday, Cash, you're going to meet someone and she'll change your views on relationships."

No matter how vehemently he claimed to be happy single, she could tell he wasn't. Not truly. There were days when she caught him watching her and Colt with an almost wistful expression. He seemed … sad. Lonely, even. Colt didn't agree with her assessment, but maybe he was too close to see it.

Cash made a face. "Never going to happen."

"Haven't you ever heard that you should never say never? You're tempting fate." She laughed as she realized how absurd that statement was. "I guess you do that every time you climb on a bull, don't you?"

"Yep. Anyway, bulls are less complicated than women. At least when I climb on a bull, I know what to expect."

The first notes of the song she and Colt had settled on for her to walk down the aisle to began, and Grace sucked in a breath, suddenly struck by nerves. Her pulse kicked higher in anticipation, and her stomach quivered. She almost felt like she was going to be sick.

Cash bent toward her ear and whispered, "Relax."

She tossed him a grateful smile as he started them forward, slowly leading her toward Colt and her future.

Chapter 39

"THAT DRESS LOOKS GREAT on you, Mrs. Boone," Colt whispered as he and Grace swayed in time to the music. "But I bet it'll look even better on the floor at the hotel."

"I'm ready to go whenever you are, Mr. Boone," Grace whispered back. "We've done the toasts, cut the cake, and now we're having our first dance. What's left?"

"My dad wants a dance. He said since your dad can't be here to dance with you, he'll stand in for him."

"Oh." She waved her hand at her face and blinked rapidly. "That's so sweet."

Colt nodded and leaned his cheek against the top of her head, listening to the music. He'd given her free rein to pick the song for their first dance, and she'd surprised him. While he'd expected her to choose some pop love song, she'd picked Kane Brown's "What's Mine Is Yours" instead. She claimed it was their song. He couldn't deny that it was as perfect now as the first time he'd played it for her. Maybe more so if he was being honest.

The dress she and Amy had picked out really was stunning on her. However, he was pretty sure she could have married him in filthy barn clothes and he'd still find her as spellbindingly beautiful as he did right now.

He ducked his head toward her ear, his breath teasing the tendrils of silky black hair that framed her face. "I love you."

"I love you too." She moved in closer, molding her body to his, and rested her head against his chest.

He savored the feel of her in his arms. Simply saying he loved her didn't seem quite strong enough of a sentiment, but since he was far from a poet, it was the closest he could come to describing the emotions she evoked in him. She'd healed his heart. Soothed his soul. Because of her, he felt whole again. Happy. Alive.

Her hand glided down his back to his jean-clad ass and gently squeezed as the dance ended. "I hope you slept well last night; sleep isn't on the itinerary for tonight," she whispered, before releasing him and stepping back.

Colt chuckled huskily as his body stirred at the promise in her voice. "Is that so?"

She smirked and nodded. Oh yeah, he loved this woman.

"Good thing our flight isn't until noon, then."

"We can sleep on the plane," she said, a laugh in her voice. "It's a long flight to Ireland from Montana."

Colt's father swooped in and swept her away for his own dance before Colt could respond.

Whatever his dad said to Grace as he led her away drew a laugh from her. The air filled with the melodious sound of it, and Colt's lips curved upward. The only sound he loved more was hearing her scream his name as an orgasm crashed over her. Hopefully, he'd be hearing that multiple times later tonight.

Colt sauntered over to the bar the catering company had set up earlier and ordered a drink. His gaze rested lightly on Grace while he sipped at his whiskey. When was it appropriate for him to grab her and escape to somewhere more private? With their five-bedroom home swarming with guests, he'd rented them the honeymoon suite at the ritziest hotel he could find in the neighboring city. The limo ride wouldn't be exactly short, but it would be plenty comfortable. At least, he hoped for as much as the company charged.

From the corner of his eye, he saw Cash approach. Colt turned to look over at his best friend. The knowing look on Cash's face was curious. "Hey."

"Hey yourself," Cash answered, leaning closer to Colt. "I'll make excuses for you two if you want to make a break for it after this dance," he whispered.

"Shit. How'd you know I was wondering how we could escape?" Colt asked with a laugh.

Cash rolled his eyes. "We've known each other how long now, dude? I know you."

Colt tossed back the rest of his whiskey then straightened. "Well, I appreciate it." He clapped a hand on Cash's shoulder as the music ended. "Thanks, man."

"Don't mention it." Cash chuckled and shoved Colt toward Grace. "Go get your girl and get the hell out of here."

Epilogue

This was what he lived for. Well, what he lived for now.

Colt stood at the top of the chutes, looking out over the practice arena with one arm around the petite woman standing beside him. On her hip, she held their two-year-old son. Together, they watched as Cash ushered a young bull into one of the arena's two chutes.

Cash was here today to help with dummy bucking the first of Colt's homebred prospects. The best of the bunch would begin their careers next season. Among the most promising was a two-and-a-half-year-old bull Grace had named Skeleton Key. Bred to buck, he knew his job well. Sweet as apple pie in the pen, he was full of cayenne in the arena. Colt couldn't wait to see how he bucked with weight on his back.

It was this particular animal that was standing patiently in the chute now while Cash and a hired hand strapped a remote-operated bucking dummy on his back, followed by the buttery soft flank strap that would allow the young bull to know it was time to work. None of it hurt him. The bucking dummy was to get him used to the weight of a rider while the flank strap was no different than putting on a work uniform.

The pampered animal snorted as the strap was tightened around his loin, but stood quietly—waiting. As soon as the gate opened, Skeleton Key exploded from the chute with an enormous leap, followed by a buck that sent him near vertical. His hindquarters twisted off to the side. That would be the buck that would have sent his rider flying if he'd had one.

Colt pressed the button to release the dummy from the animal's back, and it fell harmlessly to the ground. The bull whirled around as the hired hands opened the gate that would return him to his pen.

The power the animal possessed made Colt almost wish he'd be among the cowboys to try him. If he bucked like that with a real rider, he'd be a challenge and a half for sure. Colt had no genuine desire to ride again, though. If he was being truthful, he was enjoying this side of rodeo almost more than he had riding.

Neither he nor Grace had returned to the circuit after their honeymoon. Instead, he'd worked on acquiring the first of his bucking stock cows, and she'd made plans for her own herd of roping horses. She'd gotten pregnant three months later. It'd been easier to quit riding—permanently, this time—than he'd expected.

He watched as Skeleton Key ran through the gate. Several hired hands moved in to check the animal over, remove the flank strap, and feed him a few carrots. No doubt Grace would be down at the pens later herself to give the animal some treats too.

Colt smiled and turned to look at Grace. "I think you were right about that bull. He's going to pose a heck of a challenge for a lot of cowboys." She'd been the one to recognize the animal's potential. Though she'd argue otherwise, she had one hell of an eye for picking bulls.

She bounced their little boy on her hip. "What do you think, Austin? Is your daddy's bull a keeper?"

Austin bobbed his head in enthusiastic affirmation.

Colt ruffled his son's black hair as Cash boarded the steps to join them at the top of the chutes. "Think your Uncle Cash will ride Skelly to the buzzer next year?"

"No!" Austin's vivid blue eyes widened a bit the second he spotted Cash.

Cash covered his heart with both hands and staggered back a step dramatically. "Oof, so little faith in me, little buddy?" He took Austin from Grace and tossed him into the air, eliciting giggles from the toddler. "You're lucky you're so cute."

He tossed the little boy into the air again, then slung him over his shoulder like a sack of potatoes before glancing from Grace to Colt. "I'm stealing your kid and your truck. We're going to go check out the new ice cream parlor in town."

Colt tossed him his truck keys in response.

Since Austin was born, Cash had come around to spoil the hell out of him often. It'd grown to be a normal thing for him to take off with the boy, and since the car seat was in Colt's truck, the truck too.

Cash snatched the keys from the air with one hand, then bounded down the steps with Austin still on his shoulder. The little boy's laughter drifted on the wind as the troublesome duo disappeared from view.

Grace turned to look up at Colt, a contented smile curling on her lips. Her arms slid around his waist. "Cash will have another one to spoil next year."

It took a second for her words to sink in. When they did, a broad grin broke out on his face. "You're pregnant?"

"I am. I took a test this morning." She laughed cheerfully. "Two tests, actually. I wanted to be super sure before I told you."

Colt whooped and fist-pumped the air.

She laughed again, harder this time. "I guess that makes your thoughts about it obvious."

He cradled her smiling face in his hands and planted a kiss on her lips before scooping her into his arms. "I fucking love you, Princess," he told her fiercely as he cradled her tenderly against his chest, carrying her toward the house.

She slung her arms around his neck and rested her cheek against his shoulder. "I freaking love you too, cowboy."

⸺⬦⸺

Thanks for reading *A Bull Rider's Grace.* I hope you enjoyed it! Want more? Cash and Honor's story, *A Bull Rider's Honor*, is expected to be published in late spring/early summer 2025.

Each book in the Bulls & Butterflies series features a separate couple, a complete story, and always ends with a Happily Ever After.

About the author

A born bookworm, H.M. Hoy began weaving words into intriguing tales at a very young age. At first, she wrote short stories, primarily about horses and the people who love them. Later, sentimental poetry filled to the brim with angst. She has long had a love for thick romance novels that tug at one's heartstrings and leave you wanting more. It was a natural leap for her to become someone who writes them.

When not burrowed between the pages of a book or writing one herself, H.M. Hoy enjoys nature photography, spending time with her daughter, and cuddling her pets. Visit her website at www.hmhoybooks.com !

f facebook.com/hmhoyauthor/

instagram.com/author.hmhoy

Love this book and want sneak peeks about upcoming stories?

Join the official Reader group for H.M. Hoy on FB at:
https://www.facebook.com/groups/352634240708439/

www.ingramcontent.com/pod-product-compliance
Lightning Source LLC
Chambersburg PA
CBHW061903310726
48972CB00004B/1146